Praise for

THE MORNINGSTAR STRAIN...

THUNDER AND ASHES

"Shamblers, sprinters, and a generous helping of guts, brains, and heart—for those who believe sequels never outshine the original, *Thunder and Ashes* is just the cure."

—D.L. Snell, author of *Roses of Blood on Barbwire Vines*

"Reading *Thunder and Ashes* will once again make you turn your lights on. Just when you thought that *Plague of the Dead* could not be bested, along comes the sequel..."

—J.L. Bourne, author of *Day by Day Armageddon*

THE MORNINGSTAR STRAIN

THUNDER AND ASHES

Z.A. RECHT

edited and
designed by **Travis Adkins**

cover art by **Christian Dovel**

Permuted Press
The formula has been changed...
Shifted... Altered... *Twisted.*™
www.permutedpress.com

A Permuted Press book
published by arrangement with the author

The Morningstar Strain:
Thunder and Ashes

©2008 Z.A. Recht. All Rights Reserved.

ISBN-10: 1-934861-01-4
ISBN-13: 978-1-934861-01-1
Library of Congress Control Number: 2008922642

PROLOGUE

Hyattsburg, Oregon
January 22, 2007
2213 hrs_

THE TOWN WAS DEAD—mostly.

Vehicles lay abandoned and silent in the streets, and loose trash fluttered about in the cold winter breeze. Electricity still ran through the wires overhead, and most of the street lights still worked, cutting swaths through the gloom. A lone figure came hobbling into one of the circles of light, casting quick glances over his shoulder and leaning heavily on a Winchester repeating rifle. His leg was wrapped in a tight bandage, and dark red blood was beginning to soak through.

"Over here! Come on, you rat-eating pieces of half-decayed shit! This way! Hop to it! Let's go! Let's go!"

Private Mark Stiles breathed heavily, gasping. He'd kept up a steady run for several blocks, putting plenty of distance between himself and his pursuers, but he was running out of steam, and his wounded leg wasn't helping matters either.

Stiles cast about, left and right, looking for a way out of his predicament. He settled on a narrow alleyway on the side of the street, and limped toward it, gritting his teeth against the pain. The morphine injection the group's medic Rebecca had given him was wearing off. Behind him, in the darkness, rasping moans filled the air, mixed in randomly with full-bodied roars of fury. He risked another look back at his pursuers.

In the darkness, Stiles could make out a line of silhouettes that stretched from one curb to the other. All were in constant motion, though some were clearly faster than others. He estimated a good forty, maybe fifty infected were close on his tail. It was the third-largest mob he'd laid eyes upon, with numbers one and two being at Suez and Sharm el-Sheikh, respectively.

The first of the infected tore into the circle of illumination, swinging its arms in an exaggerated parody of Stiles moments earlier. It sniffed at the air, pulled its face back into a grimace, and turned to face the alleyway. It growled, a low, rumbling sound deep in its throat.

A moment later its head snapped back and a loud report sounded, echoing off the brick buildings. It slumped to the ground, blood pooling around its skull. In the alley, Stiles levered a spent cartridge free and racked in another. A wisp of smoke blew away from the barrel of his weapon.

"Come on, you bastards!" Stiles yelled again. He reached out with his free hand and tipped over a set of metal trash cans that stood in the alley's entrance. They clattered to the ground, spilling month-old refuse on the pavement. Stiles backed deeper into the alley and wrinkled his nose against the stench.

Three more sprinters appeared in the mouth of the alley, faces drenched in sweat and spatters of blood from earlier victims.

"*Shit, shit, shit,*" Stiles mumbled. He looked over his shoulder, trying to find a doorway or even a manhole he could escape through. Only brick wall and solid pavement met his gaze. He grimaced, raised the Winchester to his shoulder, and let his weight rest on his injured leg. It shuddered under the strain, but held him up. He let his eyes flick down to his wounded limb. "Only have to work a little while longer, baby, then it'll all be over."

He sighted in on one of the sprinters and fired, catching it a little low, in the torso. The infected looked down at the bloody hole in its chest, pawed at it, then sank to its knees and collapsed face-first on the pavement, dead—but not for long. Stiles knew it would be back up again within minutes. The virus that had been coursing through its bloodstream would reanimate it as a slow, doddering carrier, still hard-wired to prowl for victims. The Morningstar strain didn't let go of its victims easily.

The shot gave his position away to the remaining sprinters, and they spun to face him, uttering low growls of challenge.

"Come and get it, fuckers, I ain't going anywhere," Stiles said. He backed up another step, fired again, and then continued to fall back as the pair charged him.

One of the sprinters caught its leg on the fallen trash cans and tripped, slamming into the pavement. It grunted in pain. The other nimbly hopped the cans and came straight for Stiles, arms reaching out to grab hold of him.

Stiles waited until it was nearly on top of him, then fired. The round entered through the carrier's mouth, traveled straight through and blew out the back of its skull. Stiles sidestepped as the body collapsed past him, its forward momentum expended. He felt his mouth twitch upward into a grin. That one wouldn't be getting up again. Head shots put the infected down for good.

The last carrier was pulling itself to its feet. Stiles worked the rifle's lever again, but the infected closed the distance before he could bring the barrel to bear.

Stiles fell heavily onto his back as the infected tackled him, and the rifle went flying from his grip, clattering to the pavement behind him.

The carrier grappled with Stiles, and the soldier found himself hard-pressed to keep the gnashing teeth and fingernails at bay. The two struggled for a short while, neither gaining an edge. The infected, frustrated with its prey, leaned in close and roared point-blank in Stiles' face.

Stiles dropped a hand to his side, fumbled with his pistol belt for a moment, and then grinned, holding up his bayonet between their two faces.

"Yeah, well, fuck you, too!"

Stiles slammed the blade up under the carrier's chin, pinning its upper and lower jaw together and spitting its brain like a shishka-bob. The carrier's arms went limp and its eyes rolled back up into its head. Stiles grunted as he heaved the body off, then rolled to his feet, gritting his teeth as he put weight on his leg. He retrieved the Winchester, and hobbled down to the end of the alleyway, still brandishing the bayonet.

The alley opened up into another street, just as debris-strewn and uninviting as the last—but here, at least, there was no mob of infected.

Stiles spared a glimpse over his shoulder to check on the progress of the horde that had been following him. The first shambler was just rounding the corner of the alley. He grinned, and limped around the corner. Here were more stores—these few blocks made up all of downtown Hyattsburg. None looked to be as useful as the sporting goods store he'd raided hours earlier. He spotted a bridal boutique, an ATV dealership, and a comic book shop. The rest were too shrouded in darkness to make out.

Stiles tried the first door he came to, but found it locked. It looked as if it led up to apartments. He frowned, and limped down the sidewalk to the bridal boutique. He rattled the doorknob, but it, too, was secured fast, with bars bolted in the windowframes. Groans drifted out of the alleyway, and he redoubled his efforts.

The next store was the comic book shop. He hobbled to a halt in front of it, narrowing his eyes. The front door hung ajar.

Stiles glanced over his shoulder once more to make certain he didn't have any infected barreling down on his six, raised the Winchester to the ready position, and nudged the door open the rest of the way with the barrel.

"Beggars can't be choosers," he said to himself, edging into the store. He used his wounded leg to kick the door shut behind him. Still keeping his eyes fixed on the dark interior of the store, he reached behind his back, feeling around for the deadbolt. He found it, gave it a twist, then yanked on the door again to test it. It didn't budge. He was locked in. More importantly, the carriers were locked out.

"All right, Stiles, stay frosty, you're not out of the shit yet," he mumbled, reaching up to his webgear for a flashlight, recently liberated from the sporting goods store a few blocks away. He clicked it on and let the narrow beam play over the interior of the store.

A counter stocked with collectible cards and snacks stood at the far side of the floor. Between Stiles and the counter were several double-sided shelves all lined with comics and game books. Stiles let the light shine on the floors, checking for any carriers that might have been incapacitated before they'd turned. The floor was clear—clean, even. The sporting goods store he'd been in earlier had been completely trashed, with shelves overturned and boxes ransacked, but whatever riot had hit the sporting goods store had spared this humble comic shop.

"That's not surprising," Stiles said to himself. "It's not like anyone would have much use for—" he let his eyes play over some of the titles. "—*Weapon-X* in this brave new world."

A faint moan drifted through the air, and Stiles snapped back to attentiveness, peering out the shop's front windows. He was lucky in that regard. The windows were half-covered in thick black paint to block out sunlight. He backed away from the front of the store and made his way to the register counter in the rear. He leaned over, checked the narrow space behind the counter, and levered himself up and over, swinging his legs across with a hiss of pain. He dropped down behind the counter and grimaced.

Stiles let the Winchester rest on his shoulder and sighed, stretching out his wounded leg in front of him. He fished around in the front pocket of his BDU's for a crumpled pack of cigarettes. He'd been saving the last one for almost a week, and now seemed as good a time as any to light it up.

He pulled a lighter from the same pocket, thumbed it open, and gave it a flick. It sparked, but no flame. He flicked it again, and a third time, but the flame refused to catch. Stiles frowned, held the lighter up next to his ear, and gave it a shake.

"Damn," he mumbled, around the cigarette. Empty. He tossed the lighter to the floor. "Well, at least I won't go hungry."

Stiles spat the cigarette onto the floor and reached up to retrieve a candy bar from the display case, then ripped the packaging open with his teeth. He took a bite, chewed, and swallowed, barely tasting the chocolate. His eyes were fixed on his wounded leg.

He'd been bitten by a shambler a few hours prior. It was as undignified a way to go as any, he felt. Shamblers were slow and uncoordinated—stupid, even. They were little more than the reanimated husks of the people they had once been, stiff, decayed, and stinking. Worse, a bite was a guaranteed way to contract the disease. No one he'd ever seen get bitten had survived.

"How long do I have?" he wondered out loud. He knew he was finished. Morningstar didn't let you go once it grabbed you. He knew the virus was circulating in his bloodstream, replicating, multiplying. Pretty soon he'd join the ranks of the infected outside, just another sprinter like the ones he'd just finished dispatching. Just another lousy sprinter, a moving target for some other survivor, or maybe that same survivor's doom.

He probably had four or five days, he figured. The infected soldiers on the USS *Ramage* had taken that long to turn, and they'd all had minimal exposure to the virus.

What a way to go, Stiles thought. *Slowly turning over the course of a week. First'll be the fever. Then, delirium. Next I'll get the shakes, won't be able to keep anything down, and finally, I'll snap, lose my mind—become one of them.*

Suddenly there came the sound of feet scraping against wooden floorboards.

Stiles froze, candy bar half-in, half-out of his mouth, and slowly leaned his head back to stare up at the ceiling. The noise had come from upstairs. No mistaking that.

He reached up a hand to the countertop and pulled himself to a standing position. There was a narrow doorway in the rear of the shop. Stiles had assumed it led to a stockroom and nothing more, then flinched at his own train of thought.

"What's that they say about assumptions being the mother of all fuckups?" he whispered to himself. "All right, Stiles, if you've got company in here, let's evict the bastard already."

He grabbed up his Winchester, holding it at the ready, and limped slowly out from behind the counter. The doorway in the back of the store was half covered with a ratty old blanket, attached to the doorframe with tacks. Stiles reached out a hand and ripped the blanket free, sending what could have been years' worth of accumulated dirt and dust flying. He choked back a cough and pulled the neck of his t-shirt up over his face. It wasn't just the dust that made him put on the mask. A powerful, nearly overwhelming stench came flowing out of the back room, sickening and sweet at the same time. Stiles knew that smell. It was death. Old death.

He inched his way into the small back room and let his flashlight illuminate the interior. It was a stockroom after all; unopened cardboard boxes filled the shelves and a forgotten dolly lay on its side at his feet. A *Sports Illustrated* calendar adorned the wall above a tiny clerk's desk. Whoever had owned the store had faithfully marked off each day with a thick X in permanent marker all the way up to January 3rd, almost three weeks previous. Whatever had happened in Hyattsburg must have begun then.

The sound of feet scraping on wood came again, and Stiles jumped, swinging the Winchester around. He found himself staring down a wooden door, tucked away in a corner of the stockroom. The sound came a third time, and Stiles zeroed in on it. It was definitely coming from above him, in the direction of the door.

He made his way over to it and knelt, ignoring the pain in his leg. He pressed an eye to the old-fashioned keyhole and tried to see through, but it was pitch black on the other side. Stiles sighed, looked over his shoulder, and grimaced. He couldn't very well go to sleep down here if there was an infected upstairs. Sure, he knew he was going to join their ranks in less than a week, but, by God, he wanted that last week. It was his. He sure as hell didn't want to spend it as a quick snack for a sprinter.

Stiles checked his weapon, taking a moment to reload the rifle to full capacity. He tentatively grasped the doorknob and gave it an experimental turn.

It was unlocked.

"That's more like it," he murmured, turning the knob the rest of the way. He slowly pulled, opening the door inch by inch, and cringing every time the frame or floor creaked or the hinges squeaked. Finally, he finished, and exposed before him was a narrow staircase leading up to the second floor of the building. He clicked on his flashlight, still clipped to his webgear, and adjusted it so it pointed straight ahead. He'd need both hands to wield the rifle. Indoors wasn't the best place for a long arm, but he didn't have a pistol anymore. Sherman and the rest had taken them all.

Stiles made his way up the stairs one at a time, listening carefully for any clues as to the location of his unwanted guest. Whatever had made the noise was staying quiet for the time being. It felt like it took hours, but Stiles arrived at the top of the staircase in just a few minutes.

A hallway ran off in either direction. Framed photos hung on the walls and posters had been slapped onto doors, held down with copious amounts of clear tape. This was where the owner of the store below must have lived.

Stiles stepped out into the hallway—and immediately froze. His foot had come down on a loose board and the resulting creak seemed as loud as any rifle report in the silence of the night. He winced.

Sure enough, the response from his uninvited guest was immediate, though unfocused. Off to Stiles' left, in one of the rooms, he heard a grunt and the creaking of feet on floorboards. They were quick, but didn't seem to move any closer or farther away. It sounded almost like the infected was turning in a circle, looking for the source of the noise. Seeing nothing, the infected began to calm down, and the footsteps slowed, then ceased. The grunting, however, continued, and Stiles could hear the sound of snorting and sniffing thrown into the mix. He swallowed, took a deep breath, and sidestepped toward the door nearest the source of the noises. He could feel his heart pounding in his chest, and he willed it to slow to a manageable rate. No such luck.

The stench in the upstairs hall was nearly unbearable, even with Stiles' shirt pulled up over his face. It made his eyes water and his stomach do somersaults. He felt like he had to vomit, but fought against the sensation. Part of him wanted to protect his location, and another part was simply telling him to avoid doing anything that added to the smell.

When Stiles was in front of the door he froze again.

What was behind the door? It could have been just one sprinter, but the stench told him there was a corpse in there somewhere. Was the corpse a shambler, or was it truly dead? Or, perhaps, was there more than one sprinter behind the door, and he'd only heard the one?

Stiles' hand hovered over the doorknob for a while, then pulled away. No, that was too risky. Better to fight them on his terms.

Stiles backed away, put a brace of meters between himself and the door, and knelt down on the floor. He took aim at the doorway, took another deep breath to steady himself, and then flat-palmed the wall repeatedly, making the hallway shudder. He whistled a piercing note, held it for as long as he could, and then started the litany of insults he'd used in the streets all over again:

"Hey, hey fucker! Yeah, you in the room! You ugly, mangy, infected bastard! How about a quick snack, huh? You want a Stiles steak? Well, you're going to have to work for it, you rotten piece of god-da—"

The door blew off its hinges, hanging limply, and the infected came crashing into the hallway. It was large—at least two hundred pounds—and had the look of a linebacker, complete with a bloodstained, ripped sports jersey.

It swiveled its head in Stiles' direction, fixed him with a baleful stare, and roared.

"Hi," Stiles said.

The rifle was already leveled.

All he had to do was squeeze the trigger.

The round caught the infected in the side of its forehead, and its head snapped back. A look of confused frustration played across its face, then it wobbled on its feet and fell forward to the floor. The whole hallway shuddered with the impact.

Stiles levered another round into the chamber and rose to his feet, keeping the rifle trained on the body. He held his position for a few seconds, but the corpse didn't move. Blood, black in the dimness, began to spread out in a pool under the infected's head.

Stiles sidestepped the corpse and made his way to the room the infected had occupied. He peered around the corner, aimed his flashlight in, and gagged.

He wasn't sure if he was looking at the infected's wife, girlfriend, or acquaintance, but whoever she had been in life didn't much matter now. The infected had torn her apart. The room was a bedroom, and the victim had been in bed, maybe even asleep, when she had been attacked. The sheets had once been white, but were now black and crusted with dried blood. The walls beside the bed were similarly marred. The only noise in the room was the sound of a pair of flies buzzing around the body in the darkness. One arm stuck up from the corpse, fingers curled and rigid in decay. The mouth hung open and a swollen tongue protruded from it, hanging over cracked lips. It looked like the corpse was pleading for some kind of release.

Stiles backpedaled and held a hand up to his mouth, then turned and bolted for the staircase leading back down to the stockroom. He made it as far as the clerk's desk before surrendering to the urge. He fell to his knees and vomited up his candy bar into a trash bin. He remained there for a few minutes, heaving every now and then, and finally fell away from the bin, his back against the wall.

"Damn it," he muttered, wiping his mouth with the back of his hand.

At that moment he comprehended that he was going to end up like the poor bastard he'd just shot upstairs, and it was only a slightly better fate than ending up like the woman in the bed. He looked down again at his leg and nearly sobbed, reminded once more of the fact that he'd be joining the ranks of the infected in a few days.

He wondered if he had the willpower to turn his rifle on himself.

He would just have to give it time and see how things turned out.

Private Mark Stiles sat alone in the darkness of Hyattsburg and waited.

CHAPTER ONE
OUT OF THE WEST

March 03, 2007
East of Aspen, Colorado
1456 hrs_

A STRANGE-LOOKING CONVOY rounded a bend on the narrow mountain road, engines roaring. In the lead was a utility truck, white panels painted over in flat greens and browns, a mottled, home-made camouflage. Barbed wire had been bolted to the sides and front of the truck, giving it a bristly, uneven look.

Next came a sedan, a battered, twenty-year-old Mercury that had been painted over in a fashion similar to the truck. Splashes of the paint had gotten on the windows, and the vehicle was filled to the brim with passengers and backpacks. A luggage rack had been strapped to the roof, and it, too, was filled to capacity with odds and ends, from tents to red plastic gas cans. The latter would have blown away if they hadn't been roped down; the cans jostled one another as the wind whistled past and rang hollow when they struck.

Third in the line was a Ford pickup truck. It had gotten the least amount of effort, it seemed, paint-wise, having only received a coat of flat green, but the tires had been replaced with heavy-duty off-road numbers, and the front grill had been reinforced with steel rebar. The bed had received work as well. More rebar had been added, making a vertical fence that ran along the outside of the truck. Barbed wire had been strung between the steel bars, wound tightly enough that it was hard to see through. Narrow slits cut through the wire on either side provided the occupants with a way of both seeing and shooting anything hostile that tried to approach.

The convoy was making good time. They'd come almost a thousand miles in almost two weeks, which was much faster than they'd thought they'd be able to maintain. They wouldn't be able to keep it up for much longer, though.

In the lead vehicle, the utility truck, Command Sergeant Major Thomas sat at the wheel, deftly negotiating the treacherous curves and dips of the mountain roads. He was clean-shaven, as was his passenger, having made it a point to maintain his appearance despite the end of the world. Old soldiers had standards. His graying hair, once kept close-cropped, was beginning to grow out, and Thomas had tucked it up under a rapidly-fading cap.

Next to him sat Frank Sherman, formerly Lieutenant General in command of the coalition forces at the Suez canal quarantine zone. He no longer considered himself an officer, but some of the survivors in the ragtag group that followed him still addressed him as one, including Thomas. He was dressed in civilian hunting clothes and dinged-up combat boots, swearing at a map he had held up in front of his face.

"This is ridiculous," Sherman said, trying to smooth out a crease in the map. "This road was supposed to intersect with an interstate a good twenty miles back. Are you sure we didn't miss it?"

"Yes, sir," Thomas said. "Didn't see no signs. No entry ramps. Nothing. We just haven't gotten to it yet, sir."

"Yeah, maybe," Sherman said, disgruntled. He looked out the window into the sideview mirror at the vehicles following behind them. "We're going to have to do something soon. How much fuel is left?"

"Quarter tank, sir," Thomas said.

"That's not much," Sherman sighed. "Gives us just under a hundred miles' range to find another gas station with something left in the pumps or we'll be walking the rest of the way to Omaha."

"Airports, sir," Thomas suggested.

"What?"

"Check on that map of yours for airports. Most of the gas stations we've passed have been picked clean by civvies running out of the towns and into the country. They're convenient and they're easy. Airports, on the other hand—"

"—most people won't even think to check those. Good idea, Thomas," Sherman said, peering closer at the map. "Yeah, perfect, looks like there's a regional field a little bit north of us. Maybe thirty miles. Have you seen any signs? What's the next road we'll be coming to?"

"Should be Route 13," Thomas said.

Sherman chuckled. "That's lucky."

"No disrespect intended, sir, but since when do you give a crap about superstition?"

"I don't, Thomas. It just struck me funny. Take 13 North."

"Yes, sir. And it could be worse, sir," Thomas said.

"How so?"

"Could be Route 666."

Sherman chuckled again. "Didn't know you had a sense of humor."

"Sometimes I feel generous, sir."

Thomas pointed out the windshield at an approaching sign that said the junction with Route 13 was a mile ahead. Sherman nodded.

"How were the food supplies looking this morning?" Sherman asked after a moment had passed in silence.

"On the low side, sir," Thomas said. "We have enough to keep us going another few days. We could stretch it to a week if we cut back on rations, but we're already on diets as it is."

"I don't think more rationing would go over very well either," Sherman agreed. "That's something else we'll have to remedy soon. Too bad airlines aren't known for their food."

"Oh, you're a riot today, sir," Thomas drawled.

Sherman grinned. "Still, let's set a detail to look for anything edible when we get to the field. You never know."

Thomas nodded and flicked on his left turn signal. The junction with Route 13 was coming up fast, and he wanted to make sure the drivers behind him followed when he took the turn.

Behind the utility truck, in the cab of the pickup, sat Ewan Brewster, riding shotgun. He tapped his foot against the floorboard in time to the beat of the country ballad playing through the speakers, and turned up the cassette player in the dash. He hung his head out the passenger window and narrowed his eyes at the utility truck ahead of them with its blinking turn signal, then turned to Mbutu Ngasy, who was sitting at the wheel.

"Looks like Thomas found the road he was looking for," Brewster said over the music. "Left turn coming up."

"Very good," Mbutu said. He knocked his hand against the rear window, alerting the passengers in the back that something was up.

A moment later, the window was pulled open, and Denton stuck his head in, looking left and right at the two occupants.

"What's up?" he asked. The Canadian photographer looked the most at home on the road out of anyone in the group; he'd gotten used to roughing it on assignments that had taken him around the world several times over before the pandemic had struck. He seemed relaxed and composed compared to the rest.

"Hold on. We're turning," Mbutu said.

"Gotcha," Denton replied. He pulled himself free and turned to the other passengers to pass the message along. "Sit down, we're turning."

"Does this mean we're not lost anymore?" Ron asked, sitting with his back to the tailgate.

"I don't know," Denton shrugged. "I hope not. We put the last of the fuel into the tanks this morning. If we don't find a station soon to get a refill we'll be hitching."

"Hell, that wasn't safe *before* the pandemic," said Rebecca Hall, fixing Denton with a stare. "It's probably *murder* now. Count me out. I'll just walk the rest of the way to Omaha."

Denton grinned at the medic. "Then we'll see you in six months, because it's going to take you that long to get there on foot."

"Better than being carrier chow," she shot back.

"Given," Denton said, shrugging.

Jack, a civilian contractor who'd proved his worth in Hyattsburg weeks earlier, was sitting along one side of the bed next to Mitsui, another contractor, trying to get the gist of the conversation across to the slight Japanese man via simple words and hand signs. He managed to communicate Rebecca's desire to walk if worse came to worst by pointing at her and then 'walking' a pair of fingers across his palm. Mitsui looked at Rebecca and grinned.

"What the hell are you looking it?" she snapped.

"Don't let them bother you," Katie Dawson said, leaning on Rebecca's shoulder. "Construction workers are all the same around the world, I guess."

"Hey, I'm not a construction worker. I'm a *government contractor*," Jack protested.

The pickup truck slowed and went into a tight turn, following the utility truck in the lead. A bright white sign with the number '13' centered on it flashed past, and the convoy straightened out on its new course, northward bound.

1701 hrs_

The regional airfield looked at first glance to be deserted, but the survivors had long ago learned to be immediately suspicious of anything that looked like a free lunch. The vehicles pulled up to the main gate and stopped. Doors opened and people dismounted, wandering to the front of the small convoy to survey what lay in front of them.

Sherman stood with his arms folded, looking through the chain link gate that stood in their way across the field to the airport itself. It was small as far as airports went: a single story, around two hundred feet long, with a control tower that jutted up from one end and a pair of modest hangars just across a narrow runway. It was built out of poured concrete, with wide, floor-to-ceiling glass panels all along the front. The doors were shut tightly. No lights lit the runway or structures in the quickly dimming evening. No noises disturbed the calm except for a few birds in the treeline off in the distance. Their calls seemed muted and reluctant.

Sherman sighed, then turned to face Thomas, who was standing just behind him, arms akimbo.

"How much fuel is left now?"

"Eighth of a tank, sir. Forty mile range, tops," Thomas said.

"Looks like we don't have a choice. Krueger! Brewster! Up front!" Sherman called out.

The two soldiers appeared immediately. Krueger saluted. Brewster waved.

"Sir?" Krueger asked.

"Get this gate open, then follow us in. We'll be staying here tonight, after we clear the buildings," Sherman said.

"Yes, sir," Krueger replied.

"You got it," Brewster said.

The two grabbed hold of the gate and pulled it open, grunting with the strain, as the rest of the group piled back into the vehicles.

"Come on, come on, put your back into it," Brewster chuckled.

"I am," Krueger said, gritting his teeth. "Heavier than I thought it would be."

"Just a little farther," Brewster said, putting in one final burst of effort. The gate slid back and caught in the open position. "There! Got it!"

The convoy roared to life, headlights came on, and the vehicles rolled forward through the breach. Krueger and Brewster snapped up their weapons, having leaned them against the fence to free up their hands, and followed them through. They stopped on the other side of the fence and grabbed the gate once more, this time pulling it shut behind themselves. The two trucks and the sedan continued on down the concrete road, eventually pulling to a complete stop in front of the main building's entrance. They angled themselves so the headlights were facing into the building, cutting a wide swath through the darkness.

By the time Brewster and Krueger had caught up, the remainder of the survivors had disembarked and armed themselves.

"Gate's shut, sir," Krueger said to Sherman.

"Excellent. The fence around the edge of this place makes for a good line of defense, but we'll still have to make sure we're alone before we can relax," Sherman said. He turned away from the group, let his eyes play over the structures in front of him, and formulated a quick plan. "All right, let's divide into three groups. One group clears the tower, one clears the terminal, and the third will clear the hangars down there, hooah?"

The survivors nodded their assent and began to break off into groups. It was an inevitable part of any group dynamic that cliques had begun to form on the road between Hyattsburg and their current location, and it was into those cliques that the survivors broke.

"We've got the tower," Ron said, pointing up at the structure with his free hand. His other gripped his weapon of choice, a dented, stained machete. Following close behind him were Katie and Rebecca.

Mbutu trailed after the trio, shouldering a rifle. He called back over his shoulder, "I will go with them."

"I suppose we'll take the hangars," Brewster said, cracking open his double-barreled shotgun and checking to make certain it was loaded. "Coming, guys?"

"Right behind you, man," Krueger said, working the bolt on his .30-06.

"Time to go play tag with Death again, eh?" Denton said, following after them.

A third soldier, Wilson, jogged after them as well.

"I guess that leaves us the terminal," Sherman said, checking his pistol and glancing sideways at Thomas, who was eyeing the building with suspicion.

"We're right behind you, General," Jack said. Mitsui needed no translation for that, and nodded in agreement.

"No time like the present," Thomas said. He pushed open the terminal doors and entered, weapon at the ready.

✮ ✮ ✮ ✮ ✮

The tower's entrance was a pair of steel double doors at ground level. They looked sturdy enough to stand up to a car running full-bore into them, but luckily, they were unlocked.

Ron pulled both of them open, allowing what little natural light remained to flood the interior of the structure. The ground floor, at least, was devoid of occupants, living or dead. A wide spiral staircase led straight up to the tower itself.

"This reminds me of home," Mbutu said, poking his head in the doorway and looking up.

"That's right, you were an air traffic controller, weren't you?" Katie asked.

"Yes," Mbutu said, "In Mombasa."

"It was one of the first cities to be overwhelmed," Rebecca added, stepping past the others and entering the tower first. "He was lucky to make it out alive."

"Let's hope that luck is sticking around," Ron said. "Let's go."

The group made their way up the spiral staircase, taking their time, using their ears more than their eyes in the dimness. No sounds could be heard ahead of them, but they weren't about to let their guard down. The stairs wound around twice before they arrived at the top.

The tower was empty. Chairs had been tucked in under consoles and screens had been covered with clear plastic sheeting to protect them against dust and time. A coffee pot sat on a folding table near the top of the stairs, clean as the day it was purchased. All the power indicators were off.

"Well, whoever was here last sure didn't leave in a hurry," Rebecca said, looking around the tower.

Mbutu nodded in agreement. "They even took the time to cover the monitors."

"Too bad there's no power," Ron said.

"There's a great view up here," Katie said, walking across the tower floor to stand next to a console. She leaned over the machine, peering out the wide glass windows. "Just the one runway. Frank wasn't kidding when he said this was just a little regional airport, was he?"

Mbutu and Ron were busy pawing through the drawers, hoping to find anything useful. Ron pocketed a lighter, but other than that, the pair came up empty.

"Hey," Katie said, still looking out the window. The others ignored her at first, content to continue searching. She glanced over her shoulder at them, frowned, and repeated herself. "Hey!"

Rebecca looked over. "What?"

"Someone's out there," Katie said, pointing.

"It's just Brewster and the others headed for the hangar," Ron said, waving a hand in dismissal.

"Really? Since when does Brewster wear overalls?" Katie asked, arching an eyebrow at Ron.

Ron frowned, shoved the drawer he'd been searching through shut, and moved to stand next to Katie. He looked in the direction she was pointing. It was tough to see in the twilight, but there was definitely a figure across the runway, walking beside one of the hangars. Brewster, Denton, and the others were nowhere in sight.

"Shambler," Ron said, narrowing his eyes. "Gotta be."

Rebecca pulled a radio from the cargo pocket of her pants and clicked it on. "Brewster."

A moment passed, and no reply issued forth from the radio.

Rebecca tried again. "Brewster. Pick up your damn radio."

Again, silence. She raised the radio to her lips to give it a third try when a static hiss cut the air and Brewster's voice came through, slightly distorted.

"What is it, over?"

"Where are you? Are you in the hangars, yet?" Rebecca asked.

A long moment passed without Brewster's reply. Finally, the soldier's voice came through again.

"Say 'over' when you're done, for fuck's sake!" Brewster said. *"And yes, we're in the first hangar. Civvies left a plane here; we're checking the tank, over."*

"Brewster, you've got company outside the hangar. We see one— walking—could be a shambler. Could also be a friendly for all we can tell; it's tough to make out from this far away, *over*," Rebecca said, stressing the last word.

"Well, all right, it's about time we got a little action," Brewster said. *"We'll deal with it. Out."*

"Watch your asses," Rebecca said. She didn't bother with 'over', and clicked the radio off instead, dropping it back in her pocket.

"Look, there they are!" Katie said from the window, pointing across the runway once more, only this time she was focused on a doorway in the side of the hangar that had just swung open. A pair of figures materialized out of the gloom, and even in the twilight the group in the tower could see they were holding weapons.

They moved along the front of the hangar slowly, sidestepping, frosty and alert. The walking figure continued to meander along the side of the structure, coming closer to the front with every step it took.

"They're going to run right into one another," Katie said, grimacing.

"No way," Ron said, shaking his head. "They'll hear it before it's on them. Won't they?"

Rebecca didn't look so sure.

Out in the cold, far below the group in the tower, maneuvered Krueger and Brewster, completely unaware that they were moving ever closer to the unidentified figure, just out of sight around the corner.

Brewster blew out a slow breath, watched it swirl away into the night air, and moved a couple of steps closer to the corner of the hangar. His boots marked each step with a steady *crunch-crunch-crunch* on the still-frozen grass. Beside him was Krueger, scanning their sides and glancing over his shoulder every few steps to make sure they weren't being approached from behind.

"Where is this guy?" Krueger whispered.

"Becky just said he was outside the hangar," Brewster replied, shrugging.

"Well, that's real goddamn helpful," Krueger said. "If it was a sprinter it could have come at us from any direction."

"We don't even know it's infected for sure yet," Brewster reminded him. "Let's check our target before we fire."

"Right," Krueger said, scoffing. "When was the last time we met someone new who didn't try to eat us, huh?"

"Hyattsburg," Brewster said, approaching the corner with his rifle at the ready.

"Yeah, and look what happened there," Krueger grinned. "Damn near didn't make it out alive—"

"*Shit!*" Brewster shouted, backpedaling. Right in front of him, rounding the corner, came the shambler. Brewster's feet got tangled up together and he stumbled, falling hard on his back and *whoof*ing as his breath was knocked out of him.

One thing the survivors had learned was that the infected came in widely varied packaging. Some of them were more or less in mint condition, having been infected 'the old-fashioned way,' through fluid exchanges, a badly-timed sneeze, and so on. Others were in less than ideal shape, having been infected via bites, scratches, blood spatter—these all bore their wounds even on through death. The truly horrifying ones wielded as powerful a psychological weapon as they did a biological one. More than once members of the group hadn't been able to stand their ground against mobs of shamblers that were missing body parts, or were far enough along in decay to turn even the most hardened stomach.

This shambler had definitely seen better days. Both of its eyes were missing. It didn't appear to have lost them in a fight; instead, claw marks and stringy bits of ocular nerve still hanging from the sockets hinted at carrion birds having had a small feast at the shambler's expense. Its death wound was a deep gash running along the top of its chest. Whatever had caused the wound had cut right through the infected's mechanic's coveralls. A bloodied bit of bandage wrapped around the shambler's left forearm hinted at the wound that had infected him in the first place.

Only a brace of feet from Brewster, and seemingly unhindered by its lack of eyes, the shambler reached out a hand to grab the soldier's jacket.

Krueger leapt forward and gave the shambler a buttstroke across the temple. The infected grunted. Its knees buckled, and it collapsed next to Brewster in the cold grass. The soldier rolled away from the shambler and came up with his back against the steel wall of the hangar.

Krueger took a couple of steps back. The shambler was already slowly pulling itself up. Krueger flicked the safety of his rifle off, took aim, and put a round through the back of its skull. The shot echoed off the terminal and tower. The shambler collapsed face-first in the grass, and didn't move anymore.

"Jesus H. Christ on a motherfucking cracker," Brewster said, staring wide-eyed at the corpse. "That thing came right around the corner—it was right on me. Good thing I have cat-like reflexes."

Krueger smirked. "You tripped backwards over your own feet, dumbass."

"Yeah, well, I'm still alive," Brewster said, waving a chastising finger in Krueger's face. "And that's what counts."

"Brewster, you there, over?" the radio hissed.

"That Sherman?" Krueger asked.

"Shhh," Brewster said, yanking his radio free from a pocket. "Yeah, Frank, we're here, over."

"We heard a shot, over."

"Oh, yeah, yes, sir—came upon a shambler out here. No injuries, over."

"And the shambler?"

"Dispatched, sir, with *extreme* prejudice, over," Krueger interjected, grinning.

"How do the hangars look, over?"

"Well, we were just taking care of that when the infected came a-knockin'," Brewster said. "But we might have some fuel out here, over."

"Excellent. Keep us posted. We're just breaking into the terminal now, over."

"Roger. Good luck over there. Out."

Across the runway, Jack and Mitsui were finishing up their unconventional method of unlocking the front doors. Too solid and too thick to break down, and with no key in their possession, the two contractors had decided to get creative. They'd attached a chain to the door handles, and looped the other end through the trailer hitch on the back of the group's pickup truck.

"All right," Jack said, testing the chain one final time to make certain it was secure. "Feels good. Okay, go! Go!"

Mitsui, looking over his shoulder from the driver's seat of the pickup, grinned and flashed Jack a thumb's-up sign, then gunned the motor. The chain pulled taut and the doors shuddered, but held.

"Damn," Jack frowned. He motioned for Mitsui to ease off the gas. "Back her up, back her up. We'll try again."

Sherman and Thomas stood off to one side, watching. Sherman had just finished his radio conversation with Brewster and now folded his arms across his chest, arching an eyebrow at the contractor's efforts.

"This isn't exactly going to leave us with a secure place to sack out tonight," Sherman said out of the side of his mouth to Thomas.

"We still have the tower, sir. Probably our best bet, anyway. Good three-sixty-degree view up top, only one staircase—that's where I'd want to bunk," Thomas said.

Sherman nodded silently by way of reply as Mitsui gunned the pickup's motor a second time.

This time, when the chain went taut the doors groaned and surrendered, popping free of their hinges.

"That's more like it!" Jack said, pumping an arm in the air.

"Shh," Sherman reminded him, resting a hand on the butt of his pistol. "We've already run up against one shambler here. Gotta assume there are more."

Jack grimaced, then nodded. "Sorry."

"Don't apologize," Sherman waved him off. "Let's just see what we can see."

The group entered the terminal, looking left and right. There was a small gift shop, sporting advertisements for liquor and t-shirts on gaudy posters plastered to the windows, and a customer service desk butting up against the far wall. A message board hung on the same wall, covered in tacked-on pieces of paper and cardboard. There looked to be hundreds of them, written on whatever material the writers had been able to find. Some were scrawled on newspaper, others on sticky pads, and one or two were written directly on the puce-colored walls in thick permanent marker. Sherman wandered over and read some of the messages as the rest of the group spread out behind him and searched the area.

Julie - waited until they were outside the gates and the rest of the planes had taken off. I am getting on the last one out. The pilot says we are going to Montana. Love you.

Brian O'Daly was here 1/12/07, bound for Canada. Good luck and godspeed!

Everyone else back home is dead but me. Hopefully I can find a way to get on one of these planes. If anyone who knows me reads this, I'm still alive as of January ninth. — D. Pulaski

Sherman sighed, turned his back on the board, and headed over to the gift shop. Jack had already forced the door open with a crowbar and was busy sifting through the contents of the shelves inside, his flashlight casting just enough light to see by.

"Anything?" Sherman called in the open door.

"Eh?" Jack asked, his head poking up from behind a shelf. "Not really. Looks pretty well picked through. Whole rack of old magazines, though. I'm grabbing a few—been a while since I've had anything decent to read."

"Knock yourself out," Sherman said. "No food at all?"

"Well, there's a few packs of chips and some crackers, but no, not really," Jack said, holding up the items for Sherman to see.

"Take 'em. Food's food. Never know, we might need it," Sherman said.

"You got it."

Jack unzipped his backpack, and Sherman heard the sound of crumpling packaging as the contractor stuffed it full of snack food.

"Sir!"

Thomas's voice. Sherman turned and squinted into the darkness of the terminal. A flashlight clicked on several meters away, illuminating the old sergeant's face. He'd been scouring the drawers and countertops at the customer service desk.

"Flightplans and passenger manifests," Thomas said, holding up a clipboard. "Out of date, but it gives us a tally on the number of planes that were here before the bugout."

"Brewster said on the radio that there was at least one plane left in the hangars. You showing that?" Sherman asked, walking over to look at the manifest.

Thomas frowned, let his eyes play over the papers, then shook his head. "If it's out there, it was supposed to have left."

Sherman dug his radio out again and called for Brewster. It took a moment, but the soldier responded.

"Brewster, you said there was a plane in the hangars?" Sherman asked. "Over."

"That's right, Sherm, dual prop, over."

"What's the ID number on the side, over?"

There was a moment of silence as the soldier looked for the markings.

"Charlie-oscar-four-zero-seven-gulf, over," Brewster read.

Thomas looked back down at the sheet, scanned line-by-line with his index finger, and halted at the matching number.

"Says here it was outbound to Montana, nine passengers and two crew," Thomas read.

"Brewster," Sherman said, holding the radio up in front of his face, "be advised you may have an additional ten hostiles in the vicinity. Stay frosty, over."

"Ten?"

"That's what I said. Look, this terminal is empty. We're coming over to back you up, out," Sherman said.

"Roger that, sir—out."

In the hangars, Brewster clipped his radio to his belt and grimaced.

"Hey guys," he called. "Guys!"

"What?" Denton replied, coming around the front of the plane. "What did Sherman say?"

"Where's Krueger and Wilson?" Brewster asked, pushing past Denton and scanning the interior of the building for the other two soldiers. He shouldered his shotgun. "We could have company."

"Oh, damn, I hate it when we have company," Denton said, jogging to catch up with Brewster. "They're on the other side of the hangar sorting through the tool lockers, trying to find a hose to siphon the gas out of the plane with."

"Krueger! Wilson!" Brewster called out as Denton explained.

"Yeah?" The reply came floating through the hangar, echoing slightly.

"Get back over here! We need to sweep this place again," Brewster said, shotgun at the ready. He looked left and right, but didn't see anything moving.

"Why? We already cleared it!" Wilson's voice shouted back.

"Sherman says he's got ten civvies that should've been here unaccounted for!" Brewster yelled.

"Oh, for shit's sake, if there were infected in here, we'd've run across 'em already!" Wilson replied.

"Yeah? What about the one we capped outside?"

"All right, all right, don't get your panties all bunched up, we're coming," Wilson said. "Ooh, a hose!"

Brewster sighed. Next to him, Denton rolled his eyes.

"Just grab it and get over here," Denton said.

"Coming!"

Krueger and Wilson rounded a line of luggage carriers, walking briskly. Wilson had a length of hose looped over his shoulder, and held up a battery-powered spotlight with his left hand, illuminating a wide swath of hangar floor in front of him. Krueger kept him covered with his .30-06.

"All right, we're here. What's the trouble?" Wilson asked, shrugging at Brewster.

"We don't even know for sure there is any," Brewster said, looking over his shoulder. "Sherman just said there might be a few more infected around, that's all. Man's never lied to us before. Figured we better double-check things."

"Okay. Fair enough," Wilson said. "Well, the tool locker and workshop area is totally clear, that's for sure. We just came from there."

"I was just looking through the luggage in the back before you called," Denton said, pointing to the rear of the hangar. "Nothing and no one there, either."

"Well, I was over by the plane. No one there, too," Brewster said, jerking a thumb over his shoulder at the silhouette of the plane behind the group.

"Maybe it was just the one guy outside," Krueger said, frowning. "He was wearing mechanic's clothes. Seemed like he belonged here. In life, I mean."

"So, false alarm, then?" Brewster asked.

"Guess so," Wilson replied. He held his spotlight up to his shoulder and panned it around the hangar. The beam passed over half-empty steel shelving units, more luggage carts, spare parts. He directed the beam up slightly. "Did anyone go in there?"

Brewster, Krueger, and Denton turned to look at Wilson's target.

The beam was hovering over the airplane's single hatch.

For a moment, the small group was silent. Brewster looked left at Denton and right at Krueger, but both of them shook their heads.

"Oh, goddamnit," Brewster said. "No, I guess not."

"Well, don't you think we should check?" Wilson asked.

"Fuck no," Brewster protested. "First of all, there's nothing in that plane that we can't find lying around out here. Secondly, we don't need to go into it to get to the fuel tanks. And thirdly, if it is full of fuckin' infected, I'll be damned if I'm going to be the one to climb up there and open the hatch. Any one of you sad motherfuckers volunteering?"

Denton inched away from the soldier. Krueger and Wilson exchanged a glance, then fixed Brewster with a reluctant look.

"Yeah, that's what I thought," Brewster said. "Let's just leave 'em in peace, what do you say?"

"I say we should at least look in the windows, Private," came a new voice.

Brewster and the others turned to see Sherman and Thomas standing in the doorway to the hangar.

"Well, just as long as I don't have to go opening any doors," Brewster said, sighing. "Someone help me push these stairs over."

Brewster and Denton laid their rifles on a luggage crate and grabbed hold of a set of rolling stairs. Denton kicked the locks loose and the two pushed and pulled the heavy steel construct up against the side of the dual-prop plane. Another set of kicks locked the stairs in place once more and Brewster grabbed the handrail, climbing slowly.

"Brewster," Wilson said, whistling for the soldier's attention.

When Brewster looked down, Wilson held up the spotlight, then tossed it in the air. Brewster reached out and caught it with his free hand.

Brewster took a deep breath as he approached the top of the stairs and held it in unconsciously, clicking the spotlight back on. He raised it slowly until it was level with one of the windows, and peered inside.

Almost immediately, a pale hand plastered itself against the inside of the window. Brewster jumped, but kept a solid grip on the handrail.

A low moan, faint and distorted, filled the air inside the hangar. Slowly, other hands appeared in the plane's windows, followed by sunken faces.

"Well, there they are," Krueger said from the hangar floor, arms folded across his chest. "Guess we can stop wondering about that, now."

"How many can you see, Brewster?" Sherman called up.

"Uh, hang on, sir," Brewster said, trying to track the various infected on the other side of the windows. "Six...seven...eight..."

"How many?" Thomas repeated.

"I'm counting, I'm counting!" Brewster protested, waving a hand at Thomas. "Uh, eight. I see eight. All shamblers."

"Eight?" Sherman asked. He pressed his lips together and furrowed his brow. "How many were there total again, Thomas?"

"Eleven, sir. Nine passengers, two crew."

"We killed one outside," volunteered Brewster from the top of the stairs, still peering intently into the windows. "He was dressed like crew."

"That still leaves two," Thomas said.

The group members looked at one another uneasily, hands falling to rest on weapons. They turned to face the darkness of the hangar, standing almost back-to-back. Brewster flipped the spotlight around in his hand, using his elevation to get a good angle on the hangar floor. The wide beam of light darted around the interior of the structure.

"Bastards could be anywhere," Wilson said. "Could be sprinters, could be shamblers. Maybe they wandered off—"

"Quiet!" Sherman barked, drawing his pistol. "Listen!"

Silence.

"I don't hear anything, Frank," Denton said after a moment.

"I know. Shut up," Sherman said.

More silence. Then—

A single footstep. More of a scrape than a footstep, really. It may as well have been a gunshot. Every living set of ears in the building turned toward it immediately. It had come from the direction of the lines of luggage containers. Brewster shone the flashlight toward the containers, panning it slowly left and right.

"There," Krueger said softly, thumbing the safety of his rifle off. "In the middle of all that junk. The shamblers' noises must've stirred it up."

The barrel was trained on the floor. Krueger had picked out a single white tennis shoe, nearly invisible between the containers. The shoe moved forward, scraping along the cement floor with just the barest of noises. Brewster shifted the spotlight up a degree and lit the break in the containers where the infected would appear. A moment later, a hand groped around the corner, grabbing the edge of the container with white knuckles, and slowly pulled the rest of itself into view.

This had been the pilot. A sunken face, swollen tongue and rolled-back eyes attested to a slow death by dehydration. Not the most pleasant way to go for an uninfected human. It had probably taken weeks for the infected to die that way. Sherman remembered some of Dr. Demilio's briefings on the virus. It slowed the host's metabolism and bodily functions, stretching out life as long as it could. This one had probably been a sprinter until recently, same as the rest in the plane.

Brewster mentally kicked himself for not having looked in the narrow spaces between the bins. The thing must have been laying in there, dormant, until the moans of the shamblers in the plane had alerted it to prey.

"Sir?" Krueger asked. He was holding his rifle steady, having drawn a bead on the infected's forehead.

Sherman nodded, then realized Krueger couldn't see the motion with his eye pressed up to the scope. "Drop him."

Krueger fired a single shot, and the infected's head snapped back. It vanished, falling back in between the luggage containers. A muted thud echoed through the hangar as the body hit. The white-shoe clad feet were still visible, the left twitching a few times before settling into death.

"One more down," Brewster said from the top of the staircase, still fixing the corpse with the beam of the spotlight. "That leaves us one unaccounted for, right?"

"Right," Denton said, releasing a breath he hadn't realized he'd been holding. "And it won't be a crewman."

"Better get the gas while the gettin's good, sir," Thomas said, gesturing at the plane.

"Good idea, Thomas. Wilson, Brewster, Krueger, get the fuel," Sherman said. "Denton, Thomas, let's get back to the terminal, move everyone over to the tower, and button it up. If there's another shambler wandering around this place I want a defensible perimeter."

"Yes, sir," Krueger said, grabbing the loop of hose from Wilson's shoulder and jogging over to the plane. "Wilson, grab a couple of those empty cans on top of that dolly and bring 'em over here!"

Brewster slid down the staircase and ran over to join Krueger by the plane's fuel tank, holding up the spotlight to give the soldier some light to work by.

Behind the trio, Sherman, Thomas, and Denton ducked out of the hangar, jogging across the runway toward the tower.

"How many gallons do you think this plane holds?" Wilson asked, dropping off a pair of empty five-gallon fuel cans and running back for more.

"I don't know," Krueger replied, feeding one end of the hose into the open tank. "It sure ain't a Geo, that's for sure. Gotta be a hundred gallons or more."

"Damn," Brewster whistled. "If we're catching this fucker at full cap, it'll get us most of the rest of the way to Omaha."

"Keep an eye out, Wilson," Krueger said, pointing over Wilson's shoulder at the rest of the hangar. "Don't want to get snuck up on."

"Right," Wilson replied, turning his back on Brewster and Krueger and scanning the darkness with narrowed eyes.

Krueger sucked on the end of the hose until he got a mouthful of fuel, spat it out with a grimace, and fed the tube into the first gas can. The soldiers could hear the sound of sloshing as the can filled up. For a few moments, the gasoline and hushed breaths were the only sounds in the hangar. Then Krueger nudged the can with his boot to check its fullness, crimped the hose, and shoved the can across the floor to Brewster.

"What do you want me to do with this?" Brewster asked, hefting the heavy can in his arms.

"Find something to put it in," Krueger stage-whispered back.

"Like fucking what?" Brewster asked, gesturing around himself.

"Get a luggage cart, dipshit," Krueger said, pointing over Brewster's shoulder. "We'll run 'em across five or six at a time until this tank's empty. Wilson. Wilson!"

"Huh?" the soldier started, dropping his gaze from the windows of the plane. He'd been staring at the infected, still pounding away slowly from inside.

"You want to pay attention?" Krueger admonished. "You're going to get us turned into carrier chow."

"Sorry."

★ ★ ★ ★ ★

A pounding on the metal staircase alerted Rebecca, Mbutu and the others that Sherman's group had arrived in the tower.

"Ahoy the tower!" came Denton's voice. "How're things looking up there?"

Rebecca leaned out over the railing far above and shouted down, "Desolate!"

"Wish we had some lights in this place," Ron added, poking his head out next to Rebecca's.

"What, and advertise a free buffet to any infected nearby?" Sherman said, grabbing hold of the handrail and taking the stairs two at a time. "Hope you lot enjoyed your break. Time to get back to work. We're going to camp up here for the night. That means we need to set a guard down below and figure a way to lock those doors."

"That will not be a problem," Mbutu said from the other side of the tower floor. Sherman looked over to see the tall man spinning a keyring on one finger and grinning. "These places, they are the same the world over. The supervisor had these in his desk. They should take care of the doors."

"Outstanding," Sherman nodded. "Don't lock up yet; we're still waiting on Brewster, Wilson, and Krueger to get back from the hangars."

"They did find gas, right?" Katie asked.

"Yes," Sherman replied. "And a plane full of infected."

Mbutu frowned. "Is it safe to stay here if...?"

"Oh, yes," Sherman went on. "They're locked up tight. And even if they did manage to break free—which I doubt, seeing as they've been in there a good month—they wouldn't know where we'd gone to."

"I'd sleep a lot better if they were dead," Ron said. "Why don't we go in there and wipe 'em out?"

"Unnecessary risk," Sherman replied, shaking his head in a negative. Behind him, Thomas nodded slowly in agreement.

"Here comes Krueger and the others," Katie said, leaning over a console and pointing out the tower window.

Sherman walked over to join her, followed closely by Thomas. Far below, they could see the three soldiers moving quickly across the runway, pushing a loaded luggage cart in front of them. It was filled nearly to the brim with red plastic gas cans. They seemed to be having a bit of trouble keeping the cart on an even keel. It wobbled slightly and continually pulled to the right. Wilson was having to throw his entire body weight into the side of the cart to keep it headed in a straight line toward the terminal and tower.

"Looks like we've got enough fuel in that thing to get us out of these damn mountains," Denton said, grinning.

"You're Canadian," Rebecca ribbed. "Thought you were used to mountains."

"I'm used to lakes," Denton corrected. "Lakes and snow."

"And maple syrup and bad beer and hockey," Ron added, chuckling.

"Hey, hey, hey," Denton said, glaring. "Watch it with the beer commentary, eh?"

The soldiers vanished from sight below as they drew nearer the tower. Sight was replaced by sound; the group in the tower could hear the rumbling of the cart's wheels and the curses of the soldiers as they rounded the structure and made a beeline for the vehicles parked behind the terminal.

"Thomas, do me a favor—run down there and tell them not to bother fueling the vehicles tonight. Just get 'em in the tower. We'll button up and settle in for the night, get some rest. We'll take care of the rest of the work tomorrow morning," Sherman said.

"Yes, sir," Thomas grumbled. He took off down the stairs at a run, glad to have an order to follow—even if it was phrased as a suggestion.

Sherman turned to the remaining group members. "Well, pick a spot and sack out, folks. We did pretty well for ourselves tonight. No fatalities, and we're coming out ahead in fuel and food."

"If you can call it food," Denton said, pulling bags of potato chips from his pack and tossing them around the tower.

Ron caught one of the bags and tore it open with his teeth. "Hey, food's food. I'll take what I can get."

"It ain't the Atkins diet," Katie said, frowning at the label on her bag. "But I agree, I'll take what I can get."

Rebecca waved off Denton and unstrapped her sleeping bag from the top of her pack, throwing it out in a corner of the tower. "I'm fine."

"You sure?" Denton asked, waving the food in her direction.

"Yeah, I'm sure," she replied.

"Suit yourself," Denton said, opening the bag and digging in.

The sound of feet on metal from below meant the soldiers had entered the tower. The structure reverberated slightly as the doors were slammed shut.

"Mbutu," Sherman said. He held up his hands. "Keys."

Mbutu tossed the keys to Sherman underhanded. He caught them, turned, whistled to get Thomas' attention, and dropped them over the side of the railing. Below, Thomas grabbed them as they fell, then turned and sorted through them one-by-one until he found the one that matched the tower doors. He locked them, pulled on them to double check they were secure, then turned to face Brewster. He shoved the keyring into Brewster's chest and grinned.

"First watch, Private," Thomas said, then gestured for Wilson and Krueger to follow him upstairs.

"Oh, that's fucking bullshit," Brewster said, looking up after the Sergeant Major. "I ain't in the Army anymore, *Sarge*!"

Despite his bluster, Brewster lowered himself onto the stairs, sighed, and settled in for a guard shift, scratching at an itch on the back of his neck.

Rebecca awoke suddenly, sitting bolt upright and clutching her sleeping bag to her chest. She took a deep, shuddering breath and let it out slowly.

"Must've been a bad dream," she whispered to herself.

She looked around the darkened tower. The group's flashlights had been turned off to save battery power and the only light came from the waxing moon, half-full in a cloudless sky. The group lay sleeping around her, some in bags, others stretched out between blankets.

She slowly laid herself back on the floor and closed her eyes, determined to fall back asleep.

Her eyes shot back open a moment later. Something was wrong.

She sat up again and studied the scene in front of her. Everyone was accounted for. Nothing was out of place. Must have just been her imagination.

Then it hit her-Ron wasn't snoring. The man was notorious for it. Nearly every night someone had to wake him up or kick him to get him to roll over, and those were on the nights when he didn't wake himself up with his racket. Once she noticed that, she began to notice other things that were awry. No one was moving, not even those subtle, tiny sleep movements—a twitch of a finger, a reflexive swallow, a mumble. More than that, though. No one was breathing.

Rebecca felt fear solidify in the pit of her stomach, but she had long since learned to deal with fear. She rationalized it, shoved it into a corner of her brain and made it work for her instead of against her. Fear just let a person know they were still alive. She narrowed her eyes and rooted around in her sleeping bag until she came up with her flashlight, but didn't click it on immediately. She reached behind her back, feeling around in the darkness until her fingers bumped into the leather of her holster and pistol belt. She dragged it closer, grabbed for her weapon, and froze.

Her pistol was gone.

Now the fear threatened to overwhelm her. She hadn't been without a weapon since she'd shot Decker on the USS *Ramage,* and she realized she felt completely naked without one.

"Okay, okay, stay calm—everyone up here has a weapon. Get one of theirs. No problem," Rebecca whispered to herself.

She pushed herself to her feet, held the flashlight out in front of her and clicked it on, playing the beam over the floor in front of her. Her eyes went wide.

The beam had landed on Thomas' face first. His eyes were sunken, half open, and rolled back into his head. He looked long dead. Rebecca blanched, swallowed, and let the beam play over Thomas' gear, searching for his weapon. She located his holster, but it, too, was empty.

Krueger was at Thomas' head, stretched out in his sleeping bag. His face was just as pale and unmoving as Thomas', eyes open and pupils fixed and dilated. Rebecca knew Krueger never let his rifle out of arm's reach. He lived with his rifle, loved his rifle, took better care of his rifle than he would a wife, most likely—yet it was nowhere to be found.

Rebecca felt her breath coming in short gasps, realized she was on the verge of hyperventilating, and worked on slowing herself down, taking deeper, longer breaths.

One by one, she checked the members of the group. All dead. No weapons. Not a mark on them.

"The food," she said to herself. "I was the only one who didn't eat the food."

She stopped, struck by a thought. What about Brewster?

She stepped gingerly between the bodies, moved over to the railing, and leaned over, shining the flashlight down into the darkness.

"Brewster?" she called out. "Brewster, are you down there?"

There was no reply.

"Oh, no," she said, crumpling to the floor and holding onto the railing with a white-knuckled grip. "Am I the only one left? Am I—"

Booted footsteps rang out on metal from below, clear, slow, and steady.

Rebecca's face was a mask of apprehension as she shifted the flashlight in her hand, playing the beam along the stairs.

"Brewster?" she called out once more.

The beam fell on Brewster's face, halfway up the staircase.

"Oh, shit," Rebecca breathed.

Brewster was just as dead as the rest of the group. His jaw hung open, his tongue lolled out the side, skin pale as the moonlight outside. Well, perhaps not just as dead—he was shambling up the stairs, stumbling a bit but making steady progress.

"Oh shit, oh shit, oh shit," Rebecca chanted like a panicked mantra. She dropped the flashlight and began desperately tearing through blankets and sleeping bags, not caring if she disturbed the bodies within. She needed a weapon, any weapon. She'd settle for a knife. The sound of booted footsteps grew ever nearer.

"Come *on!*" she screamed, upending a backpack and sending odds and ends skittering across the floor. "Where are the guns? Where are all the *fucking guns?*"

A sound behind Rebecca attracted her attention. She froze, eyes wide, and slowly turned her head to look.

Brewster stood at the top of the stairwell, blocking her only escape route. He seemed to grin.

"Brewster," Rebecca started, holding up a hand to ward him off.

The soldier said nothing in reply. He merely opened his jaws and leaned in for the kill.

0921 hrs_

"Rebecca! Rebecca! Jesus, wake up, for fuck's sake!" Krueger said, shaking Rebecca's shoulder.

Rebecca shot awake, grabbing at Krueger's arm. Her eyes were wide and her sleeping bag was half soaked-through with sweat. Krueger had a sympathetic look on his face.

"Another dream, huh?" he asked.

Rebecca didn't answer right away. She looked around the tower. Morning sunlight was burning away the last vestiges of fog outside, and the group was already active. Only Wilson and Ron remained asleep. Everyone else was on their feet, stretching, sighing, and working out kinks developed from spending eight hours laying on concrete. Sherman, Thomas and Denton were missing, probably outside already. She looked over her shoulder at her pistol belt. The weapon was right where it was supposed to be.

"Yeah," she said, nodding. "Yeah, another dream."

"Must've been a bad one," Krueger said. "You were mumbling to yourself."

She nodded again, taking a deep breath to steady herself. They'd all had dreams over the course of the past month or so, but that one had felt extremely real. It was unsettling. If she hadn't had an appetite the night before, she sure didn't have one now.

"Come on," Krueger said, standing and offering her an arm. "We're going to head down and get the vehicles fueled up and ready to go. Sherman said he wants to get on the road after we eat."

The mention of eating sent Rebecca's stomach to twisting again. She grimaced, but accepted the offered arm after buckling her pistol belt securely around her waist. Krueger snapped up his rifle and pack, having already strapped his sleeping bag across the top, and helped Rebecca do the same. He nudged the still-sleeping Wilson with his boot as they passed.

"Wake up, sleepy-head," Krueger said. "Don't waste the day."

Wilson murmured something, still only half-conscious, and managed to flick Krueger off. Krueger chuckled and jogged down the tower stairs. They passed Brewster, leaning against the support column that held up the tower. He looked bleary-eyed and tired, having spent the night on watch. Rebecca clenched her jaw as she passed him, glancing at the soldier out of the corner of her eye.

Brewster caught her expression and arched an eyebrow. "The hell was that look for?"

Rebecca didn't reply, and instead followed Krueger out into the sunlight.

"Well, good fuckin' morning to you too, beautiful!" Brewster called out after her. He shook his head. "Some people."

Denton was standing next to the pickup, upending a can of gasoline into the tank. Three empties lay in the grass next to him, and the cart of still-untouched cans was a few feet away. He waved as Krueger and Rebecca approached.

"This one's just about full now," he said. "And there are eleven more cans in that cart. Figure four to fill up the utility truck, three for the car, leaves us with twenty spare gallons to use on the road. Not a bad haul, eh?"

Krueger grinned. "Should last us a couple more full days of driving."

"A good four hundred more miles, you bet," Denton said. "'Course, we still have twice that to go."

"So we raid one more airport along the way. Problem solved," Krueger said, raising his arms in a victory sign.

Denton chuckled.

"Where are Sherman and Thomas?" Rebecca asked.

"In the terminal," Denton replied, pointing. "They're packing up what's left of the food in that little souvenir store."

Again with the food, Rebecca thought. "Anything we can do to help?"

"Oh, no, I've got this taken care of," Denton said. "Though I bet Sherman and Thomas could find something to occupy you if you're looking for something to do."

"Thanks," Rebecca said, turning and heading towards the terminal.

Krueger hung behind, leaning up against the back of the pickup and sighing. "Whaddaya say, Denton?"

"Eh?" Denton asked, looking up from the gas can.

"Just making smalltalk. Nice weather today, huh?" Krueger asked, grinning impishly.

Denton frowned at him. "Smalltalk doesn't befit you."

Krueger chuckled. "It's been a while since we all had a regular morning. You know, wake up slowly, stretch, eat, chat. It's good to pretend things are normal for a change."

"I don't know," Denton said. "I'm not a huge fan of pretending. Makes me feel like an ostrich."

"Ostrich?" Krueger asked.

"You know, head in the sand?" Denton replied. "Ostriches—actually, I'm not even sure if they really do this or not, but it's common knowledge—when they feel threatened, they bury their heads in the sand and pretend like the danger isn't really there, because they can't see it anymore. Just because you can't see the danger doesn't mean it isn't going to bite you in the ass."

"Reminds me of something Sherman said," Krueger said after a moment had passed in silence.

"Oh? What's that?"

"Well, after we got out of Hyattsburg and got on the road, I heard him talking with Thomas," Krueger went on. "Turns out this lady we're trying to meet up with, what's her name, uh, Demilio—she tried to warn people about Morningstar before the first outbreaks in Africa. No one listened."

"Eh, that's just politicians for you," Denton said. "They don't see problems in terms of potential. They can't. If they spend a bunch of money preventing something, and that something never harms so much as a fly because of their farsightedness and caution, then they get accused of wasting resources. On the other hand, if they wait too long, they can be accused of being uncaring bastards. The trick is to find a happy medium."

"Happy medium," Krueger repeated, arching an eyebrow.

"Yeah," Denton said. "You have to let a problem get in a bite or two, and *then* kick it's ass. That way you can say, 'Look, it was *definitely* a threat, and I *definitely* dealt with it before it got out of hand. Vote for me!'"

Krueger laughed out loud. "I'd say they fucked that one up pretty good, at least as far as Morningstar's concerned."

"Oh, yeah." Denton nodded in agreement. "Majorly. I'm just saying, maybe people *did* listen when Demilio tried to warn them, but they chose not to do anything at first."

"Guess we'll never know," Krueger said.

The doors to the control tower were pushed open, and Brewster, Wilson, Ron, and Katie came ambling out. Brewster blinked heavily, holding a hand up to block out the sunlight.

"Damn, man, don't know how Thomas expects me to function with no sleep all the time," he complained.

"Sleep on the road," Ron suggested. "We'll be riding all day again."

"But I get motion sickness if I try to sleep in a car," Brewster protested, holding a hand over his stomach.

"Then stay here and sleep while the rest of us go," Ron said, throwing up his arms in exasperation.

"Hell no, I'm not staying at this creepy-ass airport," Brewster said.

Ron rolled his eyes and kept walking.

In the terminal, Sherman and Thomas had kept themselves busy, rooting around the small storage room behind the counter in the souvenir store and coming up with another couple of boxes of snack food. Thomas wasn't elated at the find ("I prefer a little more starch in my diet, sir."), but Sherman shrugged and cut the tape on the boxes with a pocketknife, dumping the contents onto the countertop.

Rebecca wandered in, nodding to Thomas and waving at Sherman.

"Good morning," she said, letting her eyes wander over a rack of postcards. "Sleep well?"

"Better than I have in the past couple of weeks," Sherman replied. "It's amazing what a set of locked doors can do to your sense of security."

"I would've slept better if I'd left someone besides Brewster on guard duty," Thomas said.

"You've got no one to blame but yourself for that one," Sherman said, shrugging. "Besides, he's not such a bad guy. Been pulling his weight just like everyone else."

"He's too damn distracted all the time," Thomas frowned, then gestured straight ahead with a free hand. "Needs to focus."

"Well, that's your job, Sergeant," Sherman grinned. "Keep the boys in line."

"Don't remind me, sir. I feel like a failure enough already. Krueger's the only one of 'em left worth half a damn," Thomas grumbled.

"Hate to interrupt," Rebecca said, clearing her throat. "Most of us are up and about out there. I was wondering if there was anything I could do to help move things along...?"

"Oh. Sure," Sherman said. "Here, grab one of these boxes and take it out to the vehicles."

He lifted a large box and handed it over. Rebecca nearly lost it, surprised by the weight, but recovered. Sherman had hefted it like it was nothing. She reminded herself once again not to underestimate the older man's athleticism. She passed by several others on their way in. Ron held the door open for her.

"More potato chips?" he asked, tilting his head to read the label on the side of the box. "Awesome."

"All right, where's the bathroom?" Katie asked, looking left and right as she entered the terminal. "There has to be one in here. I wonder if the water's still on?"

"Probably," Wilson said, pushing past her. "I remember reading somewhere that something like three-quarters of all the plumbing in the United States is gravity-fed, not pumped."

"Well, I have no idea what that means, but cool," Katie replied, shrugging.

Ron disagreed, shaking his head. "Yeah, but look where we are. Mountains, remember? They probably have to pump the stuff uphill. No electricity, no pumps, no water."

"For once I'm hoping you're wrong and Wilson's right," Katie said, poking Ron in the chest. "Aha! There they are!"

Katie made a beeline for the women's room, shoving open the door and vanishing inside. A moment later, a loud squeal erupted from behind the closed door. Ron and Wilson's hands went straight for their weapons, and they ran toward the restroom. Ron kicked the door open—and made Katie jump a foot in the air in surprise. She was standing in front of the sink, a grin plastered on her face. She gestured at the running faucet.

"Water," she said, laughing. "What's with the guns?"

Ron sighed and Wilson shook his head, holstering his pistol.

"You just about gave us a heart attack," Ron admonished.

"Sorry," Katie said, but she didn't sound it.

"And on that note, I think I'll repair to the men's room myself," Wilson said. "Wash up and change."

"I'm with you," Ron added.

They let the restroom door swing shut and walked away, shaking their heads. Sherman and Thomas came out of the souvenir store, each bearing a box of assorted food, and spotted Ron and Wilson walking toward the men's room.

"Hey," Sherman called out. The two men looked over. "When you're done in there, would you mind heading into the store and grabbing a couple more of these boxes?"

"Sure," Ron said, nodding. "We'll meet you out by the cars in a couple of minutes."

"Don't take too long," Sherman said. "Don't want to waste the daylight."

"Four, five minutes, tops," Wilson said, holding up a hand.

He leaned his back on the men's room door, pushing it open— and fell right back into the arms of an infected wearing civilian clothes. It roared in his face, grabbed at his shirt, and sank its teeth into the back of his neck, immediately drawing blood. Wilson didn't even have time to react.

"Shit!" Ron yelled, throwing his bag to the ground and fumbling for his pistol.

Across the terminal, Sherman and Thomas dropped their boxes and came running toward the pair.

"Wilson! Wilson! Throw it off! Get it off!" Sherman yelled, gesturing wildly.

Wilson was screaming in pain now, grasping at the carrier, which had latched onto his back like a humanoid leech. This one was still alive—a sprinter, with all the strength and speed of a normal human. Moreso, even, allowing for its fevered strength. Wilson slammed his back against the wall over and over, trying to dislodge the infected. It barked short grunts of pain as it hit the wall, and its jaws came loose from Wilson's neck, but its hands still grabbed at the soldier.

Ron ran forward, giving up on trying to find a clean shot, and drew his machete. He wound up, watched Wilson's movements for a careful moment, and swung. The blade bit into the infected's shoulder, spraying blood against the white tile of the bathroom wall. Ron wrenched the machete free, and the infected came loose, hitting the floor heavily. It twisted and spasmed, grasping at its shoulder with its uninjured arm, still roaring in defiance.

Sherman came up behind Ron, reached around him with a hand that held a locked and loaded pistol, and fired twice, sharp staccato bursts in the enclosed space. Both rounds took the carrier in the chest, and it spasmed once more, then settled into death.

Wilson stood in the bathroom, holding a hand to his neck and staring at the corpse on the floor. When he pulled his shaking hand away, it came free covered in blood. The soldier choked back a sob.

"That's it, man," he said after a moment. "I'm done. It got me. I'm infected."

He looked up at Sherman, Thomas, and Ron in the doorway, but none of them offered any rebuttal. They just looked back at him with sad, sympathetic expressions on their faces. Wilson swallowed, slowly drew his pistol, and walked over to the corpse of the carrier on the bathroom floor.

"Fucker," he said, and fired into the infected's head. He fired again, and again, and again. The body jerked with the impact of the rounds and blood and brain matter splashed Wilson's boots. The three men in the doorway backed away slowly, unwilling to get any of the infected blood on themselves. "Fucker."

Wilson stopped firing before his pistol ran dry. He took a deep, shuddering breath, still holding onto his neck, and looked back up at Sherman.

"Guess this is goodbye, sir," Wilson said. "I ain't getting into a vehicle with you all if I'm infected."

Again, no one offered any argument. Wilson wasn't the first of their number to be bitten. It was a death sentence, plain and simple. Wilson might have a few days left to him, but eventually, he would turn, and when he did no one around him would be safe.

"Been a slice, Wilson," Ron said after a moment, then extended his hand. Wilson shook it with his right, his left keeping pressure on the bite.

"Good huntin'," Thomas said. He nodded, then turned and strode away. It was as tender a goodbye as any the old sergeant had offered before.

"Sorry, Wilson," Sherman said, frowning. "Wish it didn't have to be like this."

"Me too, sir," Wilson said, chuckling. "Me too."

Ron collected Katie from the women's restroom and retreated with Sherman to the terminal's main entrance, sparing one final glance over his shoulder at Wilson. The soldier was standing in the doorway of the bathroom, waving with a hand that still grasped a pistol.

They pushed their way out of the front doors and into the sunlight.

Brewster and Denton had taken cover behind the bed of the pickup when the shots had rung out, and the small group exiting the terminal found themselves staring down the barrels of rifles.

"Hold up," Brewster shouted out. "Friendlies."

The survivors slowly appeared from behind the vehicles. The back of the utility truck opened up and Jack and Mitsui poked their heads out.

"Heard shots," Denton yelled to Sherman. "What happened?"

"Remember that last carrier we couldn't find last night?" Sherman said, grimacing. "Wilson found it."

"Is he...?" Brewster started.

Another shot rang out, this one muted but still loud enough to cause the group to cringe. It had come from inside the terminal.

"Yeah," Sherman said after the sound had faded away.

Brewster scowled and looked down at the ground. "Goddamnit."

"There's nothing more we can do here," Sherman said, sighing. "Mount up, people. We have a lot of ground to cover before we get to Omaha."

CHAPTER TWO
OUT OF THE EAST

```
Point Pleasant, West Virginia
March 05, 2007
1312 hrs_
```

"I THINK WE SHOULD HAVE spent a little more time trying to get the car back on its wheels again," said Julie Ortiz, sinking gratefully onto a bench and breathing heavily, holding her side and shaking her head. "I'm not cut out for this hiking shit."

"We can go over that again and again but it won't bring our vehicle back," said Mason, lifting a pair of binoculars to his eyes and scanning the horizon. "Besides, we tried. Even with all three of us, it wasn't budging."

"Maybe if we used, I don't know, a big lever or something," Julie said, throwing up a hand in exasperation.

Anna Demilio looked at the journalist out of the corner of her eye and smirked.

"I saw that," Julie said, frowning at Anna.

"I'm not the one who rolled it," Anna said in her own defense, nodding in Mason's direction.

"And I already told you both, those two sprinters came out of nowhere. It was reflexive. Either one of you would have done the same thing," Mason said, not looking up from his binoculars. After a few moments, he spoke, still peering through the lenses. "Well, ladies, I have bad news, and I have more bad news. Which do you want to hear first?"

"Eh," Julie let her mind work over her choices. "Let's go with the bad news."

"Bad news it is," Mason said. He let the binoculars drop to hang from his neck. The three were sitting in a park on a hillside, overlooking the town of Point Pleasant on the border of West Virginia. They'd made good time in a month, first clearing the suburbs of Washington, D.C., then the rural communities of Maryland, and finally the Appalachian mountains of West Virginia. They were nearing the plains, heading due west, when they'd lost their car in an accident. They'd been walking for the past week. Supplies were running dangerously low, and they were all sorely in need of a rest.

Mason's black and gray urban camoflague was ripped and torn at the knees and elbows, and mud smears marred the pattern. He'd appropriated street hockey pads in one of the smaller towns and strapped them on, but they were already dinged up. He wore a simple baseball cap on his head, and a black rucksack on his back. A submachine gun was strapped across his shoulders and a Beretta rode comfortably against his thigh. He leaned back against a maple tree and sighed.

"Bad news is there's only one way out of this town, and that's across a bridge," he said, pointing straight ahead. "It looks pretty well jammed up with abandoned cars and debris, so it could be a little treacherous."

"And the other bad news?" Anna asked. Of the three, she still looked the most presentable. Somehow along the way she'd continually managed to find clean t-shirts to wear, and refused to share her secret with her two companions. Julie and Mason suspected she was sneaking off in the night to loot stores as they passed through towns, but if she was, she kept it to herself.

"I think we'll *have* to cross the bridge," Mason said. "We're a good three, four miles from that river and I can see without the binoculars that it's trying to jump its banks. Spring thaw. Current'll be fast and dangerous. No way we're swimming it, and unless we find a boat with a working engine, we'll have to take the bridge."

"That's fine with me," Julie said, stretching her legs. "Maybe we'll find a working car somewhere down there."

"One can hope," Anna agreed.

"I'm more worried about food, personally," Mason said, looking over his shoulder at the women. "In case you've forgotten, we ran out yesterday. I can live with walking. I can't live without food."

"Well, we picked a decent place to run out," Anna said, gesturing at the town below them. "There has to be something down there."

"Yeah," Mason scoffed. "Carriers, most likely."

"Now's the best time to go through," Anna continued. "It's just past midday, we've got a good five hours of daylight left, and the infected seem to prefer darkness. If we're quiet and careful, we should make it through all right."

Mason considered this a moment, then nodded. "Okay. I'm up for it. Julie?"

"No time like the present," she said, groaning as she climbed to her feet. "I would kill for a cup of coffee and some tylenol."

"You may yet have the chance," Mason said. "Onward and downward!"

The trio kept to the streets, walking steadily downhill toward the river. Mason led the way. He unslung his MP-5, a compact but powerful nine-millimeter sub machinegun, and held it at the ready, scanning the side streets, alleys, and doorways for any signs of movement.

"Oh, look, a Bennigan's," Julie said, pointing. "Wish they were open. I could use a burger."

"Don't remind me," Mason said. "And keep it quiet."

"Sorry," Julie added, a bit sheepishly.

More than once Mason stopped the group, holding up a closed fist and staring off at seemingly innocent buildings, or empty parking lots. Anna and Julie knew better. Mason wasn't the type to halt them over nothing; invariably, he would alter their course slightly after each stop, putting a few damaged, abandoned vehicles between them and the offending building, or taking them down a side street instead of continuing on course. He never offered an explanation as to what spooked him, and neither woman asked.

After nearly an hour of walking, the terrain began to level out, and the sound of the rushing river grew louder. Mason began to pay attention to street signs, and after spotting one that seemed particularly interesting to him, he halted the group again, knelt, pulled out an atlas from his rucksack, and checked their position within the town.

"Nearly there now," he whispered over his shoulder. "Four more blocks."

"Please let there be a car we can hotwire on the bridge, please, oh, please God," Julie said.

"Quiet!"

"Sorry."

They rounded the final corner and the bridge came into sight. Cars were backed up on both sides of it for blocks in either direction. Mason halted the group again, scowling at the congestion. Vehicles of every make and model, most with luggage strapped to the roofs or spilling out the back windows, littered the road. Several were left with their doors hanging open, and suitcases lay upended on the pavement, evidence of the panicked flight of the occupants.

"See any you could hotwire again, Mason?" Julie asked hopefully.

Mason shook his head slowly. "Maybe that Festiva over there, but the door's open. The battery's probably dead. Besides, look at it—it's blocked in on all sides. We'd never get it free, even if it did start."

"Oh, damn," Julie moaned, stomping her foot. "And we haven't even seen anyplace to find food—unless you count the Bennigan's, but you weren't having that, were you?"

"I hate chains," Mason said, shaking his head. "Besides, all the food in there would have spoiled by now."

"Let's just cross the bridge and get back on the road," Anna said. "We'll find something."

"I'm with you," Mason agreed.

He jumped up onto the hood of a sedan, looking to hop from roof to roof to make the crossing easier.

Instead, he froze in place, staring across the bridge with a clenched jaw, looking very much like a lifelike statue. He narrowed his eyes.

"What?" Anna asked, looking back and forth between Mason and the bridge. When Mason didn't reply, she repeated her query. Mason stared straight ahead, not bothering to answer. "What is it, already?"

Suddenly, Mason leapt off the side of the sedan, falling into a crouch. He gestured for the two women to do likewise.

"Get down, get down!" he called out.

They hastened to comply, crouching with their backs against the side of the car.

"What is it? You've got my heart going a mile a minute," Julie protested.

Mason's voice was grating, just barely above a growl. "It's Sawyer."

"What?" Julie asked. "Where?"

She poked her head up above the car's engine block and peered across the bridge. Mason grabbed the back of her collar and yanked her back down with a yelp.

"Hey!" she said, slapping his hand away.

"What do you want to do, get yourself shot?" Mason asked angrily. "He's watching the bridge."

"How do you know that?" Anna asked, pistol drawn.

"I saw the reflection of the sun off a scope when I jumped on the car," Mason explained. "They're on the hillside across the river, watching the bridge."

"Mm-hmm," Anna said, arching an eyebrow. "I repeat: how do you know that's Sawyer and not just something randomly reflecting the light?"

Mason frowned at her. "Have I ever led you wrong before? All right, look: it's too convenient. First, this is a perfect ambush site, a bottleneck. Second, he's right where I'd be if I was the one setting the ambush. And finally, it's been two weeks since we've run across him and his posse, which makes us overdue for another encounter. I've actually been wondering these past couple of days when or if we were going to bump into him again."

Sawyer had been a thorn in the trio's side since before they'd left Washington. He was a dyed-in-the-wool All-American who, like Mason had, worked for the National Security Agency. His last assignment had been to interrogate Anna Demilio and provide his superiors with information about the Morningstar strain in order for them to better combat the virus. His methods had been brutal, and his personality suggested someone who was willing to do just about anything to get the job done, up to and including murder.

When Mason had helped Anna and Julie escape the NSA facility, Sawyer had followed, intent on recapturing his charges and bringing Mason to justice—albeit his own, twisted form of justice.

"Oh, damn it," Anna said, sighing. "I thought we'd lost him back in Maryland."

"Apparently not," Mason replied. "I'm beginning to think Sawyer knows where we're going."

Julie scoffed, shaking her head. "How could he possibly know that?"

"I don't know, *you* tell *me*," Mason said, looking pointedly at Julie. "The only place our destination was written down—at least to my knowledge—was on that computer you accessed in the safehouse back in D.C."

"It took me an hour to get into that system and I knew what I was looking for," Julie protested. "There's no way he—oh."

"Oh?" Anna asked, raising her eyebrows.

"Oh," Julie repeated. "I may have left the system on when we had to run out in that big hurry."

"Great," Anna said, rolling her eyes. "Now we can't lose the bastard. He knows where we're headed, so he can just keep leapfrogging ahead of us any time we get away from him and set an ambush. We're dead."

"Not necessarily," Mason said, considering the situation. "He's waiting for us right now. He thinks we'll definitely try to cross that bridge to keep heading west. After all, it's the only one for miles and miles in either direction, so it's a pretty reasonable deduction. But if we slip past without him realizing it—"

"—he'll just keep waiting for us," Julie finished, grinning. "He'll never realize we've moved on."

"Ah, well, let's not go too far," Mason admonished. "Eventually he'll realize we gave him the slip, and he'll pick up and come after us again. That, or he'll think we bought the farm somewhere and give up, but I wouldn't want to assume that. Sawyer's far too obtuse to let this little grudge of his go that easily. He'll want bodies. Proof."

"There's a pleasant thought," Anna said, imagining a triumphant Sawyer standing over their corpses.

"This guy is a major league asshole," Julie said. "This is, what, the third time he's caught up with us? Doesn't he have anything better to do? I mean, the world's falling to shit, the dead are walking, and this guy wants to arrest us? It's pretty sad, if you ask me."

"It's not sad to him," Mason said. "Besides, I'm starting to get the vibe that this isn't *just* a grudge. Sawyer may be an asshole, but he's a smart asshole. He isn't the kind of person to throw his life away just to get even with someone. I'm betting he has orders."

"Orders?" Julie asked. "From who?"

"From a higher-up. Brass. You don't honestly think Morningstar wiped out everyone but us and Sawyer, do you?"

"I agree with Mason," Anna said, nodding slowly. "I'm betting there are some pretty powerful people still out there calling the shots, and there have to be just as many not-so-powerful people willing to have their strings pulled."

"Like Sawyer," Mason said.

"Like Sawyer," Anna agreed. "And as much as I hate to say this, his orders probably have a lot to do with me."

"Little narcicissm for breakfast, Colonel?" Julie said, grinning.

"Seriously," Anna said. "I wasn't the only doctor researching Morningstar before the pandemic, but I *was* the most knowledgeable. That's no conceit. I studied my ass off. I already told you how those interrogation sessions of his went back in the District. Not a question about you, Julie, and not a question about why we leaked that intel. It was Morningstar. Day after day, it was Morningstar. 'Will this work?' 'Will that work?' 'Do we have a snowball's chance in hell if we try this, or that?' They were *using* me to fight the virus."

Mason nodded in agreement. "That's true. Sawyer kept you to himself, wouldn't let Derrick or me near you after the initial questioning. We thought maybe he was gunning for a promotion, keeping us out of the loop and all, but it's just as likely he was getting orders from higher-up."

"Okay, okay," Julie surrendered, holding up her hands. "I get it. So what are we going to do?"

"Well," Mason said, sighing heavily and letting a frown crease his features, "We can't cross the bridge."

"No shit," Julie remarked.

Mason shot her an annoyed glance before continuing. "We go with Plan B. We give him the slip. We'll have to find another bridge, or a working boat, and get across the river. If it was midsummer, I'd say we could swim it, but right now that's damn near impossible. River's way too high and running way too fast for that. We'd be drowned or swept downstream before we made it halfway across."

"South," Anna said, pointing. "We head south. The river cuts east just a couple miles north. We'd end up doubling back on our own trail if we went that way."

Mason considered this a moment, then nodded. "All right. South it is. Let's go."

He rose into a crouch and took off at a jog, still heading toward the water, but at an angle that would take him away from the bridge and toward the river's banks. He made sure to keep buildings and trees between him and the spot on the hillside where he'd seen the glint of sunlight on glass. When the road ended near the river, he slid on his backside down the steep grassy slope, stopping himself neatly at the bottom and turning to make sure the two women followed successfully.

A few industrial buildings littered the riverbanks, prefabricated sheetmetal structures that were eaten through in a few places by rust. Mason was inwardly pleased by these new surroundings. They would provide plenty of cover for the trio as they moved away from Sawyer's planned ambush site. Materials—rolls of rusted steel, rebar, small mountains of sand and gravel—were stacked nearly in rows between the buildings, affording even more cover. Mason led the women across an unpaved parking lot and along the side of one of the longer warehouses, moving at a dogtrot.

When Mason came to the first doorway, a wide two-story cutaway large enough for construction machinery to pass through unhindered, he skidded to a stop, pressed his back against the wall, and knelt down. He leaned out fractionally from his cover, just enough to peer into the building with one eye. Left, right, up, down—he scanned the interior for hostiles. Seeing nothing out of the ordinary, he leaned back, nodded his approval to Anna and Julie, then resumed his dogtrot.

They had made it a little more than halfway through the industrial park when Mason slowed to a walk, furrowing his brow.

"What is it?" Anna asked.

"Hold up," Mason said, drawing to a stop. Anna halted, and Julie, who had been looking over her shoulder to make certain the group wasn't being followed, had to skid in the gravel to keep from plowing Anna and Mason over. "I could have sworn I heard something."

"What was it?" Anna whispered.

"Footstep, I thought," Mason said, voice just as low. "On gravel."

The trio stood in place on the side of the building a moment longer, Mason tilting his head to the side to hear better. Sure enough, the crunch of a booted foot on gravel came to their ears, distant and indistinct. It was either coming from a long way off, or someone nearby was taking pains to remain as quiet as they were. With the metal walls of the warehouses all around them, it was tough to get a fix on the direction the sound was coming from.

"Stay close," Mason said, and carefully thumbed the safety on his MP-5 from 'safe' to 'semi'. He stalked slowly along the outside of the warehouse, peering down the barrel of his weapon. Anna was right behind him, pistol drawn and held at the ready. Julie brought up the rear, casting nervous glances behind herself.

They reached the corner of the building, and Mason brought them to a halt once again. He seemed undecided, eyes flicking between the ground at the building's edge and the corner of the structure itself. Anna could see his jaw clenching and unclenching.

"Just do it," she whispered.

That seemed to do the trick.

Mason gritted his teeth and swung out from the wall, rounding the corner in a flash and holding his MP-5 in front of him. Anna and Julie were right behind him.

They found themselves staring down the barrels of rifles.

Suddenly, everything was a blur of movement and shouted commands.

"*Freeze!*"

"*Drop your weapons! Drop your weapons!*"

"*Do it now!*"

"*Get on the ground! Move!*"

Anna, Mason, and Julie had rounded the corner and come face-to-face with another group of survivors, also numbering three. All were armed, and all were just as startled as the trio to suddenly be facing live opposition. Neither side showed any intention of lowering their weapons, and after the shouted threats had died down, the six survivors realized they were stuck in a Mexican standoff.

Mason narrowed his eyes at the leader of the opposing group, a tall, thin man with shoulder-length hair and the beginnings of a beard. "We don't want any trouble, chief. Just lower your rifles. We'll do the same, then we'll be on our way."

"Fuck you," said the scraggly man. "You lower your weapons first, then we'll lower ours."

"Not going to happen," Mason said.

One of the other two newcomers, a young man wearing a hooded sweatshirt, twitched his aim fractionally to draw a bead on Mason's head in silent response. Anna and Julie replied with adjusted aims of their own.

"All right, all right, let's everyone just relax," the scraggly man said. "Matt, ease up on that trigger finger. Ease up!"

The young man in the sweatshirt looked anxious, but his index finger slowly lifted off the trigger.

"Okay," the scraggly man said, sounding relieved. "I'm going to lower my rifle now. Think you can manage doing the same?"

"I think so," Mason replied, easing off his own grip on the MP-5's trigger.

The man's rifle barrel lowered fractionally. Mason dropped his own aim, matching the man's movements perfectly. Looking like mirror images of one another, they lowered their weapons until they were pointed straight at the ground. Seeing the two men back down, Anna, Julie, and the scraggly man's companions all dropped their aims or holstered their pistols. The six survivors heaved a collective sigh of relief.

"Glad that's over," the scraggly man said. "Can't say I enjoy the feeling of having a gun pointed at me."

"Me neither," Mason said. "Though it sure ain't the first time."

"Name's Trevor. Trevor Westscott. You can call me Trev," said the scraggly man, holding out his free hand.

"Greg Mason, NSA," Mason said, shaking Trev's hand.

The newcomer's eyes widened. "NSA?"

"Well, as of last month, anyway," Mason said, shrugging. "I'm pretty sure I'm fired. This is Julie Ortiz, formerly of Channel Thirteen News, and Lt. Colonel Anna Demilio, USAMRIID."

"Well, hell," Trev chuckled, shaking their hands as well, "It seems we've run across some white collar survivors, lady and gentleman.

This is Matt Tanner, and Junko Koji, both students. Well, they *were* students, anyway."

"Hello," said the short, dark-haired female, nodding.

"Hiya," waved Matt, slinging his rifle.

"What did you do?" Mason asked Trev.

The scraggly man grinned by way of reply and shrugged. "Little of this, little of that."

Mason knew how to read people well enough to know Trev wasn't just being facetious; the man was actually hiding something. He decided he didn't want to risk their newfound friends' ire and chose not to press the issue.

"What brings you three into town? With those jobs, you're obviously not from around here," Trev added.

"Just passing through," Mason admitted. "On our way west."

"What about you three? Towns aren't exactly the safest places these days," Julie asked.

"Shopping," Matt said with a grin.

"He means looting," Junko interjected. Her voice had a slight accent to it. "We're getting to be pretty good at it, too."

"That's right," Trev said. "Got as much non-perishables as three grown people can carry. It's not much, but it'll keep us alive a bit longer."

"Really," Mason said. His stomach growled slightly at the mention of food. "Uh, I know we just met and all, but we actually ran out of food ourselves a few days ago, and—"

"Forget it," Matt interrupted. He turned to look at Trev. "This is why meeting new people is a bad idea, Trev. Eat us out of house and home. Let's just go."

Trev looked sheepish. "Hate to say it, Mason old chum, but he's right. We barely scratch out a living ourselves. We can't feed three extra mouths."

"We're not looking to impose," Mason said. "We'd be happy to trade."

"I'm not sure you have anything we'd want," Trev said after a moment of consideration. He shook his head. "No, no, sorry, but we'll have to pass."

"Ammunition? We've got boxes," Mason suggested.

"We have plenty," Trev said.

"How about a GPS?" Anna offered.

"What, and have it kick the bucket on us in a couple weeks when the satellite falls out of proper orbit? No thanks. Besides, we already know our way around here well enough to get by," Trev said.

"Clean socks?" Julie asked, but she knew it was a stretch even as she said it.

Trev chuckled by way of reply. "I hate to leave you high and dry, folks, really I do. You're funny," he said. "But I have to look after me and mine first, you know?"

Mason nodded slowly. "I guess I understand."

"Got ourselves a little cabin outside of town," Trev went on. "If you can find your own food, you're welcome to stay the night. Just follow the logging trail up the mountain—it's the first dirt road on your left once you pass city limits."

"Thanks for the offer," Mason said.

"My pleasure," Trev replied. "Well, it's been fun. Take care, folks."

With that, Trev threaded his way between Mason and Anna and began walking off to the east, resting his rifle on his shoulder. Junko and Matt followed closely behind him. Mason turned to watch him go, a frustrated expression on his face. He glanced at Anna, and his eyes lit up.

"I have an idea," Mason said in a low voice, flashing a lopsided grin at the doctor.

"Oh, no," Anna said, studying his face. "What is it?"

"Just take your cues from me," Mason replied, still grinning. He raised his voice to normal conversational volume. "Damn, doc, if we don't find you some food soon, the world'll be out it's best shot at finding the vaccine."

Anna sighed and shook her head, completely missing Mason's intent. "We've been over this. The chances of me actually being able to sequence a vaccine once we get to Omaha are somewhere between infintesimal and imp—"

"Vaccine?" came an interested voice.

Anna, Mason, and Julie looked over to see Trev's group halted in its tracks. Trev had turned and was facing them, an inquisitive expression on his face. Matt looked dubious, but he, too, had stopped and turned. Junko's eyes were narrowed, and she was studying Anna intently.

Mason feigned surprise at having been overheard, and nodded. "Yeah, the doc here is trying to get to some lab where they've been stockpiling info on Morningstar. She's a bit of an authority on the subject."

"One of a few authorities," Anna admitted. "I mainly focused my attention on the various manifest symptoms of the virus as well as the epidemiological ramifications of—"

"Whoa, whoa, whoa, slow down there, professor," Matt said, holding up a hand to forestall any further exposition by Dr. Demilio. "What was that about a vaccine? That was the interesting part."

"Well, there isn't one," Anna said. "Not yet, anyway."

"That's right," Trev said, as if he'd expected to hear it. "Viruses. Tough to find cures for them, right?"

"Yes," Anna agreed. "Not like bacteria. Those are pushovers by comparison. Your run-of-the-mill broad spectrum antibiotic can wipe out just about any bacterial infection you come across, but with viruses, you have to specifically engineer a vaccine for each individual viral strain."

"Yeah," Trev grimaced, glancing at his companions. "That's why the polio vaccine was such a big deal when it came out."

"Right, and flu shots," Junko agreed, speaking up for the first time since the group had stopped. "Each year they need to re-engineer the vaccine to fit the mutations of the influenza virus. Or, well, they did. Before all of this."

"Exactly," Anna said, raising her eyebrows. She hadn't expected such an astute crowd.

"But you think you're on to something?" Matt asked.

Anna shrugged. "Maybe. Like I said, I mainly kept my focus on the epidemiological aspects. But there was a laboratory in the Midwest that was focused on finding a vaccine. I'm not sure how much progress they made, or whether or not they're still alive and working or all dead now, but the idea is to get out there and pick up where they left off."

Junko once again let a suspicious expression crease her features. "I took a few biology courses last year. The only place they'd work on a virus like Morningstar is in a biosafety level four laboratory, right?"

"That's right," Anna nodded.

"Well, there are only two in the United States," Junko said, treating Anna to an accusatory look. "One's in Atlanta, the CDC, and the other is USAMRIID's."

"Wrong," Anna said, smiling pleasantly. "There are three. The CDC operates one, USAMRIID operates another, and the two share joint responsibility for a third facility outside of Omaha, Nebraska."

"Then why haven't I ever heard about that one?" Junko asked.

"Because you were never meant to," Anna said. She sighed. "I guess security clearances don't matter now, what with things the way they are, so I may as well just tell you. That facility researched possible real-world uses of various viruses and bacteria. Everything from agricultural uses—bacteria as fertilizer—to more offensive adaptations."

"Wait, what?" Trev asked, narrowing his eyes. "You mean to tell me people were fucking around with Morningstar before this shit hit the fan—and they were considering actually *using* it as a *weapon*? Infecting innocent people with *this*?"

"No, no, that was just a very small portion of the overall research," Anna protested. "Yes, that was one of the possible outcomes, but more interesting to the staff both at the Omaha facility and USAMRIID were Morningstar's ability to alter a victim's metabolism and basic brain functions. Some thought that there was a chance we could actually use the virus to permanently slow an individual's metabolism and make it possible for that individual to live on, say, one-fifth their normal food intake. The final objective there, of course, is a solution to world hunger, or at least a way to put a serious dent in the problem. Victims also display a heightened sense of hearing, smell, even sight—you've noticed they don't like daylight much."

"Yeah," Matt said, jerking his thumb in the direction of the afternoon sun. "That's why we're here right now."

"They're photosensitive," Anna went on. "At least the living ones—though even the dead ones seem to avoid the light when possible. It causes them a certain degree of discomfort. Some hypothesized that we could find a way to reduce the loss of hearing and sight with age using the virus. That sort of thing. Weapons research did occur, and possibly was still occurring at the time of the pandemic, but it made up a fraction of the overall project. Please don't judge us just on that fraction."

"Besides," Julie said, speaking up in Anna's defense, "it's not like that weapons research started the pandemic. That was totally natural, a fluke of nature."

Trev considered this for a long moment, then nodded. "Okay. I see what you're saying. Bottom line, now—if you got to Omaha, what's the chance you'd find this vaccine?"

"Percentage-wise?" Anna asked.

Trev shrugged.

"One percent?" Anna said, cringing.

Matt sighed and shook his head. Junko tapped her fingers against the stock of her slung rifle and glanced at Trev to observe his reaction. Surprisingly, he didn't seem fazed at all. In fact, his eyebrows were raised and his face spoke of someone who'd just received wondrous news.

"I'm sold," Trev said after a long moment. "I mean, assuming you're all on the level."

"We are," Julie said quickly. "Why wouldn't we be?"

"Because you're out of food, we have our packs full, and you'd like to eat tonight," Trev riposted, staring at the reporter. "Hunger'll make a person say just about anything, promise the world, just for a bite—hunger'll turn a saint into a sinner."

"He's right," Mason said, earning irritated looks from Anna and Julie. He noticed their expressions and rushed to defend his apparently traitorous comment. "No, really, he is. We used to use hunger to extract confessions from suspects. It's incredibly effective. Julie, you should know. We barely fed you when you were in the dungeon."

"Thanks for reminding me," Julie said, looking away. Mason was referring to Julie's time in one of the NSA's Washington, D.C. facilities months earlier, after she and Anna had both been arrested for treason for releasing documents and research that showed Morningstar reanimated infected bodies after death. The 'dungeon,' as it had come to be called by the agents and staff at the facility, was one of their best weapons against stubborn suspects. Mason had explained it to the two women on the road.

"It was actually a wine cellar back in the early 19th century," Mason had said. "Part of some sprawling colonial estate. It was willed to the federal government by its owner, and they converted the place into a training facility for U.S. Marshals. Time passed, the city grew, and the mansion was razed and replaced with the NSA facility that stands there now. Or, well, used to stand, for all I know—those fire-bombs we saw being dropped on the city probably burned it to the ground. Anyway, the cellar was converted into a cellblock around 1960, and we added controls to modulate the temperature, lighting, even the relative humidity. It was all designed to be as psychologically distressing as possible. And it worked, too."

Julie, who had spent a much longer time in the dungeon than had Anna, was not comforted by the history lesson. Anna had found it intriguing.

In the present, more pressing matters than history demanded the trio's attention.

"So how do we earn your trust?" Anna asked Trev.

"That's a tricky one, isn't it?" Trev answered. "I guess the only way you'd be able to prove anything of what you just told us would be for us to actually see this facility."

"And that's hundreds of miles away, isn't it?" Matt asked.

"Omaha," Junko added, nodding.

"Yes," Anna agreed. "You're right. I guess we really can't prove it here and now. You'd have to take us at our word. And I really wouldn't blame you if you didn't."

"Hold on," Trev said, holding up a single finger in front of Anna's face. He turned to Junko and Matt. "Guys, group conference. Over here."

Trev led his two companions a short distance away from Mason and the others. They huddled like an underpopulated football team and began to confer, glancing every now and then over their shoulders to make sure they weren't being eavesdropped on.

"You know," Mason said to Anna and Julie after watching Trev's group for a moment, "even if they do help us out, we might be doing them a real disservice by bringing them along. It's not like food and infected are our only problems."

"Huh?" Julie asked.

"Sawyer," Mason said, glancing at her.

"Oh," Julie breathed. "Him."

Julie furrowed her brow and kicked gravel. Mason looked over his shoulder and stared in the direction of the hillside where Sawyer was waiting, out of sight behind the rusting peaks of the warehouses and facilities in the industrial district.

"I guess you're thinking right about now that it would have been a lot better if you'd just killed him back in D.C., aren't you?" Anna asked Mason.

"Yes and no," Mason replied. "If I had, I really would have been a murderer. I've said it before, but I'll say it again. He might be an asshole, but he's an asshole following orders. I can't fault him for that. At the same time, he is getting to be a little overzealous, and I have no doubt he'd kill me and Julie in the process of netting you. So, yeah, I guess I do regret not killing him when I had the chance— but only a little."

"Given another chance, would you?" Anna asked, staring at Mason.

The man sighed heavily, stared once more in the direction of Sawyer's planned ambush site, and slowly nodded. "I think I would, yes. It's down to survival, now. We've escaped him a few times, now, by the skin of our teeth. We might not be as lucky in the future. If I had the shot, yeah, I'd take it."

"All right," Anna said gently. It was obvious that, to Mason at least, the moral implications of killing an agent on the job were distressing. "Then I don't see why we should burden our possible allies with that little tidbit of trouble."

Julie looked mildly surprised, and Mason swung his head around to fix Anna with a narrow-eyed stare. "If we don't tell them, and they end up helping us, and then Sawyer comes down on their heads, it would be just as bad as if I'd shot them myself. We have to warn them."

"No, we don't," Anna insisted. "You just said yourself, if Sawyer comes around again and you have the chance, you're going to finish it. It's our problem, and if Sawyer does catch up and try again, *we'll* deal with it."

"And what if he catches up, say, in the middle of the night, and offs them while they're sleeping?" Mason challenged.

"We'll just have to be extra careful," Anna said.

Mason shook his head and bit his lip. "I don't like it."

"Neither do I, but let's face facts," Anna said. "We're out of food, we have no vehicle, my GPS says we're still weeks, probably months, away from Omaha on foot, and the three of us alone are damn tired from walking twelve hours a day and then pulling rotating three-hour guard shifts every night. We could definitely use a hand. If we add Sawyer into the equation, they might back down from even considering involvement with us."

Mason looked to Julie for support, but the journalist was fixedly ignoring both of her companions, suddenly seeming much more interested in her bootlaces than either of them. He grimaced and finally nodded.

"All right, we'll keep it to ourselves," he said, head hung slightly, sounding quite dejected. Then he looked back up and added in a firm voice: "For now. If Sawyer realizes we've slipped his noose here and catches back up with us, I'm giving them a full run-down! It's only fair."

"Deal," Anna said, sounding satisfied.

Trev and his companions looked as if they, too, were close to reaching a consensus. Matt seemed to be the odd man out, as he kept lifting his head from the huddle, shaking it as if greatly displeased, and then ducking back in. Trev repeatedly jerked his thumb over his shoulder in the direction of Mason, Anna, and Julie and must have deftly countered whatever argument Matt was putting up, because the younger man's shoulders sagged, and he finally nodded. Trev's head turned in Junko's direction, but the young woman was already bobbing her head in agreement. Trev slapped both of them on the shoulders and straightened himself out, turning on his heel to head back towards where Mason and the others stood next to the rusted warehouse wall. Junko and Matt followed closely behind. Junko seemed to be attempting to reassure Matt with a playful shove and a smile.

"Well," Trev said as he approached, "we've talked it over, and we figure that if the only way to learn whether you're telling the truth or not is to see it for ourselves, so be it. After all, what's a little food in exchange for a shot at a vaccine?"

"A one-percent shot," Matt muttered. Junko frowned at him, and Trev glanced back.

"Like I just got through explaining," Trev replied, "it's a hell of a lot better odds than the lottery, and what else are we going to do? Sit in our cabin and rot for the rest of our lives?"

"We have to do something," Junko said, agreeing. "Anything's better than this, just scraping by, barely living, and definitely not *feeling* very alive."

"All right, all right," Matt acquiesced. "I'm good to go."

"Great," Trev said, grinning at him. He turned back to face Mason. "So, like I was saying, we'd be happy to provide you with some of our food. In return, however, you're going to have to let us come along to Omaha to protect our investment."

Mason, Anna, and Julie exchanged glances. The former NSA agent stepped forward with a hand extended. "I don't think we have to have a huddle to make our decision. Welcome to the cause."

Trev accepted Mason's hand and the pair shook, a single up-down.

"We better get walking," Mason said. "We've got a long way to go."

"Walking?" Trev said, laughing loudly enough to cause all five of the others to flinch. "Brother, you're traveling with Trevor Westscott and his merry band now. We have a truck with a tank full of gas back at the cabin—we'll be riding the rest of the way to Omaha."

Julie and Anna exchanged elated grins behind Mason's back. Coming through town instead of taking the long route around was one risk that was certainly seeming to pay off.

CHAPTER THREE
SKIRMISH

DENTON LOUNGED IN THE REAR of the Ford pickup, legs stretched across the bed and crossed at the ankles. He held a chipped, battered Nikon in his hands and was carefully cleaning the lens as the vehicle rumbled along a stretch of swiftly-straightening road. The group was emerging from the Rockies and making their way onto the Midwestern plains. Denton was glad of it; despite being acclimated to cold weather due to his nationality, he had no love for it. He had even less love for the curving, unpredictable mountain roads that made land travel a veritable roller-coaster ride.

"What's that you're doing?" Krueger asked, sitting across the bed from Denton. The soldier had his rifle laid out across his lap and had was wearing a faded boonie cap on his head, strap looped around his neck.

"Keeping my gear in shape," Denton replied, holding the camera up to catch the light. He caught a stray bit of dust on the lens and puffed out a breath, sending the mote flying.

"Well, yeah," Krueger replied, "but why? Didn't you run out of film?"

"Not all of it," Denton said. "I have a couple of rolls left."

"What I don't get is why anyone would want to take a picture anymore," Brewster said, sitting cross-legged near the front of the truck bed, looking downcast. "Who'd want to remember this shitty little period of time in human history, huh?"

Brewster's attitude had been on the antagonistic side for the few days since Wilson's death. Months of traveling together could make anyone friends, and Brewster and Wilson had been no exception. Nor, for that matter, had Denton and Krueger. All of them still felt as if Wilson should still be riding in the truck bed with them, ready to interject with a witty comment or carefully timed smirk.

"Anyone who survives, my friend," Denton said, answering Brewster's question. "Think about it. Who'd want to remember the Hindenburg? Hiroshima? The Holocaust?"

"No sane person," Brewster grumbled.

"No, no," Denton disagreed, "Every sane person. Pictures are a moment in time—just one little moment—but it's *truth*, Brewster, pure *truth*—you don't get a lot of absolutes in this world. A photo is a little slice of solid, absolute truth. That's why I want to keep taking pictures. If any of us survive this and the good old human race pulls through, a hundred years down the line someone's going to ask the question, 'I wonder what the truth of it was, back then?' And then they'll break out my pictures and there it'll be in all it's shitty glory. The truth."

The truck hit a small pothole in the road and bounced the occupants of the bed. Brewster re-adjusted himself and sighed.

"Guess I see what you're saying," Brewster said. "It's just getting harder and harder to find a reason to care about the future, you know?"

Denton couldn't blame the soldier. At Suez, the coalition force numbered in the thousands. Brewster's attitude then had been that of a cynical, jaded, couldn't-care-less jokester. By the time Sharm el-Sheikh had rolled around, the number of soldiers had been pared down to just over fifty. During the journey on the USS *Ramage*, their numbers had been reduced even more. A further dozen were lost in Hyattsburg, Oregon. Others had been killed in their eastward-bound flight since then, and now, including Sherman and Thomas, only four soldiers remained.

"Doc Holliday syndrome," Krueger said, still lounging comfortably. He had been just as upset over the loss of Wilson as Brewster had, but he had somehow managed to bury it.

"What?" Brewster asked.

"What you're feeling," Krueger explained. "Feeling about the future. What's the point, and all. It's called Doc Holliday syndrome."

"The gunslinger?"

"The same," Krueger said. "I used to read about him. Not just him, I mean, but cowboys in general. I was a big wild west fan as a kid. Holliday had tuberculosis. I think it's pretty rare these days, but it was a lot more common back then. Anyway, it's fatal. So, here's Doc Holliday, and he knows he going to die from this disease sooner or later, and so he starts to take all kinds of crazy risks. He figured he was dead anyway, so why bother worrying?"

"So what happened?" Brewster asked.

"He died of tuberculosis," Krueger said with a grin. "Managed to make all those risks pay off."

"All right," Brewster said, nodding slowly. "So what are you saying? That I can take a ton of risks but in the end I'm going to end up a carrier?"

Krueger raised his eyebrows, considered the question, and shrugged. "Just saying that maybe you feel like you don't care because you *figure* you're going to end up a carrier."

"Hey, man, I see a really old version of myself when I think about the future," Brewster protested. "I'm just wondering what that old version of me's going to be doing. What'll be worth doing, you know?"

"Rebuilding," Krueger said. "I guess—and we're talking a couple of decades down the line at least, right?—we'll all be rebuilding. Working on putting what's left back together. It's all we can do. This is a big thing we're living through, man—when people open up a history book a few hundred years from now the big event, the one recurring theme will be this pandemic and its effects, just mark my words."

"I'm surprised," Denton said with raised eyebrows.

"What, that I'm a far-thinker?" Krueger asked. "I'm a far-shooter, too. Maybe it's a genetic thing."

"No, not that," Denton said, waving a hand in dismissal. "I'm surprised you think there'll still be history books being written in a few hundred years."

"I take it you don't have quite the same vision of the future in mind?" Krueger asked, wincing as the truck hit another pothole.

"Call me a pessimist if you want," Denton explained, "but I just can't see what's left of humanity banding together to rise like some kind of a phoenix from the ashes out of this disaster. It's not in our nature. We've got a good thing going right now with our little group. We help each other out. We look out for one another. I'm betting that's not how things are working out in the rest of the world. I'm betting that most of the places that haven't been overrun with carriers by now are tearing themselves apart from inside. Remember Cairo."

"That was panic," Krueger said, shaking his head. "People have had more time to cool down and think straight now."

Cairo had been a disaster among disasters in the early days of the pandemic. The civilian populace was already on edge. Their city sat just a few hundred miles from the nearest cases of Morningstar and the virus was creeping closer every day. It only took a spark—literally—for Cairo to destroy itself. A fire had started, spread, and burned out of control. Hundreds, perhaps thousands, had burned to death, and thousands more were killed in rioting and panicked flights from the city.

"If you want to know about Cairo, ask Rebecca," Denton said. "She was there. Yeah, there was panic, but people had just—what's the word I'm looking for here—shifted their perspective from being members of a community to being lone wolves, looking out for number one. You can't blame them, but it's no way to build or maintain a society when the surviving human race is stuck in survival mode."

✼ ✼ ✼ ✼ ✼

The three men in the back of the truck hadn't the foggiest idea of how relevant their conversation was to the little convoy's situation, cut off as they were from a view of the road ahead. In the cab of the utility truck, the lead vehicle of the convoy, Sherman and Thomas grimaced simultaneously as they rounded a bend and saw what lay ahead of them. Three vehicles were parked across both lanes of the blacktop road at the edge of a bridge that spanned a two-hundred-foot wide gulley and stream. There was no way to circle around them and continue on their way without tumbling into the gulley and trapping themselves.

"Tell me that's just the leftovers from an accident," Sherman said. In his heart, however, he knew the answer.

"That's a roadblock, sir," Thomas said, shaking his head and applying the brake. The utility truck slowed to a halt, still a good distance from the vehicles.

Sherman heard the familiar snick-snack of a round being chambered and looked over to see Thomas holding his Beretta close to his lap, thumbing the safety off. The General frowned inwardly. Two of his dwindling group of survivors had an uncanny knack for spotting danger before anyone else noticed the threat. Mbutu Ngasy was unsettlingly accurate when it came to the infected. He could spot an ambush before the group was even in a position to be attacked. Sergeant Major Thomas, on the other hand, was unsettlingly accurate when it came to people in general. The middle-aged NCO had been in Vietnam and Iraq and had no trouble knowing when he was being set up.

If he was going for his weapon already, the situation couldn't be good.

"Might just be a town's first line of deterrence," Sherman speculated.

"Might be," Thomas grumbled, then slid out of the driver's side door and walked around the front of the truck, eyeing the vehicles ahead of him. Sherman joined him after a moment.

Behind them, Ron and Mbutu jumped out of the front seats of the sedan and came walking up, narrowing their eyes at the roadblock.

"Seems abandoned," Ron said, looking sideways at Sherman.

"That's why I don't like it," Thomas growled. The vehicles blocking the road were dirty, but otherwise seemed to be in good condition. You just didn't leave a good truck sitting out as a roadblock; you used cement barriers or junkers. And if you *were* going to use a decent truck as one, you wouldn't simply abandon it there.

In the back of the pickup, Denton, Krueger and Brewster were straining to see what was going on through the narrow firing slits in the barbed wire.

"Looks like we've got trouble," Brewster said, peering out at the trucks blocking the road ahead of them.

"Carriers?" Krueger asked.

"Negative," drawled Brewster.

Suddenly there came the roaring of an engine gunning behind them. Sherman and the others spun around, hands going to weapons. Thomas already had his pistol raised and ready to fire. A good fifty yards behind the little convoy, another pair of trucks had appeared, pulling out of the brush that lined the road near the gulley and creek. They screamed to a halt on the road, rocking slightly, and the doors opened as men spilled out, taking cover behind their trucks. The glint of sunlight on steel gave away their shouldered rifles and pistols.

"Worse than carriers," Brewster said in the back of the pickup. "Bandits."

"They're blocking off our retreat, sir," Thomas said, gritting his teeth. "This is an ambush, sir. We don't control this situation. Recommend we bug out."

"I'd be inclined to agree with you," Sherman said, "but there's nowhere for us to go."

Sherman was right. The creek bed was impassable except across the bridge, which was sealed off by the first roadblock. The new additions had blocked off the road to their rear, and the thick stands of brush and pine trees that grew close to the road prevented an off-road escape.

They were trapped.

Brewster and Denton kicked open the tailgate of the truck and scrambled out. Brewster knelt by the rear of the vehicle and held his double-barreled shotgun to his shoulder, aiming at the trucks that had blocked their retreat. The knowledge that the distance between him and his targets was enough to render the double-ought buckshot mostly ineffective didn't comfort him much. Next to him, Denton raised his pistol. The pair felt horrendously under-armed as they stared down the a barrels of scoped hunting rifles.

Krueger was still in the back of the pickup, mostly hidden from view by the thickly strung barbed wire. He calmly and carefully loaded his .30-06, racked a round into the chamber, and lowered his eyes to peer through the scope. He relaxed his breathing, felt his chest rise and fall in carefully measured breaths. In the scope, he watched as the crosshairs danced, then slowed, and finally settled on a burly-looking man with a large-bore rifle taking cover behind one of the enemy trucks. Krueger felt his finger brush the trigger, but he halted himself, waiting for a proper moment.

A voice from the direction of the bridge drew the attention of Sherman and the others near the front of the convoy.

"Well, what have we here?"

The voice belonged to a tall man with a medium build who had the look of a farmer, but moved with the swagger of a man who was used to getting what he wanted. He walked out from behind the trio of vehicles blockading the bridge, a pump-action shotgun in his hands.

"Just a group of honest travelers looking to get back East," Sherman cautiously said.

"Didn't anyone tell you?" the man asked, grinning. "This is a toll road now."

Another five men appeared out of hiding, using their vehicles as cover and aiming weapons at Sherman and the group.

"This isn't good, sir," Thomas whispered out of the side of his mouth.

"I know. Just stay calm. Maybe they'll be rational," Sherman whispered back, then raised his voice to address their accoster. "Last I heard the interstate highway system was toll-free. What's your price?"

"What've you got?" the man asked, earning a few laughs from the bandits behind him. "We're not picky."

"Little we can spare," Sherman said. "Look, friend, we're not after trouble. We're just looking to pass through. If giving you some of our food or ammunition can get us going on our way without a firefight, I'm all for it. So name your price, and we'll see if we can meet it."

"Come on, George, let's get this done!" called out one of the bandits from behind his cover, addressing the man who was negotiating with Sherman.

George held up a hand in the direction of his men, forestalling any further protest. He looked Sherman over and quirked a grin.

"I like you," he said after a moment. "You sound reasonable. We don't get a lot of reasonable people through these parts these days. But here's the thing. We don't normally just take a bit and go home satisfied. I've got eleven men with me here, and another couple of dozen back home, and they've all got to eat. So I'm afraid when I said 'What've you got?' I meant it. Unload your vehicles and we'll clear the road for you. No one'll get hurt."

Sherman's expression darkened and George took a quick step forward, lowering his voice somewhat. Thomas kept his pistol pointed downward, but didn't take his eyes off of the man. He didn't even blink.

"Listen, guy, I just made a *very* reasonable offer to you given the circumstances. You're at our mercy. Usually we kill people who give us lip or get in our way, and as I said, I like you, so I'm giving you the chance to drive out of here with your lives and your vehicles—just not your food or your ammunition."

"You might as well be killing us," Sherman said. "Sending us out there without food or weapons is a death sentence."

George frowned and stepped back. "We can do this easy or we can do this hard, friend."

The bandits glowered from behind their cover and the sound of safeties being flicked off and the distinctive clack-clack of shells being racked into chambers echoed across the road. Sherman and his group of survivors bristled, backing closer to their own vehicles. Rebecca aimed her pistol through a half-open window on the sedan, sweat breaking out on her forehead. She'd shot carriers before, but had never faced down living, uninfected humans. She wondered for a moment if she'd be able to handle a fight in which her targets were actually shooting back.

George began to raise his shotgun. "Just a heads-up: the hard way ends with you all dead."

"Then there's no way we can do this peacefully?" Sherman asked one last time.

"'Fraid not," George said, shaking his head. His bandits laughed mirthlessly.

"Well, that's too bad," Sherman said.

A single shot rang out loud and clear, startling everyone on the scene, most of all George himself, who had suddenly sprouted a miniature crater in the middle of his chest. Dark red blood quickly soaked through his shirt and ran down his side. George looked down at the wound with a bewildered expression on his face, reached up a hand to touch it, and looked back at Sherman and his group.

"Where?" was the only word he managed before pitching, face-first, onto the pavement.

In the back of the pickup truck, still half-hidden by the barbed wire, Krueger grinned to himself and racked another round into the chamber of his .30-06.

A moment passed in stunned silence. Then the bandits recovered their senses, and gunshots began to ring out in an accelerating staccato. Sherman, Ron, and Mbutu ducked down and ran around to the back of the utility truck as rounds skittered off the pavement and ricocheted off of the grille of the vehicle, shooting sparks. Thomas fell back into a shooter's stance and began returning fire with his pistol, presenting as small a target as he could manage.

Brewster and Denton found themselves hard-pressed at the rear of the convoy, facing down the five bandits who had cut off their escape.

Brewster fired both shells in his double-barreled shotgun, cracked the weapon to reload, and suddenly found himself the target of a fusillade of rounds. He heard what sounded like a hornet fly past his right ear and realized it had been as near a miss as any he'd ever experienced. Momentarily panicked, he dropped the shotgun and dove for cover behind the rear tires of the pickup.

Denton fell back, hoping to take cover behind the open passenger door, firing his pistol one-handed as he moved.

Another loud report sounded from within the back of the pickup, and a bandit at the rear of the convoy screamed out in pain, clutching at his throat and falling out of sight behind his cover. His rifle clattered to the ground. Krueger was in his element, sniping away.

Beneath the pickup, Brewster recovered his senses, grimaced, and reached out a hand from behind the wheel to retrieve his shotgun. Almost immediately, a bullet ricocheted off the pavement inches from his hand, kicking up tiny bits of asphalt shrapnel that tore into Brewster's hand. He grunted, pulled his hand back, and gritted his teeth. Blood seeped out from between his fingers.

"Goddamnit," Brewster growled.

The soldier was angry now. He shot out his other arm, ignoring the sound of bullets whizzing by, and grabbed his shotgun, pulling it in close and yanking free the two spent shells with his wounded hand. He slammed in a fresh pair, snapped the weapon up, and sent more buckshot downrange. The shot shattered the side window of a bandit vehicle and the raiders firing from behind it reflexively ducked.

Ron went down with a yell of pain, dropping his pistol and clutching at a bloodied leg as Katie screamed out his name. He crawled backwards, trying to roll behind the utility truck and remove himself from the line of fire. His pistol lay forgotten in the middle of the road.

In the back of the pickup, Krueger let his crosshairs settle on the face of a moustached bandit wielding a semiautomatic carbine and fired a third time. Through the scope, he saw the man's head snap back as the round slammed home. His target slumped forward over the bed of his truck.

"Keep up the fire!" Sherman yelled over the gunfire. "Keep their heads down!"

Rebecca had been firing slowly, a shot every third or fourth second, trying to take careful aim in the direction of the assailants. At Sherman's command, however, she picked up the pace, squeezing off rounds with less care as to whether they hit or not.

Thomas ran his second magazine dry and skipped backwards to where the General was taking cover behind one of the utility truck's open doors. He knelt beside Sherman, dug a fresh clip free from an ammo pouch on his belt, reloaded, and resumed firing.

Jack and Mitsui had been in the front of the pickup, still inside, when the shooting had first started. Jack felt woefully under-armed with his small-caliber pistol and Mitsui was still a shaky shot with his hunting rifle, but the two jumped into the fray nonetheless. Mitsui's shots went wide, skittering off the pavement or flying harmlessly through the air above the bandit's heads. One of his shots flattened a tire on a bandit truck.

Under the pickup, Brewster found himself the bandits' favored target. His shotgun blasts had nearly taken the head off of one of the raiders and had peppered the entire side of one of their vehicles with shot. Three of them focused their fire on Brewster's position.

The soldier jumped as rounds flew anew in his direction, spanging off of the pickup's bumper, popping the tire and digging chunks out of the asphalt all around him. Brewster curled up as small as he could manage and did his best to stay hidden behind the rear wheel.

"Krueger!" Brewster yelled as another round impacted the road near him. A sliver of street embedded itself in his cheek, and blood tricked down his face. "Krueger! Little help!"

Directly above Brewster in the bed of the pickup, Krueger heard the cries and spun in a circle, trying to locate the soldier. "Brewster! Where are you?!"

"Right below you, numbnuts! Come on, put some fire on these trucks behind us! They're tearing me up down here!"

Krueger looked in the direction of the trucks and spotted three of the four remaining bandits aiming in Brewster's direction. He nodded to himself, worked the bolt on his rifle to chamber a fresh round, and took careful aim. He let his breathing calm, waited for the crosshairs to settle, and—

"Krueger! Krueger! Come on, man!" Brewster's sudden exclamation caused the crosshairs to jump.

"Shit," Krueger muttered, then raised his voice somewhat. "Brewster, don't interrupt the artist-at-work."

Beneath the truck, Brewster grimaced and rolled his eyes. "Leave it to Krueger to go all primadonna in the middle of a firefight."

Krueger's shot rang out a moment later—and missed, his first errant round of the day. It impacted the outer edge of the left-hand truck's cab, inches from a bandit's head. Paint chips and metal shards sprayed the side of the bandit's face, and the man yelled out in pain, dropping his rifle and clutching his cheek.

The wounded bandit grabbed for his fallen weapon, snatched it up and wavered in place a moment, seemingly undecided as to whether he should press the attack or break and run. Self-preservation won out over profit and the bloodied raider turned on his heels, running full-tilt into the thick underbrush lining the roadside. His fellow bandits yelled after him, one shouting for him to return to the firing line and another cursing him for cowardice.

The man's panicked flight coupled with the three men Krueger had already killed seemed to be enough to break the remaining morale of the highway bandits blocking the convoy's rear, and one by one they backed away from their cover, still firing, then turned and ran full-tilt into the pines, following in the footsteps of the wounded man.

Only four bandits remained now, and all four were situated at the front of the convoy, behind the vehicles blocking the bridge over the wide creekbed. Thomas managed to wing one of the men in the arm, drawing a shouted curse from the enemy line. Mbutu had run out of ammunition, and knelt behind the utility truck to check on Ron.

As bullets whizzed around them, Mbutu pried Ron's white-knuckled grip away from his bleeding leg and looked at the wound. He grimaced at the sight, but nodded to himself. It wasn't a fatal hit. It could have been if it had hit closer to the center of Ron's thigh, but the bullet hole was off-center and the blood was not the bright red it would have been if the femoral artery had been hit.

"You will live," Mbutu said, slapping Ron on the shoulder.

"Doesn't fucking feel like it," Ron said through gritted teeth. "My whole leg is on fire."

"Rebecca will bandage you," Mbutu assured him. "And give you a shot to dull the pain."

"Looking forward to that," Ron said, managing a half-grin.

An errant round shattered the left headlight of the utility truck, and Sherman ducked reflexively. "We have to finish this!"

"Right there with you, sir," Thomas said. "Wish we had more long arms right about now.

"Krueger!" Sherman yelled over his shoulder. "Krueger, up front if you're not pinned!"

Back in the pickup, Krueger shook his head and sighed as he worked at reloading his rifle. "No rest for the weary. On my way, sir!"

Denton and Brewster had extricated themselves from the truck and were moving briskly toward the vehicles the bandits had abandoned, weapons at the ready. They rounded the side of a black Ford and swept left and right. No sign was left of the opposition save for the body of one of the men Krueger had sniped. The soldier's bullet had torn a hole through the man's throat, and he lay in a wide pool of his own blood, hand still clutching his death wound. His eyes were wide open and his face wore an expression that spoke of surprise and fear. Near him lay a bolt-action hunting rifle.

Denton holstered his pistol and scooped up the rifle, checked to make certain there was a round in the chamber, and jogged to catch up with Brewster. The private was standing near the edge of the underbrush, in a half-kneel, squinting into the trees to see if he could spot any of the bandits.

"See anything?" Denton asked as he moved to stand alongside Brewster.

"Nada," Brewster replied. "I guess they really did bug out. I was worried for a second they'd regroup and come back for another go."

"Same here. Got some new hardware," Denton said, hefting the rifle.

Brewster looked back in the direction of the bridge, where gunshots were still ringing out. "Let's put it to use."

"I'm with you."

The pair turned and ran toward the lead utility truck, feet slapping on the pavement. As they passed the pickup, they heard the familiar sound of Krueger's rifle firing and the now equally-familiar sound of a yell of pain from the bandit's firing line. The soldier had scored another hit, but it hadn't been a fatal one from the sound of things. The yell of pain had quickly turned into a string of shouted curses.

Brewster and Denton arrived at the utility truck, sharing Sherman's cover.

"The guys that came up behind are taken care of," Brewster said. "They had enough of Krueger's sniping and took off into the woods."

Thomas grunted, firing another pair of rounds in the direction of the bandits. "First good news all day."

Jack and Mitsui had also shifted their attention from the rear of the convoy to the front, but neither was scoring much in the way of hits. Mitsui was quickly running out of ammunition and Jack's pistol just wasn't accurate enough at the distance between his targets and himself.

Sherman spared a moment to look around and take in the situation. Things had started out looking grim for the group; now the tide had turned.

"Cease fire! Cease fire! Cease fire!" Sherman yelled out, waving his arm in a 'cut-off' motion.

One by one, the survivors' weapons fell silent. The raiders continued to send rounds raining down on the convoy for a few more moments, but then they, too, realized that they were not taking anymore fire and slackened off. For the first time in several minutes, silence fell over the miniature battlefield.

"Hello out there!" Sherman called, still crouched behind the open door of the utility truck. When he got no response, he tried again, raising the volume of his voice. Finally, someone shouted back.

"What do you want?" came the reply.

"Look around you," Sherman yelled. "Your buddies behind us have been run off. Your leader's dead. You've got wounded. We outnumber you now."

"What's your point?" was the terse reply.

"My point is take your men and get out of here!" Sherman shouted back. "Just turn around and go on your way!"

"Fuck you, cockbreath!" came the shouted reply, and a renewed volley of bullets rained down on the convoy. Sherman ducked lower as the window above him was shattered out. Thomas cursed as a round skipped off the pavement and grazed his boot.

"Cease fire, goddammit!" Sherman yelled from behind his cover. One by one, the bandits complied, almost sulking as they laid off their barrage. "Look around! You're not going anywhere! Your backup's gone! Your leader's down! Just take your lives and go!"

For a long moment, there was only silence. Sherman imagined the bandits were talking it over. Hopefully, they'd take the deal and go on their way.

"What do you say, guys?" Sherman shouted over his shoulder. There was no response. He waited a moment longer, then repeated his query. Still, nothing.

Thomas risked raising his head above the level of the door, peering through the shattered window in the direction of the bandits' roadblock.

"Sir," Thomas grumbled, "looks like it worked."

"What worked?" Sherman asked.

"They're gone, sir," Thomas said, pointing at the bridge.

Sherman slowly pulled himself to his feet and surveyed the roadblock. The bandits had indeed used the momentary lapse in combat to turn tail and beat it across the bridge. Sherman could just barely make out a roadside shrub still waving where a bandit must have grazed it in his flight.

"Jesus." Sherman breathed a sigh of relief. "That could have gone a lot worse for us."

"Went worse for some of us than others," came a pained interjection. Ron was still laid up behind the utility truck. Rebecca had abandoned her cover and run over to him, and was even now busily cutting away Ron's pants leg to get a better view of the bullet wound he'd suffered.

Brewster sat down heavily on the roof of the sedan, nursing his bloodied hand and daubing at the slice on his cheek with an old sock he'd pulled from his rucksack.

"This is not my best day ever," Ron groaned, clutching at his leg. Blood oozed from the bullet wound.

"Relax," Rebecca said. "It's not that bad. I've got an exit wound here, so the bullet didn't lodge in your leg anywhere. That's a good thing. Straight in and straight out. You could probably use a couple of stitches. I'll get you some antibiotics just in case—want something for the pain?"

Ron fixed her with a sideways glance. "Hell yes, I want something for the pain. Feels like my entire leg is on fire."

Thomas and Sherman came strolling back over from their inspection of the bandit's line and took in the sight of their wounded comrades. Thomas knelt next to Ron.

"First time being shot, eh?" Thomas said, quirking a grin.

"First time," Ron said, nodding. "Hurts like a bitch."

"Doesn't hurt any less the second and third time, either," Thomas said, still grinning, then straightened himself out, clasped his hands behind his back, and strolled off to inspect the rest of the convoy.

"That guy," Ron said through gritted teeth, "doesn't have a goddamn idea how to inspire confidence, does he?"

"He's just having a bit of fun with you," Sherman said, arms folded across his chest and a soft smile planted on his face. "It's his way."

Jack and Mitsui had both run to the front of the convoy, where a pair of corpses (courtesy of Krueger) lay. They occupied themselves with grabbing up the weapons left behind by the dead men and searching the raiders' pockets for anything useful. Jack scored a pocketknife and a box of ammunition, as well as a short-barreled carbine to replace his small-caliber pistol. Mitsui struggled with removing a gear harness from another bandit and grinned as he tried it on, marveling in the plethora of pockets and pouches it afforded him. He grinned and gave Jack a thumbs-up. Jack responded by raising his new carbine and grinning in return.

Mbutu watched the looting with a carefully neutral expression on his face. He'd barely said a thing during the entire engagement. Sherman had noticed, and ambled over to the tall man, standing by himself on the edge of the road, staring into the trees.

"What's on your mind?" Sherman asked, clasping Mbutu's shoulder.

"I am thinking of these raiders," Mbutu said after a moment. "They said they had more men to feed. I wonder where those men are."

"What do you mean?"

"I mean, General, that they are most likely living nearby," Mbutu explained. "They would not want to go too far from their home. I worry they will be back, and with greater numbers. We should leave. Now."

Sherman grimaced. Mbutu was right, naturally. The man had definitely shown his farsightedness to be useful in the past and Sherman was more than willing to trust his opinion.

"All right, gentlemen and ladies," Sherman said, spinning on his heel and heading back toward the convoy. "Let's pack it up and get moving again. Denton, Jack, Mitsui—get those vehicles out of our way. Let's put some miles between us and these bandits before they decide to come back and try again. And where the hell is Krueger?"

"Here, sir!" Krueger replied, jumping out of the back of the pickup and shouldering his rifle. Sherman fixed him with a stare.

"Damn fine shooting, son. You probably saved our asses back there," Sherman said, nodding.

"Hoo-ah, sir."

Denton and Mitsui were busy trying the ignitions of the trucks left behind as roadblocks. The first truck didn't even sputter; it flatly refused to start. The second chugged and chugged but refused to catch. The third sputtered, coughed, and caught.

"Well, all right, looks like we're up another pickup," Denton said from the driver's seat. "Clear behind; I'm going to pull this truck onto the bridge."

Jack backed away from the vehicle as Denton spun the wheel and ran the truck forward onto the bridge, pulling it alongside the cement barrier and shifting it into park.

"What about these other two?" Jack yelled, pointing at the pair of trucks that refused to start.

"Must've damaged them in the firefight," Denton called back as he slid out of the driver's side door and jogged back over to what remained of the roadblock. "Shift 'em to neutral. We'll push 'em off the road."

As Denton, Mitsui and Jack went to work, Rebecca put the finishing touches on Ron's leg. She'd injected him with a local anesthetic, having run out of the morphine she'd managed to purloin from the USS *Ramage* months earlier, and closed the wounds with stitches. A clean gauze bandage put the finishing touches on her work. A bit of blood seeped through the white cloth, but other than that, the wound seemed stabilized.

"Don't try to walk on it for a little while," Rebecca said. "You'll re-open the wound. We'll have to find you something to use as a crutch in the meantime."

"Thanks, Becky," Ron said, nodding at her. "Feels a lot better now."

"That's the anesthetic. It'll start to wear off in a few hours. When it does, let me know and I'll give you another dose."

"Hey, hey," came a call from behind them. It was Brewster, waving his bloodied hand. "How about patient number two? No love for Brewster?"

"None at all," Rebecca quipped. "Besides, I'm running triage. Ron got the worst of it, so you'll just have to wait."

"I've been waiting," Brewster whined. "Is it my turn yet?"

"All right, all right," Rebecca sighed, shouldering her bag of medical supplies and moving to where Brewster sat on the hood of the sedan. "Let's see what you've got."

Brewster held out his hand toward her, and Rebecca carefully turned it in hers, inspecting the wounds.

"Looks like three bits of shrapnel," she said. "Move your fingers for me."

Brewster flexed all five of his fingers, grimacing at the pain it caused him.

"Well, that's good," Rebecca said. "Didn't sever any tendons, and from the amount of blood you've got here it doesn't look like you're in any real danger. Give me a moment."

Rebecca dug around in her bag and came up with a pair of long, thin tweezers. Brewster eyed them with trepidation.

"What're those for?" he asked.

"Well," Rebecca said, "I can't bandage this hand while you've still got pieces of bullet in there, can I?"

"Can't you give me some of that anesthetic you gave Ron first?"

"Oh, don't be such a baby," Rebecca replied, frowning at him. She grasped Brewster's hand firmly, took the tweezers in her other hand, and jabbed them into one of his wounds. Brewster hissed through his teeth at the pain and grimaced. After a moment, Rebecca yanked the tweezers free, displaying a chunk of bent metal that had embedded itself in Brewster's hand. "There's one of the culprits."

"Let's just hurry up and get the rest of them out so this can be over with," Brewster groaned.

A crash sounded from the direction of the bridge, causing the group to look over their shoulders. Mitsui and Denton had succeeded in pushing one of the disabled trucks off the road. It careened down the ledge and crashed into the gulley below, rolling over onto its top. Jack was right behind them, struggling to push the second vehicle over in the same spot. Mitsui and Denton joined in the effort, and the second truck came crashing down on top of the first. The roadway ahead was clear.

"All right, ladies and gentlemen, let's get saddled up and move on," Sherman said. "Don't want to be here if those bandits decide that they're going to try again."

Thomas slid into the driver's seat of the utility truck and turned the key. The engine whined, sputtered, coughed, and died. Frowning, the Sergeant Major tried again, with the same result. "Sir."

"Yes?" Sherman asked, turning to face Thomas.

"Problem here. The truck's dead."

"Pop the hood. Let's have a look," Sherman said. "Anyone here know much about engines?"

"I've got you covered, Sherm," Jack said, still brushing dust from his hands after pushing the dead vehicles over the embankment. "Did a stint as a mechanic before I took up my welding."

"Come and have a look at this, then," Sherman asked, beckoning Jack over. Thomas popped the hood of the utility truck and Sherman raised the hood, latching it open.

Jack leaned on the front grille, peered in at the engine and frowned. "Oh, damn."

"Damn?" Sherman asked.

"This thing's been torn up something bad, General," Jack said. "Looks like it took a lot of rounds in that firefight. Look, here—one of them sliced clean through the fanbelt. Hell of a shot. Here's two more holes in the radiator. And it looks like one of the cylinders took a shot, too."

"So what's the verdict?" Sherman asked.

"Uh, off the top of my head, this thing isn't going anywhere, at least not without some replacement parts. We'd need a new belt—which shouldn't be hard to find. Might even be able to pull one off one of those dead trucks we pushed over the edge. The radiator and the cylinder will be harder."

"Can you get it running again?" Sherman asked.

"With the parts I have here, and the tools we've got, barring any other problems that I just can't see with my naked eye—"

"*Can you get it running again?*" Sherman repeated.

"Uh, no," Jack admitted. "She's a goner."

"Damn it all," Sherman said. "What about the other vehicles?"

Katie had already taken some initiative and jumped into the sedan. She gave the ignition a try. The engine caught almost immediately and purred contentedly. "This one works, Frank!"

The pickup was in worse shape. When Mbutu tried the engine, it started, but both of the rear tires had been popped during the firefight and the underside of the vehicle was pockmarked with bullets that had ricocheted off the road.

"So we're down to two vehicles," Sherman said. "We've got that truck the raiders left and the sedan. That's no good; we can't all fit in both of those unless we pack ourselves in like sardines—and if we did that I'm not sure where we'd put our gear. No, we'll have to get one of these trucks repaired."

Mitsui, who couldn't understand much of what was being said but had a pretty solid grasp of the situation by looking over folks' shoulders, suddenly became a whirlwind of action, slapping Jack on the back and gesturing wildly at the raider's black pickup Denton had pulled onto the bridge, then pointing back at the utility truck.

"What?" Jack asked, throwing up his arms. "Slow down, man, slow down. What?"

Mitsui spoke in rapid-fire Japanese, pointing at the black truck once more and then pantomiming pulling the utility truck with an invisible rope.

"You want to...pull the truck?" Jack guessed. Mitsui shook his head rapidly and jogged over to the working, undamaged pickup. He leaned down and tapped his hand against the towing stud attached to the truck's rear bumper, then ran back to the utility truck and slapped his hand against the two towhooks there. He straightened himself out, folded his arms across his chest, and looked victorious.

"Oh, I get it! I get it!" Jack said. "He's saying we should tow the utility truck with the raider's truck until we figure a way to repair it."

Mitsui nodded, despite not having understood a word Jack had said. "Tow," he said, still nodding.

"Good idea," Sherman said. "That way we should be good, space-wise. As long as we don't lose another vehicle we should be fine."

"All right, people, we've got a plan. Let's get to work," Thomas growled.

1534 hrs_

There had been a moment of uncertainty as the group attempted to hitch the utility truck to the working pickup when they realized they didn't have any chains. Denton had solved the problem by rooting around in the beds of the disabled raider vehicles and came up with a heavy chain that served the purpose beautifully.

The convoy had crossed the bridge and put several miles between them and the raiders when they came upon another obstacle in the middle of the road. This one, however, had less of a look of a roadblock and more of a checkpoint air about it. A pair of hastily constructed guard towers flanked the road and a heavy wooden bar blocked the road.

Beyond the checkpoint lay a small town, completely cordoned off by chain-link fences topped with barbed wire. It was a survivor's encampment.

Thomas voiced concern that they might have come upon the bandit's home base, in which case Sherman expected them to be fired upon at any moment, but no rifle reports sounded and the only activity was a flurry of movement between the guard towers as the small convoy, truck in tow, rolled up to the gate and stopped short of it by a good two hundred feet.

A sign next to the side of the road proclaimed that this was the town of Abraham, Kansas, population 900. Someone had come out with red spray paint and put a large X through the "900" and replaced it with "830." A further addendum reduced the population to "621." Below that was yet another addition, this one claiming the population of the town to be at "363." The town might have survived, but not without paying a price, it seemed.

Sherman dismounted from the black pickup and walked around to the front of the vehicle, hands on his hips.

"Stand where you are!" came a commanding shout from one of the guard towers. Sherman froze in place. He knew better than to set an armed guard on edge by disobeying commands. "Hands in the air!"

Sherman slowly raised his hands above his head.

"Turn in a circle!" commanded the voice. It belonged to a man bent over the edge of the tower, eye to the scope of a rifle he had trained on Sherman's chest. "Slowly!"

Sherman obeyed, turning around so the man could see what he was carrying and whether or not he was a threat.

"Disarm!" came a third command.

Sherman reached a hand down slowly to his hip holster, unbuttoned it and pulled free his pistol. Just as slowly, he leaned forward and deposited the weapon on the ground.

"All right," shouted the guard. "Move on up closer."

Thomas started to get out of the truck to follow Sherman, but the General waved a hand at the Sergeant Major, telling him to remain where he was. Thomas sank back into his seat with a clearly displeased expression on his face. Sherman approached the guard towers alone. As he got closer, he let his eyes take in the sights.

The towers were made from the trailers of 18-wheelers, turned upright and supported with steel rebar. Platforms and a makeshift roof had been welded onto each one, providing some protection from the elements for whomever was on duty within. Beyond the barred checkpoint Sherman found he had a better view of the town. A main street ran straight through the little burg, lined with shops and apartments. Further out were several blocks of small, single-family homes, interspersed with trees and power lines. Sherman spotted an armed man with a leashed dog walking the perimeter of the chain-link fence.

"All right, stranger," came the voice from the guard tower. "Why don't you explain who you are and why you've come here?"

"Francis Sherman," Sherman said, looking up at the man. "Formerly of the U.S. Army. As for why we've come here—well, we didn't mean to. Just looking to pass through. We're on our way to Omaha. May I ask who I'm speaking to?"

"Sherman," said the guard thoughtfully, rubbing his stubbled chin. "I knew a Sherman before this shit jumped continents. He was in charge of some operation around Suez."

"That was me," Sherman said. "Lieutenant General Francis Sherman, at your service."

The guard chuckled. "Pleased to meet you. And I'm Emperor Hirohito."

Sherman shook his head and grinned. "If you say so, Emperor. Look, we're not here to cause any trouble. We just want to head through."

"I'd love to let you, Francis, but we've been having some problems of our own recently. I think you're familiar with them."

"Bandits," Sherman said.

"Exactly. Mind telling me where you got a hold of one of their trucks?" the guard asked, pointing at the black pickup that now led the makeshift convoy. "Because my gut's telling me I'm looking at a Trojan horse. What if I let you in and you start tearing up our town?"

"No tricks," Sherman assured him. "We had a run-in with your raiders a few miles back at a bridge crossing. We took a couple of them out. The rest ran. They dinged up our vehicles and wounded a couple of our people. The truck's what you might call a spoil of war."

The guard looked back and forth between Sherman and the convoy, where the other survivors were milling about, watching the exchange intently. He seemed undecided for a moment, then snapped up his rifle and shouldered it.

"Name's Keaton Wallace. Acting Sheriff of Abraham. You and your people can enter—but you'll have to surrender your weapons at the station before you'll be allowed access to the rest of the town."

"Sounds fine, Keaton," Sherman said. "You wouldn't happen to have any mechanics in town, would you?"

"Might," Keaton said. "Whether or not he'll be willing to work for you is another thing. He lost his wife to Morningstar. Lost his daughter to the raiders. He's a little on edge, if you follow."

"I follow," Sherman said, nodding slowly. "We'll have a talk with him."

"Good luck," Keaton said, scoffing. "In the meantime, welcome to Abraham."

Keaton signaled a fellow guard to raise the bar that crossed the road. Sherman stepped back and waved the convoy onward. The vehicles rolled slowly past the towers and into the security of the chain-link fence that surrounded the small town. Guards directed them to park alongside a squat concrete structure just within the town limits that was marked clearly as the Sheriff's office and dispatch center. Grass had already begun to grow up in the springtime air, and had gone uncut. No doubt the townsfolk thought gasoline was better spent on vehicles and generators than lawnmowers.

The survivors dismounted as Sherman caught up with them. Denton jumped out of the rear of the pickup and pulled a pair of sunglasses from his wide eyes, taking a moment to survey the town they found themselves in.

"This is incredible," Denton said, shaking his head. "I can't believe this is an actual town—a living town. How did Morningstar miss this place?"

"It didn't," came the answer. Sheriff Keaton was following closely behind Sherman and had heard the photographer's comment. "We got hit, just like everyone else."

"How did you survive?" Rebecca asked, shutting the door to the sedan behind her.

"We contained the infection," Keaton said, a hard look crossing his face. The survivors grimaced. 'Contained' could only mean they had executed anyone who had become infected and, most likely, burned the bodies.

"I like your defenses," Sherman commented, pointing over his shoulder at the towers and fencing.

"Thank you," Keaton grinned, loosening up somewhat. "Took half the town the better part of a month to put up, but they've been worth it. Guard towers at each road in or out of town, fencing running along the entire town's perimeter. We have guards on rotating shifts. All volunteers."

"What do you do for food?" Brewster asked, helping Ron down from the back of the utility truck. "Not a lot of fields in town, looks like."

"No, but there are acres and acres of arable land just outside of town. That's one of our problems, actually. Story for another time," Keaton said. "In the meantime, let's get you settled in. We don't get a lot of visitors around here, and, frankly, we're suspicious of any we do get. It's nothing personal," he rushed to assure the group, "but we'll have to have your weapons. Follow me, please."

Keaton led the group into the sheriff's office. It was a modest affair. The front desk butted up nearly against the main entrance and Keaton led them through a locked door and down a narrow hallway to a door marked 'Weapons Locker.'

"I promise you," Keaton said as he unlocked the door and swung it open, "No harm will come to your gear while it's in here. My deputies and I have the only keys, and most of the population here is privately armed. There's no reason anyone would want to mess with your weapons."

"I don't know, man, it's been months since I haven't had a weapon on me," Krueger said, shifting from foot to foot.

"Krueger," Sherman said, eyeing the soldier. "Do as the Sheriff says. We're guests in his town right now."

Krueger made a sour face, but nodded and acquiesced, handing over his rifle to Keaton. The process continued as pistols found their way into lockers, rifles were placed onto racks, and ammunition was locked away and stored. The survivors disarmed themselves completely. The last of the group to surrender his weapons was Jack. He handed over the semi-automatic carbine and his ammo pouches to Keaton, then turned and joined the rest of the group in the hall outside.

"Well," Keaton said as he re-entered the hallway and locked the door to the weapons room behind him. "Now that that's taken care of, you're all free to move about the town. Just remember, you're not here to stay. If you can get your vehicles fixed and move on, great. If not, well, I hear walking's good for the heart."

"What's there to do in a burg like this?" Brewster asked, grinning.

"We're not New York," Keaton started.

"...which is good, because New York's probably a dead zone," Rebecca interjected.

"We're not New York," Keaton continued, glancing at the medic, "but we've got our share of entertainment. Eileen's down the street is where most of us go. Her husband ran a microbrewery just a few blocks away. Still does, when we can get him what he needs. There's no power, so the beer's warm, but it still packs a punch. Hope you like lager."

Krueger and Brewster glanced at one another and grinned. It had been quite a while since either had gotten their hands on something alcoholic.

"That's where we'll be," Brewster said, jerking a thumb over his shoulder. "If you need us, just call. I've got my radio on."

"Whoa, whoa, wait for me," Denton said, jogging after the pair. "It might not be Canadian beer, but I'll take what I can get."

"Canadian beer sucks ass," Brewster taunted, voice fading in the distance. Just before their voices were lost Sherman could hear Denton tossing a snappy comeback Brewster's way.

"And that leaves the rest of us," Sherman said, surveying the remainder of his group. "Sheriff, if you don't have anything pressing to take care of, I'd love to take a tour of your little town here. I'm amazed at how well you've done so far."

"Be happy to oblige you, Sherman," Keaton said. "We don't much use cars anymore—guzzle what's left of our gas—but we have a couple golf and lawn carts that serve the purpose just as well. Meet me around front. I'll pull one around."

"I'll go with you, sir," Thomas said.

Keaton stopped mid-stride and turned to face Thomas. "Ah. Don't believe we've properly met, yet. Keaton Wallace, Sheriff."

Keaton extended a hand in Thomas' direction. The old sergeant pretended he didn't see it. Sherman coughed and performed the introductions himself.

"Keaton, this is Command Sergeant Major Thomas, US Army. He's been with me for years. Pardon his demeanor," Sherman said, casting a sidelong glance at Thomas. "His bark's worse than his bite."

"My bite's pretty bad, too," Thomas growled.

"Ah, yes, well," Keaton stammered, dropping his hand. "Pleased to meet you, anyway. If you two would like to meet me out front...?"

"We'll be there. Where are the rest of you going?" Sherman asked the remainder of the group.

"I'm going to find a bench somewhere and sit down," Ron said through gritted teeth. He was using a warped branch as a crutch to support his wounded leg, and it was extremely uncomfortable.

"I'm with Ron," Katie said, shrugging and smiling.

"What about the rest of you?" Sherman asked, gesturing at Jack, Mitsui, Rebecca, and Mbutu.

"Well, I can't speak for all of them, but I'm going to go exploring," Jack said. "Been a while since I've had a chance to meet anyone new."

"I'm up for that," Rebecca said. "Let's go."

1623 hrs_

The golf cart tour had turned out to be a grand idea. The little vehicle's top speed was a modest ten miles per hour, and Sherman lounged in the passenger seat, listening to Keaton ramble on about the history of the town and its current state.

"We were founded in 1905, so that puts us just over a hundred years old," Keaton said. "Pretty young in the scheme of things, but we've built a lot of history in the time we've had. That over there is the city hall and courthouse," he said, pointing.

The large, two-story brick and stone structure dominated the other, single-story buildings of downtown Abraham and featured a clocktower and steeple. Wide stone steps led down to a grassy park area, which had been plowed through in places to allow vegetables to be grown. A few townsfolk, wearing dirtied clothing, worked the half-acre, sowing seed for the upcoming growing season.

"We're using whatever land we can find that's safe to grow food," Keaton explained, nodding in the direction of the townsfolk. "In the early days, right after Morningstar hit the area, we got together and raided a distribution center about ten miles north of here. We got away with a few truckloads, enough to feed the people for several months, but when we went back to get more we found it had been occupied."

"Let me guess," Sherman said. "The raiders?"

Keaton nodded slowly. "Not sure where they came from, originally. Must have been on the road a while and when they found the distribution center they decided to set up camp. Good spot, actually. Just as secure as our little burg. Fences all around, guard shack at the entrance—they boarded it up tight, made it their personal fortress. Enough supplies in there to last a year. Just the same, they're not satisfied. We've run them off three times now, but they're still harrassing our outlying farms."

"Was that the trouble you were referring to earlier?" Sherman asked.

"Yes," Keaton replied. "It's dangerous to leave the perimeter we have set up here. And it's not just the raiders we have to worry about, either. Some of the other nearby towns weren't as lucky as us. There's quite a few infected wandering around these parts. Occasionally a few will wander up to our fence. That's what the roving guards and dogs are for. If they spot one, they take it out and then we send out a detail to burn the body. If you were to walk the fence you'd see a lot of burned-out spots on the ground outside—one for each carrier."

Sherman let his eyes wander as the golf cart continued down the main street. "I see a lot of your businesses are still open."

"Well, we're trying to keep some semblance of civilization going here," Keaton said. "Money's worthless, of course, so we're back to the old barter system. It's been working well so far."

"Damn fine work you've done here, Sheriff," Sherman said, nodding in approval. "Much better than a lot of other places have managed."

"Speaking of which," Keaton said, "We're kind of starved for news here. Like I said earlier, we don't get a lot of visitors through these parts anymore. Hell, we didn't get many visitors before the pandemic. What's life like out there?"

"Hanging on by its fingernails," Sherman replied. "We've been circling around most of the towns we approach. Yours is the first we've come across that seems to have survived. The roads are dangerous and cities are deathtraps. Basically, outside your fences, it's no-man's-land."

"Any word from the major cities?"

"They were the first ones to go," Thomas grumbled from the back of the golf cart. "Last we heard on the radio, San Francisco was under siege and Los Angeles was a lost cause. Not sure about the East Coast, but I'm guessing it was about the same there."

"What about Denver?" Keaton asked.

"Dead," Sherman replied, shaking his head. "We gave that town as wide a berth as we could.

"Damn," Keaton said, gritting his teeth. "I was hoping we weren't the only ones left."

"You're probably not," Sherman assured him. "If Abraham made it, other towns might have made it. It's just a question of finding them, and hoping that they're still as accommodating as you all have been."

"Then there are the raiders," Keaton said. "People like them make travel next to impossible."

"There will always be those who prefer to take rather than produce," Sherman said. "Always someone out there who thinks it's better to steal than to craft or to rob rather than build."

"How about that mechanic, sir?" Thomas asked from the back seat. "Might want to pay him a visit and see if he can fix the utility truck."

"Good idea," Keaton said, pre-empting Sherman's response. "I'll take you by his shop. Now, remember, this guy has lost his wife and his daughter. He's not exactly on an even keel, if you get my meaning."

"We'll see what we can do with him," Sherman said, and then sighed. "Makes me wish we'd brought Hal along."

"What, that old screw-up?" Thomas answered, scowling. "Better off without him."

"If he could fix a destroyer's engines, I'm sure he could fix a truck engine," Sherman said in the man's defense. Hal was a retired Master Sergeant who knew Sherman and Thomas from the days of the Gulf War. He'd been a tank mechanic then and had since retired and moved to the islands of the South Pacific, bought a patch of land on a remote isle overlooking the ocean and dubbed it 'Hal's Paradise.' The man was a true eccentric, always working on this invention or that, and had a lasseiz-faire attitude toward just about everything. Sherman found the man entertaining and trustworthy. Thomas saw him as undisciplined and annoying, although worthy of respect due to his service. Hal had been recruited to fix a fuel pump on the USS *Ramage* during the survivors' trans-Pacific journey months before.

The golf cart pulled into a narrow alleyway flanked by two poured concrete buildings that had cracks running through them in places. Keaton dodged a half-full dumpster and pulled the cart to a halt in front of a pair of garage doors built into the side of one of the buildings. A faded sign above the doors read, 'Arctura's Bodyshop.' Directly below that, in red spraypaint, was scrawled, 'Closed until further notice.'

"Closed, eh?" Sherman asked. "We come at a bad time?"

"No," Keaton reassured him. "He's in there. Just not a lot of business these days, plus the guy likes to keep to himself."

Keaton approached one of the garage doors and banged on it with a closed fist.

"Jose! Jose! It's Keaton! Open up!"

A long moment passed without any sign of acknowledgement from the other side. Keaton repeated the pounding and raised his voice another level.

"Come on, Jose! Open the doors! You've got customers out here!"

From inside, muffled by the closed doors, the small group heard a response.

"Don't have no customers. Don't have nothing. Go away and leave me alone."

Keaton frowned and looked over at Sherman. "See what I mean?"

Sherman stepped forward and leaned in close to the door. "Jose, is it? I'm Frank Sherman. Look, we ran into some raiders before we got here and they busted up our vehicles something awful. We sure could use your help getting them back on the road."

"Raiders are everywhere," Jose said from the other side of the door. "Raiders, raiders, bandits, raiders. Killing, looting, stealing, killing some more. Not my problem."

"Well, we killed a couple of them, but they've pretty much stranded us unless we can get our utility truck running again. What do you say? Will you help us out? We're desperate, here."

There was a moment of silence on the other side of the garage doors, then came a quiet, curious question.

"Killed some, you did?"

"That's right. Three or four. The rest ran. Anyway, look, we've got a busted radiator and a torn fan bel—"

Sherman's sentence was cut off as the garage door suddenly rolled up with a clatter, revealing an oil-stained, ill-kempt mechanic wearing a pair of filthy overalls and sporting weeks' worth of beard growth. He didn't look as though he'd seen the sun in days.

"Killing raiders is a good thing," Jose said, approaching Sherman slowly. The General didn't back away, despite the man's overripe smell. "Raiders took my girl."

"That's what the Sheriff told me," Sherman said, jerking his thumb in the direction of Keaton.

"Sheriff," Jose said, nodding at Keaton. Keaton nodded back.

"I'm sorry they killed your girl, Jose, but we really need to get back on the road, and you're the only man around who might be able to do that for us—" Sherman started.

Jose cut him off.

"Who said anything about them killing her?" Jose snapped, eyes suddenly full of fire. Then his shoulders sagged and a look of profound sadness crossed his face. "I said they took her. Took her to that place of theirs, and they're doing god knows what to my little girl. She's only seventeen, *dios mio*, how can this happen? I'm a good man, never did hurt anyone, and she—she is an angel, would never harm a fly. Why did this happen to us? Why?"

"I can't answer that," Sherman said quickly, putting a hand on Jose's shoulder. "And I'm sorry for what's happened to you."

"Sir," Thomas said softly, "the trucks?"

Jose looked over at Thomas with sudden interest, eyes taking in the man's posture and the respectful way in which he addressed Sherman, but said nothing.

"Jose, we'd really like to hire you to fix our vehicles," Sherman pressed on. "We have a good bit of supplies we can offer in trade— ammunition, clothing, food, weapons, whatever you—"

"Kill the raiders," Jose said softly, still looking at Thomas. His eyes flicked back over to Sherman. "Kill the raiders. That's my price. Kill the raiders."

Sherman seemed taken aback for a moment. He glanced at Thomas, who seemed just as surprised at the request.

"What makes you think we—"

"I'm not a fool," Jose said, eyeing Thomas once more. "You're soldiers, aren't you? I can tell."

Thomas nodded curtly.

"Not all of us," Sherman said. "Just a few of us, and certainly not enough of us to mount an attack on a raider fortress. We'd be cut down."

"Then get me my daughter back," Jose said. "If you can do either of those things, I'll fix your trucks. No, wait—I'll do one better. I'll make your vehicles better. Better tires, better parts—you'll get everything."

"Jose, I can't—" Sherman started to say, but Thomas cut him off.

"We'll see what we can do, Jose," Thomas said, nudging Sherman's boot with his own.

Jose nodded slowly, looking down at the ground. "You come back when it's finished. Don't come back if it's not."

With that, the mechanic backed into his garage, reached up, and slammed the door down. They could hear the sound of a lock being turned inside. Just like that, they were dismissed.

"Charming fellow," Sherman said.

"Can't blame him," Keaton replied. "He's lost his entire family. That's enough to drive anyone to the brink."

"Thomas, what was the nudge for?" Sherman asked, turning to face his longtime companion.

"I think we can meet his price, sir," Thomas said.

"Explain."

Thomas turned to the Sheriff first. "Keaton, how many times have you attacked the raider compound?"

"Attacked them?" Keaton asked, then laughed out loud. "Never. I'd lose too many of my people. There are about thirty of them in there, all armed."

"And how many times that you know of have they been attacked in general?"

Keaton shrugged. "I'd say never. I mean, I'm sure they get shamblers and sprinters along their perimeter from time to time, just like we do, but they probably just put 'em down and move on."

Thomas turned back to Sherman. "I'm thinking that they won't be expecting us, sir. No one's been stupid enough to attack them before. They're probably feeling very safe and secure in their little makeshift fortress."

"So you're in favor of taking on thirty armed bandits with less than a dozen armed volunteers, one-third of which have had any kind of military training? It'd be suicide, Sergeant. Not going to happen," Sherman said, folding his arms across his chest and shaking his head.

"No, sir," Thomas said. "I'm in favor of going at night, maybe three of us total, getting in there and bringing this man back his daughter, if she's still alive. I want to get these trucks fixed and get back on the way to Omaha, sir. I don't fancy spending the rest of my days in Abraham, Kansas. No offense, Sheriff."

"None taken," Keaton shrugged. "We're not everyone's cup of tea."

"Thomas, do you really think we could pull off that kind of an assault? I mean, assuming we did, for a moment. What do you think the bandits are going to do once they realize we've paid them a visit? They'll come gunning straight for Abraham," Sherman said. "They'll be out for blood."

"Now, that is a worry, isn't it?" Keaton said with a laugh. "As long as they see you they'll recognize you're not from this burg. There's probably a couple of dinged up survivors from your little road encounter embellishing the gunfight right now. I'm not too worried about an attack here yet. But don't ask for our help on your little endeavor," Keaton continued. "I can't in good conscience send out our townsfolk to help you. You're still strangers to us. Sorry."

"Nothing to be sorry for," Sherman replied. "I understand your position."

1702 hrs_

"What this place needs is music," Brewster slurred, slumped halfway over the bar in Eileen's Pub. The electricity had been out for months, but large candles suspended in makeshift chandeliers gave the bar a dim, flickering light that added to the atmosphere. Denton and Krueger sat on either side of Brewster on their stools, nursing dark, malty brews.

A few locals populated the pub, sitting in darkened booths or at tables around the bar and discussing the day's events in low, murmured tones. The bartender, presumably Eileen herself, was a stout, middle-aged woman whose service was quick but lacked a smile. The locals didn't seem to mind as long as the alcohol kept flowing.

"I don't care if it's bitter, it's beer," Krueger said, taking another quick gulp from his mug and grimacing at the taste. "It's been too long since I've had one of these."

"Almost like old times," Denton agreed. "We might as well be out on Saturday night. I'm telling you, guys, sometimes, despite all the shit outside, life's good."

"Music," Brewster repeated, annoyed that his comment had been ignored. "This place needs music."

"And right you are, compadre," Krueger said, slapping Brewster on the back and causing him to slosh his lager on the bar. "Unfortunately, the jukebox went out with the power, so we'll just have to do without."

"You know what I miss?" Brewster asked, taking a sip of his lager. "I miss cold beer."

"Don't we all," Denton said. "But, like the jukebox, the refrigeration is out. We've been over this."

Brewster was too far gone to notice. His shoulders jerked in an exaggerated shrug.

"I never used to like beer," he rambled on. "I used to like liquor. Whiskey. Figured you could drink less of it and get just as drunk. Nasty-tasting stuff, alcohol."

"Unless you mix it right," Krueger said around the rim of his glass mug.

"Then I started drinking beer, and I figure, hey, this stuff is like water compared to whiskey," Brewster said, waving his mug in front of Denton's face. "You have to drink more, but it's not so bad."

"That's right, Brewster, it's not so bad," Denton said, humoring the private.

Brewster had gone to work the moment the three had entered the bar, drinking twice as much as Denton and Krueger in the same amount of time. He wasn't quite plastered, but he'd passed the line from tipsy to drunk a while back.

"You know who liked beer? Wilson liked beer," Brewster said, suddenly sober. He stared at his mug. Denton and Krueger also felt the mood go from jovial to mellow. "He'd have liked this place."

For a moment, the trio was silent, reflecting on the loss of their friend. Suddenly, Krueger broke the reverie.

"A toast!" Krueger said, raising his mug. "This one's for Wilson!"

"For Wilson!" Brewster shouted, raising his mug and clinking it against Krueger's. Denton followed suit and the trio tipped back their glasses, draining what remained of the warm, dark beer within.

"Hey, hey, hey, Eileen," Brewster slurred, holding up his empty mug. The bartender looked over at him lazily, hand on her hip. "Refill, please."

"We don't run tabs here, guy," Eileen said, tilting her head at Brewster. "What've you got?"

"What've I got?" Brewster asked, laughing. Suddenly a puzzled look crossed his face and he looked side to side at his companions, serious in tone. "What've I got?"

"Check your pockets," Denton said. "No, wait, actually, I've got the next round. Swiss Army knife."

Denton pulled the blade from his pocket and dropped it on the bar. Eileen inspected it, decided it was good enough for another round of brews, scooped it up and went to fetch the beer.

"Maybe we'll get lucky," Brewster said. "Maybe we'll get stuck here for a couple of weeks and—"

The door to the bar swung open and in strode General Sherman, a very official expression on his face. Brewster, Denton, and Krueger looked over at him. The two soldiers groaned at the sight, well-used to the look of an officer who needed 'volunteers' for something.

"There you are!" Sherman said, striding over to the bar. "We've got a small problem. Krueger, Brewster, I need both of you."

"I knew it," Brewster lamented. "I knew this was too good to last."

Krueger sighed but nodded. "All right, sir. What can we do?"

"Well, to start with you can come with me. Let's take a little walk."

Krueger hopped off of his stool and lent a hand to Brewster, who was moving rather unsteadily on his feet. Sherman led the pair of soldiers out of the pub and into the darkening streets. A moment later, Eileen returned with three full beer mugs to find that two of her customers had flown the coop and only Denton remained. She looked at him and raised an eyebrow.

Denton caught the look.

"Leave 'em," he said, gesturing at all three glasses. "No point in letting good beer go to waste, eh? God, my head is going to hate me in the morning."

1735 hrs_

Brewster had a canteen upended in front of his face, rivulets of water running down his chin as he tried his best to chug the contents as fast as possible.

"Come on, come on, get hydrated, already," Thomas growled, standing in front of Brewster at parade rest, staring down the private. "Drunk on duty. Typical."

"Duty?" Brewster coughed up a bit of the water as he finished off the canteen. "I haven't been on duty since Suez, sarge. Come on. Forgive me if I wanted to loosen up a little bit."

"Well, you loosened up, all right—now it's time to tighten back up. We're going to need you at one hundred percent for tonight," Thomas said.

"About that, sergeant," Krueger spoke up, sitting next to Brewster on the back of the black pickup they'd taken from the raiders. "What's the score?"

"Once the General gets back from the Sheriff's office he'll explain," Thomas said, looking off in the direction Sherman had taken.

"Have anything to do with us getting the truck fixed?" Krueger asked.

"Might," Thomas answered tersely, then glanced back at Brewster. "Come on, Brewster, drink up."

"Aw, Thomas, I just finished an entire canteen. If I drink another I'll puke," Brewster protested.

"Yup," Thomas nodded. "Now get to it."

Brewster grumbled, unscrewed the top to another canteen and took a tentative sip. He grimaced. "There has got to be a better way to sober up than this. Maybe some coffee, or a Bloody Mary."

"Nothing beats hydration," Thomas said. "Good old water. Mmm-mm."

"You know," Krueger said, nudging Brewster with his elbow, "he's right. You get hangovers because alcohol actually dehydrates your body, right? So water's the best cure, really."

"That's right, private," Thomas said, nodding at Krueger. "Ah, here comes the General."

Sherman and Sheriff Wallace came walking toward the truck, each bearing a black tote bag over their shoulders.

"How'd it go, sir?" Thomas asked.

"Well," Sherman replied, nodding in Keaton's direction. "The Sheriff was kind enough to return some of our hardware to get the job done, and even threw in a few extras just in case we need them."

"What kind of extras?"

The Sheriff set his tote bag on the tailgate of the truck and unzipped it, revealing a small cache of weapons. "Mostly small arms. I noticed you all were using different calibers and makes, and I figured a little standardization wouldn't hurt, so I pulled a few pistols from our armory. They're nine-millimeters. We're too small of a town to have a S.W.A.T. team so I'm afraid I couldn't get you anything with more punch, but we've got a couple of surprises up our sleeves."

"Wait, wait, wait," Brewster interrupted, still sipping on his canteen and rubbing his temples. "I still don't even know what we got yanked out of the pub for. Anyone mind filling me in?"

"Sherman?" Keaton asked, yielding the floor to the General.

"Well, boys, as you know, the little firefight we had earlier today damaged our utility truck. We could tow it the rest of the way to Omaha if we had to, but that would put us in a bit of a pickle, having only two reliable vehicles instead of three—not to mention the extra strain it would put on the working truck, having to tow all that weight behind it."

"Following so far, sir," Krueger said.

"Well, we got lucky when we came across this town, and the people have been more than helpful—all except for one. That one happens to be the only qualified mechanic," Sherman went on.

"Sounds like our luck," Brewster commented.

"He wants us to do him a favor before he'll do one for us," Sherman said. "And that's where these weapons come in."

"What're we, mercenaries now?" Krueger asked. "Who does he want us to kill?"

"Remember those raiders we ran into?"

Brewster held up his bandaged hand and pointed to the cut on his face by way of reply. "Sure do, General."

"That's who he wants us to kill."

"Whoa, hey, now," Krueger said. "Correct me if I'm wrong, but I'm counting five of us here. More raiders than that bugged out of our little encounter earlier today, and I'm betting there's three times as many wherever they're holed up. Are we going to go basically commit suicide just to get a truck fixed? I vote we just tow the sucker."

A loud report echoed across the street and the four gathered soldiers instinctively ducked their heads down just a little. Only Keaton remained at ease.

"Relax," he told them. "That's just one of our border patrols taking out a carrier that wandered a bit too close. Happens a few times a day."

"And that's another thing," Brewster chimed in, "What about the infected?"

"That could be a problem," Sherman admitted. "We'll be doing this at night, when they're more active, so we'll have to keep our eyes open. Now, how about the rest of those surprises you were mentioning, Sheriff?"

"Right," Keaton said, digging through his tote. "The raiders are holed up in a distribution center. It has a fence and guard posts running around it, just like we have here in Abraham. It's about ten miles away, but getting in could be a problem. I thought maybe these would be handy."

Keaton produced a pair of wire cutters from the bag.

"You can cut your way through the fence with these. Since you'll be facing superior numbers, I thought you might also find these to be useful. We got hold of a few after 9/11. You have pork-barrel funding to thank for 'em."

Keaton dug out a few gas masks, followed by a pair of cylindrical canisters marked with blue paint. Krueger's eyes widened a bit.

"Tear gas," he said, picking up one of the canisters and studying it. "Could come in handy."

"That's what I was thinking," Keaton said. "If you're discovered, put on the masks and toss the grenades. It might give you enough cover to get back out without being shot."

"Which is always a good thing," Brewster quipped. "Sarge, can I stop drinking this water now?"

"Just as soon as you stop the goddamn slurring," Thomas growled.

"One other thing," Sherman said, and the other three soldiers turned to face him. "The mechanic said his daughter was taken by the raiders earlier on in the pandemic. We're not sure if she's alive or not, or what condition we might find her in, but if we do, our objective is to rescue her."

"I'm confused," Krueger said. "Are we killing raiders or rescuing damsels in distress?"

"Either-or," Sherman said. "If we can't find her, we drop however many raiders we can and get out. If we do find her, we shift from a hunt-and-kill to a rescue mission. Hoo-ah?"

"Hoo-ah," Krueger echoed.

Brewster raised his canteen in a salute, then took another tentative gulp. Thomas simply nodded and fell back into parade rest.

"We leave in half an hour," Sherman said. "Get geared up."

1801 hrs_

Rebecca had broken off from the rest of the group to wander the town on her own. It was a marvel to her that the place had escaped the total destruction they'd seen in countless other towns and cities on their way toward Omaha. They had passed within a hundred miles of Denver, but it had been close enough to see the smoke hanging in a pall over the mountaintops, and they guessed the city had been leveled.

"Probably firebombs," Sherman had figured. "Burn out the infection. Burn the city to the ground in the process, too, but if that's the price that has to be paid to get rid of the infected, I suppose it's worth it."

Now, here in Abraham, Kansas, Rebecca felt as far removed from the destruction as she ever had. The place was still full of life. She wandered into a small, half-acre park near the town's center and sank onto a bench, crossing her legs and leaning back with a sigh. Across the street, townsfolk were still busy hoeing troughs in the dirt for a crop of vegetables. They were all dressed in simple clothes, wearing simple shoes and speaking of simple things. It was quite a change from the way they would have been behaving months earlier, before the pandemic.

Rebecca closed her eyes and imagined the town before the plague. In her mind's eye, the freshly plowed field filled in and grew over with grass and wildflowers. Streetlights lit up the evening. Cars tooled up and down the main street, honking at acquaintences on the sidewalk. Mothers and children filtered in an out of the storefronts, bringing with them bags for their purchases and all looking forward to a nice, home-cooked dinner.

She snapped her eyes open and looked out at reality. The streetlights were dark, the field was once more dug up and prepared for planting, and no cars rolled down the streets, no horns broke the quiet and stillness. The only sounds were those of distant conversation among the gardeners, cursing about weeds and stones.

Behind her, a pair of children played on a set of see-saws, looking vaguely bored. She could empathize. These were the children of the videogame generation, the television toddlers. Deprived of their usual entertainment, they were still adapting to their new way of life.

"Hello," came a familiar voice from over Rebecca's shoulder. She turned to see Mbutu grinning down at her, hands in his pockets.

She smiled back, but didn't say anything.

"May I join you?" he asked, gesturing at the bench. Rebecca nodded, and the tall man slid into the seat next to her, surveying the landscape in front of him. "It is truly remarkable what people can accomplish when they work together."

"I was just thinking that," Rebecca said, smiling grimly. "I just wish more towns had survived."

"I wanted to talk to you," Mbutu began, "about the past few weeks."

"What about them?"

"You have seemed more and more...what is the word? Reserved," Mbutu said, nodding to himself. "We are becoming worried about you. We think you need to cheer up."

"I'm as cheery as I can be, given the circumstances," she snapped, then caught herself and shook her head. "Sorry. I know what you mean. I'm just having a tough time adapting, I suppose."

"How are you sleeping?" Mbutu asked, an innocent expression on his face.

"Sleeping?" Rebecca repeated. "Fine."

"Please," Mbutu said. "You can confide in me. You've been having dreams. We all have. It is a natural response to what we have seen recently."

"How did you know?" Rebecca asked, eyeing the man with a furrowed brow.

"You talk in your sleep," Mbutu replied with a grin.

Rebecca flushed. She hadn't been aware of that. "I do? So everyone knows? What have I been doing, waking everyone up every night? Why didn't someone say something to me—"

"Relax," Mbutu said. "I think I may be the only one who paid any attention. Brewster snores. He is surely waking up more people than you every night we sleep in the same room."

Rebecca chuckled despite herself. "Well, at least I'm not the only one who's putting undue pressure on the group."

"The only pressure you're putting is on yourself," Mbutu said with a slow nod. "My mother used to tell me that nightmares are our mind's way of telling us what not to do in life, or how to avoid a bad situation. Other times, nightmares force us to relive moments we are not proud of, so that we may better confront and understand them."

Rebecca thought back to the moment on the *Ramage* when she'd been forced to shoot Decker. It had been necessary, and he had been a carrier of Morningstar, but she'd been carrying the burden of guilt ever since. She had felt a bit like a murderer. Then again, none of her dreams since had featured the dead sergeant or that defining moment.

Mbutu took her silence as a sign she was considering his words and pressed on.

"Would you like to tell me about them?" he asked. "Your dreams, I mean. Sometimes, getting another opinion can be a key to sorting out what they mean."

"If they mean anything," Rebecca scoffed. "More likely, they're just products of an overactive imagination."

"Perhaps," Mbutu said. "Perhaps not."

A long moment of silence passed between the pair. Finally, Rebecca couldn't stand it any longer. She sighed and turned to the man, her lips pressed tightly together and look of embarrasment on her face.

"All right," she said. "This is how it goes:

"Usually the dream starts normally. I'm with the group and everything's just fine. But then something goes wrong. Everyone dies, everyone except for me and one other person. Whoever it is that doesn't die changes from dream to dream—last time it was Brewster but it's also been Sherman and you and Thomas and just about everyone else.

"Anyway, in the dream I'm looking for a weapon, but I can't find one. And then I find the other survivor, only they aren't alive anymore, they're a shambler and they're coming for me. I can't get away, no matter how hard I try, and I can never find anything to fight back with. The dream always ends with me being bitten, and then I wake up."

Mbutu leaned back on the bench, sighed, and considered Rebecca's words. Rebecca sat patiently next to him, waiting to hear his thoughts. When the moment dragged on into minutes, she began to get impatient, and finally spoke up.

"Well?" she asked. "What's it mean, Mr. Mystic?"

"There are several possibilities," Mbutu said, shrugging. "One way of looking at it is that you fear the loss of your friends. Another way of looking at it is that you fear the possibility of becoming infected with Morningstar. Both of those are dreams that every one of us has had since this began, I assure you."

"And that's it?"

"I have one other idea," Mbutu admitted. "You said in your dream you couldn't find any weapons, and you couldn't escape. Your mind may be telling you that no matter how badly you want to destroy the infected in your dream, you can't bear the thought of having to shoot a friend."

But I've already shot one, Rebecca thought, flashing back to Decker once more.

"You're right," she admitted after a moment. "I don't know if I could. I joined the Red Cross so I could help people. I never thought I'd have to kill them. It wasn't in me. I don't like it."

"No one truly does," Mbutu said, clasping her shoulder. "Some of us can accept it, others cannot, but none of us enjoy it. Your dreams are just preparing you for the possibility, so that if the time does come, you will be able to accept it."

Rebecca smiled up at him, nodding her head slowly. "I suppose that makes sense. Thanks, Mbutu."

"I am glad I could be of assistance," he said, rising to his feet. "Now, the rest of the group has gone to the pub to join Denton. Would you like to come?"

Rebecca looked out across the street to where the gardeners were wrapping up their evening chores.

"No," she said, shaking her head. "I think I'd like to just sit a while longer."

"As you wish," Mbutu said, turning and heading in the direction of the pub. He waved a hand over his shoulder. "You know where to find us."

"Always," Rebecca murmured, eyes still fixed on the townsfolk across the way.

CHAPTER FOUR
THE LION'S DEN

Ten miles north of Abraham, Kansas
March 07, 2007
2100 hrs_

BREWSTER, KRUEGER AND THOMAS crawled on their stomachs to the top of a gently rolling hill overlooking a sprawling distribution complex. The place was simply massive, with multiple storehouses and dozens of bays for tractor-trailers to load and unload their cargo. Apparently, the residents of the complex had a generator set up, because spotlights lit the exterior of the buildings in a warm yellow light. The three soldiers were still a good two hundred yards from the outer perimeter, well out of view of the guards that roamed the fenceline.

"All right, boys, we're on recon now," Thomas said, nodding in the direction of the complex. "Keep an eye on any guards you see and get me a good, solid count. I don't want any surprises when we go in there."

Krueger fished around on his webgear for a small pair of binoculars and held them up to his face.

"Looks like two towers near the main entrance. There's one guard in each. Armed. Can't tell with what, but they're longarms. Probably hunting rifles. Got to figure they'll be the best shots," Krueger said.

"We'll give them a wide berth," Thomas said.

"Look down there," Brewster said, bereft of binoculars but blessed with excellent eyesight. "Is that a roving guard by the fence, near the corner?"

Krueger shifted his binoculars to the right and then shook his head. "No, just looks like one of the raiders needed a spot to take a piss. Yep, there goes the fly. And there he goes back inside."

The distant figure vanished into one of the warehouse buildings, letting the door slam behind him with enough force that the three soldiers on the hill could hear it.

"Keep looking, Krueger," Thomas murmured.

"On it, sarge—holy shit!" Krueger exclaimed. "Sergeant, I think you may want to have a look at this. Near the main entrance, far side, ground level."

Krueger handed the binoculars over to Thomas, who accepted them and looked in the direction Krueger had indicated.

"Well, if that don't beat all, I don't know what does," Thomas said, grimacing behind the binoculars.

"What is it?" Brewster asked, craning his neck to see.

"Looks like our raider boys haven't been bothering to exterminate their infected company. They've got the main gates reinforced and lined on either side with more fencing. Looks like they have, what, thirty, maybe forty carriers caged up down there," Thomas said.

"What the hell would they be keeping them alive for?" Brewster wondered out loud.

"Security, I'm betting," Thomas said, scowling. "Anyone approaching would see a horde of the pusfucks at the main gates and turn right around without even bothering to try to take the place."

"Not a bad idea, actually," Krueger said, shrugging.

"Doesn't matter anyway," Thomas said, cutting off the banter. "We're not going in the main entrance. We're coming in from behind. Weapons check."

The two soldiers with Thomas turned over on their backs and began a thorough inspection of their gear. Sheriff Wallace had provided them with semiautomatic pistols as backups. Krueger had retrieved his bolt-action rifle and the Sheriff had been kind enough to loan him a night-vision scope to attach to the rails on top of the weapon, giving him an added edge in the darkness. Brewster had been handed his double-barreled shotgun back, but he'd managed to beg it off, saying that he'd rather have something that he wouldn't have to stop and reload after every two shots. After some deliberation, he traded the weapon off for a 12-gauge pump-action Remington that held seven shells.

The soldiers checked their magazines, racked rounds into chambers and re-holstered their sidearms. The rifles were similarly checked, cleared, re-loaded and held at the ready.

"Check masks," Thomas ordered.

The two men with him opened the bags that hung from their belts and donned the close-fitting black rubber masks, checking to make certain the seals were intact. Thomas joined them in this step, donning his own mask and checking its functionality. Satisfied that they held working equipment, the men replaced the gear in their pouches, bags, and holsters, and returned their attention to the facility across the field from them.

"Remember, we don't make a move until Sherman provides us with our distraction," Thomas said.

The small group had gone over several versions of a battle plan before finally settling on one they all felt (more or less) had a chance of success. The raiders would likely be settling in for the night, which aided them in their attempt to take them by surprise. Brewster had tried to argue once more that they should just tow the utility truck and avoid the danger, but Sherman had been adamant about having all their vehicles functional in case anything else came up down the road.

Thomas hadn't said anything, but he suspected Sherman's interest in this excursion amounted to more than just fixing vehicles. The General had a tender streak, and the mechanic's story compounded with the tales of hostility by the raiders they'd heard from Keaton was probably Sherman's main motivation in going forward. To strike a blow for the good guys, as it were. Sherman probably couldn't resist, no matter what he said or showed on the outside.

The plan they had finally settled on was almost elegant in its simplicity. They figured they had a miniscule chance of rescuing the mechanic's daughter. The facility before them was simply too large to clear before the raiders would locate them and cut them down. Instead, their orders were to get inside, wreak as much of the place as possible, and get back out. If they did sufficient damage to the raiders who had caused the mechanic and the town of Abraham so much grief, maybe they would be able to get the help they were after. Sherman would provide them the key they needed to get in without being spotted and shot.

Even as the three lay in the cool grass, Sherman was busy half a mile away. He'd accepted the Sheriff's offer of equipment but selected only one item for himself: a large-bore flaregun, the kind rescuers or victims used to signal for help in the wilderness, as well as a small box of flares. The idea was to launch the flares in rapid succession, hopefully drawing the attention of the raiders in his direction. They might not sally forth from their fortress, but they would certainly be curious, and that might just be enough to allow Thomas and the others to slip in unnoticed

The one big worry Sherman had was the other attention he might draw: that of nearby infected. Therefore, the older General had spent the last twenty minutes heaving himself upward, branch by branch, into the middle of an ancient pine tree. As far as he knew, the infected couldn't climb. He'd fire the flares and wait to hear whether the mission was a success over his radio.

Leaning comfortably back in the crook of a branch and the tree's trunk, Sherman popped open the box of flares and calmly loaded one of the shells into the gun. He took aim at the night sky and let fly with the first of the flares.

It popped with the sound of a shotgun being discharged, arced into the sky, and burst into color, a bright orange that must have lit up a square mile of the countryside.

"*Godspeed, soldiers,*" Sherman whispered to himself, and watched as the flare sizzled and died in the darkness. He reached down and began to load the second.

On the hillside, Thomas spotted the flare with ease. It cast a dim glow over the entire field.

"There's the signal," Thomas said, pointing. Brewster jumped up, ready to run for the fenceline, but Thomas stopped him short. "Wait. Wait for them to notice."

Krueger was busy studying the guard posts through the binoculars. He grinned behind them, nodding in approval.

"The bastards are looking mighty intrigued," Krueger said, still grinning. "They're all pointing at the flare and talking. One of them's on a radio. Brewster, scan your channels, let's see if we can pick them up."

Brewster reached down to the radio on his webgear and began cycling through channels. Most of them were picking up nothing but static. Once he hit channel 14, however, voices came through loud and clear.

"—*like a flare out over the woods to the south,*" came a voice. "*Might be someone in distress.*"

"*Easy pickings,*" came another voice. "*Should we get the crew ready?*"

"*No, no, stand down!*" came a third, a strong, authoritative voice that must have been the gang's leader. "*It's night and that flare will have infected running from miles away. We've already lost some good men today, let's not lose any more.*"

The second flare burst then, filling the sky with more of the orange brilliance.

"*Sure is pretty—like the Fourth of July,*" came the first voice again.

"*Knock off the chatter, Yoder, keep the channels clear,*" came the leader's voice.

"*All right, all right. I'm off.*"

"He might be off the radio, but he's sure not taking his eyes off those flares," Krueger reported. "Sergeant, I think we've achieved distraction."

"Roger that," Thomas said with a half-grin. "Let's go."

The three soldiers were up and on their feet in a moment, sprinting across the field toward the fenceline. Off to their left in the distance were the guard towers and the fencework swarming with infected. Even the victims of the virus seemed entranced by the bright lights of the flares, and were jostling one another, pushing against the fence as if they wanted nothing more than to run to the source of the flares and investigate it themselves.

Once the soldiers reached the fence, they went straight to work, silent as ghosts except for the clink and clatter of various bits of gear. Krueger unclipped the wire cutters from his belt and quickly snipped a straight line upwards through the fence until it was large enough for the soldiers to fit through. He pulled the fence sections apart and let Thomas through, followed closely by Brewster.

The pair came up on the other side of the fence with weapons drawn and at the ready. Brewster held his shotgun out in front of him and Thomas scanned the dark corners of the buildings and containers with a keen eye and primed pistol.

Krueger came through after them, his rifle catching momentarily on the fence and jingling the steel. The motion earned him a quick "Ssh!" from Thomas, and Krueger nodded in acknowledgement. The trio moved straight for the nearest entrance. It was a heavy steel door with a solid-looking lock on it, and none of them had any keys. Brewster, however, had his shotgun.

"Did the Sheriff get you any breaching rounds for that thing?" Thomas asked Brewster, pointing hurriedly at the soldier's shotgun.

Brewster nodded once. "Frangible slugs. The guy thinks ahead."

"Roger that. Take aim at that lock. Krueger, get your pistol out. We might need some rapid fire if the room on the other side of this door is occupied. Brewster, wait for the next flare to pop and use the noise to cover your shot," Thomas ordered.

Krueger slung his rifle and drew his pistol as Brewster stepped back from the door, cocked his shotgun, and took careful aim. The trio waited. They weren't stuck out in the open long. Sherman's third flare popped, and the moment the sound reached Brewster's ears, he fired. The slug tore into the locked door, shooting sparks and shrapnel in all directions. When the smoke cleared, the lock had been reduced to scrap metal.

"Breach it! Go, go, go!" Thomas stage-whispered.

Brewster drew back a leg and gave the door a heavy kick, sending it crashing open, and the three soldiers barreled into the room, weapons at the ready. They panned their weapons left and right, scanning for targets and finding none. They'd entered a storeroom filled to the ceiling with cardboard boxes sealed in plastic and stacked nearly to the ceiling.

"Someone will have heard that door getting kicked in," Thomas said. "Spread out and find cover. Clear the room."

"Roger," Krueger said.

Brewster nodded and slid off to the right, vanishing between stacks of boxes. Krueger kept his back to one wall, inching along. Thomas moved at a crouch, covering Krueger's other side.

Krueger let out a low whistle, catching Thomas' attention. The old sergeant looked over at the soldier.

Krueger gestured straight up. Thomas followed the gesture with his eyes and spotted a ladder hanging down from a catwalk that overlooked the entire room. The catwalk itself sported a second ladder, one that ran up to the roof of the warehouse itself. Thomas dropped his gaze back to Krueger, who was patting the rifle on his back and pointing again at the catwalk.

Thomas nodded. Krueger wanted to move to a better sniping position and cover the movements of Thomas and Brewster below. That was a strategically sound move, and Thomas approved.

Krueger nodded, swung up onto the ladder, and began to swiftly climb.

Brewster, meanwhile, was nearing the far end of the large room before he finally heard any noise other than his own breathing. Footsteps, sounding like a pair, were moving quickly toward the room from a wide hallway that branched off of the warehouse. The soldier froze in place, shotgun at the ready. After a moment, he heard voices as well.

"I'm telling you, man, I heard something in here," said the first.

"You're always hearing things in this place at night," said the second. "This ain't a haunted complex, you know. There ain't nothing here at night that ain't here in the day."

"That's not what I'm talking about, Dan. I'm saying I heard something loud, like thunder."

"Oh, Jesus. That's the flares outside. Didn't you hear on the radio? Someone's out in the woods popping off flares. Poor bastard. Won't be long before the infected get him. Though, on the upside, tomorrow we'll get to have our pick of whatever he was carrying, once we find his body."

"Maybe you're right," said the first voice. The footsteps slowed, then stopped. "Probably nothing."

Brewster relaxed somewhat. The two might not enter the warehouse room after all.

"Better safe than sorry, though," said Dan. "Come on, let's check it out."

Well, shit, Brewster thought. *Here goes our element of surprise.*

The two men came ambling into the warehouse, obviously at ease. Each was wielding a rifle, but neither held them at the ready. They were slung over their shoulders, and from the look of them, they weren't expecting trouble.

Whether or not they were expecting it, they got it.

When they were ten feet from Brewster's hiding place, the soldier swung out from behind the stack of boxes, leveled his shotgun, and fired.

The blast caught one of the men square in the chest, lofting him backwards several feet to land in a ragged heap. What was left of his ribcage poked out at odd angles, bits of bone and blood sticking up through his ripped clothing.

"Holy shit—" began the other, reaching up to swing his rifle into a firing position.

Brewster pumped his shotgun, but the spent round caught in the chamber, jamming the weapon. He cursed, re-cocked the weapon, and managed to eject the spent shell and shove in a new one. By that time, however, the surviving raider had brought his weapon to bear. Brewster looked up and found himself staring down the bore of a weapon.

A blast sounded, and Brewster cringed, expecting to feel the warm sensation of blood flowing out of his new wound. Instead, he felt nothing, and after a moment he opened one eye. The raider lay several feet away on his side, a pool of blood forming around a fresh head wound. The man's rifle had clattered to the cement floor. Brewster checked himself for bullet holes and breathed a sigh of relief when he couldn't find a single one.

"You owe me," came Krueger's voice.

Brewster looked up to see Krueger laying flat on one of the catwalks high above, waving from behind the scope of his .30-06.

"I'll get you a beer at Eileen's if we make it back to town," Brewster promised.

"I'm holding you to that," was Krueger's reply.

"Soldiers! We've got incoming!" Thomas said, pointing at the wide hall from which the two raiders had appeared. The sound of harried voices and the stomp of running feet echoed throughout the complex. "They heard those shots!"

"I've got the hallway covered," Krueger said, staring through his scope. "Brewster, give me backup with that scattergun of yours."

"I'm on it," Brewster said, kicking a small pile of boxes over to serve as a makeshift bunker. He hunkered down behind them and took aim. "Thomas! What're you doing?"

"Completing the mission," Thomas said. He'd backed away from the hall and was trying the other doors that led out of the warehouse. Most were locked, but when he found one that opened for him, he turned to face the two soldiers guarding the hall. "I'm going to see what kind of damage I can do. As far as they know, you're the only intruders. Hold them off until I get back or until I call you to join me. Hoo-ah?"

"Hoo-ah!" Krueger chimed.

"Sure," Brewster said in a much less enthusiastic tone. "Happy to hold off the horde for you, Sarge."

The first of the raiders appeared in the hall, clutching an AK-47 to his chest and shouting orders to the men that were, no doubt, closely behind him. He made it three steps before Krueger's rifle round caught him in the chest and dropped him to the floor.

"Too easy," Krueger boasted, grinning as he locked and loaded another round.

"Don't worry, brother," Brewster called up, pointing into the hall. "There are more!"

Raiders began pouring into the hallway, wielding all kinds of weapons, from rifles to shotguns to machetes and even a heavy machine gun that made Brewster wonder just where the men had been picking up their hardware.

Bullets began to fly into the warehouse as the raiders knelt and took cover in the hall, exchanging fire with the two defenders within.

Brewster fired another slug, watching with satisfaction as it knocked over a rifle-wielding raider. His death rattle echoed as loudly as the gunshots being exchanged. Krueger's next shot was at the man setting up the heavy machine gun, but the shot went wide, catching another raider in the shoulder and spinning him in place before he fell to the floor, clutching at the wound and groaning in pain.

The machine-gunner finished setting up his weapon and let loose a fusillade of bullets. Brewster abandoned his cover and dove to the side as the rounds ripped through the cardboard boxes and whatever it was inside that was being stored, ricocheting off of the cement flooring and tearing up the warehouse. Brewster clapped his hands over his ears to block out some of the deafening noise.

Krueger fired again, winging the machine-gunner and causing the man to drop his weapon with a curse. The momentary distraction allowed Brewster to swing back into action, firing another pair of shells down the hall. The fragmenting slugs wreacked havoc among the tightly-gathered raiders at the end of the hallway. Several grabbed at wounds and shouted taunts and curses reached the ears of the soldiers.

"What was that?" Brewster yelled back, firing a third slug down the hall.

"I said once I get done with you, I'm gonna find and fuck your mother, you piece of shit!" came the reply.

"And thank you very much for letting me know where you are," Krueger murmured from the catwalk above. He fired, and the taunter doubled over, clutching at a stomach wound.

"I'll let her know you're interested!" Brewster yelled back, firing another shell.

The soldier swung away from the hall, plastered his back against the wall and fished around in his pockets for some more shells. He began to reload his shotgun. "Krueger, cover me while I reload!"

"On it, bro," Krueger replied, firing again. Brewster couldn't see the results of the shot, but he guessed it had been a hit. Krueger's accuracy was only getting better as he had opportunity after opportunity to practice.

"Thomas better hurry the hell up!" Brewster yelled up to Krueger. "I don't have infinite ammo down here!"

☆ ☆ ☆ ☆ ☆

Thomas was, indeed, hurrying the hell up. He'd run flat out down the side hall he'd discovered, trying doors and listening for the sounds of company. He guessed he'd taken a turn that led him away from the main body of raiders, and that was just as well with him. The lights overhead gave him plenty of illumination to see by. He guessed the raiders had a generator set up somewhere.

Thomas slowed to a fast walk, considering the idea. If the raiders did indeed have a generator, they'd have to have fuel for it.

He ran over his mission objectives in his head, almost hearing Sherman's voice repeating them.

Get inside, wreak as much of the place as possible, and get back out.

Thomas allowed himself a rare grin. If he could find the generator room, he'd be able to do a substantial amount of damage. The only question was which way to go.

The Sergeant Major came to a T-intersection and looked left and right. The halls were empty. He had to make a fast decision, and went with his gut, heading left. There were only three doors in this section of hallway. He tried the first two and found them locked. The third was open. He eased the door open slowly, then moved in, pistol at the ready.

What he saw before him made the bile in his throat rise. Before him were a number of makeshift cells, all made from chain-link fence. Within each of the cells was a narrow, dirty cot and a pile of discarded clothes. Each cell also held a woman. Some were in better shape than others. Seeing Thomas, they all recoiled to the rear of their cells, whimpering. Whatever the raiders had been doing to them, it had been enough to traumatize them.

"Relax," Thomas growled. "I'm not here to hurt any of you."

His disgust for the raiders quickly grew into a festering hatred. This was a harem. They'd kidnapped women and kept them around just to have their way with them at their leisure. They were scum. Thomas' plan of wrecking the facility was put on momentary hold. He holstered his pistol.

"My name is Command Sergeant Major Thomas, United States Army," he said, striding forward. "And I'm going to get you out of here."

One by one, the women began to realize that this man was not one of their captors, and he had not come to avail himself of their presence. They pressed forward against the front of their cells, reaching out toward Thomas as he walked by. Many looked skinny and underfed, and more than one had bruises or cuts on their faces and bodies. Most were underclothed, wearing only thin robes or tattered shirts and underwear. Their treatment had obviously been horrible.

"Keys," he said, looking left and right at the women. "Where can I find the keys?"

"The wall," said one of the women, pointing at the far end of the room. "They keep them hanging over there, on the wall."

Thomas jogged over and retrieved the keyring. It had several keys on it, one for each of the locks on the makeshift cells. He released the woman who'd spoken up first, then handed her the keyring.

"Go around and unlock the rest of these cells, then meet me at the door. I'm going to watch the hall. I have two men engaged in a firefight, and I need to get back to them as fast as possible."

The woman nodded, swallowed, and accepted the keys, running from cell door to cell door, releasing the other captives. Once the last had been freed, they crowded around Thomas, who was standing in the doorway keeping a careful eye on the hall.

"Do any of you know your way around this place?" Thomas asked, glancing back at the women.

"I do," said the one who had directed Thomas to the keys. "I used to work here before the virus hit. My name is Marie."

"Marie, I noticed this building still has power. I'm guessing there's a generator in here somewhere."

"That's right," Marie said, nodding. "It's in the basement. I can show you."

"Do they store the fuel for it there, too?" Thomas asked.

"I think so," she said, unsure of where he was going with his train of thought. "Unless they've moved it."

"Good enough," he said. "You're with me. The rest of you, I want you to head to the main warehouse. Head down the hall, make your first right, then go straight. There's a firefight going on in there. Stay behind cover and pray to whatever god you believe in that my men can hold off the raiders until I get back."

The women stood still a moment, looking back and forth at one another, unsure of themselves.

"Go! Now!" Thomas shouted, jolting them into action. They took off, some running, others limping from injuries sustained during their captivity.

"Sergeant, the basement stairs are this way," Marie said, taking Thomas by the arm and guiding him down the hall. She took him down the opposite direction of the intersection he'd come to before, leading him to an unmarked door about halfway down the hall. "This is it."

Thomas tried the door handle. It was unlocked. He swung it open, pistol aimed, but only empty stairs, leading downward, met his eyes.

"The generator's in the other room," Marie said, and started down the stairs. Thomas grabbed her by the shoulder, holding her in place. "What is it?"

"Me first," Thomas growled, passing her by. He took the steps slowly, checking his corners carefully for signs of hostiles. The basement was finished, painted in bright white, and kept quite clean and clear of debris. Janitorial supplies lined one wall, stacked high on shelves that reached to the ceiling. In another corner, water heaters and plumbing access points jutted out of the walls and an employee laundry was set up in another corner. Farthest from the entrance was another heavy door.

"It'll be behind there," Marie whispered from behind Thomas. She extended a thin hand and pointed at the door.

Thomas strode boldly over to the door and pulled it open. The hinges creaked and hinted at a lack of oiling over recent years. As the door opened, the noise from the generator increased until it filled the basement with a dull roar. Exposed in front of Thomas was the generator room. Off to his left stood the large machine, taking up most of a section of whitewashed, cement-block wall, and to his right was a cage stacked with steel drums, all sealed and marked with sticky signs that read 'flammable.' Thomas almost grinned; the room was exactly as he had hoped it would be.

Directly in front of Thomas, however, was an unexpected occupant of the room. Sitting with his back to the door was a raider, lounging in a simple wooden chair with his feet propped up on a desk, smoking a cigarette despite the hundreds of gallons of gasoline in the room with him. He was apparently the man assigned to keep the generator running at night, feeding it with fuel when needed and taking care of any problems that might arise.

The man was also apparently a slacker, because he had hooked up a VCR and a small television set directly to the generator and was chuckling to himself as he watched reruns of M*A*S*H* on the little screen. The noise from the generator had covered Thomas and Marie's entrance, and the man was none the wiser as the older sergeant walked into the room. Thomas let his eyes wander downwards. The man had a Kalashnikov assault rifle propped up against the desk.

Z. A. RECHT

Thomas looked back at Marie, over at the generator, right to the fuel, and then back at the man lounging in front of him. Without any further hesitation, Thomas raised his pistol and fired a single shot into the back of the man's head. Blood sprayed the television screen, interrupting Hawkeye's speech about never carrying a gun.

Marie stood behind Thomas with the back of her hand held over her mouth, staring at the dead man slumped over the desk.

"Get used to it," Thomas growled. "Brave new world out there. Now give me a hand."

Marie recovered from her shock quickly enough—quicker, in fact, than Thomas had expected, raising his opinion of her a notch. Thomas busied himself by removing the protective plastic sheeting that covered the barrels upon barrels of fuel. Marie tried to help him roll the barrels to space them around the room, but had less luck in that department: the barrels were heavy and even Thomas struggled to move them.

Over the course of several minutes they had managed to uncover, open, and reposition the barrels in the miniature fuel depot; nearly fifty in all. Thomas unscrewed the cap of one of the barrels and began furiously searching the room.

"What are you looking for?" Marie asked, coming up behind him and casting curious glances over his shoulder as he looked through moldy cardboard boxes in the corner.

"Fuse," Thomas grumbled. He turned, set his hands on his hips and puffed out a short breath of annoyance. All that work and no fu—

Suddenly Thomas' eyes fell on the slumped form of the man he'd killed. The man had been wearing a t-shirt, overshirt, and a pair of dirty, oilstained camouflage pants. Thomas strode over to him and yanked at the overshirt, pulling it off of the corpse and holding it up to inspect it. Beside him, the jostled body slumped to the side and fell out of its chair, crumpling to the ground. Marie swallowed and averted her eyes as blood pooled from the man's gory head wound onto the concrete. Thomas didn't even seem to notice.

"This will do," Thomas announced, nodding at the shirt.

"Do for what?" Marie asked.

"Like I said," Thomas replied, sounding annoyed, "I needed a fuse."

Marie looked around the room at all the barrels, watched Thomas knotting and braiding the large shirt into a three-foot cloth fuse, and finally made the connection.

"You're going to blow this place up!" she said, watching wide-eyed as Thomas stuffed one knotted end of the shirt into the nearest barrel of fuel.

"No," Thomas growled. "I'm not."

"Then what the hell are you doing?" Marie asked, gesturing wildly at the shirt, the barrels, and Thomas himself.

"Setting the place on fire," Thomas said, glancing in her direction. It was a minor correction, but Thomas was a stickler for details. "Not enough explosive power here to level the place. But there is enough to set it to burning—and burning fast and hard, too. First blast ought to cover our escape."

"Uh—look, I've seen a lot and I'm not stupid, but will that shirt give us enough time to get out of here before—"

"Before it blows?" Thomas asked. He shrugged. "Yes and no. I'm going for a delayed detonation here. See that gas can there?"

Thomas pointed behind himself, toward the generator. A three-gallon fuel jug sat next to the generator's tank.

"Yes," Marie said. "What do you want me to do with it?"

"Fill it out of one of these barrels. Get ready—we'll be running out of here in a minute."

Marie did as she was asked, re-filling the jug with gasoline from one of the barrels with some difficulty, then set it at Thomas' side.

"All right," Thomas said, making certain his makeshift fuse reached from the top of the barrel to the cold concrete ground. "Now it's time to get down to business. Marie, here's what I want you to do. I'll go first, and cover us. You follow right behind me with that fuel jug. Keep pouring, just a little at a time. I want you to leave a trail of gas behind us, get me?"

Marie nodded. She saw what he was getting at.

"If anyone tries to get in our way, I'll worry about them. You just worry about that line of gas."

"Okay, Thomas. I'm behind you," Marie said, nodding once more.

"Good," Thomas grumbled. "Let's get to work."

Thomas scooped up the dead guard's AK-47, checked to make sure there was a round in the chamber, and made for the door. He signaled an all clear to Marie, and the woman began her slow retreat, splashing little bits of gasoline behind her as she went, leading from the tail end of the cloth fuse along the floor.

Thomas led the way up and out of the basement. They didn't encounter a single guard until they reached the main hall above. Apparently, one of the raiders had gone to check on the harem and hadn't liked what he'd seen. He was standing at the far end of the hall, scratching his head at the sight of the empty cells when Thomas and Marie came into view.

"Hey!" yelled the raider. "Stop right there!"

The raider went for his pistol, drew it and fired three shots before Thomas was able to react. The old sergeant cursed as he flattened his back to the wall, listened as the rounds ricocheted in the corridor outside, then swung around the corner and returned fire. The raider wasn't stupid. He'd also taken cover inside the harem room, firing from around the edge of the doorframe. Thomas let two more rounds fly in his foe's direction before ducking back into the stairwell. Marie had halted beside him, a glistening trail of gasoline leading down the stairs behind her and off across the basement floor.

"We're in trouble," Thomas said. "He's got a good position. Listen close, girl, we're going to take a risk. This rifle can fire on automatic. I'm going to switch it over, and then we're both going to run for the T-junction. I'll be firing full-auto to make that man keep his head down. You stay right the hell behind me and for God's sake don't leave a gap in that line of gas you're leaving behind."

"Right," Marie nodded. "I'm ready."

Spunky, Thomas thought. *Might've made a good soldier.*

Three more pistol shots echoed in the corridor as the raider returned Thomas' fire. Thomas flicked the selector on the rifle over to auto, held up three fingers, and silently counted down. When he got to zero, he swung out from his cover and depressed the trigger.

The AK-47 belched forth round after round in full auto, and Thomas charged down the hallway. The bullets peppered the harem doorway, leaving pockmarks and smoking craters all around it. The raider inside dove for cover.

Thomas made it to the junction and ducked into it. Marie was right behind him, still carrying the fuel jug.

"How much left?" Thomas asked, breathing heavy and nodding at the jug.

"Maybe half," Marie said.

"Gotta keep moving," Thomas said. Now that they were closer to the warehouse, Thomas could hear Brewster and Krueger, still firing away. The pair hadn't been taken out yet, and were, from the sound of things, holding their position in the warehouse as ordered.

The pair moved down the hall at a steady jog. Thomas skipped backwards, watching the intersection for signs of the raider who had been taking cover in the harem room. Once, the man dared poke his head around the corner. Thomas sent a pair of bullets his way that missed by a very narrow margin. Thomas winced as he fired, praying that the sparks wouldn't set off the gasoline trail prematurely.

Thomas and Marie burst into the cavernous warehouse and the sound of gunfire increased immediately.

"Do you know how to use this?" Thomas asked, unholstering his pistol and handing it, butt-first, to Marie.

"I've fired them before, years ago," Marie answered, unsteadily accepting the weapon.

"You'll pick it up again fast. Point and shoot. No one comes down this corridor."

"All right," Marie answered, setting down the gasoline jug and taking up her position as rear guard.

Thomas turned and sprinted toward where he'd left Brewster and Krueger. He found the pair had been busy holding off their company. Krueger was still on the catwalk above, sniping away, and Brewster kicked heavy boxes into the entrance to the corridor the raiders were coming from, providing obstacles for them. A fine grayish-green mist was seeping out of the hall, and both Brewster and Krueger wore their gas masks. Even as Thomas noticed this, he sniffed the air and picked up on the familiar scent of a far-off campfire as the first tendrils of fog reached his nostrils.

Brewster and Krueger had remembered the CS tear gas.

Thomas fumbled at his belt and donned his own mask before proceeding to the front line, where Brewster was hunkered down behind a thick stack of boxes busily reloading weapons.

"Where the fuck have you been?!" Brewster shouted over the gunfire at Thomas, his voice muffled behind his gas mask.

Thomas decided to save the dressing-down about showing respect for later.

"Finishing the mission," Thomas shot back. "Report!"

"Report is half the goddamn raider army is trying to get into this room! Krueger picked off a couple that tried to circle around back! I ran out of shotgun shells a while back and had to pull these off of a couple of guys who got too close! Take your pick, Sarge, we've got a hell of a fight on our hands!" Brewster gestured at a small selection of rifles and pistols he'd accumulated.

"Not necessary!" Thomas yelled back. "We're ready to bug out! Did you see the girls?"

"Girls?" Brewster asked, firing a pair of shots down the fog-enshrouded hallway, gratified to hear an accompanying scream of pain. "Oh, you mean the skin-and-bones ones! Yeah, they came through about five minutes ago! We gave 'em a couple pistols and told them to run for the ridge south of here, where we were scouting!"

"Goddammit!" Thomas cursed. "Those raiders could be picking them back up right now, or worse, you idiot! What if some infected come along!"

"Pardon me, sarge, but fuck you!" Brewster yelled. "I've got a lot on my hands here right now and I can't be playing nursemaid!"

As if to enunciate his point, an enemy shotgun blast obliterated the corner of one of the boxes he hid behind, showering the pair with scraps of cardboard and plastic, reduced to little more than confetti.

"Come on!" Thomas said, grabbing Brewster by the collar and hoisting him to his feet. "We're out of here! Krueger!"

"Sergeant!" Krueger replied from the catwalk above, still firing.

"Get down and bug out! Move back to the rendezvous—the hill where we did the scouting! Protect the women if they're still there! Brewster, that goes for you, too."

"Happy to oblige, sarge," Brewster said, following Krueger out the rear entrance. The pair were sending rounds down the hostile corridor all the way. Thomas retreated to where he'd left Marie. The woman was kneeling, and her pistol was slightly smoking.

"One tried to come down," she explained. "I fired at him. I don't think I hit him, but I—"

"No time to talk," Thomas growled. "See that open door across the way?"

Thomas pointed at the kicked-in door where the trio had originally breached the facility.

"Yes."

"Get out through there. Straight across from it is a hole in the fence. Go through it and meet up with the other women and my soldiers. You'll see them."

"But what about—" Marie started, pointing toward the gasoline trail, but Thomas cut her off.

"Leave it to me," Thomas said. "Now go! Go!"

Marie turned and bolted for the exit. Thomas watched her until she made it through the door, then turned back to the gas can. He dropped the AK-47, picked up the can, and began to backpedal towards the exit, spilling what remained of the fuel behind himself. Bullets whizzed around him from the tear-gas filled corridor, and the sounds of retching and coughing reached his ears. If it hadn't been for the CS tear gas he'd probably already have been dead.

The gasoline ran out about halfway through the warehouse, and Thomas threw the can aside, kneeling next to the pool of fluid.

Kidnap women, murder travelers, steal from them—that's not a very nice occupation, Thomas thought. *You people don't deserve a place like this.*

Thomas reached into his pocket, pulled free a tarnished old Zippo lighter, sparked it, and held it near the pool of gasoline.

Almost immediately the fuel caught, sending a blast of hot air washing over Thomas' face. The fire took off, following the trail left along the floor, and Thomas did likewise—only in the opposite direction. He ran straight through the warehouse, was vaguely aware of something that felt like a tug at his arm, and dove through the kicked-in door. He came up in a roll and headed for the cut fence.

Inside the facility, the trail of fire reached the stairwell. It hesitated a moment, then jumped down the first stair, fumes catching the fuel. It jumped from step to step until it reached the bottom, and raced away once more toward the generator room.

Outside, Thomas wriggled his way through the cut fence, aware that the entire facility had now been alerted to their presence. Searchlights sought him out. He pulled himself free and began the long sprint toward the hilltop where he hoped the rescued women and his soldiers were waiting for him. He made it ten meters before a spotlight landed directly on him.

Shouts filled the night and were followed up immediately by the sound of rapid gunfire. Chunks of grass and dirt kicked up all around Thomas as he ran, hunched over, toward his goal.

Inside the complex, the trail of fire met the wool fuse, caught, and slowly began to climb toward the top of the barrel.

Outside, Thomas continued his run, knowing that sooner or later one of the dozens of rounds that were seeking him would find him, and that would end him. Ahead of him came the crack of a rifle, and the spotlight that was framing Thomas went out. That would have to have been Krueger and the night-vision scope the Sheriff had loaned him. Bullets still poured around the old sergeant, and within a moment, a second searchlight had snapped on and had framed him in a circle of illumination.

Inside, the flame reached the top of the barrel, flickered for a moment, and then caught a fume leaking out of the top of the drum. The dozens of other drums nearby sat silently, waiting with patience for just that moment.

The entire basement of the complex went up in a white blast of heat and light. The facility seemed to shudder, and roiling explosions of black smoke and red fire burst forth from the center of the complex, rising high into the night sky. The searchlights snapped off all at once, as did the interior lighting and security lamps outside.

The fire from the raiders halted almost immediately as they cast about in confusion for what had caused the sudden catastrophe. An entire section of their compound had been reduced to flaming debris in an instant. One or two of them shouted about warplanes and another said something about terrorists.

In the meantime, Thomas made it to the hilltop. He was gratified to see that not only had both Krueger and Brewster survived their escape, but so had Marie and most of the other women.

"Most?" Thomas asked Marie when she had told him not all of her friends were present.

"Some were taken again before they got out of the facility," Marie said, her voice stone-cold. "But most of us made it. That's something."

"And no carriers to speak of," Krueger threw in, scanning the horizon through his night-vision scope. "Two approached the gates, but they haven't noticed us."

Thomas nodded, hands on his hips. He turned to survey the distribution facility. Black smoke, visible even in the night, rose up in a solid plume. He judged his handiwork acceptable.

"Damn fine job keeping the back door open, soldiers," Thomas said, glancing over his shoulder at Krueger and Thomas.

"Thanks, Thomas," Krueger said, then narrowed his eyes. "Sergeant, your arm. You're bleeding."

Thomas looked down at his right arm to find that he'd been hit in the crossfire. Dark red blood coated the sleeve of his shirt, and as he became conscious of the wound and the adrenaline of the firefight wore down, he began to feel pain. He pushed the sensation to the back of his mind and forced himself to shrug.

"It's not bad," he said. "Not bleeding too much. I'll get it fixed up later."

"Uh, sarge?" Brewster asked, raising a hand. "Two questions now that we're out of here."

Thomas only grunted by way of reply.

"Firstly, what about these women? We didn't come out here with a vehicle because we thought the raiders would hear it. We walking them all the way back?"

"That's right."

"Secondly, sarge, I know this was a slapdash plan and all, and I can appreciate that, given the circumstances—but what about Sherman? Shouldn't we check and make sure he can make it back?"

Aw, shit, Thomas thought. *And this was Sherman's plan to begin with. Leave it to him to forget himself in all his planning.*

"Damn it," Thomas said out loud. "All right, new plan. Marie, you can handle yourself. Do you know the town of Abraham?"

The woman walked over to Thomas and nodded. "I've only ever visited, never lived there."

"Any of you other women know Abraham?"

Three of the remaining women raised their hands.

"Okay, here's the deal," Thomas said. "Those of you who know it, lead the way. Get all of yourselves there in one piece. When you get to the main gates, tell 'em Thomas sent you and that you're from the raider's base. Got it? They'll take care of you."

The women nodded slowly, looking back and forth at one another.

"Krueger, Brewster, on me," Thomas said. "We're going to go get the General."

★ ★ ★ ★ ★

Over a quarter of a mile away, Francis Sherman felt as if his time was running out. The flares hadn't brought any of the raiders running, but they had certainly attracted the infected. He'd been worried about as much and was glad he'd taken the time to climb up into the tall pine in which he sat. So far, his theory about the infected not being able to climb was holding out.

The problem was they had no compunctions about using the bodies of their own comrades as a kind of macabre ladder.

The first few had shown up just a brace of minutes after he'd fired the first of the flares. They were sprinters, looking every which way as they tore through the forest trying to locate their prey. When Sherman had fired another flare, they had zeroed in on him and within moments were scratching and pawing at the trunk of the tree he was in, growling up at him with a look of unabashed hatred in their bloodshot eyes.

Sherman had fired one more flare, then drew his pistol and dispatched the infected. The shots had been easy: the infected were directly below him. The bullets had entered the top of the infected skulls, exited through the bottom, and sent the carriers slumping to the ground against the tree trunk, silenced forever.

Then more had begun to show up.

They came as singles, or in small groups of two or three, always seeming to prefer to stick together when possible. Most were sprinters. The shamblers just couldn't cover the distance from wherever they had been lurking to the source of the flares as fast as their living cousins. When Sherman had exhausted his supply of flares, there were nearly twenty of them gathered around the base of the tree. Sherman had killed as many as he could with his first magazine, then stopped to reload and consider his situation.

The infected he'd killed were trod upon by their brethren as if they were nothing more than cobblestones. Each body added a few inches of height to the pile, and by the time he'd racked a round into the chamber of his weapon for a second go, the infected could reach the lowest ring of branches.

One grabbed hold of a branch and nearly managed to pull itself up, making Sherman hold his breath for a moment. If they figured out how to climb, he was royally screwed. Luckily for him, the sprinter lost its balance and tumbled off the other side of the branch, crashing to the ground below. He breathed a mental sigh of relief.

The sprinters were growling and jostling one another, and every now and then they would let up a wailing, bone-chilling howl, all staring at Sherman with those piercing, bloody eyes.

Sherman had grown very familiar with that howl over the past several months. Every time he'd heard it, another group of infected hadn't been far behind. The survivors referred to it simply as "The Growl." It was an alarm, a beacon, a signal for every infected in the area that here was prey—come and get it. Sherman cursed himself for not taking more time to properly plan the assault—even if the men attacking the raiders' base got out without a hitch, he was stuck in a tree and surrounded by infected.

One of the infected took a running start and launched itself up the tree trunk toward Sherman. The infected's hand came close enough to brush the General's boot. Sherman felt a look of disgust cross his face as he fired, sending the sprinter tumbling back down the tree to land in a jumble on top of the pile at the base.

Sherman checked his supply situation and found it grim. He had two full magazines and four rounds left in his current one. That wasn't a lot. He had no armor of any kind and no way out of the tree.

He had just begun to work through possible plans to get himself out of the tight situation when gunfire erupted from across the darkened forest meadow. Below him, the sprinters jerked and spasmed as rounds passed through them, spattering blood on the tree trunk and remaining carriers. After the thunder of the first barrage faded, leaving a slight ringing in Sherman's ears, only five of the sprinters remained on their feet. All five had shifted their attention from Sherman to whomever it was doing the firing.

They looked out into the darkness, growled deep in their throats, let fly with the loudest roar Sherman had heard so far that night, and charged across the meadow.

They made it less than halfway before being cut down.

In the ensuing silence, Sherman sat in his crook in the tree, breathing a heavy sigh of relief. He kept silent. His rescuers might be raiders, after all, and he still didn't feel right giving up his position until he heard a familiar voice.

"General! The way is clear!"

It was Thomas.

"Thomas! Holy hell, am I glad to hear you!" Sherman shouted back. He holstered his pistol and swiftly descended the tree, carefully avoiding any smears of infected blood he came across. He dropped to the pine-needle coated ground and ran toward the source of Thomas' voice. He came upon Brewster, Krueger, and Thomas, all looking on edge and scanning the darkness with their weapons for further threats.

"Good to see you three," Sherman said, breathing heavily after the run. He glanced over the group, taking in their state. "Thomas, you've got red on you."

Thomas held up his wounded arm, shrugged, and went back to scanning the darkness.

"How did the mission go?" Sherman asked.

"With all due respect, sir, I think we should save that for when we're safe back in town," Thomas said.

As if to enunciate his point, the thrashing sound of vegetation being trampled reached the group's ears, and a moment later Krueger fired a shot into the darkness. A heavy thud followed a moment later, signaling a hit.

"They'll be coming from all angles," Brewster said, sounding anxious. "We should move. We should move now. They'll be coming!"

"Keep it calm, private," Thomas said. "All right, doubletime, back to Abraham—can't be more than a few miles. We can make it."

The group moved off at a dogtrot. Krueger brought up the rear, constantly scanning the darkness with his night-vision scope for any hostiles. Occasionally he would halt, kneel, fire, and then run to catch back up with the group.

It was nearly pitch-black in the forest, and though the group knew which way to go, it was hard to make out their surroundings.

Sound became their worst enemy, moreso than any of the infected. Sprinters and shamblers from all parts had responded to the rattle of gunfire and the brightness of the flares, and many, especially the shamblers, were wandering aimlessly through the underbrush, looking for their prey. Sounds of snapping twigs, thrashing shrubs, and the rustle of leaves left all four feeling frazzled and nervous before they'd gone half a mile.

A crashing noise off to their left drew Brewster's attention, and he swung his weapon—a purloined carbine he'd picked up from one of the dead raiders—and fired three shots in rapid succession. His timing had been perfect.

Out of the darkness loomed a sprinter, jaws wide and arms outstretched, no more than ten feet from the group. At least one of Brewster's rounds struck home. Blood blossomed out of the infected's back and it fell, skidding to a halt nearly at Brewster's feet. The soldier stepped back from the body, put a second round through the infected's skull, and spat on the remains.

"Missed me, fucker," Brewster taunted.

Behind him, Krueger knelt and fired again. "I hate to rush things, but we're getting more and more company on our tails."

"All right, keep a move on! Let's go!" Sherman said, waving on the small group. They continued in more or less the same fashion, moving as fast as they dared while still trying to keep an eye on all four angles of approach. Three more times a carrier loomed up out of the night to attack, only to be gunned down before it could reach them.

The group reached the bottom of a small hill that Sherman remembered.

"This is it," he said, hands on his knees as he tried to catch his breath. He was in great shape for a man of his age, but a multi-mile run in the dark, with full gear and while under attack was enough to exhaust anyone. "I remember this hill."

"Tell me the town's on the other side," Brewster gasped, leaning on the butt of his carbine.

"Not quite," Sherman huffed, "but it opens up into a field—then we get to the town."

"Better than...all these trees," Krueger said, also out of breath. "Can't see...the fuckers coming."

A loud snapping drew their attention, and Krueger brought up his rifle again, scanning the undergrowth. After a moment, he lowered the weapon. "Nothing. Let's keep moving."

The four began to climb the hill, which was rocky and supported dozens of thick vines that curled up and around the trash trees that had managed to take root there. About halfway up, Krueger snagged his foot on the root of a vine and sprawled flat on his face with an oomph of pain. His rifle clattered to the rocks.

"Come on, pal, come on," Brewster said, turning to help Krueger up. He froze, staring down the hill.

At the bottom of the rise were three shamblers. They'd come out of the brush at an angle Krueger hadn't scrutinized, and were now working their way up the hill toward them, foot by foot. One of the shamblers leaned its head back and moaned, a loud, mournful tone. In the distance, they could hear the howls of sprinters responding to the call. They would have even more company soon. Brewster redoubled his efforts to get Krueger up.

"Come on!" Brewster shouted. "We're out of time!"

"My fucking foot is stuck!" Krueger said, pulling at his leg. His foot had lodged in the roots of the vine and become mired. "Help!"

Thomas and Sherman had nearly reached the top of the hill when they heard Brewster and Krueger's exchange. They stopped, turned, and made their way back down to where the soldier lay stuck.

Sherman opened fire on the shamblers. His first shot struck one in the side of the chest. The creature recoiled, but remained on its feet. Slowly, it righted itself, staring at Sherman with its decaying mouth pulled back in a rictus of a grin, almost taunting him.

Sherman's second shot took the thing right between the eyes.

The first of the sprinters caught up with the group, bursting through the foliage at the base of the hill and snarling. Its head looked up, saw the four on the hillside, and it widened its eyes. It growled, showing teeth, and began to charge up the hill. Thomas dropped Krueger's arm and grabbed for his pistol. He managed to pull it and fire as the thing approached, dropping it with a pair of shots to the chest. It would be up again as a shambler, but not before the survivors made it out of there.

"Come on, pull it out!" Brewster said, grabbing at Krueger's foot.

"The boot! The boot!" Krueger said, fumbling with his laces. "Help me take the boot off!"

Sherman fired twice more, killing another shambler. Two sprinters appeared out of the darkness, roared up at the group, and began their climb. Thomas winged one in the shoulder, and it spun with the impact of the round, rolling back down to the bottom of the hill. It jumped back up to its feet, roared again in defiance, and began its climb anew.

The second was struck in the stomach by Sherman, and it doubled over, faceplanting in the dirt. For a moment, Sherman had thought he'd killed it, but then he saw it raise its head and stare at him. It still moved forward, dragging itself up root by root, rock by rock, snarling all the way. The bullet had severed its spinal cord, disabling its legs. The rest of it still worked fine, however, and it wasn't giving up.

Krueger managed to unlace his boot and pull his foot free. He grabbed for his rifle. "Come on, come on! I'm out! Let's go!"

The four fell back, firing downhill at their pursuers, and finally burst free of the treeline at the top of the hill. Far in the distance, across several acres, were the guard towers of Abraham, Kansas.

"Looks like a little slice of heaven," Brewster heaved, taking a moment to appreciate the sight of salvation.

"No time for discussion," Thomas said, firing a shot back into the woods. "We're still being hunted."

Krueger took off first, shouldering his rifle and moving with an odd limp. Sherman wondered about it a moment, then realized the soldier was only wearing one boot. He would be the slowest of them.

"Thomas, don't overtake Krueger," Sherman ordered. "Keep his back covered."

"Yes, sir," came the monotone reply.

By the time the group had covered half the distance to the town's main gates, the full force of sprinters on their tails was exposed, pouring out of the woods. By the look of it, they had stirred up enough infected to populate a crossroads village. Between the ones they had already shot and the ones running after them in the dark fields, Sherman estimated well over a hundred of them had crossed their paths tonight.

"Last magazine!" Sherman announced, shoving in his final clip.

Thomas had already thrown aside his own longarm, having run out of ammunition for it. He'd drawn his pistol again and was rapidly going through ammunition. Brewster had run out completely. Krueger was of little use in the firefight as the pace-setter for the group. He was busy running full-tilt.

Sherman fired three rounds in the direction of a nearby sprinter. One of the rounds must have hit, because the infected pitched into the tall grass of the field, thrashed about a bit, and was still. Thomas took another kill of his own, a female infected that loomed just a little too close. Thomas took his time lining up the shot and dropped the woman before she reached them.

"We're going to run out of ammo before we run out of sprinters!" Brewster said, taking in the situation.

"Noticed!" Thomas grumbled back.

"Look there!" Krueger said, eyes widening as he ran toward the town. "The gates! Look there!"

Ahead of them at the town's gates, a commotion was stirring. In the darkness it was hard to make out who was who, but Sherman guessed the women they'd saved had made it back and now the gate guards were expecting the soldiers' arrival. Out of nowhere, small spotlights low to the ground lit up the night, swiveled in the group's direction, and illuminated the fields. The sounds of engines being revved up met their ears.

"Don't stop to think about it," Sherman said, seeing Krueger's stride shorten. "Keep running, keep running!"

The lights wavered as the engines in the distance picked up speed. Reinforcements were apparently on the way.

The infected were closing in. There were about twenty in full view of Abraham's spotlights, and more along the treeline. Thomas and Sherman picked up their rate of fire. Sherman sent another sprinter sprawling to the ground before his pistol's slide locked back. He had not a single bullet left.

"I'm out!" he shouted.

"Got you covered, sir!" Thomas said, taking over. He sent a barrage in the direction of a pair of sprinters that were coming up directly behind the retreating foursome, scoring hits on one but only grazing the other. His pistol clicked on empty and he cursed, pausing to eject the magazine and slam home his final clip.

Thomas brought his weapon back up just in time to get off a shot that impacted the carrier's solar plexus, knocking it backward to slam hard on the ground as if punched by a giant, invisible fist.

A moment later, the revving of the engines reached a fever pitch and a pair of Jeeps pulled up alongside the winded survivors, outfitted with off-roading tires and spotlights along their tops.

Sheriff Keaton leaned out one of the driver's side windows.

"Come on, come in, get in already! You've got half the damn state behind you! We have to get behind the fences!"

The survivors didn't argue. They jumped and clambered into and on the vehicles as fast as they could manage. Deputies that had ridden out with the Sheriff fired parting shots with the sprinters as the Jeeps turned tail and gunned it back to the gates of the town.

They roared onto the road, scattering gravel and debris behind them, and squealed to a stop just past the guard towers. The deputies swiveled the spotlights to face the fields and guards in the towers raised their rifles.

"Defend!" Sheriff Keaton yelled up. Though no verbal response was given, the men seemed to understand. Sherman guessed they had done this before over the course of the preceding months.

The carriers that had been following grew closer and closer until the group of men and women near the town's gates could hear their labored breathing. Only then did the men in the guard towers and along the edge of the fence open fire. Carriers dropped left and right as bullets tore through them.

It took less than five minutes for the citizens of Abraham, Kansas to kill the carriers that had been pursuing Sherman and the rest. When the last infected had died, silence fell over the little town. It was the first time in hours that Sherman, Thomas, Krueger or Brewster had heard true silence. Their ears were ringing from the dozens of gunshots they'd fired and their lungs and legs burned from the long run. They met the silence as a leper meets a cure, whole-heartedly and with warm thoughts.

The battle was over.

The looked around at one another, nodding thanks or appreciation.

"All right," Sherman said after they had caught their breath. "Now maybe it's time you told me about the mission."

Before Thomas could respond, an exultant cheer swept the silence away. Dozens of voices raised in praise and admiration. The four soldiers stood upright and looked around. Half the town, it seemed, had turned out to greet them upon their return. Off on one side, sitting on a sidewalk, were the rescued women, being tended to by townsfolk and Rebecca, who had quickly found her way to them with her medical kit.

Sherman recognized Jose Arctura as one of the men gathered around the women. He was embracing one of them with tears in his eyes, and Sherman could only guess that it was his daughter. He felt a surge of relief at the sight. There were few enough reasons to feel good in the brave new world, and he was more than happy to have provided one.

Such was the reason the town had turned out to greet the saviors of the women. Young, old, male, female, it seemed the citizenry would never stop cheering. They pressed around Sherman and his small group, patting them on the back and expressing their thanks or offering them home-made dinners from home-grown ingredients. By the fence near the guard towers, aloof from the group, stood Sheriff Keaton, shotgun over his shoulder and a small smile on his lips.

Keaton let the throng lead the soldiers down the street, then turned to one of his deputies, his smile fading.

"You saw the explosion?" he asked, nodding in the direction of the raiders' complex.

"Sure did, Sheriff," the deputy said. "They really did a number on that place."

Keaton sighed heavily and gritted his teeth. The strangers from the west had done Abraham a great service in returning their captive women and dealing a blow to the raiders that had plagued them for so long, but the very same action may have doomed more lives.

"Double the guard along the fences," Keaton said askance to the deputy, staring out into the darkened fields. "Twenty-four hours a day. Call in the reserves and have Grimes do an inventory and cleaning on our weapons."

"Sheriff?" asked the deputy. "Problem?"

"Maybe," Keaton said. "Maybe not. But let's be prepared either way."

They sure stirred up a hornet's nest, Keaton thought. *Let's just hope these hornets have the good sense to stay and rebuild...and not come looking for vengeance.*

CHAPTER FIVE
LANDFALL

Coast of Oregon
March 09, 2007
0956 hrs_

A MONSTER LURKED OFFSHORE. It wasn't a monster of flesh and blood. Instead, it was a monster of steel and wiring, a hulking shape in the early morning fog. It approached the rocky shoreline slowly, carefully. As it approached, it began a slow, ponderous turn to port, giving the men onboard a clear view of the coastline. As the ship came out of the fog, the words upon its bow, at first wispy and enshrouded, stood out bold and clear:

DDG-61

U.S.S. RAMAGE

On the bridge, Captain Prescott Franklin stood with folded arms, staring out the windows at the shore, a distant look in his eyes. All around him, the crew went about their normal business of making certain the ship was in a safe position, then proceeded to drop anchor.

"Ship's secure, Captain," reported Franklin's second in command, a slightly built man with a receding hairline named Harris.

Franklin nodded to himself and sighed heavily. This was a day he had hoped would never come.

"It's time, then," he said out loud, hanging his head. "Give me the comm."

Commander Harris picked up a radio handset, dialed out so the Captain could speak to the entire ship, and handed the transmitter to Franklin. Franklin accepted it and slowly brought it up to his lips. He hesitated a moment, shoulders sagging, then clicked the handset.

"Crew of the U.S.S *Ramage*, this is the Captain speaking," he began. He let a moment pass before clicking the handset again and continuing. "I know we've been through a lot together these past few months. We've seen and done things we all prayed we would never have to do. We've seen things come about that we all prayed never would. And now I'm going to give the one order I prayed I would never have to. There's nowhere left for us to go, sailors. We're low on rations, low on fuel, and there's not a friendly port that can accomodate us left in the world. Therefore, I've brought us back home."

Franklin let go of the handset and sighed again. Harris stood closely behind him, hands clasped behind his back.

"Give the order, sir," he quietly said.

Franklin nodded slightly, held the handset back up to his lips, and clicked the transmit button.

"All hands, prepare to abandon ship. I say again, abandon ship. This is the Captain."

Franklin let the handset drop to the surface of the console next to him, turning away from the bridge to stare out the windows once more. Around him, the crew responded to the order, taking off headsets and leaving the bridge. Harris remained behind, supervising the exodus. Franklin barely moved at all as his men prepared to leave their floating home behind. Duffels had been packed days before. The crew had known the order was coming.

Things moved swiftly. Within minutes, the remaining sailors of the Ramage as well as one civilian stood on the deck of the ship, waiting to be offloaded and ferried to shore.

On deck, the sailors were both excited and nervous about what lay ahead of them. The decision to leave the ship behind had not been an easy one, and it hadn't been made overnight. Since leaving Sherman and his group of survivors behind on this very same rocky stretch of land, the crew had been through a lot. They hadn't merely been sailing the oceans, safe from the infection.

The U.S.S. *Ramage* had been waging war.

After Sherman and his crew had disembarked months earlier, the naval destroyer turned southward, toward San Francisco harbor. Their orders had been to assist the Army in securing the city. By the time they had arrived, the city had been overrun. There was no Army commander to report to. He had been infected. The Ramage and the other four Naval ships in the bay loitered around for several days, occasionally picking up an uninfected survivor that had made it out of the city, but otherwise doing a lot of nothing.

Then an outbreak had occurred on one of the other destroyers in the bay, and the sailors hadn't been able to contain it. The vessel was overrun within a day. When all radio contact had been cut off for five hours, the sailors presumed her lost. Seeing one of their ships effectively destroyed by the virus, the remaining four Captains held a meeting.

They concluded, after nearly twelve hours of argument, that they were the sole remaining effective force in the area. That gave them operational command of the efforts to control the Morningstar strain in San Francisco. Therefore, they decided, they would carry out their orders to the best of their ability, and may God have mercy on their souls.

Within moments of the meeting's adjournment, the four remaining destroyers turned their weapons on the city of San Francisco.

Missiles rained down on the metropolis. Skyscrapers came crashing down. The suburbs burned like a wildfire, consuming everything. The ships laid waste to San Francisco as might an angry Olympian god, and left behind only smoldering craters when they sailed out of the bay the next morning. The sailors could stand on the deck of their ship and watch the smoke rising up into the sky for hours afterward, long after the city itself had vanished over the horizon.

The four destroyers had parted ways soon afterward, each bound for a separate target. Two Captains decided to go and see what was left of Los Angeles. Another plotted a course for Seattle. Franklin went to Portland.

Franklin and the Captain of the destroyer bound for Seattle lost radio contact with the two L.A.-bound ships three days later, and they were presumed lost.

The *Ramage* had approached Portland slowly, scanning radio frequencies for any contacts. There were none to be found. The ship pulled in as close as it could and visually surveyed the city from on deck. Gangs of infected roamed the streets, and small fires were burning throughout the city. Franklin tried for two more days to raise someone in the city by radio, and then gave the order to drop what remained of the ship's ordnance onto Portland.

Franklin and his sailors stood on the deck that night and watched Portland burn. It was one of the quietest nights of Franklin's life. None of the sailors spoke to one another. Only the gentle sound of waves lapping against the hull of the ship broke the silence. All of the men simply stood and stared.

The next morning, Franklin tried to raise the Captain of the destroyer bound for Seattle and got nothing. The ship had simply vanished. Franklin left the *Ramage* sitting just offshore of Portland for an entire day, repeating calls over the radio in vain. Not a soul responded. Franklin and his crew felt as if they were the only people remaining on the planet.

A pervasive sense of loneliness and emptiness washed over the sailors. Morale was at an all-time low. Fights were breaking out, and even the Chief Petty Officers were having a hard time keeping the seamen in line.

Finally Franklin decided that what the men needed was a purpose. He turned the ship westward, and headed back out across the great Pacific Ocean. His destination was a speck of an island that they had visited once before, when Sherman had still been onboard. They'd received repairs and supplies in return for trade items from a man on the island named Hal Dorne. Franklin had remembered how much the men had enjoyed the tropical atmosphere and was banking on being allowed a return visit.

He was doomed to disappointment.

Hal Dorne himself was quite welcoming when the *Ramage* showed up once more off the shore of the little island he'd come to call home. The native islanders, on the other hand, were not. They had one radio that they used to get news and updates from around the world, and when they had stopped receiving transmissions altogether, they had decided that the best way to protect themselves was to continue doing what they had always done: mind their own business and keep any outsiders away.

Hal had argued on behalf of Franklin and his crew, trying to convince the locals to allow them sanctuary. When the argument turned into a shouting match, Hal suddenly found himself evicted. He'd stood on the deck of the *Ramage* making rude gestures at the locals until the ship had moved far enough away from the tropical paradise that the people on the shoreline were out of sight.

At first, Hal was the most irate, unbearable guest Franklin could have ever wished for. He cursed the crew of the ship up and down for "ruining his retirement" and kept going on and on about how he could be "laying in a hammock drinking rum" instead of being "trapped on this goddamn rustbucket."

As time went on, however, Hal calmed down and accepted his fate as a new member of the crew. During an outbreak onboard months earlier, the ship's mechanic had been killed, and Hal had done his time in the Army as a tank mechanic, so it seemed only fair for him to don the title of chief engineer. Franklin didn't doubt the man's ability. The ship had been damaged during that same outbreak, and Hal had been the one to come onboard and fix the problem. In a matter of hours, no less. The Captain of the *Ramage* had every confidence in his new crewmember.

Then morale began to sink again. There were murmurs floating around the ship. Some of the sailors thought that they would be onboard until they died. Others thought they would drift aimlessly from port to port until the ship rusted out from underneath them. Still others claimed that they wanted off, to take their chances at surviving on solid ground and maybe having a future.

As the days and weeks passed, those few who claimed they wanted to leave grew in number until most of the crew stood behind the idea. Even Franklin considered it reasonable. As far as he knew, he was all that remained of the U.S. Navy. They wouldn't be able to last forever onboard a destroyer. The men, he had to admit, were right. They had to leave the ship behind and find someplace more permanent, a place where they might have a future.

And so Franklin had turned the ship eastward again, and headed straight for the coast of Oregon. He still had the exact coordinates where he had dropped off Sherman and his men, and intended for his crew to disembark at the same location. Franklin didn't know what had become of Sherman, but he did know several things.

Firstly, he knew Sherman was heading east, toward Omaha, Nebraska. For what purpose, Franklin could only guess. He knew, however, that Sherman was hoping to meet up with a doctor, one who might know a thing or two about the Morningstar strain.

Secondly, he knew that if Sherman and his men had managed to survive heading eastward from that cold, foggy point on the Oregonian coast, his men stood just as good a chance.

And finally, if Sherman hadn't made it east but had instead holed up somewhere along the way, maybe the crew would run into them and join forces. That, however, was a pipe dream: the continental United States was massive, and there were hundreds of routes Sherman could have taken to get to Omaha.

And so Franklin stood on the bridge of his vessel, looking down at the assembled sailors (and Hal), wishing that it hadn't come to this. Wishing that the pandemic had never occurred. Wishing he didn't have to do what he was going to do next.

He spun neatly on his heel to face Harris, who was still standing at ease, waiting for orders.

"Commander, are the men ready to disembark?" Franklin asked.

"Aye, Captain. All present and accounted for," Harris said, nodding.

"Good," Franklin said, settling down with a sigh into a console operator's chair. "Go down and join them. You're in command of them, now, Harris."

"Sir?" Harris asked, furrowing his brow at Franklin.

"You heard me," Franklin snapped, flicking his eyes up to meet Harris' gaze. "Get down there and oversee the debarkation. Make sure everyone's armed and outfitted properly, just like we went over, and then get them onshore and headed east. But I'm not going anywhere. I'm not leaving my ship."

Harris stood silently for a moment, opened his mouth as if to say something, then shut it again. He nodded curtly.

"Aye, sir," he said, then turned and strode off of the bridge to join the men below. He shut the bulkhead gently behind himself.

Franklin sighed and folded his hands in front of him. It would be very quiet on the ship after the men had gone.

He'd use the time to catch up on his reading.

✯ ✯ ✯ ✯ ✯

Commander Harris strode out onto the deck of the destroyer with a purpose, shouting orders and berating any seaman who wasn't in perfect readiness.

"Secure that weapon! Double-knot those boots, son, what do you want to do, have them come off in the mud? Oh, Jesus, give me strength, sailor! You wear the damn webgear like this!"

Harris moved up and down the line, adjusting the equipment on the men and checking their packs. A few of the sailors were sent back off into the bowels of the destroyer to retrieve pieces of gear that they had left behind ("Decided not to pack that extra set of batteries, did you? That's fine, sailor, that's just fine—you'll have to stumble around in the dark, that's all.")

Hal stood apart from the sailors, leaning up against a rail with a heavy pack strapped across his shoulders and midsection and a pistol on his waist. His arms were crossed and he watched Harris' efforts with a carefully concealed look of amusement. Being a civilian, he was exempt from Harris' inspection and was enjoying watching the dressing-down the commander was giving the sailors.

Finally Harris deemed the men ready to debark. Cargo netting had been lowered over the side of the ship to allow the men to climb down into the small boats that would ferry them, ten at a time, to shore. In total, there were just under fifty sailors leaving the *Ramage*.

Though the men hadn't talked it over, both Hal and Harris harbored the thought that after a few weeks ashore, that number would likely be much lower.

One of their problems was a lack of weaponry. Months back, when they'd originally picked up Sherman and his troops off of the Arabian coast, they had already run dangerously low on 5.56 ammunition, the standard round for the M-16 assault rifle. As a result, the ship's armory had a fair store of the rifles, but nothing to load them with. They did, however, have a healthy supply of nine-millimeter rounds and a full complement of standard-issue Beretta sidearms. Every sailor was going ashore armed, even if only with a pistol. Three of the sailors carried MP-5 submachine guns, which also fired nine-millimeter ammunition: they were the heaviest weapons the group was bringing along.

Another problem was food. The *Ramage* had been running low for weeks. Even so, the men had been allowed to raid the larders. All of the canned and fresh food had been eaten, but boxes of M.R.E's still lined the shelves in the ship's mess. The sailors stuffed as many as they could comfortably carry into their pockets and backpacks.

The third problem was where to go.

Hal, Harris and Franklin had discussed that item at length. Franklin believed that Sherman would take the most direct route to his destination—Omaha—and traced a rough route on a map. Harris disagreed, and drew a separate route that was much longer but stayed far away from any major city. Franklin's route took Sherman near Denver. Hal elected to not speculate. He said he didn't know enough about the situation to make a prediction that lives might depend on.

In either case, both Franklin and Harris had agreed that Sherman would take a route that would head due East for at least fifty to a hundred miles to get away from the more heavily-populated coastlines. The two Naval officers went over the roads near their drop-off point and traced the initial path the sailors would follow. Once they were far enough into the country, it would be up to them to decide which route was best for them to take.

Hal pointed out that the officers' path led straight through an Oregon town called Hyattsburg, but the officers shook it off. They said that if the town looked like a risk, the sailors could always go around and pick up the road on the other side. Hal had shrugged and accepted it.

One thing that would work in their favor was communication. One of the sailors carried on his back a heavy field radio with a range of miles. If there were any operating relays in his broadcasting area, his signal would be bounced even further. Franklin had ordered the man to try and raise anyone on the radio at least twice a day, scanning the channels for transmissions. For the first few days, the sailors would all be in range of the *Ramage* and would be able to get updates from their home base as they traversed the terrain.

Hal watched as the first group of sailors climbed down the cargo netting and into the boat that would ferry them to shore. He scanned the faces of the men waiting to debark, and noted anxiety, excitement, and caution displayed on the faces of the sailors. They were more than ready to leave the ship after months onboard, but were worried about what they would face once they did.

Hal couldn't agree with them more.

Hal wished for a moment that he were back on his island, back in his hand-built hut, sitting in his hammock and drinking something—anything—alcoholic. Reality was getting too weird for him. He was supposed to be retired, for fuck's sake. He dismissed the train of thought as unproductive and shifted the pack on his shoulders as the second group of sailors began to climb down the cargo netting.

In the poet's words, they had miles to go before they slept.

CHAPTER SIX
MEMORY LANE

"YOU DO KNOW WHERE WE'RE GOING, RIGHT?!" Gregory Mason shouted over the sound of whipping wind. He had poked his head into the cab of Trevor Westscott's pickup truck from his designated spot in the bed.

"Hell yes," Trev said back, barely glancing at the intruder in the cab. "Interstate 74 will take us most of the way. Then what, Juni?"

Junko, sitting next to Trev with crossed legs, looking very at ease, reached under her seat and pulled out a faded, folded map of the nation that looked to be nearly as old as the truck itself.

"We'll be getting onto Interstate 80 West," Junko announced, nodding once to herself. "Relax. Enjoy the ride."

"Uh-huh," Mason said, raising his eyebrows. He pulled himself free of the window and collapsed back into the bed of the truck, wincing a bit. "I swear, my ass couldn't be sorer if I was riding a goddamn horse to Omaha."

"I don't care," Julie said, shaking her head as she rested against the side rail of the bed, eyes closed. "I'm just glad I'm not walking anymore."

Anna was busily studying her PDA. She'd struck gold when she realized the truck had a cigarette lighter; in the pack she'd taken from the safehouse in Washington was a power adapter for just such an outlet. She'd plugged the PDA in and was even now recharging the batteries, going over what fragments of research Julie had managed to download at the safehouse, and was working hard at keeping the adapter's cord from getting into anyone's face. The three shared the truckbed with Matt, who still didn't seem all that enthralled at the idea of having new companions. He'd barely said a word all day.

"So, Matt," Mason said, trying to spark up conversation. "What did you do before all this?"

"Student," came the terse, one-word reply.

"What were you studying?" Mason pressed, leaning forward and resting his elbows on his knees.

"Engineering," Matt said. "I wanted to be an engineer."

"What, and you can't be one now?" Mason asked, smiling in a friendly manner.

"Look around, asshole. World's gone. No need for engineers out here," Matt said.

"Actually, that's not so," Anna said suddenly. She didn't even look up from her PDA as she continued, "The bell curve—as it pertains to intelligence and aptitude—applies in this case to fatalities as it would in any other situation. There are few enough educated people in this world and, if we assume that deaths have been taking place regardless of economic situation or geographic location, then there will be barely anyone left with any kind of real education."

Matt simply stared at the woman with raised eyebrows. She didn't even glance at him, but, in her unnervingly astute way, guessed at what he was thinking.

"What I'm saying is that most of the smart people are dead and you're still alive. Whether or not you have a degree, that makes you one of the world's best engineers," Anna said, nodding once and tapping the screen of her PDA to bring up another page of data. "Just a matter of the process of elimination."

Julie, still leaning back with her eyes closed, shrugged at the thought. "Never did think of it like that. I guess that makes me prime material for this year's Pulitzer prize for broadcast journalism."

Mason grinned and shook his head despite himself. "I can't believe you're making yourselves feel better by using the deaths of all these people."

"Oh, don't try and play Mister High-and-Mighty over there, Mason," Julie said, opening one eye and staring accusingly at him. "I see that grin of yours."

The truth was Mason was happy because the rest of the people in the bed of the truck were happy. He was a natural morale-evaluator, always feeling what the group felt. When they were down, he was down. When they were happy, he was happy. And now that they had a truck and were putting miles between themselves and Sawyer's last known position, they all felt a load lift off their backs— or at least, Anna, Julie and Mason did. Their new companions still didn't know about their pursuers.

"What about you, Julie?" Matt asked, looking over at the journalist. He seemed to be taking an interest in her—not just because there were so few people to talk to, but because he was a young man and she was an attractive woman. "What all did you do before this?"

"Haven't you been listening?" Julie asked. "I was in journalism."

"What, like Clark Kent journalism?" Matt retorted.

"No, broadcast—" Julie cut herself off, heaved a sigh, and sat up straight, looking over at Matt. "I was a news anchor. Other people go out and find the news, bring it to me, then they turn on the cameras and I read it to the world."

"Oh, that kind of journalist," Matt said, nodding. "Sounds cool. Kind of like being a movie star."

"Not really," Julie said, shaking her head. "You want to hear about something you'll think sounds cool, ask Mason about what he did before all this."

Matt looked over at Mason, who met his gaze with a look that said, 'Don't bother.' Matt returned his attention to the journalist.

"I don't know, journalism sounds cool, too. I mean, it's your job to tell the world what's happening in the world. Or it was. It's like you're the entire intelligence agency for the citizens of a country. It's a big responsibility."

"Stop trying to butter me up, bucko," Julie said, grinning lopsidedly at Matt. "You need to work on your flirting technique."

Matt stopped trying to talk to her and faced forward, cheeks flushing. "Sorry."

In the cab of the truck, a more serious discussion was taking place.

"So what do you think of them?" Trev asked Junko, glancing askance at her profile.

The Japanese girl quirked the corner of her mouth upward as she thought, considering the question from every angle.

"I think that if they were nothing more than thieves, they would have killed us and taken the truck by now," she said, but ended her sentence in such a way that made Trev think she had something more to say. He was right. After a moment, she continued. "At the same time, I don't know about their whole vaccine story. It just seems to be so convenient."

"I think so, too," Trev said. "But we're both in agreement about them not being with the demons, at least."

Juni turned in her seat to face Trev, a serious expression creasing her pleasant features. "Trev, we've talked about this. You can't—"

"I know, I know, I've heard it," he said, furrowing his brow. "Why can't I call them that? Why can't I call them what they are?"

"Trev," Juni said gently, placing a hand on his shoulder. "Maybe they are demons. Maybe they're not. But most people aren't ready for that idea. They can barely handle the idea of them being victims of a virus. You can't tell them what you think. Not yet. Keep it to yourself, please?"

Trev murmured something under his breath that Junko didn't quite catch.

"What was that?" Juni asked.

"I said '*What's the goddamn point of ever leaving that hospital if I'm back to pretending it's all a fantasy again?*'" Trev said, a little too loudly. Mason glanced in the direction of the cab from the bed, but otherwise seemed unconcerned.

"You're not pretending," Junko hurried to explain to him. "You're not pretending at all. You're humoring them. It's not about you. I've seen you fight the infec—the demons. You're amazing. You just let that rage take you over and there's no coming back for the demons once they meet you."

Trev sighed and shook his head. "I just don't like calling them 'infected' or 'victims' when they're just so clearly demons."

"It's semantics," Juni said. "Whenever you meet one, call it what it is. Call it a demon. When you're with others, call it an infected. What is that expression you Americans have—it's about pronunciation. Something about vegetables."

Trev grinned despite himself and chuckled. "You mean po-TAY-to and po-TAH-to. All right, all right, I get it. I'll call the damned things infected if it'll make the others feel better."

"Thank you," Juni said, clasping the man on the shoulder again and breathing a deep inner sigh of relief.

She'd come upon Trev months earlier, wandering the streets of a dead town wielding nothing more than a nightstick and wearing little more than a patient's gown, stained with the blood of infected. At first, Juni had thought to shoot him down as one of the enemy, but then he had spoken to her.

"Your eyes," he'd said. "They're not bloody. You're not a demon, are you?"

"No," Juni had replied. "I'm not a demon."

That had been the dubious beginning of their alliance. What had begun as convenience had blossomed into friendship and friendship had blossomed into true camaraderie. The pair trusted one another and relied on one another, though Trev had never once tried to move on Junko. She suspected it was out of respect, and didn't mind the fact that sex wasn't there to get in the way of staying alive on the move. It also helped when she reminded herself that Trevor Westscott was a mental patient.

The man truly believed that the infected were demons, sent by the Devil to ravage the Earth pre-apocalypse, just as Revelation had promised. He was a strange blend of a man. Junko never saw him pray, nor did she ever hear him reference God. He was wholly concerned with God's antithesis, and never went much into his motivations for it. Junko suspected it had something to do with the reason why he was a mental patient in the first place.

She did find it very odd that Westscott chose to call the infected demons and somewhere, in some laboratory in some other part of the world, a researcher had decided to call the virus that created the infected "Morningstar," which was just another name in Western society for the Devil. Secretly she wondered if there might have been something to Trev's ramblings, but just as quickly she cut herself off from that train of thought. The virus was perfectly natural. There was no supernatural force driving it, no shadowy government agency responsible for it—Trev's choice of words was a mere coincidence, though an unnerving one.

Aside from his odd convictions, Trevor Westscott was a solid companion and a good friend. He was intelligent, thought fast on his feet, and had a penchant for the dramatic. Junko had endeavored to keep his questionable sanity under wraps for as long as possible. After all, she reasoned, he wasn't out to hurt so much as a fly. He was out to hurt the demons. And who wasn't, these days?

Trev gunned the motor of the pickup truck, increasing his speed somewhat. Junko looked over from the passenger seat at the speedometer and frowned.

"If there were still cops you'd be getting a ticket right now," Junko scolded. "You're pushing ninety."

"Ha ha!" Trev said, grinning widely. "But once I reach 88 miles per hour, the flux capacitor will take us back to..."

He trailed off as he saw that Junko had no idea what he was referencing.

"Never mind," he said, waving a hand and smiling. He eased his foot off the accelerator some. "We'll just cruise and conserve some gas, then. You're no fun, Juni."

She grinned and punched him in the shoulder by way of reply.

"No, seriously," Trev pressed. "Here we are, not a car in sight, the entire Interstate Highway System is at our feet—and you want us to go the speed limit."

Trev blew a raspberry in Juni's direction. She stuck out her tongue at him in reply.

"Now, maybe we'll find a nice dealership in one of these little dead towns and get something with some real power," Trev prattled on. "A V-8. Hell, a V-16. Zero to sixty in point five seconds. Ha! I have to put that on my list of things to do once we clear out the demons from some of these towns down the line."

In the back of the truck, the conversation had fallen flat. The four occupants lounged around, each engrossed in their own thoughts and activities. Julie dozed in the corner, hair whipping around her face as she rested. Mason was systematically disassembling, cleaning, and reassembling his pistol, repeating the process over and over. It was a trick to keep all the pieces together in the jouncing bed of the truck, but to Mason, it merely added a degree of challenge to an activity he could (literally) do blindfolded.

Anna was still engrossed in her PDA, gratified at the full charge it had acquired from the truck's cigarette lighter. She checked their position on the GPS feature and smiled to herself. In one day they'd covered more distance than they had in two weeks on foot. She switched back over to her research notes and continued to read. She felt it was her duty to keep the data as fresh as possible in her mind.

July 23, 2004 - Log Entry #792

Have assigned Joseph and Virginia to run the RNA sequencer on the Marburg strain samples again to check for possible errors. We've been experiencing a lot of employee turnover recently and I really didn't want to have to give them that order. It's extremely dull work and you have to do it all in an environment suit, which is hot and stuffy and more than a little claustrophobic. Most of our researchers don't last long in Level 4. They always request transfers to Levels 2 or 3 after a while of dealing with these organisms.

But the funny thing is, it's not the organisms themselves that are driving researchers away from my department. It's the department itself. Isn't that ironic? The environment designed to keep you safe from the living things you're working on is what sends you running from those living things. I wax pedantic.

We received and processed tissue samples today from two apes who are suspected victims of hemhorrhagic fever from a zoo in China; I have made running those samples top priority. If they come back positive for anything that's contagious and deadly in humans we'll have to issue a quarantine order for the zoo and maybe for the city it's in.

As far as Morningstar goes, we've made little progress. I honestly can't understand why they've assigned this virus to our team, too. We already have enough on our plates. Besides, from what I've heard through the grapevine, the Deaucalion Co-op and the Centers for Disease Control are already researching the bug.

Probably it's political. In fact, I virtually guarantee it. They just need to cover their asses if there's ever an outbreak. They said Ebola would never break out, and it did, several times—they finally got wise and started researching it seriously so they could point and say, "Look, we've done all we can."

I wish I could get the Deucalion Co-op to share what they have on the virus with me. I know next to nothing about it besides it's a filovirus and a nasty one. The brief I received said, and I'm writing this quoted word for word, that "the Morningstar strain possesses an infectious nature and fatal potential that has not yet been exceeded by any other known virus."

That makes me damn curious. Even though I resent the extra workload, I can't wait to see what this little bug can do.

In the bed of the truck, Anna sighed and rolled her eyes after reading her own words. Even though they were only a couple of years past, they seemed like a lifetime ago, and she felt like an entirely different person.

I can't wait to see what this little bug can do.

She almost laughed out loud at the absurdity of the line.

Matt was facing away from the group, sitting cross-legged at the rear of the bed and staring at the road as it receded behind them, occupied with his own thoughts.

"So what's on the docket today, Doc?" Mason asked without looking up from his pile of gun parts. "Anything interesting?"

"Not really," Anna drawled. "Just my daily log entries. I just read an entry dated right after I first was assigned to Morningstar. It's almost funny how naive I was."

"Well, you got a lot better fast, if it's any consolation," Mason said.

"A little," Anna grinned. "Still, I just don't know where to begin when it comes to this vaccine. My data's incomplete. Maybe if I had the hard drives from the CDC, USAMRIID, and the Deaucalion Co-op all together, along with a team of skilled researchers and proper facilities—maybe then I'd be able to get something real done."

"Give it time, Doc. Right now your only lab is that little gizmo of yours. You'll find a way," Mason said.

"Wait a minute," Matt said, looking over at Anna with a quizzical expression on his face. "What's a Deaucalion Co-op?"

"The third facility," Anna said.

Matt stared at her blankly a moment. "What?"

"The third facility," Anna repeated. "Remember that whole conversation we had back in town when we met? About there only being two Biosafety Level 4 labs in the US and I said there were three, and the third was a joint operation?"

"Oh, yeah," Matt said, nodding. "Yeah, I remember that. So the third one calls itself the Deaucalion Co-op. What's the significance of that?"

"They were feeling a little ambitious in their naming," Anna said wryly. "The staff there is made up of private-sector employees, military doctors, and representatives from the CDC. They called themselves Deaucalion because they were focusing on ways to use the viruses to, ah, improve humanity. Or at least, that was their foremost stated goal."

Matt shook his head, still confused. "I still don't get it. Deaucalion?"

Anna lowered her PDA to her knees, sighed, and launched into her explanation. "Deaucalion was a man in Greek legend who was sort of like Noah. The Gods decided that the human race was too weak to survive. It had been crafted out of the living clay of the earth, but was vice-riddled and crime-torn."

"Sounds like pretty much any city today," Mason murmured.

"The Gods decide that they're going to kill all of the human race, but they save Deaucalion and his wife, who had remained above temptation and were, you know, worthy of being saved. Problem was, once the extermination was complete, Deaucalion and his wife were pretty lonely, what with being the only human beings left on the planet."

"Sometimes I feel like that, at least these past few months," Mason interjected once more.

Anna went on as if Mason hadn't spoken.

"The Gods took pity on Deaucalion and his wife and they said, 'Pick up the bones of your mother and throw them over your shoulders, and you will have companions.'"

"The bones of their mothers?" Matt interrupted, a scowl crossing his face. "Those old myths sure can be foul, man."

"Wait, wait," Anna said, waving a hand. "The Gods weren't being literal. The mother of all humanity is the earth, and the bones of the earth are rocks. They didn't mean literally throwing the bones of their mothers over their shoulders."

"Small mercies," Matt snorted.

"So Deaucalion and his wife pick up handfuls of stones, throw them over their shoulders, and sure enough, up springs twenty men behind Deaucalion and twenty women behind his wife. Since the old race that was made of clay had been destroyed, this new race was made of stone and was supposed to be able to withstand vice and evil better than, for lack of a better term, Humanity version 101," Anna explained. "So these people call themselves the Deaucalion Co-op because they're looking for, and this is a stretch of a metaphor, a way to change humanity from clay to stone."

"Ah," Matt said, nodding slowly. "So they're arrogant bastards, is that it?"

That brought a hearty chuckle from Anna, and even Julie grinned as she leaned back against the side rail of the bed again.

Anna tapped the screen of her PDA and brought up a list of her journal entries. She sighed, watching the list scroll by slowly, entry after entry. She had diligently added her thoughts into her files at the end of every day, entertaining the vague notion of perhaps condensing them into a book or research manual for future generations. Now she was simply hoping to milk any last bit of data about the virus out of them.

September 12, 2004 - Log Entry #821
   I halted the studies on Marburg and Sudan today. Lassa will probably be up next on the chopping block. I've been getting a lot of pressure to focus on Morningstar and I can't keep running my researchers ragged. The more I learn about this virus the less I want to admit it even exists. It multiplies like Ebola, similar initial symptoms, but instead of crashing and bleeding, the victims go feral. We're guessing the fever has something to do with it, but it's a really a very effective technique for spreading the virus. The feral hosts attack whatever is nearby. They'll bite and scratch and spread infected fluid that way.
   We've got fully half the lab dedicated to Morningstar research now. I'm still keeping myself busied running epidemic simulations and the results are never pretty. We used a colony of mice to simulate an outbreak in a rural village. It was tough getting a properly controlled environment for the project since we couldn't exactly build a miniature replica of the Congo River basin in the BSL4 lab, but we made do with some large clear plastic cages and some tubing.
   We put one infected mouse in with fifteen others and observed the results. At first, the mice accepted the infected newcomer as one of their own but as symptoms began to develop

the healthy mice reacted unexpectedly. As far as we as humans know, animals are ignorant of the knowledge of disease and how to react to it. Despite this, the healthy mice forced the infected one into a kind of "quarantine." It was something worth a National Geographic article, I'm sure. They ostracized the mouse, kept it away from their food and water sources and generally refused to play nicely with it. They seemed to want it out.

The data suggested by this reaction indicates that the healthy mice had some recognition of the infected mouse's illness. We wondered what might happen in the wild: whether if, when one animal is infected, the rest put enough distance between themselves that the infected creature dies without being able to spread the disease. That might explain why we haven't seen a major outbreak of it yet.

Of course, humans are another story. As far as I know we don't possess any kind of sixth sense that lets us know when a fellow human is infected. And we're just dumb enough to get close to the poor bastard when he goes feral, too.

Anyway, the infected mouse's harassment by his peers lasted three days before the virus had replicated enough to cause the feral reaction I was speaking of. When that happened, that poor, tormented little rodent got his revenge: by the end of the day all fifteen healthy mice had been infected with Morningstar. No matter where they went in the cage and its tubes, the infected mouse found them, one by one, and systematically infected them all.

It was disturbing to watch. It's as if the little bugger developed one hell of a predatory instinct, as if the virus erased all that was that made him a mouse and turned him into a killer.

I'm really not liking this assignment right now. It's keeping me up at night.

Anna swallowed. Her throat felt dry and scratchy, and she lowered the PDA to her lap to retrieve a canteen of water from one of the bags in the bed of the truck. She unscrewed the cap and took a long, satisfying gulp, a small rivulet of water running down her neck. She sighed, replaced the canteen, and looked around the truck.

The occupants were all still busily doing plenty of nothing. Mason was on his umpteenth repetition of disassembling and reassembling his pistol. Julie looked as if she was completely asleep, her head lolling back and forth gently and her mouth hanging open slightly. Matt sat cross-legged in the rear of the bed where he had always been, still staring at the road behind them.

Anna suddenly felt a tremendous rush of responsibility fall over her. It was heavy and smothering as a blanket soaked in cold kerosene. The lives of billions had ended over the past few months and she, one of the chief researchers into the problem, hadn't been able to do a damn thing about it.

Then again, she thought to herself, *I did warn them. Several times.*

Just as suddenly, the heavy weight lifted, and Anna felt as if she could breathe again. It was wrong of her to blame herself for the outbreak. She'd had nothing to do with it, and even the governments she'd tried to warn had done their best once they'd begun to take her seriously. This was nature's way, and nothing one small species could do could stop it.

Unless I find the vaccine.

And that was the ringer, Anna thought. The big If. From an epidemiologist's point of view, she figured the human race had two options.

First, they could hole up wherever they could stay alive and bolt the doors, wait out the pandemic. It would, as with all pandemics, burn itself out after enough time had passed. The problem with this idea is that even once all of the carriers had died, including the shamblers, whether it be from violence or pure decay, infectious material would be scattered all across the globe.

A spot of blood from an infected man might have landed in a warm, shaded puddle or some other natural petri dish and the virus would continue to exist. Outbreaks of Morningstar would be never-ending for the human race. Generations down the line, men and women would have to fight off the virus over and over as Anna and her friends were attempting to do now.

The second option was for her to create a vaccine. The pressure of that Herculean task was not lost on her and weighed down on her just as much as the guilt she'd felt when she'd momentarily blamed herself for the pandemic. If she succeeded, she would be responsible for immunizing the human race to the Morningstar strain. Never again would a carrier be able to infect a human being. The only worries the survivors would have would be the physical threat of feral infected biting, clawing, or otherwise mauling them to death—not pleasant, but no less so than the thought of infection.

The pressure was doubled by the fact that Anna Demilio had never focused her research on finding a vaccine. That responsibility had rested with the Deaucalion Co-op and their plethora of experiments. They had certainly not succeeded, Anna rationalized, given the current infected state of the world, but they might have made progress.

Anna was banking on them having made boatloads of progress. She was hoping that most of the work had been done—the RNA sequencing, genome investigations, blood and serum tests. In order to make a vaccine work, she had to figure out how to disable the Morningstar strain's virulent properties. She knew from reading the regular updates that circulated between USAMRIID, the CDC, and Deaucalion that the first attempt at a vaccine using killed cells of the Morningstar strain—much the same as a flu shot might—had no effect whatsoever. The human immune system attacked the dead viruses, of course, but no immunity was built up from the injections.

Her better shot was to try and create a vaccine that used a live virus. It was riskier, but it had a better shot of success. The problem there lay in the human immune system itself. Billions of cases worldwide had proved better than any laboratory could that the human immune system couldn't fight off Morningstar and therefore couldn't build up an immunity to it.

Either she needed to find a way to reinforce the immune system or find someone whose body made them naturally immune, and use their blood to culture the antibodies she'd need. The former was the option she was considering chasing once they arrived in Omaha, as she'd never heard of so much as a single infected person who didn't succumb to the disease.

Anna picked up her PDA once more and scrolled through the entries, looking for ones that dealt with immunization and their experiments.

October 09, 2004 - Log Entry #869
Today was a busy day. Joseph didn't come in, complaining of a fever and nausea. I believe him. 'Tis the season for influenza, or getting there, anyway. I joked that he should come in anyway and offer himself as a test subject to the guys in BL2. Virginia and I were the only two researchers on duty so we thought we'd take a light day and try out a few experiments on the Morningstar strain. Our funding for Lassa research was cut off last week and handed over to another department anyway, so we figured, why not?

We'd just received a new shipment of mice. We're not mean or, what's the word I'm looking for here, sadistic, that's it, but we were extremely intrigued with the responses of healthy mice to hosts. We can reasonably hypothesize that a human reaction would be different, so we changed tactics a bit and focused on the behaviors of the infected rodents.

We set up the following variables:

Heat/cold were set in the cage, light/darkness were set up, healthy mice were kept on hand as bait, and we started to brainstorm some obstacles. We were trying to categorize the behavior of the infected mice besides a simple "feral."

We left the modified cage with our infected mouse sitting next to a cage with the healthy mice. A simple curtain device was placed between the two cages so we could cut off the infected rodent's line of sight of its prey at will.

Here is what happened as we tinkered with our variables:

WHEN PREY WAS VISIBLE:

The infected mouse was unaffected by extremes in either heat or cold. If we darkened the cages, the hostile reactions increased. We speculate that the virus, using whatever mechanism it has within it to turn a rational rodent feral, also turns them nocturnal. When we increased the brightness of light past levels of natural sunlight the reaction was opposite: the feral rodent seemed more subdued. It was still openly hostile, but seemed slower, more cautious. It spent more time looking down at the floor of the cage and less time trying to climb the sides. It seems that carriers of Morningstar are photosensitive.

WHEN PREY WAS NOT VISIBLE:

The infected mouse's behavior was still unaffected by extremes in either heat or cold. However, there seemed to be slightly more activity in periods of warmth. In total darkness, activity increased significantly. When we turned up the lighting, the host retreated to a small burrow and refused to emerge.

Generally, the feral hosts don't seem to wander around all that much, at least when you compare them to a healthy specimen. They don't use their exercise wheel and don't explore their cage. Most of the time they just sit, and wait. It's creepy—reminds me of trapdoor spiders. Patient little predators that dig a hole and just sit inside, waiting for an insect to come by to be grabbed and dragged down to be eaten.

And that'll about do it for me tonight; I'll have to check the sheets in my bed for spiders again. I hate the little things.

We're learning bit by bit how the symptoms of this disease affect the host. I'm guessing today's experiments won't be all that important in the scheme of things but, hey, I needed a light day.

Anna grinned as the she read over the log entry. The real-world laboratory they had all been a part of over the past several months had certainly vivified that particular theory. The carriers were indeed reclusive in the day, active at night, and single-minded about pursuit of their prey. She wished she hadn't had to have seen it in action on the streets of Washington, but then again, she had a lot of wishes for her life and, like nearly all wishes made worldwide, it hadn't been granted.

Her grin faded into a thin-lipped frown. For all the days, weeks, even years she'd spent working on the virus, all she'd seemed to come up with was data that any surviving human being was well aware of. She scrolled through entry after entry, reading excerpts from experiments on more of their ill-fated lab mice, bits and pieces of RNA sequencing, and epidemiological simulations. Her dark-humored mood took a turn for the worse when she came upon one of her later entries, after she'd spent every day for two months working on an epidemic projection.

May 21, 2005 - Log Entry #978
I've concluded my work on the epidemiological projections for the three strains that are remaining within our department's authority—Hanta, Zaire, and Morningstar. The simulations look grim, for the most part.

The Hanta virus, being native to our shores here on the US, isn't an unfamiliar disease. We ran worst-case scenarios and they were not particularly disturbing. The virus is hard to detect as the symptoms resemble the flu at first, but once Hanta has been identified, quick action can stop the outbreak in its tracks. Assuming the mass media was informed, simple instructions such as wearing facemasks or avoiding contact with contaminated areas showed the virus outbreak burning itself out in a minimum of three months with a maximum of eight months. Fatalities can be rated as "insignificant."

Ebola Zaire presented a trickier situation since it's hard to predict rates of infection. It is a fast killer, which means that there is a significant chance of it burning itself out before expanding from an outbreak to a full-fledged pandemic. It's native to Africa (hence the river it is named after), unlike Hanta, so we have a geographic buffer between us and the disease. Further, villages in this area of Africa are not unfamiliar with the virus and will take steps to quarantine themselves, which adds an additional buffer.

However, we ran the worst-case scenario as requested and the results were not pretty. Assuming worldwide infection and factoring in the fatality rate of the virus (90% +/- 5%) we estimated that one in three people would be killed. Fatalities can be rated as "catastrophic." Projections indicated just over two billion dead.

Finally, we ran the Morningstar simulation, complete with the data we've acquired on the predatory nature of infected hosts, and we scared the shit out of ourselves. We ran the worst-case scenario (Morningstar escaping its natural habitat, infecting major cities and travel routes, etcetera) and I felt like tendering my resignation right there and moving to the middle of the mountains somewhere, far, far away from any other people. The projection showed Morningstar jumping from the level of an outbreak to pandemic within one week. From that point, casualties increase exponentially. The fatality rate of the virus was tricky: since the virus seems to leave its host alive, is it really a fatality? We decided that, in the case of these simulations, we would count a live, infected host as a fatality.

Factoring in the rate of infection and fatality rate (100% +/- 0%), we projected a nearly total obliteration of the human species. We estimated that approximately thirty-five million people would survive the pandemic. In other words, for every one survivor, one thousand seven hundred and fourteen people would die. Most of the survivors would be relegated to rural areas, cut off by natural distance or geography from population centers.

Cities and towns that are infected give the survivors worse odds. We ran those numbers as well, using Philadelphia as a model, and found that for every one survivor, there would be five thousand nine hundred and eighteen dead.

May God have mercy on us if this son of a bitch jumps its banks.

Anna sighed, blinked slowly, and lowered the PDA to her lap.

"Why the long face, doc?" Mason asked, looking over from his pile of weapon parts.

"Nothing much," Anna replied, still staring down at the journal entry. "I'm just feeling a little bit like a prophet of doom."

"What're you reading over there?" Mason pressed.

"Daily logs," Anna said. "It was a kind of diary for me. I kept hard data in separate files but made entries into a log every day to describe what we'd accomplished. Reading over it now is making me feel like a latter-day Nostradamus."

Anna held up the PDA so the screen faced Mason. "See right here? Predicted the pandemic. Scroll up a little bit and I've got the behavioral characteristics of the carriers all spelled out. It's eerie."

"Well, that's what they paid you for," Mason said, snapping the last piece of his pistol back together and checking chamber. "You're the world's Morningstar expert."

"Yes, that's what everyone keeps reminding me," Anna drawled, shaking her head.

"What kind of hard data do you have on that thing?" Matt asked, looking over from his spot at the rear of the bed. "I mean, is it useful stuff? Things you can turn against the virus? Like, maybe instead of a vaccine, we could make something that destroys the virus so it doesn't matter where you shoot them, they go down."

Anna grinned and Mason actually chuckled out loud. Matt looked hurt for a moment, but Mason jumped in to explain their reaction.

"We've thought of it," he said. "And, actually, it's a great idea. I mean, if we can't find a way to keep the virus from hurting people, maybe we can hurt the virus, right? Thinking of that option just shows you're brighter than average."

Matt looked pleased at the compliment.

"Then again," Mason went on, "Anyone left alive by now had better be brighter than average."

"So, where are we, Doc?" came Julie's voice. The journalist was still reclining in the corner of the bed, eyes closed, but apparently had been following the entire conversation. "Take a break from those notes and load up the GPS."

"We're well on our way, Julie," Anna said, frowning. "Relax."

"Come on, humor me," Julie pressed. "Humor me or I'll start repeating, 'Are we there yet? Are we there yet? Are we there yet? Are we—'"

"All right, all right!" Anna snapped. "Give me a second."

She busied herself with loading up the requested program on the PDA, taking care to save her notes as they were. Matt seemed to have lost interest in the conversation and was back to staring at the road behind the truck, resting his chin on closed fists.

Mason noticed the intense look in the young man's eye, but thought nothing of it.

"Here we go," Anna said, squinting at the PDA. "Well, damn. I can't get a connection. Maybe that satellite's finally moved out of its proper orbit. We might have to rely on old-fashioned maps again if it doesn't come back up."

Matt leaned forward against the tailgate, staring back down the road, eyes half-closed against the sunlight.

"Smack it a couple times," Julie said, smiling widely. "That's how I used to get my cellphone to pick up a signal."

"It should be working just fine without resorting to physical violence," Anna retorted.

"What's so interesting, Matt?" Mason asked, ending the banter. Both women looked over at the young man, intently studying the road behind them.

Matt looked over his shoulder at the trio and shrugged. "Not sure. I thought I saw a flash of light back there. Maybe it was just a heat wave. There aren't any other cars out on this road but us and the junkers."

Matt nodded toward one of the abandoned cars they'd dubbed the 'junkers' as they passed it by, a bright blue flash of a battered sedan turned up on its side off the edge of the interstate.

Mason moved to sit next to Matt and began rooting around in his backpack.

"What're you doing?" Matt asked.

"Hunches are a good thing to follow up on," Mason said, locating the binoculars he'd been searching for in his pack and pulling them free. The strap caught on the zipper and he impatiently yanked it loose, holding the lenses up to his face and studying the road as it led off into the distance behind them.

"See anything?" Matt asked after a moment of silence.

"Road," Mason quipped from behind the binoculars, a grin appearing on what was visible of his face. Suddenly, the grin was gone, replaced by a look of apprehension. "Uh-oh."

Far in the distance, just cresting a hill that sloped so gently it was nearly unnoticeable, came a glint of sunlight off of a windshield.

"Is that a car?" Matt asked, pointing.

Anna and Julie had abandoned their respective projects and were now crowded around Matt and Mason, looking over their shoulders with anxiety written on their features.

"No, it's not a car," Mason said. His teeth ground together. "It's a Land Rover. Black."

Anna and Julie looked at one another silently, eyes wide with fear.

"Does that mean what I think it means?" Julie whispered.

Mason let the binoculars drop to his lap and turned to face the two women. He drew his pistol, so recently cleaned and oiled, slapped in a magazine, and racked a round into the chamber. "Yep. Sawyer's back."

CHAPTER SEVEN
SIC VIS PACEM, PARA BELLUM

Abraham, Kansas
March 08, 2007
0923 hrs_

Francis Sherman stood near the border of Abraham, looking out through the chain-link fence as the sun burned the last of the spring fog off of the fields. His hands were clasped behind his back, unconsciously at parade-rest, as he surveyed the surroundings. The night before had been one to remember.

Unfortunately, he doubted half his entourage would have the capacity to remember it once they woke up. Eileen's husband's beer would have seen to that.

Sherman's raid on the bandit headquarters had ended up saving the lives and freedom of eleven women and cost the bandits, at their best estimate, a dozen of their number, not to mention a significant portion of their makeshift fortress.

The people of Abraham were more than overjoyed to hear that news. They'd been taunted and terrorized by the raiders since shortly after the pandemic struck, and five of the rescued women were citizens of the town itself. Further, some of Abraham's men had been killed when they had defied the raiders abroad. The town was looking for vengeance, and they had found it in Sherman and his soldiers. They had found more than that, though: they had found heroes.

The night before was a virtual whirlwind of celebration. Cheers and rallies in the streets led to Sherman and the rest attending a dinner in their honor, with freshly-baked bread and spring vegetables lining the table. They hadn't eaten so well in months. All of their food had been pre-packaged and preserved. Some of the townsfolk had taken up their instruments and an impromptu concert sprung up. The men and women played whatever tunes they knew, and the people of Abraham had danced and eaten and drank more than their normal share over the course of the evening.

Especially drank, Sherman thought. Brewster had picked up where he'd left off, downing pint after pint of Eileen's bitter brown lager, and the last the General had seen of him, he was dancing with one of the girls of the town, barely managing to stay on his feet. Thomas, in true form, had remained aloof, eating quickly and with purpose, politely declining all offers to dance, and then vanished to seek out a bunk to sack out in for the evening.

Krueger and Denton had spent their evening egging on Brewster and getting the soldier to drink more than he could handle. Sherman had sat close enough to them at the banquet table to overhear them placing bets on the soldier.

"My good knife says he passes out before six pints," Denton had said, slapping a K-Bar combat knife down on the table.

"I'll see your knife and raise you a survival compass, complete with waterproof matches, that says he makes it to at least seven," Krueger had said, adding his items to the table.

"Bet?"

"Bet."

Sherman had chuckled at the scene. He hadn't paid enough attention to Brewster afterward to find out who was able to collect and who went home the loser, but he'd had enough on his hands.

The Sheriff, Sherman had noticed, was conspicuously absent from the banquet and as soon as he was politely able, Sherman had excused himself from the celebration and gone off to find the man. He'd failed, and eventually he had turned in, accepting the offer of a bunk at the town mission.

He'd awakened as the sun rose, did his morning calisthenics in the tiny room in the mission house, dressed, and went outside for a long walk. He'd walked down one side of main street, up the other, and around several of the surrounding blocks, thinking over their current situation.

The mechanic, Jose, had been so overjoyed at the return of his daughter that he'd nearly kissed Sherman the night before and had promised that he would keep up his end of the bargain and throw in more to boot. He said it would take around a week to effect the repairs, and in the meantime, the group should relax and rest.

Sherman was just going over the mechanic's promise when he found himself at the border of Abraham, staring out over the fields at parade rest. The mornings in Abraham were quiet. Nearby, a guard stood in one of the two makeshift towers that protected the only real entrance into Abraham, but the man paid the General no heed. He simply looked out over the same field with a pair of binoculars. Sherman was used to more hustle and bustle in the mornings.

On the road, when the group began to awake, things always happened very fast. Gear had to be packed up, people had to wash (if possible) and change their clothes, and banter would invariably be shooting back and forth like a ping-pong ball at the Chinese championships. Here in Abraham, people woke up at their own pace, in their own homes. It was almost like things were back to normal—if only the ten-foot chain link fence and makeshift guard tower weren't there to remind Sherman otherwise.

"Good morning!" came a familiar voice from behind the General. He turned to see Sheriff Keaton approaching, a rifle slung over his shoulder.

"Good morning yourself, Sheriff," Sherman said, shaking the man's hand. "I have to tell you, your people sure know how to play host."

"What, that little party last night?" Keaton asked, chuckling. "Not my idea. Sort of an impromptu display of our appreciation, as it were."

"I noticed you missed it," Sherman said. "I was looking for you."

"Sorry," Keaton replied. "I was out patrolling the borders."

"Well, the whole thing was very much appreciated," Sherman said, nodding his approval. "My people really needed something to bring their morale up a bit."

"Uh-huh," Keaton said, also nodding in agreement. He seemed to be holding himself back, and Sherman noticed.

"Is there something on your mind, Sheriff?" Sherman asked.

"Well," Keaton started, then trailed off. "Probably nothing."

"Nothing's nothing," Sherman disagreed. "Come on, what're you thinking?"

"Well, Sherman, you fellows dealt one hell of a blow to those raiders last night," Keaton said. "It'll be months before they feel like the kings of this county again."

"It was our pleasure, Sheriff," Sherman said.

"No, it goddamn well wasn't," the Sheriff snapped, suddenly angry. He caught himself, took a deep breath, and apologized. "I'm sorry about that, Sherman, but let's face it, it wasn't your pleasure. You did what you did because you needed Jose's help with your big truck. I'm not saying there's anything wrong with that," Keaton went on, holding up his hands to forestall protest, "but it wasn't because you're our friends, if you follow."

"I follow," Sherman said, nodding slowly. He felt somewhat subdued. The Sheriff's remarks were dead-on. "Though I'd like to mention that if things keep going the way they're going, it won't be long before we're doing things to help you truly because it is our pleasure to do so, as friends."

Sheriff Keaton grinned and nodded. "I wouldn't be averse to the idea, Sherman. But I have a problem. Or I *might* have a problem. And, frankly—with no offense meant by this—it's *your* fault."

Sherman took a step back, his eyes widening somewhat. "Our fault? What? What's the problem?"

Keaton folded his arms across his chest and stepped forward, looking out through the chain link. "You rattled the hornet's nest, Sherman. Stirred up those raiders. I didn't tell you this because it didn't matter to your mission last night, but I know the leader of those scavengers. He's a real hard case. Locked him up three times for drunk and disorderly. Once for armed robbery. He was just about to come to trial for sexual assault when the pandemic hit. He goes by the name of Herman Lutz. Don't let the name fool you—the guy's stone cold. He should have been behind bars permanently years ago. He and his brother George put together this particular group of raiders and let me tell you—from what I know of Lutz, he'll be out for blood. Revenge. You really bloodied his nose, he'll want to bloody yours. And between you and him is Abraham. You see my problem now?"

"I'm seeing it," Sherman said, nodding. "I'm seeing it very clearly."

"So I've got a choice," Keaton said, sighing heavily. "I can hurry Jose's repairs up and get you and your compadres out of my town before Herman and George come looking for payback..."

"Or?"

"Or I can seal the gates and tell them to fuck off," Keaton said with a grim smile. "Option number one means selling you guys out, and you really have done us a favor since you've been here. I'd feel like an asshole kicking you out of here just to be hunted by those scumbags down the highway a bit."

"And what're you thinking about option number two?" Sherman asked.

"If I do that, maybe I lose a lot of friends when they come knocking on the front door," Keaton said, shaking his head.

"That's a hell of a choice," Sherman said. "If it's any consolation, I've had to make tough calls before, too."

"Oh, right, you're a 'General,'" Keaton said, chuckling. "Forgive me, but I'm still finding it hard to believe."

"That's quite all right, Sheriff," Sherman said. "You don't have to believe me. Just know that I've been there, and I sympathize. But would you be open to a little advice?"

"My mother raised me to always listen to advice. Whether or not I take it is up to me, she'd always say, but she always told me to listen first," Keaton said.

"Wise woman. Sheriff, if I were you, I'd draw your battle lines, because from the sound of these scumbags, they'll never leave you be until you show them why they should leave Abraham far behind—and that's whether or not you send us packing. Even if we're out of here tomorrow, I'd say fight these bastards. The next time they try to raid one of your outlying farms, send a vehicle with riflemen out there. Make them pay in blood. They'll learn. They'll learn fast."

"Jesus, that's cold," Keaton said softly, gripping the chain of the fence in a white-knuckled grip. "But it also makes sense. George and Herman'll just keep stirring them up until they own this town or all their men are dead."

Sherman paused a moment, still standing at parade rest, and cocked an eyebrow. "Wait one second. What were the names of the leaders again? Lutz?"

"That's right," nodded Keaton. "Herman and George Lutz. Brothers. Herman's the older. George came a couple years later."

"Oh, hell," Sherman said, posture stiffening. A hand wiped across his forehead as a sudden sweat broke out on his brow.

"What is it?" Keaton asked.

Sherman thought back to the firefight on the bridge, flashes of it playing out in his memory. Taking cover behind the open door. Trucks blocking their escape. *And a man named George demanding they surrender.*

"Keaton, could you describe these two for me?" Sherman asked.

"What, physically? Sure. I know them by heart. Herman Lutz is a big fellow, about six feet, two hundred pounds. Thinning brown hair. Large nose. Bit jowly. Starting to get a stomach. George Lutz was thinner, about the same height, maybe thirty pounds lighter. Longer brown hair. Same exact nose, no jowls. More of a square-jawed type, George," Keaton said, rambling off the physical characteristics of the felons purely from memory. He was a small-town cop, and they tended to file away their repeat offenders in their heads rather than their filing cabinets.

"Damn," Sherman said, shaking his head. The description of George Lutz was nearly a perfect match to the features of the man that Krueger had killed on the bridge during the firefight.

"What is it?"

"Sheriff, I think we've already killed George Lutz," Sherman said. He went on to explain again about the ambush on the bridge and the man who demanded they pay a tribute to pass. He told the Sheriff how one of the other men had called the leader 'George' and that, plus the fact that he was out in front, had made him Krueger's number one target. "If he is this Herman Lutz's brother, he's lying facedown in a ditch about ten miles west of here."

Keaton swore and kicked the chain link fence, yelling a curse at the sky.

"I don't know if Herman's heard about this yet or not, but I'm betting he has. He's going to be pissed as all hell!" Keaton said, rambling off a litany of curses that would have made a sailor blush. "He'll be coming for blood."

"Well, then," Sherman said. "I suppose we've only just begun to fight. I'm sorry, Keaton. Sorry I brought this down on your town."

The Sheriff was silent for a long while, leaning against the fence and staring at the ground. He gave the fence a final shove and spun to face Sherman, a range of emotions playing across his face. He calmed himself, took a deep breath, and spoke.

"It was coming whether or not you'd stumbled on us, Sherman," he said. "You were right. These are the kind of people who won't quit. Something needs to be done. You just provided the catalyst, that's all. We'll have to get ready. I just pray to God we make it through the storm."

1234 hrs_

Keaton had called a town meeting. The mayor, an aging man named Nathan York, had been contacted and advised of the situation. Sherman got the distinct impression that the while the mayor was technically in charge, he was acting as little more than a figurehead. Sheriff Keaton had shown initiative and intelligence in the short time Sherman had known him, and that led him to believe that the Sheriff was the true leader of the little town of survivors.

The town gathered slowly as word of mouth summoned the citizens from their homes to the freshly plowed field in front of the town hall. Sherman sat on the stairs of the old building next to the Sheriff, watching the people gather. There were hundreds of them, most with families, and all looked apprehensive. According to the Sheriff, the last town meeting had been called to decide to build the fence and quarantine the town in the early days of the pandemic. The citizenry was probably worried this new meeting also boded poorly for them.

If only they knew, Sherman thought.

Sherman spotted some of his group on the edge of the growing crowd, and excused himself from the Sheriff to go meet them. Mbutu, Ron, Katie, and Rebecca stood off to one side. They were watching the crowd with vested interest, and Sherman could see them muttering back and forth to one another as they watched.

"Good morning," Sherman said as he approached, raising a hand in greeting.

"Early afternoon, actually," Rebecca replied, smiling at Sherman.

"What's with the party?" Ron asked, leaning heavily on his crutch—a real crutch now, not a makeshift one. He had received permission from the town's registered nurse to help himself to one from the town clinic. "Did someone die?"

"No," Sherman said, heaving a breath. "At least, not yet."

"What's that supposed to mean?" Katie asked, eyeing the General warily.

"I think it means we're going to war," Sherman said. "Spent the morning talking with the Sheriff. Remember that guy named George who was leading the raiders we fought on the road? The one Krueger blasted?"

The assembled group nodded as one, and Sherman pressed on.

"Turns out he was the brother of the leader of this particular gang of scavengers and looters. The Sheriff has files on both of them as thick as dictionaries. Real scum-of-the-earth types. Keaton figures we've got a day, maybe two, before what's left of the raiders come to pay us a visit, and they won't be looking for tribute. They'll want heads."

Rebecca groaned. "Oh, no. Not more of this. I have to get to the clinic. Maybe there's something I can do there to help prepare."

She took off at a jog without bothering to say goodbye, moving fast and with a sense of purpose.

The remainder of the group looked subdued. From the party the night before to the sudden announcement of incoming war, the mood was shifting too rapidly for them to feel comfortable. They shuffled from foot to foot, exchanging unsettled glances.

"Relax," Sherman said, noticing their ill ease. "The Sheriff's already decided that the town's going to meet these bastards head-on. If they want blood, they'll get it, but it'll be their own."

"I hope you're right, Frank," Ron said, favoring his uninjured leg. "Last time I faced these guys, they took some of my blood. I hope the Sheriff doesn't think his hands won't get dirty."

"Give him more credit than that, Ron," Sherman said. "Keaton's a smart man. He knows people will die in this fight, when it comes. He's ready to accept that. If nothing's done about these raiders, they'll just keep coming and coming."

"That is true enough," Mbutu said, speaking for the first time. "They are bullies. Bullies only understand violence and strength. If you show one you are stronger, he will never bother you again."

"Exactly," Sherman said, nodding at Mbutu. "So I'm hoping they come here full of piss and vinegar looking for a stand-up fight. That way we'll be able to use a quick show of force to convince them to head somewhere else."

"What's the alternative?" Katie asked.

"The alternative is that this Herman fellow might be smarter than he seems," Sherman said. "If that's the case, we might need to get creative. I'm hoping the town will help on that end."

"Afternoon!" came a greeting from behind the little group. Sherman and the rest turned to see Jack and Mitsui approaching. Between them was Brewster, moaning and leaning heavily on the two men. Denton brought up the rear with Krueger.

"Brewster!" Sherman said, feeling a smile crease his face, "You're alive."

Brewster moaned in response and tried in vain to raise his head. "It doesn't feel that way, sir."

"Who won the bet?" Sherman asked, turning to Krueger and Denton.

"Krueger," Denton grumbled, jerking a thumb in the soldier's direction. "Brewster made it to eight pints before he threw up and passed out."

"I threw up?" a groggy Brewster asked. "Did I throw up on anyone?"

"No, it was in the grass—don't worry about it," Denton hurriedly reassured him. "And on the sidewalk on the way back to the mission house. And in the mission house bathroom."

"And in a bucket in your room about three in the A.M.," Krueger finished up, chuckling. "You know what you need to learn, Brewster? Limits. Moderation."

"Moderation is for pussies," Brewster slurred, looking dizzy.

"All right, all right, enough for now," Sherman said. He raised one finger and spun it in a circular motion. "Gather up, group. We've got a few announcements to listen to that concern all of us."

"What's going on?" Brewster asked.

"Be quiet," Denton reprimanded. "You'll make your headache worse if you talk."

"Won't talk, then," Brewster added.

"Good boy."

Nearly all of the town had gathered on the field in front of the town hall by then, and the murmur of conversation was drowning out the normal afternoon sounds of the birds and breezes. Finally, after what seemed like a quarter hour or more, the mayor of Abraham stood up on the stairs to the town hall and raised his arms for silence. One by one, the conversations dropped off until a quiet calm fell over the assemblage.

"People of Abraham," Mayor York began, "We are once more presented with a problem that may threaten our very survival. I'm asking all of you to do as we did months ago, and pitch in, do your parts. Do that, and we'll all pull through this trial as we pulled through the pandemic. Sheriff Keaton will explain more."

Mayor York yielded the floor to the Sheriff, who took his place at the top of the stairs amid renewed murmurs from the crowd.

"All right, people, here's the situation," Keaton said, raising his voice to a commanding level. The mumbled conversations halted and all eyes turned to the man addressing them. "As you know, our recent guests dealt one hell of a blow to the raiders living in the old distribution center last night."

A resounding cheer went up among those assembled, and continued for several seconds until Keaton waved his hands for silence.

"Unfortunately, that's also our problem. We've confirmed that George Lutz was one of the raiders who was killed," Keaton said. "As some of you may be aware, George Lutz is the younger brother of the raiders' leader, Herman Lutz. Less of you may be aware of the fact that Herman isn't the type to let this kind of thing go without an answer. I guarantee you, even now he's getting ready to strike back at us, and we're going to have to be ready."

A voice rose up out of the crowd.

"He's got maybe twenty men with him! We have seven hundred! We're an army! Let him come!"

A renewed cheer went up from the crowd, and this time, Sheriff Keaton had to wave his arms for twice as long before the people would fall silent.

"He may be outnumbered, and even outgunned, but what he has are vehicles, mobility, and intelligence," Keaton said. "Herman Lutz might be a criminal, but he's not a stupid criminal. We're in a static location. We can't get up and move. We'll have to watch for attacks from any angle, any location, at any time. They might try and come at night, or at dawn. We can't let our guard down. I've already doubled the watches along the town borders. However, that means my deputies are going to be strained to their limits. They'll be dog tired by tomorrow morning. I'm asking for volunteer deputies to help with the guard duties. More than that, I'm looking for volunteers to help build up our defenses. Last night, our new friends showed us how easy it is for three people to break into a facility defended exactly as our town is and wreak all kinds of holy hell on it. We can't let that happen to us."

"So what're we doing?" came a shouted question from the crowd.

"To start with, anyone of able body and mind who wants to volunteer as a deputy, meet me after this discussion. Secondly, anyone who's able to dig a trench or fill a sandbag should meet with Mayor York. We're going to start reinforcing our walls and defenses."

Suddenly the meeting was interrupted as one of the Sheriff's deputies came pulling up alongside the town hall in one of Abraham's off-roading Jeeps, squealing his brakes. He dove out of the driver's side door and bolted toward the Sheriff. Everything about his movements and expression screamed emergency.

Sheriff Keaton ran down the stairs to meet the man halfway and the two had a hurried, quiet meeting. When it was over, the deputy nodded, spun on his heel and ran straight back for his Jeep, tearing off down the streets in the direction of the main guard towers and entrance. Sheriff Keaton jogged back up to the top of the stairs to address the town.

"People of Abraham!" he shouted, quelling the murmurs that had sprung up during the interruption. "It seems we don't have that time to prepare I was hoping for. Wes in the guard tower out front says he's spotted a mass on the move coming this direction from the north. He says it looks like infected, numbering in the dozens. We're going to need riflemen—if you've served on the front line before, grab your weapon and meet us at the main gates. That is all."

Sheriff Keaton ran down the stairs of the town hall, past Sherman and the Mayor and the assembled civilians, and headed off full-tilt in the direction of the gates.

"I suppose that means we should help," Sherman said, arms folded across his chest.

"Time to play hero again," Krueger said.

"I don't know if I can handle a rifle right now," Brewster protested.

"Very well," Sherman said, quirking an eyebrow at Brewster. "Jack, Mitsui, let him drop where he's standing. Both of you get your weapons from the Sheriff's armory and meet us at the front gates, too."

The two men grinned, let go of Brewster, and headed off after the Sheriff. Brewster hovered in place a moment, knees buckling. His face turned a light shade of green at the sudden movement, and he let himself collapse to the ground, one hand clutched over his mouth and the other held over his stomach.

"Maybe that'll teach you moderation," Denton chided, looking down at the soldier.

"Fuck you," Brewster said, and immediately regretted it, fighting back a retch.

"Come on, let's go," Sherman said to the remaining members of the group. "I'm sure every rifle will be welcome."

1302 hrs_

Sherman climbed the last rung of the ladder that led up to one of the makeshift guard towers of Abraham. In the small space on top, he was met by Sheriff Keaton, Mayor York and a deputy with a hunting rifle and a large pair of binoculars set up on a tripod.

"Sherman," Keaton greeted, shaking Frank's hand. "Good to see you managed to join us. This is Mayor York, and Deputy Willis."

"You can call me Wes," said the deputy, shaking Sherman's hand in greeting.

"What's the SitRep?" Sherman asked, looking out across the flat fields.

"Well, you can just start seeing it with the naked eye now," said Wes, pointing north. Sherman squinted in the direction the man was indicating, and made out a wide line of figures heading in their direction. "Take a look through the binoculars. It's quite a sight. Didn't give these raiders enough points for ingenuity, that's for sure."

Sherman took up a place behind the binoculars. He swiveled them on their tripod and looked through the lenses. Up close, the sight was enough to turn even a strong stomach. A quick estimate told him he was looking at between forty and fifty figures, and all of them were sprinters. Their bloody, ruined clothing and hateful expressions told him they were definitely infected, and the fact that they were running gave away the rest. Sherman refocused the binoculars, zooming them out somewhat, and saw two men dressed in hunting clothes, rifles strapped to their backs, riding dirt bikes a good hundred meters in front of the small horde.

"Well, I'll be damned," Sherman whispered as he stared through the lenses. As he watched, the men on the dirt bikes revved their engines, heading straight for Abraham. Behind them, the horde changed direction to follow them, arms outstretched. Sherman could almost imagine their roars of protest each time their prey picked up and moved further away from them.

"You may indeed," Keaton replied. "It is kind of ingenious, like Wes said. They're using bikers to lead the infected right to us."

Sherman remembered Thomas' report of their action at the distribution facility the night before. The sergeant had mentioned that the raiders had two huge cages filled to the brim with infected just outside their main gates. Thomas and Krueger had guessed the infected were meant to serve as deterrents to possible attackers, but now Sherman saw that the raiders had been saving them up for an actual offensive purpose.

"They're using carriers as shock troops," Sherman said, voice awed somewhat. "They're going to actually use the infected to soften us up before they attack."

"Smart puppy, Herman Lutz," Keaton said. "Oh, but that's not the worst of it. Refocus behind the sprinters—a good half-mile back."

Sherman did as he was asked, jostled the binoculars until they focused in, and grimaced.

Well behind the mob of sprinters was a second mob, just as large, made up entirely of shamblers. Two waves, then, one hitting at full speed and another hitting at a slow walk perhaps an hour later.

Sherman stood and let the binoculars rest. He folded his arms and walked over to the edge of the tower, staring off in the direction of the incoming carriers. A thoughtful expression was etched across his features.

"What're you thinking about, Sherman?" Keaton asked, watching the General carefully.

"I'm not sure," Sherman replied. "Just a bit of a feeling."

"Well, let's hear it," Keaton said. "No secrets here."

"I'm thinking you're right about this Herman guy," Sherman said. "He's smarter than people give him credit for. Here's this horde of infected coming right down your front door, and leading them here are two men on bikes. Two. Where are the rest of his people?"

"Sitting back and waiting for us to get softened up by the infected," Deputy Willis volunteered. "Just like you said."

"The more I think about it the more it doesn't sit right in my gut," Sherman said. He rubbed his chin. "Have you given any orders to your people yet about these infected?"

"Sure have," Keaton said. "We've been on it since it was reported. All the deputies and volunteers are being armed right now and they'll be reporting here to the main gates to hold off the infected once they arrive."

"All of them?" Sherman repeated, looking intently at the Sheriff.

"Every single able-bodied—" the Sheriff began, then cut himself off, jaw dropping open as he saw what Sherman was getting at. "Wes, radio."

"Huh?" asked the deputy, busy peering through the binoculars once more.

"Radio! Give me your damn radio!" Keaton repeated.

The deputy handed over the device and went back to watching the oncoming enemy force. Keaton held the radio up to his mouth and clicked the transmit button.

"Defense detail, come in. Defense detail, come in. Sheriff Keaton here, over," Keaton spoke into the radio. A response came back almost immediately.

"We're here, Sheriff. Just arming the last of them now, and—"

"Cancel that deployment order I gave you," Keaton said. "Send half the men to the main gates. Send the other half to the back side of town. Tell them to take good cover and stay hidden."

Sherman smiled. Keaton had a military man's mind. He'd thought of the same thing as Sherman: that the infected were a diversion.

"Come again, Sheriff? We're splitting our forces?" came the reply over the radio.

"Hell yes, we are, and get to it! Tell the men you send to the backside of town to watch for an attempt at incursion. They'll be trying to get in quietly," Keaton said. "Double-time it down there. Out."

Keaton clicked the radio set off and handed it back to Wes, then turned to Sherman.

"Was that what you were thinking?" Keaton asked.

"To the letter," Sherman said. Mayor York and Deputy Willis looked back and forth at one another, shrugging. They hadn't followed. Sherman leaned on the edge of the guard tower and nodded in the direction of the approaching infected, explaining.

"I'm thinking this is a diversion," Sherman said. "Send out all the infected they've rounded up over the past couple of months straight to Abraham's front door, and send them right across these open fields, where we'll be sure to see them coming, with plenty of time to mobilize. We bring all our men here to defend against the carriers, and while we're doing that, the raiders slip in the back door and go to work on the town. At least, that's my hunch."

"What happens if you're wrong?" York asked, raising his eyebrows.

"Then we have to drive off all these carriers and an entire attacking raider force at fifty percent capacity," Sherman said. "Even if I'm wrong, we can recall the men sent to the other side of town within a few minutes. I don't think we're risking too much, and it might save us if I'm right."

"I see," York said, nodding slowly. "That makes sense, I suppose."

"Now we just have to wait and see what happens," Keaton added. "Let's hope our boys shoot straight and true today."

1345 hrs_

Once again, the battle lines were drawn. Along the western edge of Abraham, a slapdash layer of sandbags provided minimal cover for riflemen strung out along the fenceline. An eighteen-wheeler had been driven forward to fully block the roadway, and the wooden barriers had been lowered. Three riflemen were stationed in each tower, and more had lined up behind the eighteen-wheeler, laying behind semicircular bunkers made of sandbags.

Across town was the second element of the defense force. Denton and Krueger found themselves among the platoon's-worth of men who responded to the call to reinforce the rear of Abraham, as were Jack and Mitsui. Here, things looked and felt less battle-ready. No sandbags had been brought forth for cover, and the volunteer deputies and civilian soldiers instead took cover behind yard fences, parked cars, trees and landscaping, all carefully watching the fence and the thin forest beyond for enemy activity. Conversation, what little there was of it, was subdued.

Near the main gates, the revving of the dirt bike's engines grew louder as the carrier-wranglers drew ever closer. In the guard tower, Deputy Willis adjusted the range on the scope of his rifle, drawing a bead on one of the bikers as he accelerated across the field. His finger tightened on the trigger, but a hand on his shoulder stopped him. Sheriff Keaton looked down at the man and shook his head.

"Wait," he said. "Let them get a little closer first."

The bikers sped across the field until they were nearly in front of the main gates themselves. They skidded to a stop, kicking up small clouds of dirt. One of them turned and lifted the visor of his helmet so the defenders could see his face.

"Enjoy the company," taunted the man. "Lutz says you people have it com—"

"All right, he's close enough now," Keaton said, tapping Willis on the shoulder.

Wes fired, and the taunting biker was blown backwards off his vehicle. He shuddered once, tried to lift himself off of the ground, and then lay still. The bike tipped over on its side, engine still idling. The remaining biker flipped off the defenders and gunned his engine, accelerating sharply. He got on the main road and vanished within moments.

The sprinters, unaware of the verbal exchange, charged onward. They caught up to the body of the heckler and surrounded it in moments, hunching over it and tearing at the man's flesh, biting and scratching. Willis swallowed back bile as he watched.

"All right, men," Keaton said, looking left and right at his defensive line. "Careful shots, now. Drop 'em."

Rifle fire began to ring out along the fenceline as shooters picked their targets and squeezed their triggers. Several of the feasting carriers jerked and spasmed, falling to the ground. A dozen or so still approaching the scene shifted their attention from the downed biker to the riflemen along the fenceline, and turned almost as one, sprinting straight for the chain link. The riflemen in turn shifted their fire. Sprays of bright red arterial blood flew up from the backs of the oncoming carriers as rifle ammunition tore through them. Here and there a carrier dropped permanently, skulls split open by headshots. Most went down with wounds to the chest or legs.

Several of the carriers reached the fences, threw themselves against the metal and tried to rip their way through. The fences easily held up to their attempts. The riflemen on the other side had an easy time dealing with these carriers, aiming at point-blank range and dropping them with shots to the head.

Meanwhile, the two-dozen or so that had surrounded the downed biker were rapidly losing interest. The corpse of the man was thoroughly ravaged, and they began to cast about for new prey. The second biker had long since vanished down the road, and the only remaining targets were the defenders of Abraham. The sprinters turned their attention to them, roaring and running full-tilt toward the fences.

Suddenly the riflemen found not half a dozen angry infected tearing at their defenses, but nearly three dozen. Rifle shots rang out with more frequency, and the shaking of the fence increased in intensity. The steel wire holding the chain link to its posts creaked ominously.

"Put them down! Gun for the ones on the fenceline!" Keaton ordered, shouting down from the guard tower. Carriers grasping the fence were riddled with bullets. One by one, they dropped free, falling on their backs in the grass. Some twitched out of residual reflex actions. Others lay still, bullet wounds in their heads.

Thomas was in his element, bandaged arm and all, holding aloft his pistol and jogging up and down the line, shouting encouraging comments or yelling obscenities at the less adept marksmen. Every now and then, he would halt in place, take aim, and put a round through a carrier hanging on the fence.

The sudden fury of the combined assault on the section of fence near the gate was taking its toll. One by one, the steel loops used to hold the fence securely to its posts began to spring free with loud pings. The upper corner of the fence sagged free, and the riflemen redoubled their efforts.

Keaton leaned out over the guard tower to shout instructions.

"Forget the heads for now! Just gun 'em down! Get 'em on the ground! We'll clean up after! Don't let that fence fall!" Keaton shouted. He knew that if the fence went down and they left a gap in their defenses, the second mob of shamblers would have an easy access point into the town. With their force split down the middle, they would be hard pressed to kill them all safely.

The townsfolk and deputies shifted their fire, taking easy chest shots. Bloodspray filled the air beyond the fence as carrier after carrier fell to the ground. The gunfire began to slacken after a minute as the number of carriers decreased. Soon, only a handful remained, still roaring in fury and pulling on the fence with fevered intensity. They were put down one by one until not a single sprinter remained on its feet.

The riflemen looked back and forth at one another, then broke out into nervous laughter. They'd beaten back the attackers.

"Knock it off!" Keaton yelled suddenly from the guard tower, and the laughter died out. "We're not even halfway done yet! Five men with pistols, meet me at the main gate!"

Keaton descended the ladder that led from the tower with surehanded swiftness, sliding down the last few rungs and spinning on his heels. He drew his weapon, checked the chamber, and nodded to himself. He looked around for his volunteers.

Thomas was the closest and the first. He wouldn't have had it any other way. Deputy Willis tried to follow the Sheriff, but Keaton turned and pointed him back up into the guard tower, explaining that they needed his hands on a rifle and a vantage point. Keaton and Thomas were joined instead by three of Keaton's deputies, all wielding pistols. Their rifles were slung across their backs.

"All right, guys, you know the drill," Keaton said. "We go out there, moving fast, put a bullet into the head of any one of those bodies that doesn't already have one, and then get back behind the defensive line. Ready?"

The men nodded their assent, and Thomas grumbled something about always being ready.

"Let's move," Keaton ordered, ducking under the eighteen-wheeler that was blocking the road and coming up on the other side with his weapon at the ready. He shouted up to Willis in the guard tower. "Keep us covered, Wes! Let us know if we're going to have company!"

"I hear you!

The five volunteers ran around the towers to the scene of the battle. The grass was a rust brown, stained with blood, and the fence hung loose in two places. Bodies lay scattered in the field here and there, some twisted into unnatural positions, having fallen hard and broken their own limbs.

"Let's go to work," Keaton said.

The detail got down to the dirty, unenviable job of finishing off the sprinters. Thomas took his time, unhurriedly walking from body to body, inspecting the skulls, and firing once into their foreheads if he couldn't locate a head wound.

The deputies worked on the fenceline. Staccato bursts of pistolfire rang out as they finished off the bodies laying there, one after another. Keaton roamed farthest afield, checking the bodies that had been killed before they'd gotten near the defenders. He knelt next to one, turned the head to inspect it, and grimaced. He stood, took aim, and fired a round through the body's temple.

"You never get used to it," he said, loudly enough for Thomas to overhear him several meters away.

Thomas finished off another sprinter before replying. "Get used to what? Killing the infected? Gotta disagree. I'm damn well used to it."

"No, I mean finishing off the sprinters before they get back up," Keaton replied, checking another body. This one had an existing head wound, and he left it behind for the carrion crows. "I get the feeling like I'm desecrating a body. You know, there used to be respect for you when you died."

"Can't be helped," was Thomas' terse reply. He toed a corpse, then fired a shot through the body's eyesocket. "Either this or do it again when they're up and about."

"It's just that they look almost normal when they're dead like this," Keaton replied as he ambled over toward another body. "Then they—whoa!"

The body he had been walking toward suddenly snapped its eyes open and began to sit up, movements slow and awkward. The Sheriff looked over at Thomas.

"Well, they do that," Keaton said, pointing at the newly re-born shambler. "Unsettling fuckers."

Keaton's next shot took the new shambler between the eyes. The creature sat up in place for a moment, blood trickling down the middle of its forehead, then slumped backwards again to lay in almost the exact position it had been in before reanimation.

"Nice shot," Thomas grumbled. "Next time, do it before the damn thing gets back up."

Keaton chuckled by way of reply, and the pair rejoined the three deputies who were finishing off the bodies at the fenceline.

"Sheriff!" came Deputy Willis' call from the tower above.

Keaton looked up. "Yeah?"

"Those shamblers are getting to be pretty close," Wes said.

He stretched out a hand and pointed, and Keaton turned to look. The second mob, made up entirely of shamblers, had been lagging behind their faster cousins by a wide margin. Now, they were catching up. Keaton estimated they were three hundred, maybe three hundred and fifty feet away. They still had a minute or two before they would be close enough to do any damage.

"Are these bodies taken care of?" Keaton asked, whirling on a deputy.

"Yeah, Sheriff, we pegged all of 'em," said the deputy.

"You're sure? Every one?"

"Every last one. They're dead for good."

"All right." Keaton nodded his approval. "Back inside the fences, all of you. Hurry!"

The five exterminators ran back around the guard towers and ducked under the eighteen wheeler once more. When Keaton came up on the defended side, he froze. In front of him was General Sherman holding a pistol and blocking his way.

"What's up, Sherman?" Keaton asked, eyeing the pistol and, for the most fleeting of moments, wondering if this was a coup attempt.

"What's up is your feet," Sherman said. "Take a look."

Keaton, Thomas, and the three volunteer deputies simultaneously looked down at their shoes. Their footwear was coated in the shed blood of the carriers. Specks of it had landed on their pants and one of them even had a bit of spatter on his shirt.

"That blood is hot," Sherman went on. "It's infected, and unless you five deal with it properly, you'll be infected, too."

Keaton felt his own blood turn to ice. Sherman was right. He hadn't even thought about that when he'd had the men and Thomas go out into the field to exterminate the carriers. "Damn it. What do we do?"

Sherman looked over his shoulder at the town's main street, with its storefronts and supply houses. "Got any place that sells bleach?"

"Yeah, the hardware store and the market, both," Keaton said, still looking down at his feet with wide eyes. Next to him, one of the deputies was stepping gingerly from foot to foot as if trying to minimize his contact with the bloodied footwear.

"Get some. A couple gallons. And a bucket. Oh, and a hose," Sherman said. "We'll need all of that. Going to have to decontaminate you all."

"Sheriff!" came Wes' cry from the guard tower. "The shamblers are getting right up on us!"

"Damn, damn, damn," Keaton cursed. He felt like he should be up in the tower helping guide the defenders, but he knew he had to take care of the infected blood first.

"I've got this," Sherman said, clapping Keaton on the shoulder. "You make sure you get a nice bleach scrub-down. Hose yourself off afterwards, then get back on the line."

"All right, Sherman. I'm trusting you on this one," Keaton said, nodding.

"Give 'em hell, sir," Thomas added, following Keaton as he led the way to the supply store.

☆ ☆ ☆ ☆ ☆

Across town, Jack and Krueger sat behind their cover—a three foot tall, long brick wall that divided one house's lot from its neighbor's—and they were feeling very left out.

They'd heard the shots echoing across the town and figured that the main attack was underway at the town's entrance. They tried to call on the radio to get a SitRep, but the men over there were either too busy firing to answer or hadn't heard the radio call at all.

"This is useless," Jack moaned, leaning his head back against the brick wall. "We could be over there doing some good, but instead, they've got us on rear guard duty. Do you know who gets rear guard duty? The inept guy who never gets anything done right."

"Inept? Look, I'm no Narcissus, but I'm a damn good shot. They could be using me over there right now," Krueger complained. He shook his head in frustration.

Across the narrow street, taking cover behind a row of boxwoods, Mbutu and Denton disagreed, and let them know it.

"I'm just glad I'm not being shot at," Denton stage-whispered across the street. "Or being looked at like lunch, for that matter."

"I agree with Mr. Denton," Mbutu said, nodding slowly. "It is better to avoid the fighting if we can. I do not mind being at the 'rear of the line,' as you call it."

"But we're useless here," Jack countered. "Just a bunch of civvies taking up space—"

The conversation suddenly cut off as a loud rustle and snap of a branch from the direction of the woods caught their attention.

The line of defenders shifted nervously, their equipment making the barest of rattles as it clinked off of belts and buttons.

Krueger peered around the edge of the brick wall, eyes darting left and right as he tried to identify the source of the unexplained noise. He saw a grouping of shrubs rustle near the border of the town. He held up a restraining hand for the defenders to see.

"What is—" Jack started to ask.

Krueger cut him off. "Don't know. Might be a deer. Might not. Hold on."

The shrubs rustled again, and out of them appeared a man dressed from head to toe in woodland camouflage, wielding an AK-47. He waved his hand, and behind him, the forest rustled and snapped as more men appeared from behind trees and out of gullies. They were all armed, and all were moving as quietly as they could manage.

Krueger narrowed his eyes. This was why they'd been sent to guard the rear. Sherman must have suspected such an attack. They weren't the inept and the inexperienced. They were suddenly the vanguard.

Krueger picked up his radio and prayed that there was someone left at the main gates to hear his transmission.

"Krueger here, on station at the rear of the town. We have enemy contact, repeat, we have enemy contact. Do we engage or observe, over?"

He waited a moment. Only static answered him. He picked up the radio to repeat the request when a burst of static came over the radio and Sherman's voice came through, quiet but clear.

"Engage. Out."

Krueger nodded to himself, flicked the safety to his rifle off, and took aim. He looked left and right at the defenders and pantomimed shooting with his thumb and forefinger. Silent replies filtered in—a nod here, a thumbs-up there—and weapons were readied.

The first of the raiders reached the fence and knelt, pulling a pair of wire cutters from his pocket. Krueger swallowed as he watched the man work, flashing back to the night before when he had been the one cutting his way through a chain link fence on his way to mete out death and destruction. There hadn't been a sniper watching him then. His good luck.

As for the man he was staring at through his sights, well, Lady Luck just wasn't with him, it seemed. Krueger took the first shot of the engagement, killing the man with the wire cutters with a well-aimed round through the throat.

Gunfire immediately erupted from both sides. Defenders revealed themselves, popping up from behind their cover or leaning around the sides of trees and houses, and attackers rushed out of the treeline, weapons blazing.

Bullets tore into the brick wall, and bits and chunks of brick and cement sprayed up into Jack's face as he fired. He grunted in pain, dropping back down behind the wall and holding his hands to his eyes.

"I can't see! I can't see!" he cried out.

"Just stay down!" Krueger shouted above the gunfire. He took careful aim at an enemy rifleman who was lying next to a tree and sent a bullet through the man's head. The enemy jerked as the round hit him, then lay still.

Mbutu and Denton were taking turns rising up from behind the line of boxwoods, putting loads of ammunition downrange. They weren't hitting much, but they were causing the enemy to keep their heads down. The rest of the defenders were full of fighting spirit as well, having overcome the initial shock of contact. Rounds rained down on both sides.

A sudden metallic clang rang out and Denton dropped his rifle with a curse, shaking his hands in pain. A bullet had struck the weapon dead-on, shattering the chamber and shocking Denton's hands into numbness. He tried to fight off the pins-and-needles feeling as he fumbled for his backup pistol.

One of the attackers was hit at the top of the forested rise. He screamed, clutching at his shoulder, and spun to the ground. When he hit, he rolled, bouncing off of rocks and tree trunks until he came to a stop next to the chain link fence.

A defender took a bullet to the face when he jumped up from behind his cover to lay down fire. The back of his skull exploded outward and the man slumped forward over the wall, arms hanging limply.

Krueger saw the man die out of the corner of his eye and murmured a string of expletives, narrowing his eyes and sighting in on the nearest attacker, a man trying to set up an M-249 at the edge of a drainage ditch. Krueger fired, and the man fell over the weapon. "That'll teach you."

Machinegun fire suddenly erupted from the treeline, peppering the brick wall with dozens of rounds in rapid succession. The defenders lined up there dove for cover, huddling behind the bricks as powderized concrete filled the air around them.

"Machine guns!" Denton yelled. "The motherfuckers have machine guns!"

"I fucking noticed!" Krueger crowed over the gunfire. "Where's it coming from?"

"I see it!" Mbutu cried out. "Behind the tall tree!"

Krueger braved the fusillade and leaned back out from behind his cover, staring through his scope. When he put his eye to the magnifying lens, it was as if the battle narrowed down to just what he could see framed there. The sound, the chaos, all of it evaporated. There was no world. There was no battle. There was only Krueger, his crosshairs, and whatever they happened to fall upon.

Krueger scanned the treeline, letting the crosshairs drift over riflemen and pistoleers, searching for the machine-gunner. He found him exactly where Mbutu had said, perched at the top of the rise half-hidden behind the base of a towering oak. He was busy firing another M-249. Krueger sighted in, steadied his breathing, and fired. The round nearly missed, flying just a bit too high. Instead of hitting dead-on, the bullet tore off the top of the man's skull, spraying brain matter and bone fragments into the air behind him. The machinegun fire ceased at once.

The defenders, noting the sudden decrease in incoming fire, resumed their attack, popping up to send rounds off at the attackers and dropping back down to reload or take cover when rounds came their way.

"Is this the kind of fun you were hoping for?!" Denton shouted across the street.

Jack, still clutching at his eyes, answered back: "Everything except the pain part, yeah!"

⋆ ⋆ ⋆ ⋆ ⋆

Across town, the main gates were once again under attack. The shamblers had reached the town and were on their final approach toward the half-ruined fence. Already rifle shots were ringing out, but these came only from the best marksmen the town had. They didn't have infinite ammo, and, though the shamblers were slower than their cousins, only a precise head shot would drop them. Anything else was a waste of ammunition.

General Sherman was solidly in charge, barking orders that the townsfolk, perfect strangers to him a mere 24 hours previously, followed without question. His commanding presence allowed the townsfolk to work as a mostly cohesive unit, responding to threats as they appeared.

"You there!" Sherman shouted from one of the guard towers. He was gesturing wildly at one of the riflemen in the opposite tower. "Drop that shambler in the red shirt! Yes, that one! He's breaking off from the main group, and we don't want him circling around to give us grief later! Willis, concentrate on the ones heading for the damaged fence section!"

Below, volunteers were busy shoring up the damaged fence. They'd taken spools of wire and were busily cutting them into lengths, then re-tying the chain link fence to the posts that held it upright. One man wielded an acetylene torch, melting the hurried wiring together. The repairs were slapdash, but they looked to be effective. As the first shamblers came within arm's reach of the fenceline, Sherman belted out more orders.

"Repair crews, back away from that fence! Any of you with pistols, up front! Drop those shamblers!"

The men and women with the spools of wire hurriedly moved away from the combat zone. The welder snapped off his torch and raised his facemask, giving Sherman a wave. Sherman realized it was Jose, the mechanic, and gave the man a curt nod of recognition before turning back to survey the battlefield. About a dozen and a half of the shamblers had moved en masse toward the weakened section of the chainlink fence, stepping over the bodies of their sprinter cousins, and began to pull and push on the mesh once more.

Defenders stepped up to the line, firing pistols into the mass of shamblers. Three of the infected dropped backwards immediately, bullet wounds in their heads. Others were near misses, with sprays of brackish, coagulated blood flying out of torn throats or shoulders. In the field, another shambler went down after a neat shot by Deputy Willis.

"Keep firing on those shamblers by the fence!" Sherman shouted down. "Keep it up!"

The defenders were willing, but not entirely able. None were trained marksmen, and most of them unconsciously took steps backwards from the fenceline, driven away by the stench and appearance of the decaying shamblers. Their pistol shots were going wild, and although another shambler dropped dead, the remainder stayed on their feet, absorbing near misses and not reacting at all to the sound of rounds whizzing by their ears. The pulling and pushing on the fence intensified, and the makeshift welds began to snap, one after the other.

"Damn it, put those shamblers down!" Sherman screamed, watching as the fence began to come loose. He yanked free his own weapon and fired down into the mass of undead. One of his bullets struck home, punching through the top of a carrier's skull and exiting from under the creature's chin. It fell to its knees and slumped against the fence.

With a rending screech, the last of the makeshift welds popped free and the entire section of chainlink fence came crashing inward. Defenders backpedaled as the fence toppled toward them. Even so, three were caught underneath as the fence hit the ground. They tried to pull themselves free, but the weight of the shamblers stepping through the breach onto the chainlink kept them pinned. The shamblers slowed as they advanced and fell to their knees around the pinned defenders, reaching through the links to grab at them. The screams of the trapped men and women were heart-wrenching.

"Get back in there!" Sherman shouted, pointing at the swiftly retreating townsfolk. "Fill in that hole! Don't let them wander loose! Cut them down, damn it!"

It was no use. The townsfolk had seen their line breached, their friends trapped and devoured, and had cut and run for the safety of their own homes. Sherman's pistoleers had abandoned their line. He breathed a curse.

"Willis!" Sherman said, spinning in place to face the deputy, who was still taking careful potshots at shamblers on approach in the field below.

"Yeah?"

"Shift your fire! We need to kill the ones that've breached the line or they'll wander off into town and then we'll have a real hunt on our hands!" Sherman punctuated the order by unloading the remainder of his clip into the carriers below, to little effect.

Deputy Willis shouldered Sherman out of the way, rested his rifle on the edge of the tower, and began firing into the shamblers. His more accurate shooting had the immediate effect of dropping the lead shambler, who was just making its way into a nearby yard. The remainder of the shamblers that had breached the line numbered around eight, and Sherman didn't want a single one to get lost in the streets of Abraham.

✵ ✵ ✵ ✵ ✵

Halfway down main street, Sheriff Keaton and Thomas were busily decontaminating themselves. They'd dragged a metal trough into the street and had filled it halfway with water and copious amounts of bleach. The fumes rising up off the concoction made their eyes water and mouths itch.

"All right, I guess I'm first," Keaton said. He took a deep breath, held it, and jumped into the two-foot deep pool of bleach. He hurriedly splashed the mixture on his arms and legs, leaving his bloodstained shoes on to absorb as much of the virus-killing bleach as possible. Just as fast, he jumped back out. Already his bare arms and neck were turning red from exposure to the bleach—they had poured gallons of the stuff into the water. They hadn't been sure how much would have been enough, and it was always better to err on the side of caution.

"Come on, come on," Keaton said, raising his arms above his head. "Wash it off! Wash it off! The damn stuff burns!"

Thomas was happy to oblige. He held in his hands a well-fed garden hose with a spray nozzle on the end. The old sergeant almost seemed to grin with sadistic pleasure as he twisted the nozzle, sending a spray of icy-cold water all over the Sheriff. Keaton took it like a man, gritting his teeth and turning in a slow circle as Thomas hosed him down. When the sergeant had finished, the Sheriff stood, sopping wet in the middle of the road, all traces of infected blood gone from his person. He was shivering, and looked miserable. Thomas looked over the shoulder of the sheriff to the three deputies who were all waiting their turns.

"All right, who's next?" Thomas asked.

The deputies looked at the miserable Sheriff, over to the enthusiastic Sergeant Major with the garden hose in his hand, down to the trough of bleach, and back at one another. They seemed unwilling to go through the same process their leader had.

"It's either this or I get to shoot you as an infected," Thomas added, his malicious grin fading into a deadly serious expression.

Two of the deputies immediately jumped into the trough, fighting over which one of them would get to wash themselves off first.

In the distance, shots echoed from the rear of town. Keaton, who had taken a seat on the curb and was trying to warm himself up by vigorously rubbing his arms, leapt to his feet. He stared off in the direction of the gunfire.

"Well, I'll be damned," he whispered. "Sherman was right. There's an attack coming from behind!"

"Give it three minutes, Sheriff, and we'll all be back in fighting shape," Thomas said, opening up the hose on the two newly-decontaminated deputies. They grimaced and held up their hands against the blast of freezing water.

Keaton picked up his rifle, impatiently pacing back and forth behind Thomas. He wanted to get back to the conflict as soon as possible.

More shots rang out—this time coming from the direction of the main gates.

"God *damn* it!" Keaton yelled. "Now we've got a fight on two fronts at once!"

"Sherman's at the gates, Sheriff," Thomas reminded him. "He'll keep things under control."

"Ah, fuck this waiting!" Keaton snarled. He took off at a flat-out run toward the main gates, praying that the fighting at the rear of the town would go well enough without reinforcements. The Sheriff's feet pounded pavement, and a million and one grisly situations played out in his head. In one version, he saw his town overrun by the carriers, his friends and neighbors among their ranks, wandering the streets in a mindless search for prey. In another, he saw the raiders standing over the bodies of himself and his friends, burning the town, looting and pillaging. None of the fantasies ended well.

Keaton could see the tops of the guard towers as he neared the main gates, and passed a pair of townsfolk running in the opposite direction, still clutching their weapons. Keaton skidded to a halt, turning to yell after them.

"Hey! Hey! Where are you going? What the fuck do you think you're doing? Get back on the line!" Keaton's orders were all in vain; the townsfolk had seen enough and were in a full retreat. Nothing he said even slowed them down. He cursed, turned, and resumed his run. Only a block separated him from the fighting.

Keaton came sprinting around the corner and nearly collided with a shambler, only a few feet in front of him. It was a nasty specimen. The lower half of its jaw had been torn off and its chest was cratered and pockmarked with bullet holes, exposing decaying organs and fragments of ribcage. Keaton recoiled, fighting back his gag reflex as the thing's stench washed over him. He recovered himself, raised his rifle, and fired a shot that punched a hole neatly through the shambler's left eye socket. As it fell, the rest of the battlefield was revealed to Keaton, and the sight wasn't a good one.

A section of fence had been ripped free, and Keaton saw the bloodied remains of several of his volunteers trapped under the wire mesh. Shamblers seemed to be everywhere, but the objective part of Keaton recognized that there were actually less than a dozen. It was just that the dozen were spread out over an ever-widening area. Some were wandering down a side street, presumably going after defenders that had abandoned the line. Still more were clustered around the bases of the guard towers, reaching up toward the defenders within.

Those were being dealt with.

Sherman was leaning over the edge of the tower, firing straight down at the shamblers around the base of his tower. Every third or fourth round would find its mark, and a shambler would slump against the steel of the tower and slide to the ground, leaving behind bloody smears. Willis was firing after the shamblers that had broken away from the main gate area. His accuracy at long range left a little to be desired. Keaton turned to watch the effects of the man's shooting, and saw a round ricochet off the concrete near the foot of a shambler, and saw another punch a hole through a carrier's back. Neither did much to slow or stop the attacking infected.

The men in the other guard tower were busy with their own shamblers, finding it awkward to aim straight down with their longbarreled rifles, but neither position was in great danger. The infected had never been great climbers.

The Sheriff looked out into the field and ground his teeth together. Another half-dozen or so shamblers were steadily approaching across the field, heading straight for the breach in the fence. He made a decision.

"Wes!" he yelled. The deputy in the guard tower didn't hear the call over the sound of the gunfire, so Keaton called again. "Wes, damn it!"

The deputy looked up from his scope, noticed the Sheriff, and waved. "Keaton! We've got problems!"

"I fucking noticed! Take out the ones in the field! Don't let anymore of the bastards into town! I'm going after the stragglers!"

With that, Keaton snapped up his rifle and turned, running down the side street where he'd seen the group of shamblers. In the guard tower, Willis shifted his position once more, taking aim at the approaching undead reinforcements.

"This is for Mike," Wes said, referencing one of the dead defenders trapped beneath the fallen fence. He fired, blowing the back of a shambler's skull off. "And this is for Tina." Another shot, another kill. Willis paused to reload, scowling at the undead in the field. He'd killed six of them so far, and the rest of the defenders had probably knocked off another dozen or two, but that still left a full dozen up and wandering.

Keaton tore down the side street, past the modest houses of Abraham with their green yards and pruned shrubs, until finally he caught sight of them, just making a turn onto another road. They were definitely locked onto prey. Keaton was out to make sure they didn't reach it.

"Hey! Hey!" Keaton yelled as loud as he could manage, waving his arms and rifle over his head as he ran. "Over here!"

Two of the shamblers halted and awkwardly turned, eyes falling on the rapidly-approaching Sheriff. They opened their mouths and moaned, signaling the rest of their group. The remainder of the shamblers slowed to a stop and turned as well, in their stiff, jerky way to face their newfound prey.

"That's right!" Keaton yelled, slowing to a jog. "Right here! I'm lunch today!"

Keaton stopped and knelt, pulling his rifle in close to his shoulder. He sighted in as the shamblers began to work their way back towards him, and fired. His bullet took down the lead shambler. It fell into a line of tall, flowering plants and was lost to sight except for its feet, which jutted out onto the cement of the sidewalk.

Keaton grinned behind his sights, worked the bolt of his rifle to chamber another round, and fired a second time. This bullet went slightly awry, punching a hole through the jaw of a shambler and exploding out the back of the thing's neck. It collapsed in a heap. Its body was still, but the head still moved from left to right, snapping what remained of its teeth in exasperation. The round must have severed its spinal cord.

The rest of the shamblers, four in all, were closing on the Sheriff. That was fine with him. A closer range meant his shots would be easier. He racked another round into the chamber, drew a bead on the nearest shambler and pulled the trigger.

Click.

Keaton felt his eyes widen. The light click of the firing pin hitting nothing but an empty chamber rang out louder than any of the shots he'd taken so far today. He'd forgotten to reload in his haste to get back to the fighting.

"Shit, shit, shit," he cursed. He dropped his rifle and began rapidly patting himself down, feeling for extra rounds. He knew he'd stashed some on his person somewhere. The shamblers drew ever closer as he searched. Keaton patted down his last pocket, finding nothing—then he remembered. He'd taken off all his gear— ammunition, radio, equipment belt—before jumping into the bleach-filled trough. "All right, not good."

Keaton grabbed up his rifle and backed away from the shamblers, putting some distance between himself and his would-be slayers.

"All right, Keaton, this isn't as bad as it looks," he said to himself. "You're unarmed, but you're smart and they're slow. Just keep thinking."

As Keaton wracked his brain for a plan, he kept backing away from the shamblers. They followed him mindlessly, moaning out loud with frustration—the distance between them and their prey never seemed to decrease. Keaton noticed this, and allowed himself a quick grin.

"That's the spirit, Sheriff," he told himself. "Just keep them coming."

Keaton continued his slow retreat, leading the errant shamblers back to the scene of the battle at the main gates, foot by tedious foot.

At the rear of the town, the fight was turning against the attackers. The defenders of Abraham had better cover, and the attackers had been surprised by the sudden, ferocious defense. The attacking machine-gunners had been killed, depriving the raiders of their heaviest armaments.

The defenders weren't coming out of the fight unscathed, however. Even as Krueger drilled another enemy rifleman from behind the brick wall, a defender wailed as she caught a round in the stomach and collapsed to the grass, clutching at the wound. Jack, who had managed to clear the bits of debris from his eyes well enough to see, crawled over to the woman to try and help. By the time he reached her and rolled her over, she was dead, staring up at him with fixed and dilated pupils.

The attackers were yelling something back and forth between themselves. Krueger tried to hear what they were saying, but the words were lost in the chatter of gunfire. They seemed to be orders of some kind.

Krueger saw one of the men pointing at the fenceline and shouting back up the hill to a man who was well-covered behind a row of jutting limestone. Krueger took a shot at the man shouting up the hill, but missed, and the raider dove for cover of his own. Krueger cursed and chambered another round, this time shifting his aim to the man hiding behind the limestone outcropping—only to find the man had moved.

"Where, oh, where could you have gone, you little bastard?" Krueger whispered as he peered through his scope. Suddenly, the man rose up from behind the outcropping, winding up in a classic pitcher's stance. Krueger grinned and fired, the round taking the man directly through the chest. It was an instant kill—but before the man dropped, he completed his pitch. An oblong object arced through the air, landed just on the inside of the chainlink fence, and rolled to a halt against it. Krueger's eyes widened.

"Everyone down!" he screamed, ducking behind the wall. "Grenade!"

Before he could even finish his warning, the explosive went off with a concussive blast, shredding the fence and embedding shrapnel in the brick wall Krueger was hunched behind. A defender screamed as he took shrapnel to the chest, collapsing on his back in the grass. He clutched at the bit of metal protruding from his ribcage.

The grenade was probably meant to land behind the brick wall and take out the line of defenders there, Krueger realized, but his shot had taken away some of the man's momentum. Still, the explosive hadn't been rendered entirely ineffective. The end result was a section of fence that had been blown outward, warped by the blast, and shredded in several places by shrapnel.

The attackers took up a yell, charging the breach and firing their weapons full-auto.

Most of the defenders were still hunched behind cover, ears ringing from the grenade blast. Denton and Mbutu, close enough to Krueger to have heard his warning, had covered their ears and were quick to recover. They sprayed the breach in the fenceline with rifle and pistol fire, dropping two of the charging attackers. One lay wounded, crying out in pain and rolling around on the ground.

The rest reached the fenceline and started pouring through. Krueger looked through his scope and realized he couldn't count the number of attackers flooding the fence. There had to have been fifteen, maybe twenty, at least.

"Fire! Fire!" Krueger cried out, abandoning his scope. He aimed in the direction of the breach and let fly round after round, trying to suppress the charge. Other defenders joined in, rising up from behind the wall and opening up on the raiders.

Attackers fell left and right, riddled with rounds as they tried to funnel themselves through their entry point. Those that made it took cover behind trees and even a fire hydrant, returning fire. Defenders went down as the raiders fired.

Krueger's rifle clicked empty and he swore. He'd used up all the .30-06 rounds he'd taken from the Sheriff's station. He left his rifle where it lay, drawing his pistol instead. He flicked the safety off and popped up from behind the brick wall, firing a trio of shots at the raiders.

Krueger didn't stop to see if any of them hit, and dropped back down to relative safety. Return fire kicked up debris and brick dust floated over the wall, making Krueger's eyes itch. His mouth felt dry as a bone.

The raiders were now spread out on the inside of the fence, hunkered down behind cover of their own. Krueger's mind raced, and he let his infantry training take over.

He turned so his back was to the brick wall and looked left and right at the remaining defenders. None of them were military; none of them would understand what needed to be done. He was about to start grabbing random volunteers for his plan when he noticed four figures rapidly approaching down the main road, running full-tilt toward the fighting. Krueger squinted at them, and let fly a bark of laughter.

"Thomas!" he yelled, waving his hand above his head. "Thomas! Over here!"

The Sergeant Major and the three deputies, all still soaking wet from their decontamination, had chosen to run for the rear of the town and reinforce the lines there. Thomas spotted Krueger hunkered down behind a two-foot brick wall, waving his hand at him. Thomas made for the sniper, running hunched over to present as small a target as he could manage. Bullets from the raiders sought out the deputies and himself, and the whizz of near misses made the old sergeant involuntarily flinch. He made it to the brick wall, falling hard against it. The deputies dove for cover nearby as well, and began firing at the raiders.

"It's no good, Sergeant!" Krueger yelled over the gunfire to Thomas. "They're well behind cover, and so are we! It's a slugging match! We need to flank these fuckers and put some fire on them from a better position!"

Thomas poked his head up over the brick wall, eyes flicking left and right, quickly taking in the tactical situation. He dropped back down after only a moment and nodded. "Fourteen of them, all with assault rifles on the inside of the fence. Two more outside the fence with scoped rifles."

Krueger's eyebrows raised. That was quite an assessment for a three-second recon.

"I agree, Krueger," Thomas went on. "We're going to need to drive them out from behind their cover."

"Wish we still had one of those tear gas grenades," Krueger said, reloading his pistol.

"Wishes are like assholes," Thomas grumbled. "Everyone's got one and most of them are shitty. Krueger, you're on me. Deputies!"

The three men that had accompanied him looked over.

"You're with us! The rest of you, keep firing on these bastards! Defend!"

Thomas leapt up, sprinting away from the firing line. He was headed for the nearest house. Krueger and the deputies jumped up and followed as closely as they could manage. Thomas swung around the corner of the house and ran along the side, making for the back yard. Krueger was right behind him. Two of the three deputies made it. The third was hit by a raider's bullet right before he made the turn, and collapsed soundlessly, face-first, onto the lawn.

Thomas ran through the backyard, circling around the house. When he came to the other corner, he halted, kneeling behind a white fence with thick green vines entangling it. Krueger and the remaining deputies caught up and knelt beside Thomas.

Thomas looked up over the fence. Down the road about twenty meters away he could see the engagement continuing, but from this angle, he had a clear view of the raiders as they lay or stood behind their cover of choice.

"All right, listen up and listen good," Thomas grumbled, turning to face his small squad. "There aren't many of us, so we'll have to make this count. You know the rebel yell?"

"Hoo-ah, Sarge," Krueger said, readying his pistol. The deputies nodded in reply.

"Good. That's what we're going to give 'em. That and every last damn round we have in our weapons. We're not here to kill them all, we're here to drive them out of their cover so our guys down the street can finish 'em off!"

Thomas checked his own weapon, took a deep breath, and set himself in a runner's stance.

"Ready?" he asked.

The three men with him nodded.

"All right. Good luck. Go! Go! Go!"

The four men leapt the short fence and ran straight across the street, screaming at the top of their lungs a battle cry that made the sprinters' roar seem muted in comparison. They opened up on the raiders' positions, firing as fast as they could pull their triggers. The rounds skipped off cement, embedded themselves in tree trunks and kicked up chunks of dirt, doing little real damage.

From the raider's perspective things looked a mite different. Suddenly they were being assaulted from the side by several men, screaming like banshees and raining down fire on them. One or two of the raiders remained calm, trying to pick off the new targets, but the rest panicked, shifting their positions to try and avoid the bullets that Thomas, Krueger, and the deputies were sending their way. They succeeded in avoiding being shot by the flanking squad—and in the process, moved directly into the other defenders' line of fire.

Thomas and Krueger finished their run, stopping with their backs to a thick oak tree, and reloaded their pistols. The deputies followed suit, and all four once again appeared out in the open, screaming at the top of their lungs and advancing on the raiders, firing nonstop.

Mbutu and Denton rallied the defenders, seeing that the raiders were being pushed out of their position.

"Come on!" Denton yelled, waving an arm over his head. "Let's finish the bastards!"

The rallying cry was taken up all across the line, and defenders whooped and yelled, emptying their magazines into the attackers.

Raiders fell one after the other. Blood ran like red streams over the curb and down the gutters. Within minutes, the attacking force had been butchered nearly to the last man. Only a few remaining wounded were left, and those were in no position to fight.

Thomas and Krueger walked up on the raider's position, the two deputies trailing closely behind, and inspected the carnage. The other defenders rose up from behind their cover and wandered out to see the effect of their fighting efforts.

Krueger kicked a rifle away from one of the wounded raiders, a tall, heavyset man who was clutching a stomach wound and gritting his teeth.

"You pissant motherfuckers," he growled, wincing against the pain. "I'll kill you all, I'll kill you—"

Krueger kicked the man lightly in the stomach, right where the bullet had entered, and the man howled, doubling over.

"That's enough out of you, asshole," Krueger said, taking aim at the man's head.

Thomas put a steadying hand on Krueger's arm. "Don't. Betting Sherman and Keaton wouldn't mind a prisoner or two."

At the main gates, the tide of the battle had turned as well. Sherman and the men in the towers had succeeded in killing the shamblers that had remained inside the fenceline, and were now finishing off the few that were still wandering in the field outside. Infected corpses were everywhere.

The largest pile lay at the breach in the fenceline, stacked three or four thick in places. Most of those had been the sprinters from the initial attack. More lay scattered here and there inside the fence, slumped against a vehicle or facedown in a gutter. Several more were piled up at the base of the ladders leading up into the guard towers. Not a one had been spared.

It was relatively quiet now that most of the gunfire had slackened off, and Sherman was overseeing the sharpshooters as they took out the remaining shamblers.

"Lead him just a bit to the left, there, Wes," Sherman said, leaning over the shoulder of the deputy with the rifle. "Remember to breathe...and squeeze the trigger."

Wes fired, and halfway across the field, the shambler jerked and fell.

"Nice shot!" Sherman commended, slapping Wes on the back.

Deputy Willis looked up from behind his scope, eyebrows raised. "Damn, that must've been two hundred meters, easy."

"Hell yes," Sherman agreed. "Only a couple more left, now. Same drill. Take 'em down."

Wes put his eye to the scope and was about to fire again when Sheriff Keaton's voice rang out in the street below.

"Hello, the towers!" Keaton yelled. "I've brought back some old friends! Think you could give me a hand with them?"

Sherman and Wes turned as one to see Keaton striding boldly back toward the main gates. Not more than twenty feet behind him were the four remaining shamblers that had managed to wander off into town. The Sheriff seemed unconcerned with their presence, even though their arms were stretched out toward him and their disturbing moans were incessant.

"Well, that's one way to lead a horse to water," Sherman said, grinning. "Why didn't you just finish them yourself, Keaton?"

The Sheriff held up his empty rifle one-handed and grinned. "Stupid me—forgot to bring along extra ammo. Not that it mattered. These smelly bastards haven't stopped following me once I caught up with them. They're like retarded dogs, or something."

"Walk 'em over to the towers," Sherman said. "I'll toss you my pistol."

Behind Sherman, Deputy Willis fired, and across the field another shambler fell. "Thanks for the shooting tips, Sherman. I'm really starting to get the hang of this thing, now."

Keaton moved over to the guard tower Sherman occupied, taking care to avoid the puddles of infected blood and decaying bodies of shamblers that littered the area. When he was close enough, Sherman threw down his pistol. Keaton caught it deftly, one-handed, and checked the chamber. He turned to face his macabre followers, flicked the safety off, and dispatched all four, one after the other, in quick succession. Keaton flicked the safety back on, turned, and threw the pistol back up to Sherman, who caught and holstered the weapon.

"That's that," Keaton said, grinning. "Takes care of the infected problem. Any word from the rear line?"

Sherman started to reply, but held off a moment as Wes took another shot at a distant shambler. When the blast from the shot had faded, Sherman spoke up.

"Just got a radio report in," Sherman said. "They held off an attack by the raiders. The infected were a diversion, like we thought."

"Well, hell yes," Keaton said, his smile widening. "Did any get away?"

"They think a few might have bugged out before the fighting ended," Sherman said. "They took two prisoners, though. They're bringing them to the clinic to be treated for their wounds, then taking them over to your station."

Keaton nodded to himself, folding his arms across his chest. All around him was death, destruction, and chaos, but the adrenaline of battle was already fading from his head. The people of Abraham—with a little help from their visitors—had won the day and saved their town.

There was only one part of victory that left a sour taste in Keaton's mouth.

The cleanup would be a bitch.

CHAPTER EIGHT
THE FAST LANE

I-74 West
March 08, 2007
1452 hrs_

"*Sawyer*?" Matt asked, a quizzical expression crossing his face. "Who the hell is Sawyer?"

"I told you we should have told them," Mason said, shooting a recriminating glance in Anna's direction.

"I didn't think they'd catch up to us this fast!" Anna protested. "We just left a day ago! How the hell could they have figured out where we'd be so quickly?"

"That's not the point—" Mason started, then shook his head. It was no use arguing about it now.

The black Land Rover that was tailing them had picked up speed quickly once Mason had spotted it. Whoever was sitting in the passenger seat must have also had a pair of binoculars focused on the truck, and seen Mason scope them out. With their cover blown, the occupants of the SUV were going for broke. They had closed half the distance with the truck already, and were still gaining.

Mason slapped a hand on the window that led to the truck's cab. A moment later, Juni pushed it open, eyebrows raised.

"Tell Trev we've got company—the bad kind. He might want to step on it," Mason said, pulling his MP-5 from around his shoulders and checking the chamber. He'd reholstered his pistol. Something told him he might need both in the upcoming tiff.

"I heard you," came Trev's voice through the open window. "And I've been looking for an excuse to do just that for a while now. Hold on to your butts."

The pickup accelerated sharply, throwing Mason and Julie off-balance. They stumbled, but recovered quickly. The distance between the truck and Land Rover grew for only a moment. The hostile driver picked up on the difference and slammed on his own accelerator. The more-powerful SUV once more began to close. It was around two hundred yards away, and gaining quickly.

"Step on it, Trev!" Mason yelled over his shoulder.

"I am stepping on it!" came back the irate reply. "This is about as fast as this bucket can go without adding some damn jet fuel to the tank!"

"Then we're in for a clusterfuck," Mason murmured, locking and loading the MP-5. "They won't try anything too rash, though."

"Doesn't look that way to me," said an anxious Matt, peering over the edge of the tailgate with his rifle next to him. "Looks like they're planning on running us down!"

"Not as long as we have Doctor Demilio with us," Mason said, allowing himself a quick grin. "They won't try and wreck us. They'll want her alive. They'll try and stop us so they can take her."

"Who the hell are these people?" Junko asked, sticking her head out the back window of the cab.

"I'll explain later!" Mason shouted over his shoulder. "Get back in there and buckle up!"

The Land Rover was close enough now that Mason could see through the windshield to the occupants within. Neither of the men sitting in the front seat was Sawyer; that was enough for him to breathe a mental sigh of relief. Sawyer wouldn't have stopped at anything, but maybe, if they put up enough of a fight, these cronies would.

Even as he spoke, red and blue flashing lights lit up in the grille of the Land Rover and the passenger side window rolled down.

"What are they, cops?" Matt asked, eyes widening at the sight of the lights.

"Not cops," Mason said, shouldering his sub-machinegun. "NSA, probably, or FBI or CIA, depending on who's left."

"And what, do they think we're going to pull over for them?" Matt pressed. Even as he spoke, the Land Rover activated a wailing siren, pulling in directly behind the beat-up pickup truck.

"Well, we *are* speeding," Anna said wryly.

The passenger in the Land Rover leaned out the open window, buffeted by the wind. His eyes squinted against the gale as he grimaced and gestured at the occupants of the pickup, forcefully pointing to the side of the road.

"Hot damn," Mason said, chuckling. "They really *do* want us to pull over. Well, it's not going to be that easy, guys."

Mason raised himself up to a kneeling position, tucked the MP-5 in close to his shoulder, and took aim at the road between the two vehicles. He squeezed the trigger over and over, sending rounds skipping off the pavement mere inches from the Land Rover's front tires. The response from the men in the vehicle was immediate. The SUV lurched to the side and braked, throwing off Mason's aim. The man in the passenger seat disappeared inside, reappearing a moment later with a sub-machinegun of his own.

"Down, down!" Mason shouted.

His voice was nearly drowned out by the rapid fire of the enemy agent's weapon. Bullets skittered off the back of the pickup truck, and the occupants dove for cover. Only Mason remained upright, kneeling at the rear of the bed. He had been trying to disable their vehicle so they could put some distance between themselves and their pursuers, but if they wanted to play hard, Mason was willing to oblige them. He shifted his aim up from the road to the windshield, flicked the selector to three round burst, and pulled the trigger.

The weapon belched rapid fire and three craters appeared in the Land Rover's windshield, spiderlike cracks running away from each in every direction. The Land Rover bucked and lurched once more, but righted itself after a moment. Mason didn't give the men inside any more time to recover. He pulled the trigger again, and another spray of shattered glass and hot lead flew up from the Land Rover's windshield. He was trying for the driver.

Return fire came at them then, this time full-auto. Mason heard one of the women cry out behind him, but didn't allow it to distract him. He was in combat mode now. Nothing could shift his attention from his target. He squeezed the trigger twice more, and this time, the results were immediate. Two of the six rounds kicked up paint and steel from the Land Rover's hood, and the remaining four stitched upward across the driver's side of the windshield. Mason could see blood spattering the splintered glass from the inside. He'd scored a hit.

The Land Rover shuddered, lost speed, and careened off the side of the road, hitting the shoulder doing sixty miles per hour. It tipped up on its side with the passenger still firing his weapon full-auto at the truck, and, much to the surprise of Mason, continued to move on its two left wheels, balanced precariously on the edge of the road.

Then someone inside must have shifted—perhaps the wounded driver—because the vehicle suddenly lost its center of balance, tipping the remainder of the way over. It crashed into the median upside-down, glass shattering out of all the windows, and rolled several times before coming to a shaky stop on its side, smoke drifting up from the damaged engine block.

"That got him!" Mason said, pumping a fist in the air in triumph. "Wasn't Sawyer, though—it was just a couple of his buddies. We'll have to figure on them having radioed our position, so we'll—"

His voice drifted off as he turned away from the Land Rover and saw the scene in the truckbed. Matt and Anna were on either side of Julie, expressions of panic and horror on their faces.

"Keep pressure here," Anna said, grabbing Matt's hand and pressing it down firmly on Julie's shoulder. "We need to stop the bleeding!"

"What happened?" Mason asked, dropping the MP-5 and moving over next to the rest. When he saw Julie's condition, he sucked in a sudden breath.

The journalist lay on her back in the truckbed, eyes wide with fear and pain. Sweat ran down her face as she gritted her teeth. Dark red blood soaked through her shirt in two places: one wound in the shoulder, the other high on her abdomen, just on her right side. Anna was working furiously, trying to call back the lessons she'd learned in practical medicine before she'd delved into her specialties.

"Jesus Christ," she cursed, voice trembling. "I don't know what to do!"

Mason eyed the wounds. The shoulder wasn't bad. From the amount of blood pooling on the truckbed, he knew it had been a clean in-and-out shot—a survivable hit. The other, however, caused him to swallow hard.

Anna cut away the bottom half of Julie's shirt, exposing the bullet wound in her abdomen. Dark blood ran out of the wound in a steady stream, flowing down Julie's side and dripping onto the bed of the truck.

"Oh, Jesus," Anna repeated, wiping a hand across her forehead. "I think she's been hit in the liver. Don't just stand there, help me!"

"What do you want me to do?" Mason asked.

"I don't have any tools, I don't have any supplies, I don't know!" Anna yelled, clasping her hands behind her head. She clenched her eyes shut and ground her teeth together. "I just don't know."

"It's—it's—nothing to worry about," Julie said, gasping for breath. She managed a half-smile. "I've—I've never been—shot before."

Matt, still holding his hand down hard on Julie's shoulder wound, tried to grin, but failed. "I've never been shot before, either."

"Just keep her talking," Mason whispered in Anna's ear. "I've seen these kinds of wounds before. You'd need a hospital and a surgeon to treat them."

Anna looked back at Mason with a horrified expression on her face. She dropped her voice to a whisper and leaned over to him.

"What are you saying, that we do nothing? Just wait and hope she gets better?"

Mason stared hard at the doctor, then shook his head slowly. "No, Doc. I'm saying that Julie is dying."

"Well, fuck that!" Anna shouted, startling everyone, including Julie. "There has to be something I can do, some kind of—maybe I have some drugs in my bag from the safehouse or maybe we can sterilize one of your knives, Mason—we can get this fixed and—"

"Don't—don't bother," Julie said, looking up at Anna. "It's funny—it doesn't even hurt. Don't bother."

"Don't goddamn tell me not to bother," Anna said, still dumping her bags and furiously rooting through the contents for anything that might help. "I can't just sit back and watch you—"

Anna cut herself off with a shake of her head.

Julie managed her weak half-smile again and held out a bloody hand toward Anna. "What—watch me—what? Die? Like I—like I said, don't bother. Doesn't even hurt."

Mason laid a hand on Julie's unharmed shoulder. "Just relax, Julie, we're going to do what we can for you."

Julie tried to chuckle, but ended up coughing instead. Matt swallowed and looked away, hand still clamped firmly over Julie's shoulder wound. Anna came up with a syringe and a bottle of narcotics, and worked feverishly to load a dose.

Julie's bloodied arm tapped weakly at Anna's leg. "Give it—give it a rest, Doc."

"Shut up," Anna snapped, testing the needle's flow and quickly injecting the contents into Julie's outstretched arm. Within moments, Julie's panicked, pained expression eased somewhat as the painkillers took hold. She looked dreamy and almost content.

"I was—I was wrong," she said, still smiling. "I—I guess it did hurt before, but now—now it doesn't. Guess I shouldn't—shouldn't have tried to stop you, Doc."

Julie laid her head back and let out a long sigh, staring up at the sky.

"Damn straight," Anna said, rooting through Mason's pack for any medical supplies he might be carrying. She came up with gauze bandages and some surgical tape. "Next we're going to get this bleeding stopped, and once I find a couple proper tools we're going to get you all fixed up."

"Doc," Mason said, trying to interrupt Anna. The doctor was having none of it.

"Then we'll pull over and do a little surgery. I hope you trust me to try it, Julie, because the last surgery I did was in medical school," Anna rambled, pulling together her meager pile of supplies. "But it can't be too tricky. I'll get that bullet out, and we'll hole up for a bit while you heal—"

"Doc," Mason repeated, this time louder.

Anna glared at him.

"Doc, she's gone," Mason said gently, looking down at Julie.

The journalist lay still, eyes open, rocking gently from side to side with the motion of the truck.

Julie Ortiz was dead.

Anna stopped her frantic search, stared for a moment at Julie's peaceful expression, and fell back against the side of the truck, dropping her face into her hands. Matt slowly released his hold on

Julie's shoulder. The blood had stopped flowing. The young man looked at his hands, covered in the journalist's blood, and swallowed hard. Mason turned away from the scene entirely, facing the tailgate, knees pulled up against his chest. He managed to hold himself in check for a few seconds before he lost his control.

"God *damn* it!" he screamed, reeling back and throwing a powerful punch at the steel tailgate. The whole back end of the truck vibrated with the impact, and when Mason withdrew his arm, his knuckles were scored and bleeding.

He didn't even notice.

1734 hrs_

Trev had pulled the truck off the interstate two exits past the site of their engagement with the Land Rover. He'd chosen that particular exit because it connected the interstate with a rural road, without a town in either direction for miles. He drove until he found a wide gravel shoulder next to an open field and pulled off. Dust billowed up around the truck's wheels as he braked to a stop, shifting into park and turning off the engine.

The occupants of the vehicle were unnaturally silent. Even Matt and Junko, whom Trev knew loved to argue back and forth, were subdued and withdrawn. They had all seen friends and acquiantances killed in the pandemic, but those people had been felled by the Morningstar strain.

This was the first time any of them, save Mason, had actually seen a person killed by another uninfected person.

Julie lay in the truckbed, covered in a thin woolen blanket, the one she had been using as her bedroll on the long trek west. When Trev offered to help carry her, Mason and Anna glared at him, silently refusing the offer. They lifted the journalist's body between them and carried her over to the field, laying her down gently in the grass.

For a moment, the remaining five were silent, looking down at the blanket-covered body. Trev removed his baseball cap and held it over his heart.

Mason broke the silence after a full minute. "Do we have a shovel?"

Trev shook his head. "No. No, we don't. There might be a spade in the toolbox in the back, and that's about it."

Mason nodded silently, turned on his heels and strode back to the pickup truck. He rooted around in the bed, and came up with a small, handheld garden spade. Without saying a word, he fell to his knees next to Julie's body and began to dig, one tiny spadeful at a time.

Trev opened his mouth, intending to say that they would waste too much time trying to dig a grave without proper tools, then decided against it, snapping his mouth shut again. Instead, he reached down to his boot and pulled free a long hunting knife that he'd sharpened to a razor's edge, knelt beside Mason, and began stabbing at the dirt, loosening it and scooping it out with his free hand.

Mason looked over at Trev and managed an emotionless smile, a silent thank-you.

It wasn't long before the rest of them had joined in, using whatever tool they could find. Anna dug with her bare hands, still wearing an expression of frustration and anguish on her face. She felt horrible over not having been able to do anything for Julie when she needed it most.

It took two hours, but the group finally finished the grave. It wasn't six feet deep, but it was close. Trev and Mason stood in the hole while Matt and Anna handed down Julie's body. They laid her gently to rest, head supported on a small cushion of loose dirt. The pair climbed out of the hole and brushed themselves off, looking down at the body beneath them.

"Does anyone want to say anything?" Trev asked after a moment.

No one responded.

"Someone should say something," Trev pressed.

Still, no takers. Matt and Junko looked at one another, then down at the ground. Anna's face was still playing a range of regret and frustration, and Mason—burning in Mason's eyes was hatred and resolve. None of them looked up for presenting a eulogy.

Trev cleared his throat.

"Well," he said, once more sweeping his cap off his head to hold it over his heart, "If none of you want to say anything, I guess I will. There are two kinds of people in this world, at least in my experience: those that are generally good, and those that are generally bad. I didn't know Julie Ortiz very well. In fact, I'd only just met her, but in that short time I realized that she was one of those people who was generally good. She didn't deserve to die this way, just like all the good folks who have died since these bloody-eyed demons first appeared."

Junko glanced at Trev out of the corner of her eye, but none of the other survivors reacted to his slip, and she let it go as Trev continued.

"We're not just burying a woman. We're burying a friend, an ally, a trustworthy companion—and that is something that is all too rare in today's world. Julie, I didn't know you well, but I can honestly say I will miss you. Godspeed."

With that, Trev pulled his hat back down over his head, nodded once to himself, and folded his arms behind his back. The others seemed to feel that Trev's eulogy was appropriate, and knelt down next to the piles of dirt, scooping handfuls back into the grave. When they had filled in the hole, they piled rough limestone over the freshly dug earth to make certain no roaming animals would disturb Julie's rest by digging her up, and piled more stones at the head of the grave to serve as a marker. There was no way for them to inscribe her name. Julie Ortiz would rest in an anonymous grave.

When they had finished, Trev spoke up again.

"Look, guys, I hate to be the pragmatic bastard, but it's going to be dark soon. We should get back on the road, keep heading west."

Mason looked up from the cairn then and fixed Trev with a stare.

"That's a good idea," Mason said, "but that's not where we're going. We're going east—at least for a few miles."

"What?" Junko asked, incredulous. "Backtrack? But we got ambushed back there. You want to repeat—"

"Don't think for a second I don't know what I'm doing," Mason said, spinning on the young woman with a look on his face that dared anyone to disagree with him. The look in his eyes was murderous. "Those shooters will have radioed back our location, which means Sawyer will be mobilizing to come after us. That'll probably take him several hours. We have enough time to go back to that Land Rover and still get away clean."

"Why?" Juni asked, pressing the issue.

"Why?" Mason repeated. "You'll see when we get there. Come on. Get in the truck. Everyone, get in the goddamn truck. Trev, are you with me? Will you take me back there?"

Trev, with eyebrows raised, was intrigued by Mason's determination. Though he didn't feel particularly threatened by the ex-NSA agent, he did feel compelled to comply.

"I'll drive you back, top speed," Trev said, nodding.

"Good. Let's get to it, then," Mason growled through clenched teeth. "I have some unfinished business to take care of there."

The survivors loaded back up. Matt sat in the bed as far as he could from the bloodstains Julie had left behind. Anna sat right next to them, staring at the blood and hanging her head. Junko and Trev climbed into the cab together, and Trev started the engine. It sputtered for a moment, churned, and caught, and he quickly put the vehicle in gear and swung it around on the road, heading back the way they'd come a few hours previous. Junko stared out the passenger side window at the cairn of stones that marked Julie's grave until it disappeared behind a bend.

In the bed of the truck, Mason was working singlemindedly on his equipment. He was reloading his pistol's magazine round by round, each bullet making a loud click as it settled into place. His eyes were unfocused, staring through the truckbed, reloading by reflex. Anna studied his face as the truck pulled back onto the interstate. She'd seen that expression twice before: once when Mason had to hold off an attack by NSA agents at the safehouse in Washington, and once more when he'd fought Sawyer in the catacombs beneath the city.

Mason was running on autopilot, and so far, every time she'd seen him in that mode, people had died.

☆ ☆ ☆ ☆ ☆

It didn't take long for the truck to reach the spot where the Land Rover had crashed. Even though it was twilight, Mason told Trev to leave the headlights off so any survivors of the wreck wouldn't be alerted to their presence. When they were half a mile away and the tipped-over Land Rover was visible in the distance, Mason had Trev pull over and stop.

Mason jumped out of the bed, carrying with him only his equipment belt and pistol. Anna watched him as he walked toward the crash site. Trev opened the driver's side door to accompany him, but Mason spun around upon hearing the sound and pointed—

simply pointed—at the truck. Trev nodded slowly and sank back into his seat, content to allow Mason to run this one solo.

Anna, on the other hand, wasn't as willing. She jumped out of the truckbed and ran to catch up to Mason.

"What are you doing?" she asked as she came up alongside him.

Mason didn't answer for a moment. He simply frowned, swatted at a mosquito that was buzzing near his face, and continued his steady walk.

"What are you going to do?" Anna asked again, this time with more force.

"I'm going to do what I'm supposed to do in this kind of a situation," Mason said. "I'm going to interrogate my enemy."

"Not like this, you're not," Anna said, shaking her head. "You're in a bad place. You're going to overreact, you might—"

Mason moved like lightning.

He pulled his combat knife free from its sheath, grabbed Anna by the throat, and held the point of the blade less than an inch from her eye. She froze, stiffening up, and felt fear uncoil itself in her gut like an unwelcome alien presence.

"I am going to interrogate my enemy," Mason repeated. He said it slowly, word by word, still holding the knife to Anna's eye. "And you are *not* going to interfere."

Anna watched the point of the knife dance in front of her eyes for a moment, swallowed, and nodded slightly. "All right, Mason. Have it your way."

Mason let go of the doctor without another word, sheathed his knife, and continued his walk. Instead of retreating to the truck, Anna found herself following behind him. When Mason glanced over his shoulder at her, she was quick to explain herself.

"I won't get in the way," she said. "But I do want to be there. You need backup. Just in case."

Mason turned away from the doctor and lengthened his strides, boots crunching on the gravel shoulder. Though Anna couldn't see it, he quirked a smile.

"All right, Doc," he said. He heaved a sigh as he walked. After a moment, he spoke to Anna over his shoulder. "Look, I'm sorry about the knife thing. It's just that I—"

"I know," Anna interrupted. "It's been a bad day, and for you, it's probably reflex at this point. It's all right. No harm done."

Mason nodded, hanging his head a bit.

The pair made it to the crashed Land Rover. It still lay on its side, and the engine was still sputtering smoke. The driver's body was still strapped into its seat. Anna knelt in the grass and looked through the shattered windshield at the body.

"Looks like your shots killed this one," she said, staring at the bullet wounds in the man's chest.

"Yeah," Mason said, standing behind Anna with his pistol drawn. "But where's the gunner?"

The former NSA agent walked a slow circle of the vehicle, his head cocked slightly to the side, and studied the ground in the dwindling light. He found what he was looking for on his second revolution: a bit of blood staining a blade of grass a rust brown. He picked up another bloodspot a few feet away, and began to follow the trail, moving at a slow, measured pace, eyes fixated on the grass for clues.

The blood spatters were far enough apart from one another to convince Mason that the shooter—the man who had killed Julie— was in good enough shape to have walked away from the crash, but the blood also told Mason that the man was injured. He wouldn't have gone far.

The blood led up to the interstate, and Mason walked halfway across the pavement, following the trail, before he froze in place. He stared off at the thicket of trees and bushes that grew up on the far side of the interstate. Anna, who was watching from the side of the Land Rover, sucked in her breath.

Whenever Mason froze in place, Anna heard an old rhyme play in her head: '*By the pricking of my thumbs, something wicked this way comes.*' The ex-NSA agent was uncanny about spotting threats— not that it was any surprise when one considered his background.

Mason had spotted the shooter. The man lay against a tree on the far side of the interstate, a radio laying in the grass next to his left hand and an MP-5 laying next to his right. For the briefest of moments, Mason thought the man was already dead, but then he saw the man's head shift, lolling in place.

"Perfect," Mason whispered to himself. The shooter was dozing, waiting for a pickup. That meant that Mason had the jump on him— but it also meant he needed to hurry, if reinforcements were truly on the way. He picked up his pace, keeping his pistol aimed at the dozing man. His footfalls were careful heel-to-toe steps, making next to no noise. Anna followed as far as the edge of the interstate, close enough to see what was happening while still being far enough away to allow Mason to do his work uninterrupted.

Mason made it to within ten feet of the shooter before the man woke. Whether Mason had made some noise to alert him or if the man had just happened to wake up then was unclear, but Mason's reaction was immediate.

As the shooter reached for his weapon, Mason closed the distance in three long, swift strides, and kicked the weapon away from the man's hand. The shooter's other arm reached up toward his pistol belt, and Mason brought the same leg he'd used to kick away the weapon straight down on the shooter's forearm. Even from her vantage point several meters away, Anna could hear the snap of the man's wrist.

The shooter screamed out loud in pain, clutching at his left hand, now hanging limply from his wrist. Mason wasn't yet satisfied, and knelt, pinning the man's legs with his own and shoving the barrel of his pistol into the man's right eye, pressing in hard. The threat of violence went unspoken. If the shooter tried anything, all Mason would have to do was squeeze the trigger. The man stiffened up, froze in place, and for a moment, only the sound of the shooter's labored breathing and the distant calls of birds roosting for the night could be heard.

Then Mason went to work on the man, patting him down and reaching into pouches and pockets, tossing the contents over his shoulder, away from the man. He never took his eyes off of the shooter's face. Anna watched as the shooter's gear went flying over Mason's shoulder. A knife, a backup pistol, magazines, a compass, a map, a PDA not unlike her own—all of these things wound up in the grass a good distance from Mason and the shooter.

Only then did Mason speak to the shooter.

"My name is Gregory Mason," he growled, leaning in close to the shooter's face and tilting his head to one side. "Do you know me?"

The man didn't answer, and instead gritted his teeth and tried to ignore Mason and the pistol barrel being rammed into his eye socket.

"I asked you a question," Mason said. Now his voice was deadly calm. "Are you going to answer me? Do you know my name?"

The man still refused to say a word, looking off to the side.

Mason's free hand snaked out and grabbed the shooter's broken wrist. He squeezed hard, and the shooter screamed aloud in pain again.

"I don't like repeating myself," Mason said. "Do you know my name?"

"Yes, yes," the shooter said, gasping for breath. Sweat had beaded up on his forehead and ran down the sides of his face. "Gregory Mason. U.S. Marines. National Security Agency. Wanted for murder and treason. We were assigned to pick you up."

"And the woman standing behind me?" Mason pressed. "Do you know her?"

The man looked up at Anna, swallowed hard, and looked as if he was trying to decide whether or not to answer. He chose the latter, clamping his lips shut and looking away from Mason and Anna once more.

"Look," Mason whispered, leaning in close to the shooter's face. "You can answer all my questions and just ruin my evening—or you can play the hero and make my goddamn day, because by the time I'm through with you, your compadres won't even recognize you when they come to pick you up. And if they do, they'll need several little boxes to put all the pieces in—I shit you not. And you remember that little firefight we had earlier? You killed one of my friends in that fight. I'm out looking for blood and you're the only one around that I can bleed some. So one final time: do you recognize the woman standing behind me?"

This time the man turned his head to face Mason directly, and spoke in monotone, meeting Mason's gaze with a stony-eyed stare. "Waters, Desmond, agent with the FBI, 945-23-9199. And that's all you're going to get out of me, asshole."

Mason grinned. The grand old standard reply to interrogation: name, rank and organization, and Social Security number. It was as good as a "fuck you" to the person asking the questions.

"All right," he said, drawing the word out. "What did they teach you about interrogation in the FBI, Desmond?"

"Enough," spat Waters, nursing his broken wrist.

Mason, still grinning, slowly pulled free his combat knife and held it up in front of Waters' eyes so he could see it.

"I'm pretty sure they didn't show you *these* tricks at Quantico. Now, pay attention, Desmond, because this is going to hurt—a lot."

Mason leaned in over the shooter.

Anna had to look away as the FBI agent's anguished screams echoed across the interstate.

1947 hrs_

Anna had long ago left Mason and the shooter alone, and had wandered back across the interstate to sit in the grass and watch the last crescent of sun disappear over the horizon. Every now and then, a wail of pain drifted to her ears, and she did her best to ignore what was going on across the road from her.

Finally, the screams stopped, and a few moments later Mason appeared on the other side of the interstate, wiping his hands clean with a handkerchief. He tossed the bloodied cloth away and called out for Anna.

She pulled herself to her feet and walked over to stand with him. The shooter still lay against the tree, but he wasn't moving. His head hung limply against his chest and his shirt had been cut to pieces. Even from a distance Anna could make out the thin lines of cuts made by Mason's razor-sharp combat knife. He'd flayed the man alive, and done God knows what else to him while Anna had been out of their line of sight.

"I hope you're not going to give me a lecture," Mason grumbled.

"No," Anna said, furrowing her brow. "No lecture. I understand why you needed to do that."

"Thanks," Mason said. "I want you to know—it's not exactly what I call fun. But sometimes—sometimes that's the only way to get them to tell you what you need to know."

"What did he say?" Anna asked, staring at the shooter.

"Not too much, but enough to give us an edge," Mason replied. He seemed drained, spent. The rage in his eyes had faded, and he once again seemed to be his rational self. "He admitted he knew you, and that you were his primary target. You were supposed to be taken alive, just like we thought. Then I went into him about Sawyer, the state of things—got some interesting tidbits there."

Anna didn't respond at first. She was still staring at the motionless FBI agent slumped against the tree. "You killed him?"

"Oh," Mason said, raising his eyebrows. "Actually, no."

The ex-NSA agent turned and walked briskly back toward the shooter. When he'd gone about halfway, he stopped, drew his pistol, and put three rounds into the man's chest. Agent Desmond Waters jerked as the bullets struck home, then seemed to sigh as the life drained out of him. The corpse slumped down further against the tree trunk and slid off sideways into the grass.

Mason re-holstered his pistol and returned to Anna.

"Thanks for reminding me," he said, as nonchalantly as if he'd just forgotten to put a quarter into a parking meter. "He was dying, anyway. We should be getting along, now. I picked up all of his useful stuff. Did you check the Land Rover while I was busy with him?"

Anna admitted she hadn't.

"Doesn't matter," Mason said. "Probably not enough time to give it a search now. Let's get back to the truck."

As the pair walked, Anna cast a glance over her shoulder at the corpse of the shooter. "You said he was talking about the state of the world—what did he say?"

"We'll save that for when we get back to the others," Mason said, grimacing. "But I can tell you now that we were right about them wanting you. They're after you with a vengeance, Doc. There's a lot of RumInt floating around about you, apparently—"

"RumInt?" Anna interrupted.

"Rumor Intelligence," Mason explained. "The word on the street, as it were. You're becoming something of a post-pandemic urban legend."

"What do you mean?"

"I mean that Desmond back there thought you were carrying a cure for Morningstar on you," Mason said. "The guy actually thought that you were running off with the only cure to Morningstar."

"But that doesn't even exist," Anna protested as the pair walked along the edge of the interstate. "That's the dumbest thing I've heard since—"

"I know, I know, but if you look at it from his perspective—he thought he was going to save the world, and that you were some kind of villain out to make off with the cure and sell it to the highest bidder."

"Then it's twice as stupid," Anna seethed. "What the hell use is money in this world?"

Mason looked frustrated as he tried to think of a way to explain the dead shooter's motivations to Anna.

"He hasn't been living in the same world we've been in for these past few months," Mason said. "He's been living on the grounds of an Army National Guard station along with about a hundred other government employees—fighting off carriers every day and working on orders, just like before the pandemic hit, at least according to him."

"And those orders included finding me and bringing me back?" Anna pressed.

"Actually, according to Desmond back there, those are the only orders they have," Mason admitted. "That and stay alive."

The pair reached the pickup truck, where Matt, Juni, and Trev were waiting for them. The trio had spread out on the grass in the median, relaxing. Trev was smoking a cigarette, and Matt and Juni were sharing a can of Spam and crackers off to the side. When Trev spotted Mason and Anna approaching, he pulled himself to his feet and dusted off his hands.

"So what's the news? Did you get done what you wanted to get done?" Trev asked, folding his arms across his chest.

"I did," Mason said, nodding slowly. "I have some news for all of you, if you wouldn't mind paying attention for a few minutes. I've already told Anna about half of it, but the rest of you should hear it, too."

Matt and Juni looked up expectantly from their Spam, and Trev raised his eyebrows and leaned back against the pickup truck.

"Before you get into any of that," Trev said, cutting off Mason, "I think you owe us another explanation."

"About why we were attacked today," Mason said, nodding his head in agreement. "I know. I wanted to tell you earlier, but I was vetoed."

Mason glanced pointedly in Anna's direction, but she studiously ignored him.

"We're what you might call fugitives from the law," Mason explained.

"There's not much left of the law these days," Trev said. "You must have really pissed someone off."

"I did. I mean to say, *we* did," Mason admitted. "You know about Anna's background, her work on Morningstar, and the hope for a vaccine. We've told you all of that."

"Right," Trev said, nodding. "Heard it. Go on."

"So you know why she's a valuable commodity," Mason said. "She's one of maybe a handful of people on the planet with enough raw knowledge to be able to put together a vaccine. What's left of the Feds want her back—badly. She's not only one of their only hopes for a cure, she's studied the habits of the infected, their strengths and weaknesses—in other words, she's a human Morningstar strain Google. Just ask her any question."

"What's the incubation rate of Morningstar?" Matt shot out before Mason could continue. Mason was about to reprimand him and say that the last sentence hadn't meant to actually be followed up on, but Anna interrupted.

"Five to nine days if the initial contact is minimal. Incubation periods drop dramatically as the initial amount of virus introduced into the bodily system increases," Anna said, speaking without hesitation, the words flowing out of her one after another in rapid, articulate succession. "A major bite to a vein or artery can bring down the period of incubation to a matter of hours."

Matt looked over at Juni and shrugged. "All right, I'm sold on that point. Keep going, Mason."

"Anyway, there's one man in particular who wants her back. His name is Sawyer—he works for the NSA, like I did. In fact, he was on my team before the pandemic hit, along with one other agent— Derrick. He wasn't so bad a guy, but Sawyer—Sawyer could be a sadistic bastard. He really enjoyed his work. Took it seriously. Too seriously. Almost lived at the office. So when I went AWOL and busted Anna and Julie out of their holding facility a few months ago, it pissed off Sawyer something fierce," Mason said. "After all, they were both his cases."

The others were paying close attention, engrossed in the tale.

"We managed to get out of Washington all right, but we had to fight our way free," Mason said. "Sawyer was right on us the whole way. Once we got out of the city and into the country, it was easier to lose him, but he is one tenacious bastard. So far he's managed to catch up with us several times on the road and tried to take us down.

We've escaped each time, and until today, none of us were hurt or captured...or killed."

"So we've banded up with a bunch of wanted fugitives," Matt said, scowling. "That's fucking great. Now we have what's left of the Feds on our asses."

"Wait, wait," Mason said, holding up his hands. "That much is true, but we've got one thing on our side."

"And what's that?" Matt asked.

"Sawyer's gone rogue, officially," Mason said. "According to the shooter—the man I just 'talked' to back at the Land Rover—there's been a break in the Federal Government. Most of what remains is out to restore order, bring relief to the civilians—they're doing their job, in other words. Then there's a rogue faction, a breakaway group who knows about Anna's research as well as the studies done at the CDC and Deaucalion Co-op in Omaha. They want a cure, and they're perfectly willing to kill to get it. Here's our big problem with them: most of their information is nothing but rumor. Some of them think Anna's carrying a cure on her person, others think she has the blueprints for a cure on a disc she's keeping, and still others think she could whip up a batch of cure if they just captured her and put her in a lab."

"Which is ludicrous," Anna interjected. "We'd only just begun to look into a vaccine at USAMRIID. Maybe—and I stress maybe—the Deaucalion Co-op made some more progress than us. Of course we'll have to wait until we get to Omaha to find that out."

"So this is good news?" Matt asked sarcastically. "It's good that we've got a rogue faction of the surviving government out to kill us and take the Doctor here back to some lab?"

"Yes and no," Mason answered. "It's bad that they're after us, sure, but it's great to find out that they're a rogue faction."

"And why is that?" Matt pressed.

"Because," Mason said, "It means that they're just as busy fighting a civil war as they are chasing us down."

That quieted the group for a moment. The thought of what remained of the armed forces split down the middle, fighting one another instead of trying to clear cities and restore order was a sobering one.

"All right," Trev said after a moment had passed. "So here's an idea. Why don't we try and get in touch with the other faction, the one that's stayed legit? Maybe they could give us an escort, or some backup, or, hell, maybe just some information every now and then."

Mason shook his head.

"No," he said. "No, we're not getting on a radio unless we absolutely have to. We're running silent. Let the two halves figure it out on their own. Right now our best bet is to keep going forward with the plan—get to Omaha, hole up, and try to find that vaccine."

In the distance, the group heard the faint growl of a car engine. Mason looked over his shoulder in the direction of the sound.

"That's our cue to leave," he said. "That'll be the backup our friends in the Land Rover called before I sent them off the road."

"They'll find the crash," Trev said.

"Yes, they will," Mason agreed. "And they'll find the shooter I interrogated a few yards away from that. I wouldn't be surprised if Sawyer is with them."

Trev looked over with raised eyebrows. "Sawyer, the tenacious one? Why run? Why don't we head back that way and see about putting the fucker in the grave? That would solve a major problem of ours, wouldn't it?"

"It would," Mason agreed, "except Sawyer won't be alone. He's probably got a squad with him. I don't think we could put up much of a fight if we went back again. No, let's put some distance between us and him, and at top speed. We should probably take a couple of side roads for a while to throw him off, and avoid the Interstate."

"Easily done," Trev said, opening the driver's side door to the truck and fishing out the folded map Junko had been using earlier. "We'll plot ourselves out a nice backroad route. It'll take longer, and we might have to worry about fuel, but if it keep us from being jumped again it'll be worth it."

CHAPTER NINE
BOOGIE OUT OF DODGE

Abraham, Kansas
March 09, 2007
1521 hrs_

THE CLEANUP HAD GONE much more smoothly than Sheriff Keaton had imagined. The townsfolk had raided the clinic for surgical gowns, gloves and masks to keep hot blood off of themselves, and had pulled all of the infected bodies free from their tangled piles near the guard towers and crumpled fenceline.

A bonfire of human corpses had been formed on the far side of the field outside of town. Each time a new body was added, a splash of kerosene followed to make certain the body would catch. The infected weren't the only ones being thrown unceremoniously onto a burn pile. The bodies of the raiders who had tried to attack during the excitement at the front gate were all trucked across town and thrown onto the pile as well.

Sheriff Keaton had placed himself in charge of corpse disposal. He'd said that it was his duty to see to it that the people of Abraham were protected, and that extended to making sure plague-ridden bodies were properly taken care of. Sherman and Thomas volunteered their services wherever they could be used, and Keaton had sent them to oversee the repairs being done on the fence and main entryway into the town.

Krueger, Denton, and Brewster, who was still a little shaky, found themselves cleaning up the battlefield at the rear of the town, where the raiders had attacked.

"Oh, man, my head is killing me," Brewster lamented as he bent over to pick up a discarded pistol. He checked the chamber, unloaded the weapon, and dropped it into a duffel bag that hung over his shoulder. "All this movement isn't helping any."

"No one made you drink all that beer last night," Denton said, rooting through a small pack one of the raiders had dropped. "It's your own fault."

"Well, sure, but can't I bitch about it?" Brewster asked.

"No," came the simutaneous reply from Krueger and Denton.

The trio, along with several townsfolk, quickly cleared the area inside the town of debris and discarded bits of weaponry and equipment. Street sweepers were hard at work with hand-held brooms, sweeping up bits and pieces of shrapnel, tree bark, asphalt and brick that had been blown free during the firefight. Another crew was busily removing the blasted and warped section of fence that had been damaged in the grenade attack, and once they'd pulled it down and cast it aside, Krueger seized the opportunity to exit the town's perimeter and inspect the weapons and bodies left behind on the wooded hillside.

Behind him followed Denton, nudging at what few bodies were left over with the toe of his boot and occasionally stooping to add a bit of useful equipment to his slung duffel.

"Look at this, man," Krueger called out over his shoulder. "Come on, check this out."

Denton, furrowing his brow, jogged over to where Krueger knelt next to a large weapon on a bipod. Laying next to the weapon was a raider whose head had met a bullet.

"So?" Denton asked, shrugging. "Dead guy and his gun. Grab the weapon and let's go."

"No, no, man, this is U.S. Army issue," Krueger said, hefting the weapon in his arms. "It's an M-249 Squad Automatic Weapon. We call her the SAW. Where the hell did they get their hands on a piece like this?"

"Probably looted it off of some dead soldiers," Denton shrugged.

"Yeah, maybe, but then look down there," Krueger said, pointing downhill to another firing position. An identical M-249 lay there, ammo half-expended. "These guys are really well armed for a gang of bandits. Did you see the other weapons they were carrying?"

"Wasn't really paying attention," Denton admitted. "I was kind of busy not getting shot."

"Most of them were using AK-47's, but almost all of their pistols are Berettas—same issue we got in the Army."

"So they knocked over an Army supply convoy. At least they don't have these guns anymore—they're in our hands now."

"Yeah, but...I don't know, it still seems weird that they came by all this nice hardware," Krueger said. "Never mind. It's probably nothing."

"Hey, guys," Brewster called from the other side of the fence. He was sitting on what remained of the brick wall, looking miserable. "My duffel's full. Does that mean I can drop it off at Keaton's office and go to sleep?"

Krueger and Denton glanced at one another and shook their heads.

"Sure, Brewster, why not?" Denton said, chuckling. In a softer tone, he added to Krueger, "That's it for Brewster and drinking. He's cut off."

"Yep, I hear that," Krueger replied, grinning.

As Brewster wandered off in the direction of the Sheriff's office, Denton and Krueger continued their cleanup of the battlefield. A pile of weaponry was growing steadily on the lawn nearest the fence, firearms taken from both dead raiders and dead defenders. A separate pile of magazines and ammunition was growing just as steadily next to it. Every now and then, a townsperson would come walking up with one of the Sheriff's duffels, load up a bagfull of the gear, and head back across town to deposit it in Keaton's armory.

Krueger and Denton worked together to toss a body through the breach in the fence, where another pair of townsfolk were waiting to load the corpse onto an electric cart and take it across Abraham to the burn pile.

Denton counted out, "One...two...three...heave!" The body arced through the breach and landed in a crumpled heap on the other side of the fence. The townsfolk got to work hefting the body onto the cart, and Denton and Krueger went back to searching the battlefield.

Denton wandered off to the side, using a long stick to push aside leafy branches to check for bodies or discarded equipment. Krueger, a little winded from throwing the heavy body and toting the weapons back and forth, huffed and puffed his way up the rise to where the corpse of the machine-gunner lay. He knelt next to the corpse, pushed it over so it lay on its back, and began rifling through pockets.

He pulled out a few folded pieces of paper, glanced at them, and tossed them over his shoulder. A compass went into one of his pockets, as did a combat knife. The dead machine-gunner had also been wearing a watch—a nice, rubberized number with a built-in calendar and a quality wriststrap. Krueger pulled it off the dead man's wrist and slipped it onto his own. No use worrying about what the dead man would have thought. As he was adjusting his new timepiece, a bit of discolored grass on the far side of the hill attracted his attention.

Krueger squinted at it, then stood to get a better view. It wasn't a discolored bit of foliage after all—it was the tip of a dead man's boot, sticking up above the wild grass. Curious, Krueger slid carefully down the short embankment and trudged through the knee-high weeds to where the body lay.

The raider had been shot high in the chest—in fact, the round looked as if it had gone in just above the man's collarbone and right out his back. The considerable pool of blood under the corpse and soaking through the dirt around it told Krueger that the raider had bled to death.

"Not a pretty way to go, my friend," Krueger murmured, looking the man over. Something struck him as odd. Though the man was armed with a pistol, Krueger couldn't locate a rifle anywhere nearby. So far, all the raider bodies they'd searched had a matching rifle lying nearby. The men had been very well-armed. So why was this one fellow near the back lines carrying only a pistol and a backpack?

For a moment, Krueger thought he'd discovered the body of the bandits' leader. He just as quickly discounted the idea. The description Keaton had given them of the raiders' leader didn't match this corpse. The body was that of a short, wiry man in his mid-30's—almost the exact opposite of Herman Lutz's characteristics.

So what the hell was the guy doing way back here? Krueger wondered. From the look of things, the man had tried to get a view of the battle and had been hit by an errant round—piss poor luck on the raider's part. All the evidence pointed to this man being a very important part of the overall battle plan for the raiders. He'd been kept on the back lines, supposedly safe from fire, and he'd only been armed with a pistol, meaning that they hadn't expected him to do much fighting.

Krueger flipped the corpse up on its side. The body was still wearing a heavy hiker's backpack, and Krueger pulled out his knife, slicing the straps clean from the corpse's shoulders. The pack came free easily, and Krueger stood it on its end, unzipping the top and looking inside.

His eyes widened, and he froze in place. His left hand, still holding his combat knife, shook a bit as Krueger slowly backed away from the pack, still at a crouch, his hands held out in front of him as if to ward off the backpack. Once he was a good fifteen feet away, he relaxed, turning and jogging back up the rise.

"Denton!" Krueger called out from the top of the hill.

Below, busy dragging a body out of a bunch of thick brush, Denton looked up. "What is it? I'm busy here."

"Hey, uh, look," Krueger said, casting nervous glances behind himself at the backpack. "We have a little problem here. Actually, it's a pretty big problem and I'm not sure how to deal with it, so, uh, we'd better get Sherman over here. You still have your radio on?"

"What kind of problem?" Denton asked, dropping the body he was dragging and turning to face Krueger. "More raiders? Shamblers coming this way?"

"Ah, no," Krueger said. "Look, just get on your radio and get Sherman over here and tell him to bring Keaton and anyone who knows anything about bombs."

"Bombs?!" Denton said, eyes widening. "We're going to blow up?! What kind of bomb?"

"Radio!" Krueger shouted, pointing at the gadget on Denton's epaulette.

"Oh, right, right," Denton said, visibly shaken. He clicked the handset and made the call.

✵ ✵ ✵ ✵ ✵

There were a number of people gathered near the Sheriff's office. Most had come to drop off bits and pieces of gear they'd collected from the dead raiders, but some had formed a circle around Krueger's

discovery: a brown hiking pack that was crammed to the seams with plastic explosive.

As it turned out, none of the explosives were set to detonate. They'd found det cord, blasting caps and a plunger in one of the pack's other pockets. The plastic explosive was inert. Just the same, Keaton and Sherman kept the curious onlookers at bay while Thomas and Krueger emptied the contents of the pack onto a folding table brought out of the office just for this purpose.

"Jesus Christ," Krueger said, as he pulled the last brick of explosive out of the pack. He and Thomas had formed a neat stack of brown-paper-wrapped plastic explosives on the table. Each brick weighed around a pound, and they had pulled fifteen of the bricks from the bag. "That's one shitload of explosives."

"What is it, though?" Keaton asked, folding his arms and turning his back on the pressing crowd momentarily. "C-4?"

"Worse," Thomas growled, picking up one of the bricks and reading the fine print on the underside. "Semtex."

"Semtex? Isn't that military?" crowed one of the onlookers.

"No, not quite," Sherman said, leaning in close to inspect the blocks. "It's used commercially, too, but the military does use it. Strange, though—it has to be imported from the Czech Republic. It's normally relegated to special operations, at least militarily. A very powerful explosive, and there's pounds of it here. Enough to..."

Sherman let his voice trail off.

"What?" Keaton pressed.

"Well, I was going to say, it's near enough to blow up a town," Sherman concluded, then shrugged.

The crowd of interested onlookers took an unconscious step backwards from the table and quieted.

Keaton nodded to himself, picking up a brick of the explosive and examining it for himself. "Yeah, that'd be Herman's style. Come in, blow up a few of our most useful buildings, then get back out—bloody our noses, like I said."

"So that was the whole plan," Krueger said, piecing together the battle in his mind. "Send the infected as a distraction, penetrate the town's defenses as we're distracted, plant the bombs, get back out, and blow half the town sky-high. That's brutal."

"Actually, it's almost exactly what you soldiers did to Herman and his raiders the other night," Keaton mused. "He probably thought of it as poetic justice."

"Well, why don't you ask him?" said a voice in the crowd. The townsfolk parted to let through Deputy Willis. He looked haggard and worn, and sported a fresh bandage on his forearm.

"What do you mean?" Keaton asked.

"I'm just coming from the town clinic," Wes said, holding up his arm. "Got myself caught on a piece of that torn wire in the fence and thought I'd better get it cleaned up. All the wounded are there and Miss Barrington and that Rebecca Hall girl are trying to treat them all. Anyway, I'm sitting there waiting for one of them to check out my cut and I look over and see fucking Herman Lutz laying in one of the beds, dead to the world."

"Are you serious?" Keaton pressed, excited. "Lutz was one of the attackers, and we got him alive?"

"Alive? Mostly," Wes said. "The guy took a couple of bullets, but it wasn't fatal. They—Nurse Barrington and Hall, I mean—gave him a sedative to knock him out since he was apparently cussing up a storm and trying to leave."

"Well, shit on me," Keaton said, awed. "We got their leader."

This set the townsfolk gathered around to murmuring amongst themselves. As Keaton and Willis conferred, the murmurs grew into victorious whoops and shouts, and the little crowd dispersed to take the good news to their friends and neighbors.

"This'll mean the end of those raiders," Keaton said, grinning widely.

"The Lutzes were the glue," Willis agreed. "They were the ringleaders. Now George is dead and Herman's in our clinic, strapped down to a bed. We can transfer him to the jail tomorrow, at least that's what Nurse Barrington says."

Keaton seemed speechless. He grinned, put his hands on his hips, and nodded to himself.

"I don't know what to say," Keaton stammered after a moment. "Aside from the infected, those raiders were the biggest threat to our survival out here. Now—that's it, they're done with. Whatever or whoever remains out of their band will probably disperse after this. We'll have our fields back, and it'll be safer to travel. Seems like a dream come true after these past few months."

Wes nodded in agreement. "I feel like we've just been paroled—we can go out in the world again if we need to."

Keaton turned to Sherman, Thomas and Krueger. "We couldn't have done it without your help. If you want to, I'm sure you're welcome to stay in Abraham. The offer goes for any of you. You're friends here."

"I thank you, Sheriff, but I need to get myself back on the road," Sherman said. "I told an old friend I'd meet her in Omaha."

"Omaha," Keaton drawled. "Are you sure you wouldn't rather stay, Sherman? If what you told us about all the major cities is true, Omaha is probably a dead zone. You might be driving to your own death."

"Just the same, Keaton, I told her I'd be there," Sherman said.

Next to Sherman, Thomas nodded slowly in agreement.

"Look, uh, I hate to be the prying type, but I just have to know—why turn down a relatively safe town to head out to what could be your own death?" Keaton asked. "I mean, I'm not offended you're turning down the offer or anything, but I just don't see your motivation."

"Hope," Sherman said, smiling gently at the Sheriff. "*Hope*, Keaton. That's why I'm going to Omaha. My friend—the one I promised I'd meet—is a doctor. She thinks she has a chance at creating a vaccine using a facility in Omaha."

"A vaccine?" Keaton repeated, his eyebrows rising. "Now, *that's* something worth trying and dying for."

"Exactly my thoughts," Sherman said.

"Do you really think you're going to find it? The vaccine, I mean? Or even your friend the doctor?" Willis asked.

"I don't know," Sherman admitted, "but the *chance* is there and I can't give it up. We've got to try."

"Well, the offer is open to you and your people," Keaton said. "Anyway, you'll have time to think it over. I'm sure the people are going to want to celebrate this victory, too."

"Oh, another night of carousing about Abraham, a night on the town," Krueger chuckled. "Now *that* I'm up for. *Especially* if we can get Brewster to start drinking again."

2031 hrs_

Keaton's prediction about the town wanting to celebrate had come true. He'd dismissed a sulky Deputy Willis to his guard tower post just as the festivities were warming up. Someone had brought out an old iron grill and set it up over a campfire on the lawn of the town park and was busily barbecueing fresh venison, shot earlier that afternoon. Eileen and her husband had brought their pub outside—or at least rolled a few metal kegs out to the park and tapped them. One of Abraham's eldest residents, a man who told everyone to just call him Buck, sat in a rocking chair near the grill playing a fiddle without a care in the world. The town's younger folks clapped and danced in time to the music, and the smell of roasting meat and frothy beer drifted across the entire gathering.

Sherman and his survivors were once again present, only this time they were treated less as conquering heroes and more as comrades in arms. The distinction was actually a pleasant one—they all felt accepted. It was something none of them had felt in months.

Sherman sat near the edge of the party on a park bench, sipping at a pint of Eileen's bitter lager and laughing at the antics of the people arrayed in front of him.

Katie tried to drag Ron into a dance, wounded leg and all, and eventually the pair worked out a deal where Katie danced normally and Ron stayed in one spot, hopping up and down on his good leg and trying not to look too foolish.

Jack and Mitsui were sitting at a picnic table with several of the townsfolk, sampling the barbecued venison. Mitsui hadn't had the pleasure of barbecue before, and when Jack and the townsfolk figured that out the slightly built Japanese man suddenly found himself barraged with advice in the form of different bottles of sauces and which bits and pieces of the meat were best. He barely understood a word of it, but faithfully sampled each of the platters set in front of him, bowing and thanking each of the townsfolk in turn.

Brewster, fully recovered from his hangover, was sipping as lightly on his pint as was Sherman but didn't allow his lack of drunkenness to get in the way of having fun. He tried to flirt with some of the town's young women, but was rebuffed each time.

Krueger, on the other hand, leaned back against a tree and silently drank his beer—and was bombarded with requests from those same young women to dance with them. He turned down each invitation politely.

"What the fuck, man?" Brewster asked, throwing up his arms in exasperation after the fifth girl walked away from the pair. "I'm trying my best and I'm not getting shit, and you're doing shit and getting the best. What's going on here?!"

"You ever see Airheads?" Krueger asked around a sip of beer. Brewster shook his head. "Old comedy movie. Anyway, what I'm doing is 'the quiet cool.' You just lean back, act confident, pretend like nothing around you is worth your attention, and man, it drives the ladies nuts."

"So why do you keep saying no?" Brewster asked, putting his hands on his hips and glaring.

"Adds to the act," Krueger said. "Eventually word'll get around that there's this mysterious soldier who can't be charmed, even by half a dozen young ladies, and when that happens, the real beauties will start swinging by to try and get me to dance. You'll see."

"Fuck you," Brewster said, holding up a middle finger.

Denton was maintaining his distance, slowly circling the town park with his camera hanging around his neck. He'd dragged it out earlier in the day and had taken shots of the battlefield, and was now taking another opportunity to document his journey. Every now and then his flash would light up the park as he took photos of the dancing crowd, Buck the fiddle-player, a pair of young lovers on a bench, and one of Brewster glaring at Krueger, who was surrounded by adoring women.

Rebecca was nowhere near the celebration. She was still at the clinic, along with Nurse Barrington and Mbutu Ngasy. The three were doing their best with minimal supplies to treat the wounds caused by the day's violence. Two of the townsfolk had already died of their wounds, and they were put in the morgue until the next morning, when they would be buried. That still left a full dozen in the ward, and there was no real doctor anywhere nearby. Nurse Barrington was the closest thing the town had.

Off on the border of town, Deputy Willis puffed on a cigarette— one of the few remaining in town—and stared out over the open fields. Behind him he could hear the music and the laughter of the party, and grimaced again at having to pull guard duty while everyone else enjoyed themselves. Out across the field, however, stood a stark comparison to the celebration in Abraham: a pile of blackened and charred bodies, smoke still rising off of their cracked and deformed limbs.

Let that stand as a warning, Wes thought as he looked at the pile. *Anyone coming into Abraham from now on will have to pass by that shitty sight. Let 'em. I don't want to have to shoot another human being as long as I live, and if a pile of burned corpses is the only guarantee I can get, I'll take it.*

Wes spat off the side of the guard tower and rested his arms on the ledge, sighing heavily.

Near the center of town, close enough to the park to hear the music and smell the barbecue, Jose Arctura was busy in his shop. He had his end of a bargain to fulfill. His daughter was off enjoying the celebration, but he had closed himself up in his garage and was busy surveying the vehicles that Sherman and his friends had brought in.

Jose looked over the sedan, grimaced, and wrote it off as a piece of junk that wouldn't last much longer.

The black pickup that Sherman and the rest had taken from the raiders was in nearly perfect shape. A few bullet holes had dinged up the exterior, but when Jose looked under the hood, he saw that everything was in working order and nodded to himself, allowing the hood to slam down. He moved on to the utility truck, the largest of the three vehicles.

"You're in a sorry state, friend," Jose said, running his hand along the side of the boxy truck. "But we'll see if we can get you back into working order...or better than working order."

Jose turned to a cinderblock wall covered in hanging tools and equipment. He pulled on a welder's mask, freed his torch from a tangle of cables, and turned to face the utility truck. He sparked the torch and adjusted the flame, then lowered the mask over his face.

"All right," Jose said, approaching the truck with the blue-flamed torch in hand. "Let's see what I can do."

Long into the night the sound of roaring tools and the clang of metal on metal rang out from Jose Arctura's bodyshop, and didn't cease even after the party had ended and the good people of Abraham had gone, full, sated and happy, to their beds.

March 10
1032 hrs_

The town was slow to awaken the next morning, which was just as well. The weather dawned warm and humid, and low-lying clouds sprinkled the area with a steady drizzle. By the time midmorning had passed, the clouds were just beginning to break up and the first rays of direct sunlight began to shine through.

Deputy Willis had spent all night in his guard tower, and midmorning saw him leaning against one of the rebar supports, eyelids heavy and drooping. The steady clank-clank of booted footsteps on the ladder leading up roused him from his doze, and as he turned he saw Sherman pulling himself up into the tower, holding a styrofoam cup in one hand.

"Morning," Sherman said, offering the cup to Willis. Wes accepted it and sniffed at it.

"Coffee?" Willis asked. "Haven't had a cup of this in about a month."

"It's instant," Sherman warned. "Keaton broke it out at the station this morning, said we could all use a little treat, even if it is only Sanka."

"Here's to instant, then," Wes said, taking a sip from the cup. He grimaced, but swallowed it down. "It's not decaf, is it?"

"Not at all," Sherman chuckled. "So it's not a total loss. You've been out here all night?"

Wes nodded around another sip of coffee. "Keaton isn't big on set schedules for us deputies. He'll probably have a replacement around for me before noon. We tend to pull down about twelve hour shifts."

"So you missed the party last night," Sherman said.

"Yeah," Willis shrugged. "No biggie. Someone had to stay on duty. By the way, I think you might want to swing by Jose's shop sometime today. I was sitting up here at four in the A.M. and I could still hear him banging away in there. I don't know what he's up to but you might want to take a look."

"Well, he told us it would probably take a couple of days before he finished. Jack—wait, did you meet Jack?" Sherman asked.

"Taller fellow, brown hair, about 180?" Willis asked.

"That sounds like him," Sherman nodded.

"I think so," Willis said. "What about him?"

"Jack's a contractor, handy with a torch. Said he was going over there when he woke up today to see if he could help. I'll trust him to keep an eye on things," Sherman explained.

"I'm not suggesting you need to keep an eye on Arctura or anything," Willis was quick to explain as he took another sip of his coffee. "It's just that from the sound of the place he's tearing right into that job—and from what I can remember before the pandemic, if a mechanic tells you it's going to take a couple days what he really means is a couple weeks."

Sherman frowned and sighed. "Well, I can't have that. I wanted to get on the road within the next day or so."

"Good thing that Jack guy's going over there, then," Wes said. "He'll be able to move him along, keep the pace up. Though I'm betting that Jose's grateful enough for what you did for him that he'll keep up his end of the bargain."

"I'm hoping so, too," Sherman said. "Well, I'm going to head over to the Sheriff's office again and see what else is brewing—besides bad coffee."

Willis chuckled. "Thanks for stopping by. And remind Keaton when you see him that I've been up here since last night."

"I will."

☆ ☆ ☆ ☆ ☆

Sherman was greeted by the sound of raucous laughter as he entered Sheriff Keaton's station. Three of the deputies as well as Thomas and Krueger were gathered around the coffee pot sharing stories, and Keaton was in the middle of a tale about one of his small-town criminals.

"So he's just robbed Ruby's convenience store just outside of town," Keaton said between chuckles, "And I'm driving out there to respond when I pass this guy jogging in the opposite direction—completely naked!"

The deputies, who had heard this story before, all stifled their laughter. Krueger and Thomas looked at one another incredulously.

"Don't tell me it was the robber," Krueger said.

"Yeah, yeah, it was," Keaton said, trying hard not to laugh. "He's carrying a bag full of cash in one hand and his clothes in the other—only thing he's wearing is a pair of tennis shoes. So I stop him and he says, 'What's the problem, Sheriff? I'm just out for an evening jog.'"

One of the deputies lost control at that point and laughed. "Tell them the best part, Keaton."

"Turns out," Keaton went on, "that the guy realized that Ruby would call us and tell us which way he'd gone and what he was wearing—so—so," —Keaton choked back laughter— "He thought that maybe if he took off all his clothes we wouldn't able to identify him!"

Even Thomas cracked a smile as the room burst into laughter.

"Oh, morning, Sherman," Keaton said as he noticed the older man entering the room. "We were just swapping war stories from before the pandemic. Got any?"

"Tons," Sherman said. "but I thought we'd get to taking care of some business before the day's half gone."

"Oh, right, right," Keaton said. "The weapons—you're right, come on, let's get that taken care of."

The Sheriff and Sherman had come to an agreement about the weapons they'd seized from the raiders. Since Sherman's group was working with a ragtag assortment of firearms, Sherman had asked if they could pick and choose a few from the raiders' leftovers. Keaton was quick to agree, since his office's small armory room was now overflowing with rifles, pistols, and spare ammunition.

Keaton led Sherman down the hall to the armory, unlocked the door with a key that hung on a small ring from his belt, and allowed Sherman to enter, followed closely by Thomas, Krueger, and the deputies.

The Sheriff's regular weapons store was neatly arranged along one wall: a rack filled with 12-gauge pump-action shotguns and a pair of high-caliber rifles. Directly beneath that was a pistol locker filled with standard-issue Berettas and outmoded .38 revolvers. Across from these neatly-stored firearms was a hodgepodge assortment of the weapons they'd seized.

Most of the long arms were AK-47 assault rifles, but there were a few hunting rifles thrown into the mix as well for longer-range work. The pistols that had been seized were identical to the ones Keaton had locked away: nine-millimeter Beretta 92FS. Stuffed carefully into a steel locker secured with a padlock were the blocks of Semtex explosives, and on top of that locker lay one of the M-249 Squad Automatic Weapons. Conspicuously missing was its mate.

"Where's the other machinegun?" Sherman asked, furrowing his brow. "We did get two, didn't we?"

"Oh, yeah, we sure did," Keaton said, nodding. "About seven or so this morning Jose and your man Jack showed up and begged it off of us—they didn't ask for any ammunition so I didn't see why not. Besides, the way I see it, half of this stuff is yours anyway. Right of conquest and all that."

"Now what the hell are they doing with a SAW?" Sherman wondered out loud. He shrugged and filed the thought away to be addressed later. "All right, let's get down to business. Thomas, you have our weapons list?"

"Yes, sir," Thomas growled, pulling a neatly folded sheet of paper from a chest pocket and unfolding it one-handed. He looked down at it and read off the manifest. "We came in with two rifles, .30-06, scoped. One carbine, Ruger M-14. One Smith and Wesson Revolver, .22. Four pistols, assorted makes, nine-millimeter. One pistol, Cobra, .380. One shotgun, double-barreled, Remington, and one revolver, Smith and Wesson, .357."

"Al lright," Sherman nodded. "Now, how do we go about this switch-out?"

"Well," Keaton said, rubbing his chin, "I honestly don't care. Most of this town is self-armed. Second Amendment and all that. And we don't really need all this firepower sitting in here. I'd say, leave us whatever you don't want or need and take whatever you think you could use—except for one thing."

"What's that?"

"That other machinegun, the SAW—leave that one to us. I'd like to mount it in one of the guard towers," Keaton said.

Sherman nodded in agreement. "Sounds fair to me. All right, Thomas, let's get to picking and choosing."

The next few minutes were spent placing firearms into cardboard boxes and shuffling them around the room as the two parties worked through the armory. Sherman turned all of his group's pistols over to Keaton, with the exception of the .357, which Krueger insisted he wanted to keep as a backup. The motley assortment was replaced with the bandits' Berettas. Their ammunition was taken as well—an entire box full of magazines and bullets. Even so, Keaton was left with a surplus of ammo.

Krueger also insisted on keeping his .30-06, a decision Sherman didn't fight in the least. Krueger was the best shot the group had, and he wanted him to have a long-range rifle in his hands. Keaton must have been feeling generous, because he tossed in the night-vision scope he'd lent Krueger for the night raid. The rest of the longarms were turned over to Keaton, and Sherman took one Kalashnikov for each of his people minus two. He managed to wrangle two of Keaton's pump-action shotguns, one for Brewster and one for Jack.

"That'll about do it," Sherman said, surveying the boxes full of weapons he'd procured and double-checking to make certain he'd gotten ammunition for each.

"One thing left to talk about," Keaton said, holding up a finger to forestall Sherman's exit.

"What's that?"

"The semtex," Keaton said, pointing at the sealed locker in the corner. "I have to tell you, I have no use for it whatsoever and having it in here kind of makes me feel unsafe."

"The stuff's perfectly safe!" Krueger protested. "It's inert unless you add heat and pressure—then it blows. Hell, you can almost play with it like silly putty—"

"Krueger, if I hear you refer to semtex as silly putty again I'm going to have you on shit details until you can draw Social Security," Thomas growled, fixing Krueger with a stare. Krueger's talk fell off and he shrugged, hands in his pockets.

"I was just saying," Krueger protested, looking a little guilty.

"Just the same, I don't really want it. Got any use for it?" Keaton asked Sherman.

"No," Sherman admitted. "I don't really have anything to blow up. Thomas? Anything to blow up?"

"Nothing at the moment, sir," Thomas replied.

"I guess we don't need it, either, Sheriff," Sherman said. "Sorry."

"Well, just the same, I'd be much obliged if you'd take it with you. You never know—you might need it down the road and I really don't want it in my town," Keaton said. "Hell, you can dump the stuff over the side of a bridge if you want. Call it a personal favor, what do you say?"

Sherman shrugged. "I suppose so. Once the vehicles are fixed up we'll load it into one of the trucks and figure out something to do with it."

Keaton smiled and nodded in appreciation. "Oh, about that. I'll bet you're probably wanting to see if Jose's made any progress. I think you'll be surprised—the guy has a gift. He should be middle-management at Ford, not running some backwater garage in a little town like this."

"I actually would like to see what he's done so far," Sherman admitted. "Though I've heard it's bad luck to disturb an artist at work."

Keaton chuckled. "We'll see when we get there. If he's into his project, he won't even answer the door—but it's worth a shot. I'll meet you out front in one of the electric carts."

✮ ✮ ✮ ✮ ✮

The trip to Jose Arctura's shop took all of five minutes. Only Sherman and Keaton had come out to check on things. Thomas, Krueger and the deputies had remained behind to pull out the weapons and get them ready for transport.

The shop looked much the same as it had when Sherman had first seen it. It was still half-hidden on a side street, the sign was still humble and two-dimensional, and both garage doors were down and secured. The only change was in the spray-painted message on the facade. Instead of reading "closed" it had been covered over in paint and replaced with "open for business."

"Well, look at that," Keaton marveled, pointing at the paint.

"It's an encouraging sight," Sherman agreed.

The high-pitched whine and grind of a saw shearing through steel echoed from within, and every now and then a loud boom rang out. Sherman envisioned a sledgehammer hitting steel.

Sherman stepped out of the cart and walked around the front of it to approach one of the garage doors. He knocked politely, and when no one came to answer, he pounded his fist on the metal, causing the door to vibrate. From within, the sound of the saw cut off, and a moment later the side door to the garage opened and Jack appeared, careful to keep the door open just wide enough for him to stick out his head.

"Sherman!" Jack said with a grin, spotting the General. "Good morning. Come by to take a look at the progress?"

"Sure have," Sherman said, nodding.

"Well," Jack replied, an impish look crossing his features. "You can't."

"Can't?"

"Can't," Jack repeated. "It's a surprise."

"Surprise? I just wanted these damn things fixed up—tell me the truth, you've got them all torn up in there, don't you?"

Jack looked guilty for a fraction of a second, just long enough for Sherman to pick up on it.

"You did!" Sherman said, pointing an accusing finger. "You've been taking the trucks apart! Oh, come on, Jack, we're supposed to be getting them put back together, not the exact opposite!"

"If you want to make an omelette you have to break some eggs," Jack said in his own defense. "Trust me, Frank, this is going to be worth it. Give us another day in here. Jose's already got both engines running and they're purring like a cat in a lap—now we're just making a few modifications. Twenty-four hours, General. Twenty-four."

"Keaton tells me you and Jose wrangled one of the M-249's from the armory this morning," Sherman pressed. "You want to let me know what that's about?"

Jack grinned once again. "Twenty-four hours, Frank."

Jack shut the door in Sherman's face and the older man could hear the sound of deadbolts sliding into place on the other side.

Sherman was left standing in the alley facing the shut door. Behind him, Keaton sat up on the cart, biting on the end of a cigarillo and chuckling.

"A few hours with Jose and your man Jack is already starting to act like him."

"Can't say I'm not curious," Sherman said, still eyeing the closed door in front of him. "I guess we'll just have to give them their day. In the meantime, we can get ready to hit the road again."

"Did you give any more thought to my offer?" Keaton asked from the cart.

"What, about staying?" Sherman asked. "I'm still set on getting to Omaha. I let my people know, though, so they've had a night to chew it over. I asked them all to meet me at Eileen's for lunch to discuss the matter."

"Well, it's coming up on noon now," Keaton said, glancing at his watch. "Want me to take you over there?"

"That'd save me a walk," Sherman agreed. "I'd be much obliged."

"Hop in," Keaton said, settling back down into the driver's seat. "I'll drop you off."

Eileen's was mostly quiet; only a couple of the locals had come in. Most of them were still at home, either sleeping off the effects of the party or relaxing. Sherman's group made up the largest bunch of customers, and Eileen was kept busy with them. They weren't drinking much of her bitter beer, but they weren't shy about ordering food. Eileen had a working kitchen in the back of her bar, complete with a jury-rigged woodstove oven. Most of the group were busy eating fresh scrambled eggs and sliced ham when Sherman entered and joined them.

Denton signaled for Eileen to bring Sherman his breakfast, and she vanished into the kitchen to fill the order. Sherman sank into his seat with a sigh and folded his hands on the table.

"Well," he started, "we have quite a bit to discuss today."

"Fire away, Frank," Denton said around a mouthful of scrambled eggs.

"First of all, I wanted to see how our wounded are doing. Gentlemen?"

Ron and Brewster swallowed their mouthfuls of food before commenting.

"Hand's doing fine, General," Brewster said, holding up his bandaged hand. He then pointed to the taped gauze on his cheek. "The nurse down at the clinic said the hit on my face'll leave a little scar but other than that, I'm in good shape."

"My leg still hurts like a bitch," Ron said. His crutch was leaned up against the table next to him. "Apparently it'll be a while before I can walk on it properly again. In the meantime I'm going to have to rely on the crutch."

"But it's healing?" Sherman pressed.

"That's the verdict," Ron agreed. "Healing nicely; it'll just take a little while before I'm back up to speed."

"What about you, Thomas?" Sherman asked, looking over at the Sergeant Major. Thomas hadn't made much of a fuss over his wounded arm. He'd allowed Rebecca to bandage it, and accepted a shot of antibiotics, but then simply donned a long-sleeved camouflage shirt over the gauze so the wound was invisible to the casual onlooker.

Thomas looked over at Sherman. "Arm's doing fine, sir."

"No pain, aches, anything like that?"

"No, sir."

Sherman grinned. "Don't lie, Thomas, it sets a bad example. We'll need you in your best shape out there. If you're hurting at all, get a shot of local anesthetic at the clinic."

Thomas looked left and right at the group, almost embarrased to have to admit such a thing. "It's a bit sore, sir. I'll stop by the clinic later."

"Excellent. Now, on to item number two. This is the big one," Sherman said. All eyes turned toward him. "Have you all given some thought to Sheriff Keaton's offer?"

"What, about staying in town?" Brewster asked around a mouthful of ham. "No offense to him, but fuck that, I'm headin' on to Omaha. I haven't come this far just to stop here."

"I'm in, too," Denton said. "Been with this ragtag group of screwups since Suez, and I'm not leaving now."

"Who the hell are you calling ragtag?" Krueger asked, narrowing his eyes at Denton. He looked back over at Sherman after a moment. "I'm in. I'm going, I mean. You could use me out there."

"Very good," Sherman said, nodding. "Mitsui?"

The Japanese man recognized his name and looked up from his food, a wide-eyed expression on his face. Jack was his usual translator through hand motions, and the contractor was truly feeling the language barrier. He was a clever sort, however, and figured from the context of what he'd just seen that he was being asked whether he was going or staying. He called on his meager supply of English to answer.

"Yes. I go," he said. "Omaha to go."

Sherman nodded and moved on down the line. "Ron? Katie? What are you thinking?"

There was a moment of silence as Ron and Katie looked at one another, then back at Sherman.

"We've talked it over, Frank," said Ron. "We've decided we're going to stay."

"You're not coming with us, man?" Brewster asked, a pained expression crossing his face. "We've come all the way from Oregon with you two. You sure you don't want to finish up the trip?"

"Yeah, we've looked at it from all the angles," Ron went on. Katie nodded silently in agreement with him as he spoke. "With my leg I'd just slow you down out there. Plus, we're not looking for anything more than a safe place to settle down and get on with our lives. We're thinking maybe this is the place we can manage that."

"I don't really want to stay behind and leave all of you," Katie said, speaking up for the first time, "but it really is the best thing we can do right now."

"That's just fine," Sherman said, sighing. "I hate to lose you two, but I wish you the best of luck here in Abraham. I'm sure they could use you here, too."

"What about Jack and Mbutu and Rebecca?" Denton asked. "Where are they?"

"Jack's over at Jose Arctura's shop," Sherman said, "working on our trucks, and Rebecca's still at the clinic with Mbutu treating the wounded. I'm pretty sure they'll want to come along—Jack and Mbutu, anyway, I'm not so sure about Rebecca."

"She has seemed pretty uptight recently," Denton said.

"Ever since the *Ramage*," Brewster agreed.

"We'll ask her and the others when we see them," Sherman said. "For now, let's just enjoy our breakfast. We've got another day here before we have to move out."

Eileen appeared at Sherman's elbow with a plate of food for him. He moved to the side to allow her to place the platter in front of him and dug in with the gusto of a hungry soldier once she'd left.

"So what are Jack and Jose doing to the trucks that's taking so long?" Denton asked.

"I'm not sure," Sherman said, slicing up his ham. "They're being a little secretive about it. Wouldn't let me see inside; said to come back in twenty-four hours. I have to admit I'm pretty curious. Keaton says Jose's got a bit of a gift with mechanics and we all know Jack's had experience with construction and the like. I'm wondering just what they're adding or removing from those trucks of ours."

"Just as long as they're road-worthy, I won't be complaining," Brewster chuckled.

March 11
1023 hrs_

Several of the townsfolk, including Mayor York, Sheriff Keaton and Deputy Willis had shown up to see off Sherman and his group. The previous day had been spent rounding up supplies, most of which had been happily donated by the citizens of Abraham. Thomas stood off to one side with a sheet of paper taking inventory. A lot of the donations included fresh vegetables and crusty, home-baked bread, and Thomas was already listing them in his head as perishable—the survivors would eat well for their first few days on the road, then it was back to canned rations and other unperishables.

Katie and Ron had shown up as well. They'd already been offered a small house back in the residential blocks. The owners had been among the victims of the pandemic, and the structure had stood empty ever since. The town didn't mind donating it to their two new residents.

Rebecca and Mbutu had both elected to come along, and stood with the rest of the group on the sidewalk, checking over their gear one last time to make certain they were ready to continue their journey. Packs were filled with food and clothing and strapped to backs over fresh clothing donated by Keaton. Weapons were distributed. Finally, all seemed to be in readiness—all that was missing were their vehicles.

After nearly an hour of waiting, the sound of Arctura's garage doors sliding open drew the attention of the assembled group. Jack appeared in the open doorway, a wide grin plastered on his face. He was covered in grime, oil and bits of debris, having been working nonstop on the vehicles for nearly two days alongside Jose.

"You guys are in for a treat," Jack said. He looked over his shoulder into the garage. "All right, Jose, bring her out!"

The sound of a truck engine revving echoed through the garage, and Jack stepped aside as Jose drove the utility truck out of the garage and into the street—except it could barely be called a utility truck anymore. It was somewhere in between its former incarnation and a tank.

The back end of it had been gutted and then reinforced, creating a wider, more comfortable space in the back. Firing slits had been cut in the sides and those had been protected with jutting steel mesh. The tires had been replaced with larger, off-road numbers, and the front grille had been armored with iron bars. A triangular-shaped device had been attached to the front of the truck that looked like some kind of a plow. Sherman realized that was exactly what it was— a way for the truck to push its way through abandoned cars or a horde of infected. A pair of swiveling spotlights had been attached on top of the cab, and every visible part of the truck had been armor-reinforced. A rusting metal cylinder jutted out from underneath the truck, and Sherman saw it was a fuel tank from the cab of an 18-wheeler. This, too, had been armor-reinforced, and, if Sherman had to guess, most likely doubled the fuel capacity of the truck.

Most conspicuous of all, however, was the gunnery turret that rested on the roof. The purloined M-249 sat there, welded into place on a swiveling tripod. Jack and Jose had cut out a hatch that could be opened and closed from within the rear of the truck, allowing an occupant to pop up through the roof and put his hands on the firepower waiting there.

Finally, the pair of grease monkeys had redone the camouflage paint job that Sherman and the others had slapped on weeks earlier, only they had managed to make it look halfway professional—the entire utility truck was done up in woodland camouflage, all flat paint with no shine. If Sherman didn't know better, he would have guessed it was an actual military vehicle.

"Holy shit," Brewster murmured from just behind Sherman. "I call gunner."

"Fuck you," Krueger riposted. "I'm the best shot here; I call gunner."

"Ah, but wait, we're not through yet," Jack said. "Wait here a second."

Jack vanished back into the garage. A moment later, a second engine revved and out pulled the raiders' truck. The vehicle had already been massive, a gas-guzzling behemoth, but Jack and Jose had managed to make it appear even larger.

The group's old pickup—which was sitting abandoned a few miles from Abraham near the original ambush site—had seen its bed reinforced so riders wouldn't be in danger of getting snagged by an infected as they passed by. That job had been held together with spit and duct tape. Jack and Jose had done one better.

Steel rebar had been threaded through the truck's metal frame, and used as supports for the aluminum siding that now ran up all four sides of the bed. The siding, which Jack commented had been found in the alley behind the shop, had been welded together and secured firmly to the steel rebar. Firing slits similar to those on the utility truck had been cut out of the armor, though there was no matching turret. The tires had been replaced with the same large off-road numbers on the utility truck, and the paint job had been changed from flat black to the professional-looking woodland camouflage they'd managed on the first vehicle.

"I have to say I'm impressed," Sherman said, grinning and folding his arms across his chest. "You two went above and beyond."

"Ah, but there's one final thing," Jack said. He walked over to the large rusting fuel tank on the utility truck and kicked it. The kick rang solid, and the group could hear fuel sloshing inside. "Jose siphoned the gas out of a few of the impounded vehicles behind his shop and filled up both tanks with it. We've got about a 250-mile range with what we've got in the tanks, and..."

Jack let his sentence trail off as he walked around to the side of the utility truck and popped open one of the tool lockers there. Inside were a number of red plastic gas cans, all full.

"...we've got enough spare to get us the rest of the way to Omaha, provided we don't have too many more obstacles along the way."

"Well, if there's one thing I've learned since the pandemic, it's that there's always an obstacle," Sherman said. "Still, hell of a job. I don't know how to thank you both—you especially, Jose."

"It was my pleasure," said the mechanic, grinning. "You gave me back my daughter. You come back here anytime in the future, I'll fix you up for free. I'll never be able to truly pay you back for what you did for me."

"We'll consider this a bargain struck and filled," Sherman said, nodding at the vehicles. "The slate's clean."

Jose chuckled. "If that's the way you want to think of it, sure, but in my mind, I still owe you."

Sherman turned to the gathered group.

"All right, gentlemen and ladies, it's time we got on our way. Mount up!"

The group got busy, loading the supplies and tossing full packs into the vehicles. Sherman turned to Keaton.

"Thanks for taking us in, Sheriff. I have to say, we've had a good time here, except for the whole battle thing," Sherman chuckled. "All the same, it's been a pleasure, and I hope I'll see you again down the road sometime."

"Maybe you will, Sherman," Keaton said. "We'll see."

The men shook hands and Sherman moved down the line to where Ron and Katie were standing. Rebecca was busy saying goodbye to Katie, who she had become rather close with over the past few months. They were teary-eyed and looked involved, so Sherman turned to Ron first.

"Glad you came along with us this far, Ron. We'll miss you out on the road," Sherman said.

"Same here, General. If it wasn't for you, we'd be dead in Hyattsburg by now," Ron said, shaking Sherman's hand. "Like Jose said, we owe you. If you ever come back through here, look us up."

"I will."

When the goodbyes had been concluded, the last remaining group members boarded their newly-improved vehicles. Thomas took the driver's seat of the utility truck, as he had in the past, and Sherman slid in beside him, slamming shut the passenger door. In the back of the truck, Krueger and Brewster were still arguing over who would take the gunner position. Mbutu, sitting in the driver's seat of the pickup with Denton next to him, waved and flashed a thumbs-up to Sherman and Thomas.

Sherman waved a hand out his window and made a circular motion. "Let's roll on out!"

More goodbyes and well-wishes were shouted as the trucks pulled off the side street and onto the main road running through town. They turned east, and picked up speed, heading in the direction of the still-rising sun.

It wasn't far to Omaha now.

CHAPTER TEN
SHOWDOWN

```
I-80 West
March 13, 2007
1543 hrs_
```

ONCE TREV HAD GOTTEN BACK in the driver's seat and pulled the group off the main roads, the journey actually began to go smoothly for a change. For a matter of days they hadn't caught wind of Sawyer or any of his cohorts, sticking to side roads that ran parallel (mostly) to the Interstate that would take them directly to Omaha, Nebraska.

They'd covered hundreds of miles in less than a week, and the goal of Omaha was literally within sight. The terrain was flat and ahead in the distance, across a glistening river, was the city of Omaha.

Anna had briefed them all on what to expect, and the forecast hadn't been pretty.

"Omaha is a relatively major city," Anna had said. "Bearing that in mind, we're probably looking at an overrun, infected dead zone. The bad news is that the Deaucalion facility is on the far side of the city. The good news is that we can circle around pretty easily."

"Good to hear," Matt had said. "That keeps us from having to take out half the city on our way through."

"And it keeps the infected from following us to the front door of the facility," Anna agreed.

"What about the facility itself?" Trev asked. "What are we looking at there?"

"Well, one of two possibilities," Anna admitted. "First, there's a chance that Frank and his friends—that's the General I told you about who I asked to meet me here—have already arrived and secured the facility. The other possibility is that they haven't arrived yet and we'll have to clear it out ourselves."

"Do we know if it's overrun or not?" Junko asked.

"No idea," Anna said. "We lost all communication early on in the pandemic. The facility closed its doors and buttoned up."

"So that's good news," Matt said. "Maybe they survived. Maybe we'll arrive and the place will still be running."

"There's a chance that's the case," Anna said tentatively. "But we're going to have to assume that it's not. There are only five of us here and we aren't the best armed group out there, so if it's infected, we have quite a chore ahead of us."

"What about Sawyer?" Trev asked. "If it's true he knew where you all were headed, won't he be right behind us, too?"

Mason stepped up to answer that one.

"I'd say there's an excellent chance that we're going to run across him sooner or later, especially now that we're getting so close. He knows exactly where we're headed, he's determined to stop us, and he has more resources behind him than we can muster. We're just going to have to hope he isn't here yet."

"Hope's a pretty flimsy thing to hang our lives on," Matt said, frowning.

"Just be glad we've got that much," Mason replied. "All right, if we're going to do this, we're going to do it right. Like Anna said, we'll circle around the city."

"Then we all go on foot to the facility," Matt said, nodding. "Got it."

"No, no," Mason said, shaking his head. "Once we're on foot, you're all coming with me. I've done this before. Listen close to anything I say. If I stop, you stop. If I go, you go. Pay close attention to me and don't fall behind. Got that?"

"Yeah, sure," Matt said, shrugging. "Got it."

Mason leaned in closer to Matt, narrowing his eyes. "I said, 'got that?'"

Matt frowned at Mason. "Yeah, I said. I got it."

Mason sighed, then continued. "Once we reach the facility, we'll have to clear it room by room. That means we'll have to set up a safe zone from which we can operate. That'll be the main entryway, most likely, since it'll afford us a quick retreat if we need it. We'll reinforce the main doors, get situated, and then get the facility back up and running. If Sherman and his people are already there, then happy fucking day—we're in for a picnic. Anyway, that's about it. Trev, can you get us around the city?"

Trev looked over his shoulder from the driver's seat of the pickup and flashed a thumbs-up at Mason. "Not a problem. I've been reading this map while you've been talking. I see a route that should be clear."

"Great. All right, gang, here we go," Mason said, sitting down and holding on to the siderail of the pickup's bed.

Trev turned his head once more to address the passengers in the bed as the truck picked up speed, turning onto a narrow two-lane side road. "Attention all passengers: thank you for riding Westscott Roadways. We are now beginning our final approach into Omaha, Nebraska. Please keep your hands, feet, and all loose articles secured within the vehicle until it comes to a full and complete stop. In the event of an infected attack, fire at will and hope to hell you don't fall out. Once again, thank you, and have a pleasant trip."

"Now there's a morale-boosting speech," Junko chuckled.

"Mama always said I should've been a pilot," Trev said.

The truck puttered on, turning from side street to side street. They passed through suburbs, and more than once Trev had to gun the engine to outrun a sprinter that caught on their tail. Once the sprinter lost sight of the truck, it would keep heading in the last direction it had seen its prey go, allowing Trev to throw them off with relative ease.

What had once been life-filled suburbs were now silent and eerie. Vehicles sat abandoned on the curb or in driveways, and children's toys lay out gathering mildew in untended yards. Here and there were signs of violence. A burned-out car sat at one intersection, having collided with a telephone pole. Spent brass littered the asphalt in another location, and smears of blood led away from the spot, hinting at a last stand by a surrounded survivor.

The charred and gutted remains of a suburban house still smoldered off to their right. The fire hadn't spread to any of the nearby homes, but had burned the leaves from the yard's only tree, leaving behind a skeletal, haunting sight. Junko wasn't sure but she thought she saw the outline of a human body, blackened from the intense heat, leaned up against one of the posts.

There wasn't much conversation as Trev artfully dodged the obstacles left in the roadway and brought them ever closer to the side of the city where the facility was supposed to be located. Every occupant of the truck was busy in their own way; mostly, they worried over the possibility of imminent death, but others, like Mason, were once again running on autopilot, training taking precedence over normal emotion.

"We're close," Trev warned after taking a right turn onto a street running north. "Two minutes, maybe."

Mason shoved the MP-5 he'd taken from Julie's killer toward Anna, loaded and ready to fire. The other he looped over his shoulder. He checked his magazines, making certain they were topped off, and secured his sidearm in its holster. By the time he was finished running down his mental checklist, Trev had arrived at the spot he'd picked to ditch the truck.

The vehicle slowed to a stop and idled on a street corner. Trev looked over his shoulder to address his passengers.

"This is about as close as we can get without getting into the more-developed areas of the city," he said. "Anna, if your information's right, we only have about a six block walk from here."

"Six blocks," Anna repeated, nodding.

"That's actually a lot, when you think about the number of infected that could be out there," Junko mused, staring off in the direction Trev had pointed. "We'll have to be very careful."

"And that's why I meant what I said back there," Mason said, standing in the bed of the truck and flicking the safety to his MP-5 off. "Stay on me and do what I do. No talking. Don't do anything—anything—unless I O.K. it first. Are you all ready for this?"

"Ready as I'll ever be," Matt said, jumping over the side of the truck and coming up on his feet, rifle at the ready.

"Let's get to it," Trev said, climbing out of the cab. Junko followed suit. Neither shut their doors; instead, they left them barely hanging open. They made no more noise than was absolutely necessary.

Mason silently signaled for the group to file in behind him and led them down the street in the direction Trev and Anna had indicated. Here were mostly industrial complexes: large, spawling acres of factory floors, warehouses and smoke stacks. Lining one side of the road, however, was a long line of rowhouses and storefronts. Mason focused in on those buildings: if there were infected about, those would be the buildings where they'd elect to hide and wait.

They made it past the first two blocks without incident, but when they reached the third, Mason inexplicably stopped in his tracks. Anna, used to him, stopped immediately as well. Trev, Juni and Matt were less accustomed to Mason's modus operandi and bumped into Anna's back when she halted in place. Trev was tempted to ask in a whisper what had Mason spooked, but he remembered the ex-NSA agent's warning to make no noise unless absolutely necessary. He kept his mouth shut.

Mason stared off down the block, eyes focusing in on shattered glass that lay scattered across the sidewalk. The storefront the glass belonged to was wide open. The rest of the doors and windows seemed secure.

Mason turned his head to look at the group. He pointed down the street, as if to say, "Proceed," and then turned on his heel and marched briskly at a half-crouch down an alleyway, leaving behind his comrades.

"Where's he going?" Matt whispered in an urgent tone.

"Shh!" Anna reprimanded him with a sharp glare. "We keep going. He knows what he's doing."

As the main group continued to proceed tentatively down the street, Mason crept along the alleyway behind the rowhouses, eyeing each rear doorway as he passed it. He finally reached the one on the far end. Instead of passing it by, he tested the doorknob and found it to be unlocked. A small smile creased his features as he disappeared into the store.

On the street, Anna felt less and less sure of herself. Whatever had spooked Mason was now spooking her, though she had no idea what it could have been. She aimed left and right with the MP-5, checking every nook and cranny the group came across, but found nothing. As they approached the far end of the block, she finally noticed the shattered glass.

Anna grimaced and stepped off the sidewalk, intent on walking around the glass to keep from crunching it under her feet and possibly alerting any nearby infected. Unfortunately, Matt didn't notice her maneuver and proceeded straight ahead. His booted foot came down on the glass and crunched loudly.

The group froze. The sound of shuffling feet came from the direction of the storefront, and they swiveled their heads in its direction. There, silhouetted in the broken window, was the bloodied figure of a sprinter, staring at the group with wrathful, bloodshot eyes and wild, unkempt hair. It sucked in a quick breath.

Anna's eyes went wide. She knew what was coming next—the growl. The thing would roar, and every sprinter and shambler within earshot would come down on their heads.

Before the roar could come out, however, Mason appeared behind the sprinter. He'd slung his MP-5 and drawn his combat knife. In one swift motion he slit the sprinter's throat, and it gasped as blood burbled out through the cut. It slumped forward to its knees and collapsed face-first in the storefront, head and shoulders hanging out over the edge of the broken window. Mason stepped out of the storefront and knelt next to the dead sprinter, cleaning his knife on the corpse's clothing before resheathing it.

"Holy shit," Matt stage-whispered. "You knew he was there?"

"I suspected," Mason said. "Let's keep going."

The group crossed a four-way intersection. A heavy traffic collision had occurred there at some point. Empty cars were backed up half a block in each direction, and five vehicles were all piled into the center of the intersection, frames bent and windows shattered from running full-speed into one another. Mason glanced up at the dark traffic lights and wondered if the power had gone out and caused the accidents.

When they reached the next block, Anna grew visibly excited. She pointed down the street, tapping Mason on the shoulder.

"There it is!" she said. Her finger pointed out a squat brick structure that blended in perfectly with the industrial facilities around it. It stood only one story high and had few windows on the ground level. The front of the building was similarly spartan in its design: a pair of windows allowed a view of the street from within, and a pair of glass-faced double doors led the way in.

As Mason turned his head to look at the building, he could have sworn he saw a flutter of movement on the rooftop. He narrowed his eyes and stared, standing in place. The rest of the group silently waited behind him for news.

A pair of pigeons suddenly took off from the roof of the building, winging it deeper into the ruined city. Mason huffed a sigh. Nothing but birds. He waved the group onward. Only two more blocks to go.

Trev was taking note of the buildings they passed. He was the last in the line of survivors, the rear guard, and he felt a combined sense of duty to keep an eye on their asses and a sense of curiosity about the environment they were embedding themselves in. The storefronts that ran opposite the industrial zones were widely varied in their offerings and many of them were dusty and boarded up. Trev wasn't sure whether they'd closed their doors before the pandemic or after, only that they held nothing that would be of use. Two of the stores were consignment shops; Trev marked them down in his head as possibilities. After all, a person could only wear the same clothes so many times before they started to fall apart.

When they reached the final block, Mason halted the party and waved his finger in a circle, beckoning them closer. He knelt on the pavement and the others followed suit, casting glances over their shoulders every now and then.

"All right, listen up," Mason said. "We don't know what's in that building now, but we're going to assume it's full of infected, so lock and load. When we get up from this huddle, we move straight for that building and we don't stop for anything. We get inside, we clear the first room, and we lock it down. Once we're safe in that room, we plan our next move. Roger?"

"Got it," Matt said.

"I'm with you," Trev replied.

"All right," Mason said, double-checking the safety on his MP-5 to make certain it was off. "Let's roll."

The group sprung up from their huddle and darted out into the intersection—this one blessedly clear of traffic accidents and abandoned cars—and made a beeline for the building Anna had pointed out.

They made it about halfway.

A gutteral roar interrupted their run, and Mason and Trev cast about for the source of the noise. It could only have come from an infected. When they looked down the side street they were passing by, they spotted the source.

A sprinter had been lounging in the shade provided by a shop's stoop, and upon sighting the group of survivors, it had pulled itself to its feet and growled. When Mason and Trev spotted it, it was still standing in its shady spot, but it was staring directly at them, arms held out to its sides, fingers extended as though ready to claw its way through them.

"Shit," Mason murmured. He raised his MP-5, drawing a bead on the infected's skull. He knew the gunshots would bring more infected running, but he didn't see any other choice. Before he could fire, a hand reached out and lowered the barrel of the weapon. Mason looked over to see Trev.

"I've got this," Trev said, reaching down to his belt. He pulled free a simple baton, snapped it open, and waved the rest of the group on.

"Whoa, whoa, you're kidding me—" Mason started, eyes widening at the sight of Trev's choice of weapons. Melee combat with the infected was, in essence, suicide—if one got blood on oneself or was so much as scratched in the fighting, that would spell the end of the combatant. Junko stopped Mason's protests by placing herself between Mason and Trev.

"Let him," Juni said. "He's done it this way before. He knows what he's doing."

Even as Juni spoke, two more sprinters appeared in the roadway, jumping out of darkened doorways and running up out of cellars. Now Trev faced three infected, and still Juni kept Mason from involving himself.

Trev looked over his shoulder at Mason.

"Let me go, man," he said. "I can take three demons. Hell, I can take five of the fuckers. Get everyone inside—I'll do this my way. No noise, no more company."

Mason knew Trev was right: a single gunshot could have several city blocks' worth of infected bearing down on them, ironically a much louder and better-suited call to dinner than the roar of the infected. Trev's baton, on the other hand, was soundless. Secretly, he felt Trev was going to die in the process of letting the rest of the group get away.

But if that's how he wants to go out, Mason said to himself, *who am I to stop him?*

"Move out!" Mason said, shoving Anna in the direction of the research facility. "Go, go, go!"

"But we can't just—" Anna protested, pointing in Trev's direction.

"Yes, we can!" Mason growled. "Go! Now!"

The remaining four survivors ran straight for the facility doors, leaving Trev alone in the middle of the intersection, baton in one hand, the other balled into a white-knuckled fist at his side. He tapped the baton against his leg steadily, staring down the three infected.

Trev glanced up at the sun. It had already begun to slide down toward the horizon. He'd missed high noon.

Oh, well, Trev thought. *Any time's a good time for a showdown.*

"Well," Trev said after a moment, raising his voice just loud enough for the infected to hear, "are you three just going to stand there, or are we going to dance?"

It may have been Trev's voice that jolted the infected into action, or perhaps it was some unspoken agreement between the three, but all of them broke out into a flat-out run toward Trev at that moment, arms flailing wildly. The distance between Trev and the infected closed rapidly.

The entire time the infected were running at him Trev remained motionless, save for the metronome-like tapping of the baton against his leg.

Then they were upon him, and the battle was joined.

Mason and Matt were the first two to reach the main doors of the research facility. Mason fired off a quick prayer that they weren't locked, and found his prayer answered when he pulled on the left-hand door and it swung open easily. Matt pulled open the right, ushering in Juni and Anna, who both entered with weapons at the ready.

Mason and Matt followed suit, allowing the doors to shut behind them.

Mason readied his MP-5 and took in the room they found themselves in. It was a wide, open space; a reception area. A receptionist's desk stood across the room, protected by thick safety glass, and a pair of steel doors directly in front of them led to the rest of the facility. These were the first things Mason noticed.

The second thing Mason noticed was the furniture in the room, which had been dragged to either side of the main entrance and piled high to form a mish-mash pair of walls, hemming in the little group in the center of the room. Mason's stomach did a flip-flop. It didn't feel right.

Anna didn't seem to notice anything out of the ordinary. She was focused on the steel double doors and the tiny black card reader embedded in their center. The red light on the reader was out, as were the overhead lights. That was good. Security was down, which meant they'd be able to access the entire facility. She began to walk toward the double doors.

Suddenly, the room became a flurry of activity. On either side of the group, from behind the furniture-walls, appeared men in urban camouflage, wearing balaclavas and wielding assault rifles. Four had popped up on either side of the group, and for a moment, all was chaos as threats, surprised curses and orders were shouted back and forth.

"Drop the weapons!"

"You're surrounded and outgunned! Lay down arms!"

"Where the fuck did these guys come from?" Matt blurted.

"Weapons down! Down! Now!"

The room slowly silenced. The four survivors stood back-to-back in the center of the room, surrounded by the well-armed men. Mason calculated their odds of survival and swallowed. This was a perfectly executed ambush—these men had known they were coming.

That meant Sawyer, which in turn meant laying down his weapon was as good as killing himself. Sawyer would see him executed if he was caught. At the same time, though, opening fire on these men in their current situation was as good as killing himself as well.

"Mason?" came Anna's voice from over Mason's shoulder. "What are we doing?"

Fingers tightened on triggers around the room, and for a moment the only sound was the clink and clatter of gear rustling on pistol belts.

Mason frowned, feeling slightly sick to his stomach. All that traveling—only to be caught the moment they arrived.

"Lay 'em down," Mason softly said, lowering the barrel of his MP-5. He dropped it to the floor, and slowly unholstered his pistol, tossing it to the floor as well. Around him, his companions did the same, disarming themselves.

"Hands up!" came a command from one of the masked, uniformed men.

Three of the ambushers came out from behind their cover, approaching the survivors carefully, weapons still trained on their targets. They kicked the weapons away from the survivors, back toward the main entrance, and once they were satisfied, they backed away, lowering their own weapons.

The steel double doors that led deeper into the facility burst open, and the small group of survivors spun around, half-expecting a new threat of some kind. Instead, framed in the doorway was a single man, dressed in nearly-identical fatigues as the ambushers. Instead of a balaclava, however, this man went bareheaded, and instead of wielding a rifle, he merely carried a pistol in a low-slung hip holster. He walked forward slowly, fixing Mason with a stare.

"Well, I'll be damned," Mason said, eyeing the newcomer. "I didn't think you'd stick with Sawyer after all this, Derrick."

Special Agent Derrick, NSA, quirked a grin at his former partner.

"Sawyer's working for the good of the country, buddy," Derrick said. "He's out to find a cure. That's what we should all be after."

Mason chuckled. "That is what I'm after, Derrick. That's why we're here. To try to find a vaccine."

"Vaccine?" Derrick said, raising his eyebrows. "No, Mason, we want a cure. There are millions of people out there we can save. Think about it—no more of this killing, no more innocents dead—just hit them with a dart gun and inject them with a cure. Think of the lives we could save."

"You're not going to find a cure," Anna said, looking down at the floor.

"The prodigal doctor speaks," Derrick said, still grinning. He shifted his attention from Mason to Anna. "We've been after you a long, long time, doc. You know how many people have died trying to find you? You should have stayed put. We might've already had the cure if we'd had you working on our side all this time."

Anna shook her head. "You didn't hear me. I said you're not going to find a cure. You almost never find a cure for a virus. The best you can do is vaccinate the remaining population—"

"Shut up," Derrick said, his face reddening. "There is a cure. There has to be a cure. And you're going to find it—once we get you back east. We haven't just been bumbling around these past few months. We've got an entire hospital staff rounded up and ready to help you, Doctor."

"There isn't a cure," Anna said, dejected. "I don't know how to convince you."

"You can't, because you're lying," Derrick growled between clenched teeth. "I've heard it straight from other doctors, straight from our leaders—there's a cure, and you're a piece of the puzzle. You're going back east with us, Doc."

"You're the man with the gun," Anna said, shaking her head.

"That's right, I am," Derrick said, quirking another grin. "Foster!"

One of the uniformed men snapped to attention. "Sir!"

"Get Sawyer on SatCom."

The man nodded and jogged over to one of the piles of furniture, dragging out a large black duffel bag. He unzipped it, revealing a menagerie of odds and ends, the largest of which was a satellite phone. He pulled it free, set it on one of the room's couches, and worked on establishing a line directly to Sawyer.

"One minute, sir," Foster said, fiddling with the phone.

"Secure the prisoners," Derrick said, nodding in the direction of Mason and the others.

Two more uniformed men approached the group from behind, pulled zipties from their pistol belts and firmly tied the group's hands behind their backs. The plastic zipties dug into Mason's skin and hurt, but he pushed the pain to the back of his mind. If Derrick was calling Sawyer on a satellite phone, that meant that he still had a chance to get out of his current situation before he was shot as a traitor. He began wracking his brain for just such a way out.

Next to him stood Matt, eyes silently roving from one guard to the next. The young man didn't say a word and hadn't protested when the men had ziptied his hands behind his back. Now that the guards had backed off, Matt moved his hands slowly, pulling free a tiny pocketknife that had been clipped to the back of his belt. He clicked it open and began to saw away at the ziptie. It was slow going, as he had next to no leverage, but he kept going, a steady back-and-forth.

"Sawyer on line, sir," Foster said, standing up from the satellite phone and handing the receiver to Derrick. The NSA agent stepped forward and accepted the receiver, holding it up to his ear.

"Derrick here," he said.

The other end of the conversation was inaudible to the group, but Mason could guess what was being said.

"Yes, sir," Derrick said. "Flawless. They walked right into us."

A pause.

"Give me a second, Sawyer," Derrick said into the mouthpiece. He held the receiver down against his chest and surveyed the four captives. "Let's see, now. You I know, Mason. And Doc, I recognize you, too. I don't know these other two. Where's Ortiz?"

Mason scowled at Derrick and looked away.

"You shot her," Anna said, staring Derrick down. "Back on the highway a few days ago."

Derrick shook his head twice. "I didn't shoot anyone."

"One of your men did."

"Ah," Derrick said, nodding. "That explains it."

He picked the receiver back up.

"Sawyer, I have Mason and Demilio here. They have two unknowns with them. Ortiz is dead; she didn't make the journey," Derrick said. He paused, listening to Sawyer's response, and eyed Mason. "Well, at least he finished him off. One moment."

Derrick lowered the receiver again.

"Mason, I have to tell you, Sawyer's mighty pissed off about what you did to those men on the interstate, especially the one you worked over. He told me to tell you he's going to take it out on your hide."

"Tell Sawyer I said 'fuck you' for me, Derrick," Mason said, looking away.

Derrick raised the receiver once more.

"He said exactly what you said he'd say," Derrick reported, then chuckled. "Roger. ETA?"

A long pause as Derrick waited for his response. Mason was busily trying to piece together the conversation using just Derrick's end of it with little success; as close as he could figure, Derrick was merely reporting the captures and setting up a meeting to pass them off.

"That's a hell of a long time, Sawyer," Derrick said suddenly. "No, no, we can hold until then. We brought enough with us to last two weeks. The prisoners might not get much in the way of eats in that time, though."

Derrick grinned at something Sawyer said on the other end.

"Not a problem at all. Half rations it is. As long as they're in working order, right?" Derrick asked. "Roger that. Derrick out."

The NSA agent dropped the receiver into Foster's hands and faced the captives.

"All right, folks, listen up," Derrick said. Everyone including the uniformed men perked up. "We're going to dig in here for a little while and wait for Sawyer to come and take the Doc back east. We've got a nice set of windowless offices in the back we can use as cells in the meantime. Foster, Hurley, David—bring the prisoners with me. Jackson and Smith, stay here and guard the main entrance. You other three, get up on the roof and resume surveillance."

Mason could have kicked himself upon hearing that last part. He knew he'd seen something on the roof of the building, and had let the pigeons throw his instinct off-track. He should've spotted the ambush before they'd walked into it, and now it was too late, he thought, as they were led deeper into the facility, hands bound tightly, destined for their temporary holding cells.

The first of the infected that reached Trev had been a police officer. It still wore its uniform, and still sported an ugly, festering wound on its arm. Trev ducked under the infected's tackle and came up behind it, allowing it to fall forward onto the pavement, carried there by its own inertia.

The remaining two sprinters were right behind the first.

As Trev came up out of his duck, he was already attacking, bringing his baton upward in a parody of a golfer's stroke. The end of the baton caught one of the infected under the chin, and its head snapped back, spraying blood from its mouth. It staggered backwards a moment, off-balance.

Trev wheeled around, using his own momentum to maximize the striking power of the baton, and brought his weapon slamming into the side of the head of the third infected. The thing's skull cracked under the impact, splattering blood on Trev's weapon. The infected fell flat on the pavement with wide, surprised eyes, dispatched for good. Blood pooled around its skull.

Trev turned his attention to the ex-cop infected. It had regained its balance and spun to face him once more. The rage in its eyes had grown; frustration at being evaded had upped its adrenaline. Trev recognized the look, and was ready when the ex-cop sprung at him.

Trev jumped nimbly to one side, again dodging the infected's attack. He used the momentary opportunity to wheel on the bloodied infected he'd uppercutted, bringing his baton down hard on the top of its skull. Unlike the one he'd put down, this one withstood the blow, but went down to the pavement, unconscious. Trev filed that little bit of tactical knowledge away in the back of his mind—he'd have to finish it off when he got a chance.

The ex-cop turned from its second foiled attack and glared at Trev. It leaned its head back and roared once more, then charged a third time.

Trev was tiring of dodging the infected. This time, as it reached him, he simply sidestepped, held out one foot, and tripped the infected.

The ex-cop fell hard onto the street, and Trev could hear the breath get knocked out of the infected's lungs. He didn't care. He didn't give it a chance to draw another breath, much less climb back on its feet. Trev was on it before it could move again, swinging the baton overhanded and bringing it down on the infected's skull over and over until little remained but a pulpy mess.

Trev rose from the cop's body, took a deep, shuddering breath, and steadied himself. Three attackers, three victories.

Oh, wait, Trev thought. *Two victories.*

He took two steps back, eyed the unconscious sprinter, and stomped hard on the back of its neck. A quick, loud snap reached his ears.

That one won't be getting back up, Trev thought. *Now there are three victories.*

Trev straightened himself out, cracking his neck and shaking the baton free of gore. He was just about to reach down and clean it off on the clothing of one of the dead sprinters when he heard a raspy, gutteral moan echo across the street. Trev froze in place and raised his head, looking off in the direction of the noise.

Half a dozen shamblers, drawn by the roar of the sprinters, had stumbled into the roadway and were heading straight for Trev. He judged the distance between them and himself, and figured he had a good thirty seconds to kill—then he heard a second moan, and turned his attention to his left, down another street.

This road, too, was swiftly filling with shamblers. Trev's eyes went wide and he looked to his right. Even more shamblers were approaching from that direction. Trev rose to his feet and began backing toward the research facility. He had every confidence in his own abilities when it came to fighting the infected, but he knew a losing proposition when he saw one, and a losing proposition was heading toward him right then, numbering several dozen.

Trev turned, intent on jogging the rest of the way to the research facility and warning the others of the incoming threat. The street leading to the facility had likewise become infested with shamblers. Four of them were already between him and the facility.

"Well, shit," Trev murmured under his breath.

The roar had drawn all of the infected in a one-block radius from the intersection where he'd fought the sprinters.

"Now or never," Trev said to himself. He shook out the baton once more and broke into a run, clubbing the first of the shamblers out of the way and dodging between the second and third. The fourth he repeated his wind-up golfer's swing on, snapping its head back. It tipped backwards on its feet and fell motionless to the street. The way to the facility was clear.

Trev ran toward the glass double-doors, a hand outstretched to yank them open.

Several events transpired at that precise moment. Above Trev, the three rooftop guards emerged into the sunlight at the same time Trev disappeared from view below. All that greeted them upon their arrival was a view of the streets and the shamblers working their way, bit by bit, toward the research facility. Below, in the entryway, Jackson and Smith, the two guards Derrick had left behind, were just beginning to relax. Jackson was in the middle of passing a cigarette to Smith when Trev's hand gripped the door handle.

As Trev burst into the entryway, Jackson and Smith turned to look at him, surprise etched on their features. A lit cigarette dangled from Jackson's lips. For a long moment, the men stared at one another—then burst into motion.

Trev's mind, still racing at a mile-a-minute from his encounter with the infected, first guessed that these were the soldiers that Mason and Anna had kept speaking of, the ones they were trying to meet up with.

That thought was dashed when Jackson and Smith went for their pistols.

Trev dove sideways and skidded to a stop half-behind one of the piles of furniture, fumbling for his own weapon. He freed it from its holster, flicked the safety off, and took aim.

"It wasn't easy tracking you down along the way," Derrick was saying as he led the small group through the twisting, disorienting corridors of the research facility. "All those side roads we had to cover. We figured you'd use the interstate at some point, and that hunch paid off—I guess. Depends on your point of view."

Mason wasn't listening much. He was paying attention to their surroundings. They'd passed a number of offices and some storage rooms but nothing much that looked like any kind of laboratory. He guessed they were on another level—in a basement, perhaps. The facility was only one story, after all. He also paid close attention to the men escorting them. The three uniformed men and Derrick formed a diamond around their prisoners, with Derrick in the lead. Mason was right behind his former partner, with Matt off to one side and Juni to his other. Anna brought up the rear, looking rather dejected at having been caught.

Matt, meanwhile, was still sawing away at the ziptie that bound his hands together. As Derrick rambled on about their search for Doctor Demilio, he suddenly felt the plastic snap and part. His wrists were free. Matt was careful to keep his expression neutral as he palmed the knife and shifted his grip on it. He kept his wrists held tightly together behind his back to create the illusion of them being bound, and waited for his moment.

Mason, too, was waiting for his moment. Even with his hands tied, he knew he could take at least one of the guards, given an opportunity. He just hoped his companions would back him up.

In the entryway, Trev and the two guards opened fire on each other. Bullets ripped into the stacked couches and chairs and buried themselves in walls. One put a spiderweb of cracks in the receptionist's window. All three parties scrambled for better cover.

✯ ✯ ✯ ✯ ✯

In the hall, the sound of shooting suddenly reached the ears of the guards and their prisoners.

"What the hell?" asked one, turning to look back in the direction of the entryway—and providing Matt and Mason with their respective opportunities.

Mason lashed out immediately at Derrick from behind, kicking the back of the man's leg and buckling it. Derrick went down with a grunt, and Mason followed up his attack with a snap-kick to the back of Derrick's head. The man fell forward, stunned.

Matt slammed his shoulder into the chest of the guard to his right at the same moment, and the pair ran up against the concrete wall. The guard's head snapped back and hit the wall with a sickening crack. He slid down the concrete and slumped against the wall, unmoving.

"Mason!" Matt called.

Mason turned in time to see Matt, hands free, tossing him the small pocket knife. Mason half-turned just enough to catch the blade in his bound hands. He immediately began to saw away at his restraints.

Juni had thrown herself against her guard as well, but her results weren't as dramatic. The guard pushed her off of himself and backpedaled, drawing his weapon. The fourth guard, upon seeing the prisoners' sudden revolt, grabbed Anna and drew his own weapon, holding it up to the side of the doctor's head. He pulled Anna backwards, putting a few feet between himself and the fight. The guard Juni had bodyslammed fell back alongside his companion, and both guards pointed their weapons at the prisoners.

"Don't move, don't move!" they warned. "We'll wax her!"

Matt leaned down and grabbed the assault rifle off of the shoulder of the guard he'd bodyslammed and held it up, aiming at the head of the guard who held Anna. The man noticed and ducked back behind her, barely presenting a target. Matt eased his finger off the trigger, unwilling to take the shot and possibly hit Anna.

"Wax her and you wax the cure you're after," Mason said calmly, holding up his newly-freed hands and passing the knife off to Juni to free herself.

Gunfire still echoed through the corridor, hinting at conflicts yet unresolved in the rest of the facility.

"Take off!" came a grunted order from behind Mason. He turned to see Derrick pulling himself to his feet, a look of rage on his face. "I said take off! Get the doctor away from here, put her in a room, lock it, and guard it. The rest of these piss-ants are expendable."

Mason turned to face Derrick. The NSA agent was the deadliest threat in the hallway, and Mason knew it. He wasn't about to leave his back turned on the man. Over his shoulder he addressed Juni and Matt.

"Get the doc," he said. "I'll handle Derrick."

Matt and Juni faced off with the two armed guards. Anna kicked and struggled against the one that held her, but her attempts at escape were futile. The man had his arm wrapped securely around her throat; the more she struggled against him, the more she choked herself.

"Back off," ordered the guard holding Anna. He stared down Matt and Juni.

"Not going to happen," Matt said, staring down the barrel of the assault rifle.

Juni felt somewhat helpless next to him, unarmed as she was, but she brandished the pocketknife and tried her best to plaster a feral expression on her face.

☆ ☆ ☆ ☆ ☆

Mason and Derrick faced one another a few meters away. Derrick had finished clambering back up to his feet and was dusting himself off, looking none the worse for wear despite the heavy kick to the back of the head Mason had given him.

"Shouldn't have let you stay behind me," Derrick mused. "Learn something new every day."

"Here's another lesson for you," Mason said. "Don't fuck with us."

Derrick chuckled, shaking his head. "And who is 'us,' exactly, Mason? You're a lone rogue. You're nothing."

"You're wrong," Mason replied. "I've been trying my damndest to get Demilio here so she could work toward a vaccine—and now you're going to just ship her back east. Can't let that happen, Derrick.

We've come to far and we've lost too much. I'm no lone rogue. It's you and the rest of your little breakaway faction that's gone rogue."

Derrick's eyebrows raised a fraction of an inch for a split second only, but Mason caught the microexpression and grinned.

"Didn't think I was keeping up-to-date on national politics, did you? Sawyer tell you about the shooter I worked over out on the interstate? He told me some real interesting things," Mason said.

Mason and Derrick were now slowly circling one another in the hallway, each looking for an opening in their opponent's defense and finding none.

"Oh, yeah?" Derrick asked. "And what did he tell you?"

"Enough to know that you and Sawyer broke off with half of Congress and formed your own little plan to 'stabilize' the country," Mason said. "From what I heard it's bullshit. There is no cure. Hell, there isn't even a vaccine—yet. And you're getting in the way of us finding even that much."

"A vaccine won't help my infected wife," Derrick snarled, and suddenly burst into motion. His hand slipped behind his back for a moment and came up less than a second later with a compact automatic pistol.

Mason was nearly caught off-guard, but he leaned back just far and fast enough to allow Derrick's first shot to miss. Mason used his momentum to swing around and snap off a side-kick, connecting solidly with Derrick's arm. The compact pistol went skittering down the hall, ricocheted off of a doorway, and spun into an office. The two combatants fell back from one another, now both unarmed, and dropped into combat stances, hands held out in front of them and legs spread, their centers of gravity low.

"Last time I got this kind of workout I put Sawyer under," Mason muttered, referring to a hand-to-hand match he'd had with Sawyer when he, Anna and Julie had been trying to escape from Washington.

"Sawyer didn't hit the gym six times a week," Derrick countered, and attacked.

Derrick launched a flurry of punches in Mason's direction. Mason held his arms in close, absorbing the blows and keeping an eye on Derrick's legs. He'd sparred with the agent before and knew a thing or two about his style—throw off his opponent with lots of high attacks, and then leg-sweep him.

Sure enough, after the last punch had been deflected, Derrick's left leg lashed out in an attempt to trip up Mason and put him on the ground.

Mason was ready for it. He blocked the kick and followed up with a quick one-two combination to Derrick's stomach.

Derrick recoiled, the breath knocked out of him, and narrowed his eyes at Mason. The ex-NSA agent was in his combat stance, resting on the tips of his feet, ready to spring in any direction. Mason simply held out a hand and beckoned Derrick forward.

"Come on, asshole," Mason said. "You wanted a fight, you've got one."

Mason wasn't prepared for Derrick's next move. The agency had taught them a touch of jiu-jitsu, but had mainly focused on simple boxing and basic martial arts. The agency didn't make ninjas out of its agents—it made artful brawlers out of them. The one thing it definitely didn't make them was wrestlers, and that was why Mason was surprised when Derrick launched a tackle in his direction.

Mason, balanced nimbly on his feet, tried to jump out of the way in time and failed. Derrick hit Mason full-force in the chest, grabbing him in a bear hug and bringing him down hard on his back.

Mason felt his head crack off the floor and his vision burst into bright lights and twinkling stars, then swam drunkenly. The ceiling tiles zoomed in and out of focus. Derrick, straddling Mason's chest, didn't let him off so easily. He reared back and struck Mason over and over in the face with balled-up fists, bringing Mason closer to the brink of unconsciousness.

Derrick's attacks fell off just before Mason dropped off into the darkness. He stood, eyeing Mason's bloodied face, and grinned.

"Looks like this round goes to me," Derrick said, wiping blood from his knuckles.

He turned his back on Mason and looked down the hallway. *Now, which office did that pistol skid in to?*

Derrick spotted the open doorway and headed toward it. He swung into the doorway and looked around on the floor inside. There, just a few feet away from him, lay the pistol, half under a desk. He took one step toward it before a roar of frustration and rage rose up behind him and Mason appeared, full-body tackling Derrick. The two agents crashed into the office, upsetting a coat rack and the pair of chairs that sat in front of the desk.

"Jesus, you just don't give up!" Derrick cursed.

"I get that a lot," Mason replied, using his opportunity to throw a couple of kidney punches into Derrick's back.

The agent arched his back and grunted, gritting his teeth against the pain, and reached out a hand toward the desk. His index finger just barely brushed the grip of the pistol. He felt the blows of another pair of kidney punches and pushed the pain to the back of his mind, focusing on the pistol. He managed to slide it an inch closer to himself and he grabbed it up, blindly aiming it over his shoulder and firing twice.

Mason saw the pistol appear in Derrick's hand and rolled backwards off of the agent. The two shots embedded themselves in the ceiling tiles, and bits of dust rained down on the combatants.

Mason jumped to his feet as Derrick began to rise. He knew he couldn't let his opponent get in another aimed shot—it was a miracle he hadn't already been hit.

Mason tried for another snap-kick, but Derrick pulled his arm out of the way in time. The kick landed on Derrick's side, and Mason heard a muffled crack. He'd broken a rib or two with that one.

Derrick rolled over onto his back, pistol held out in both hands as he took aim at Mason. Mason had no real time to react: he simply dove across the room, praying that none of Derrick's shots would hit him. The first shot took a chunk out of the concrete wall. The second shattered the office's only window, sending shards of glass flying and leaving a few jagged edges in the windowframe.

The third skipped off the top of the desk and embedded itself in Mason's shoulder just as he came in for his landing. He grunted as he felt the round strike home, and clasped a hand to the wound. Blood oozed out from between his fingers.

Derrick pulled himself to his feet and raised his pistol, moving around the desk to get a better view of his target—but Mason was gone. For a split second, Derrick wondered where his opponent had vanished to, then got his answer as Mason appeared on the opposite end of the desk. He'd rolled underneath it and come up on the other side.

The two combatants froze in place a moment. Derrick had his pistol pointed directly at Mason's chest, with his back to the shattered window. Mason, unarmed, stood a brace of feet from Derrick, one hand still clasped over his bullet wound.

"Round one went to me," Derrick said, "and it looks like round two is going to be a K.O."

Derrick tightened his finger's grip on the trigger.

At the same moment Mason lashed out with a desperate kick, shoving Derrick backwards. Derrick's shot went off just as Mason's boot connected with his chest.

Both agents fell backwards. Mason had felt the punch of the second bullet striking home, and he wondered for a moment if it was a fatal hit. He lay on the office floor, staring up at the ceiling. He tried to draw breath and found it hard, as if something heavy were standing on his chest. He figured the bullet had pierced a lung.

Then Mason heard wry chuckling coming from the other side of the office, and he managed to raise his head just enough to see Derrick.

The NSA agent was still standing, but it wasn't because he chose to. Mason's kick had driven him back against the windowframe, and Derrick was now looking down at a large shard of glass protruding from his chest. He was pinned to the window.

"I'm sure...it's not as bad...as it looks," Mason wheezed, coughing. He felt a bit of froth and blood on his lips and knew then for certain that he had a punctured lung on his hands.

Derrick didn't respond. His free hand reached up and touched the large glass shard, coated in his own blood.

"Didn't think...I'd go like this," Derrick said, letting out a long sigh. His eyes slowly closed, and his head slumped down to rest on his chest.

The pistol slid from Derrick's lifeless hand and clattered to the floor.

Mason stared at the corpse of his former partner for a moment, and then remembered his own predicament. He coughed again, and more blood trickled out of his mouth. He knew he had a matter of minutes to get help—otherwise, he'd be joining Derrick in death.

Slowly, inch by inch, he began to drag himself toward the hallway.

✫ ✫ ✫ ✫ ✫

Juni and Matt faced off with the two guards who held Anna. They were in a kind of stalemate. The guards were backing up, heading deeper into the facility, and Matt and Juni were following cautiously. Matt still had his rifle trained on the man holding Anna,

but the guards were loathe to open fire. Both sides were worried about hitting Anna in a crossfire.

"Just let her go, man," Matt said. "We don't have a fight with you. You're free to go. Just leave us the doc."

"Can't do that," responded one of the guards. "We have our orders."

"Yeah, 'I had orders,' I've heard that before," Matt said, narrowing his eyes.

"Let's just all calm down, and try to be reasonable about this," Juni said, holding up her hands in a placating manner. "I'm sure there's a way we can work this out without—"

Suddenly a gunshot rang out in the hallway. Both guards jumped, but the shot hadn't come from Matt.

It had come from the guard Matt had knocked out and left for dead in the corridor. The man had recovered, drawn his backup weapon, and fired.

Matt blinked, suddenly feeling lightheaded. He wavered on his feet and looked down at his chest. Blood ran down the outside of his clothing, soaking it and dripping to the floor. The bullet had hit him center mass.

"Shit," he murmured.

The assault rifle fell from Matt's nerveless hands and clattered to the floor. Matt was right behind it: he dropped to his knees, looked up at Juni with surprise and regret etched on his face, and then pitched forward, laying motionless.

"Matt!" Juni yelled, dropping to his side. She turned him over, but his eyes were already glazed over and lifeless. The shot had pierced his heart. Juni nearly sobbed. Matt had been part of her group since nearly the beginning of the pandemic.

Suddenly the sound of rounds being chambered drew her attention, and she looked up. The guard that had shot Matt had recovered his assault rifle, and all three of the uniformed men were pointing their weapons at her.

"Up," said the one holding Anna. He gestured with his pistol to enunciate his words. "Up. Get up."

Juni slowly rose to her feet, hands held in the air.

"Re-tie her," said the one holding Anna.

The guard that had shot Matt pulled Juni's arms behind her back and secured her with another zip-tie. The three guards and their two prisoners picked up the pace, hustling Juni and Anna off to a deeper section of the facility.

Up on the rooftop, the three guards Derrick had sent were busily setting up their rifles on the edge of the roof, taking aim at the shamblers below. They'd heard the gunshots coming from the entryway beneath them, and had guessed those had been the beacon for the infected now making their way closer and closer.

"There weren't this many to deal with when we came through," muttered one of the guards as he opened fire on the shamblers below, dropping one with a neat head shot.

"Yeah, well, we were a lot more quiet about it," said the second.

"Jackson and Smith must have a lot of company at the front door to be firing like that," said the third, referring to the two guards in the entryway. "Derrick said no unnecessary shots."

"I'd call these shots necessary," said the first, firing again and dropping another shambler.

"No argument here, buddy. If those things get inside..."

Suddenly the three uniformed men heard the sound of an engine revving. They looked up, startled, and saw in the distance a camouflage-painted vehicle heading toward the facility, moving straight down the center of the street.

"What the hell?" asked one.

"Looks like Army," said the second, grinning. "We got that backup we called for after all!"

Behind the large assault vehicle came a second, similarly-painted truck, this one armor-reinforced. Gunfire was erupting from both of the vehicles, and they left behind a trail of shambler corpses in their wake as they approached.

The first man narrowed his eyes, squinting at the vehicles. The lead truck had just popped open a rooftop hatch, and a man wearing a BDU top but a civilian cover appeared, grasping the handgrip of an M-249 on a tripod.

"Wait a minute," he said, studying them intently. "Those aren't Army!"

He swung his rifle around, taking aim at the man on the turret.

"What if they're friendlies?" asked the second.

"You remember what Derrick said: shoot first, questions later," said the first, and took a shot at the turret operator.

The bullet spanged off the top of the vehicle, leaving a nasty dent, and immediately drew the attention of the man on the machine gun. He swiveled the barrel in their direction.

The three rooftop guards dove for cover as a virtual hailstorm of bullets rained down around them, kicking up chunks of rooftop and zipping past their ears. After a moment, the gunfire shifted, and one of the guards had the tenacity to raise his head above the roof's ledge. The turret gunner had shifted his attention to the shamblers, and was busy mowing them down.

Automatic fire tore into the infected, and brackish blood sprayed across the street as the stumbling corpses jerked and spasmed before falling. The truck was clearing a path to the research facility.

The first of the guards on the rooftop decided to try his luck one more time. He rose up from behind the ledge and took careful aim at the gunner on the turret. He didn't pay any attention to the pickup following closely behind it, and didn't notice the barrel of a rifle pointed out of a firing slit in his direction.

Before the guard could squeeze the trigger, a single shot rang out and he fell back onto the roof. A bullet had caught him just above the eye. The two remaining guards had the good sense to stay down as the vehicles neared the entrance, crushing the bodies of infected beneath their tires as they rumbled along.

✯ ✯ ✯ ✯ ✯

In the entryway, Trev felt like he was swiftly running out of time. The two guards he'd surprised had opened fire on him, and he'd returned the favor. The problem was both parties were behind good cover and Trev didn't have infinite ammunition: in fact, all he'd carried with him were two spare magazines for the pistol, plus the one in the pistol itself, and his rifle. His rifle was already empty, and he was down to his last magazine for his pistol. He had no intention of engaging the guards with his baton; that would be suicide.

As he traded a few more rounds with the guards, he heard the sound of the vehicles outside. He wondered for a moment whether he was about to be flanked, gunned down by enemy reinforcements. He dismissed the thought. If that were the case, he was done for and there wasn't a thing he could do about it.

Trev risked a glance outside and saw a large utility truck, running full-bore, slam into a group of shamblers that were closing in on the facility's entrance. A cow-catcher, welded onto the front of the vehicle, threw most of them out of the way. A pair were caught up underneath the catcher, and even inside Trev could hear the crunch of bone and flesh as the truck's tires ran them over. Their mangled bodies tumbled out from beneath the vehicle's rear and rolled to a stop in bloodied heaps in the middle of the road.

The truck slammed on its brakes and squealed to a stop. Trev heard more than saw the vehicle shift gears into reverse.

Jackson and Smith, Trev's two foes, seemed as surprised by the arrival of the vehicle as he was, but they quickly recovered and opened up on Trev's makeshift bunker with their rifles, sending couch stuffing and plastic shards flying. Trev ducked down lower and hoped one of the rounds wouldn't find him.

The truck's tires squealed again as it backed up straight into the entryway, effectively blocking the main doors. Another vehicle, a pickup truck, came screaming by on the road, shots ringing out from the bed as it passed. What few shamblers remained on the streets were being dropped one after the other. Whoever the new arrivals were, they knew how to deal with the demons.

The back doors of the utility truck were flung open and several men in mixed civilian and military garb jumped out, throwing open the facility's doors and entering with weapons at the ready. Jackson and Smith turned their attention from Trev to the newcomers, opening fire on them as they entered the room.

The response from the newcomers was immediate. Two dropped to the ground into a prone position, returning fire. The other two moved to either side, firing shots from upheld pistols.

Jackson and Smith, caught by surprise and in the open, were cut down in the hail of gunfire. Smith took a round to the chest and was flung backwards onto the floor. Jackson was stitched by several rounds, and he crumpled against a wall, sliding slowly down to the floor and leaving a trail of smeared blood behind himself.

In the ensuing silence, the four newcomers held their position, watching the bodies of Jackson and Smith for any movement.

Trev decided to take that moment to stand up from behind his bunker.

Instantly, the four newcomers swiveled in his direction, weapons leveled.

"Whoa, whoa, whoa!" Trev yelled, holding his hands and pistol up above his head. "Friendly! I think! Who the hell are you guys?"

"Who the hell are you?" came the reply.

"Trevor Westscott. I'm here with Mason and Demilio—and you are...?"

"Denton," was the response. "You said Demilio? The doctor?"

"That's the one," Trev said, wiping sweat from his forehead as he surveyed the bodies of Jackson and Smith. "You are the guys she was trying to meet?"

"That's us," Denton replied. "What's with the hostile fire? We figured we'd be coming into an infected zone but we weren't counting on the bad guys with guns."

"I honestly have no idea," Trev admitted, shaking his head. "I stayed outside to deal with a few infected, and when I came in these two bastards were waiting for me. I don't know where everyone else went. I guess they took them back through there."

Trev pointed at the double doors that Jackson and Smith had been guarding.

"All right," Denton said, nodding. "So we're not out of the woods yet. We've got the main doors blocked. One moment."

Denton plucked a radio from a pocket and clicked the handset.

"Ghost Three to Ghost Lead, come in, over," he said.

"Ghost Lead to Ghost Three, go ahead, over," came the reponse, crackling slightly.

"Sherman, we've got problems. There are hostiles in the facility; apparently, they've got your doctor friend held prisoner. Let's get everyone in here and make sure this place is secured, over."

"Roger," came the reply. *"We're coming back. Out."*

The pickup truck squealed to a stop alongside the utility truck, blocking off a set of windows. The back of the pickup popped open and another small group of survivors jumped out, all armed. They made their way to the utility truck, entered it through the passenger door, and one by one appeared through the rear doors of the vehicle and entered the facility.

"Everyone," Denton said, waving a hand in Trev's direction. "This is Trevor. He's on our side. Trevor, this is our group."

A few waves and nods completed the ad hoc introductions.

"All right, what's our situation?" said a late middle-aged man dropping out of the rear of the utility truck. "Give me a full SitRep."

Another older man, dressed in full Army uniform save for a simple baseball cap on his head, turned toward the speaker.

"Sir, we're all operational. Brewster's still manning the .249 and covering the entrance. The trucks should keep out any unwanted visitors."

"Trevor says that these shooters were sent by some guy named Sawyer," Denton added, gesturing at the corpses of Jackson and Smith. "He says there are probably more, and that the doc we're here to find is probably being held deeper in the facility."

"There are definitely more," chimed in another man.

"Explain, Krueger," said the late-middle aged man.

"Well, General, I popped one of them on the rooftop after he tried to take a potshot at Brewster. There are probably a couple more still on the rooftop and I'd bet a few more in the facility somewhere—probably right with the doc, keeping an eye on her."

"All right," said the General, nodding and folding his arms. "Thomas, take Jack, Denton and Mitsui and secure the ground level. Find Anna and bring her back here safe and sound. If anyone fires on you, kill them. Get them to surrender if you can."

"Yes, sir," Thomas growled.

"Krueger!" said the General. Krueger snapped to attention.

"Sir!"

"Take Rebecca, Trev here, and Mbutu and head up to the roof. Get rid of those guards, then hook back up with Thomas and help him finish securing the facility. We're finally here, gentlemen and ladies! Let's make it ours!"

The men in the room moved out with a purpose, slamming open the double doors and heading deeper into the facility with the practiced ease of seasoned survivors. Their weapons were all held at the ready and they moved professionally, at a half-crouch, checking each corner before taking it and covering one another with overlapping lines of fire.

Thomas and Krueger's groups split off from one another when Krueger located the stairwell that led to the roof. He nodded at Thomas—a quick gesture meant as a good-luck wish—and took off at a jog up the stairs, followed closely by Rebecca, Mbutu, and Trev.

After Krueger's footsteps had faded, Thomas continued to lead his miniature squad deeper into the facility. He came to a four-way intersection and stopped, gesturing for everyone to take cover.

As Denton squatted with his back to a wall, Thomas advanced on the object of his attention: a corpse in the middle of the hallway.

Matt's body had been left where it had fallen. Thomas checked it over, noted the civilian clothing and the lack of a weapon as well as the cut zipties lying near the young man's body.

"We've got a dead prisoner here," Thomas called over his shoulder. "Let's get a move on—don't want the same thing to happen to the doc."

Luckily for Thomas, someone had gotten close to the corpse and had stepped in the pool of blood that had spread out from the young man's torso. A few bloody footprints led off down a side corridor, telling Thomas exactly which direction the guards had taken their prisoners.

"This way," Thomas ordered, pointing off down the hall. "Go slow. Check your targets and your corners. And from here on, silence."

Denton and Jack nodded in reply. Jack turned to face Mitsui and passed the message along by holding a finger up to his lips. Mitsui nodded, a look of grim determination on his face.

The four turned down the side corridor and advanced, vanishing around a corner. They knew it was only a matter of time before they caught up with the prisoners—and their guards.

The moment they vanished around the corner, Mason's hand appeared in the doorway of the office where he'd fought Derrick. He pulled himself forward another couple of feet, succeeding in getting his head and shoulders into the hallway. He saw Matt's body and gritted his teeth, both against the pain of his wounds and the pain of seeing another comrade lost.

He thought he'd heard voices in the hall a moment before, but it was empty now, save for Matt's corpse. Maybe he was starting to hallucinate or go into shock.

Can't let either of those things happen or I'm a goner, Mason thought.

Mason coughed again, blood flecking his lips. He didn't have much longer.

$$\star \; \star \; \star \; \star \; \star$$

The door that led to the roof burst open, propelled outward by a swift kick from Krueger. He and Trev were the first two through the breach, weapons at the ready. The roof was covered in obstacles, making it difficult to get a clear view of the area. Krueger noted in the back of his mind that the obstacles he was passing by were large solar panels covering most of the roof.

Trev ducked down, looking under the panels. He spotted the booted feet of the guards near the corner of the roof and let a quiet whistle escape his lips. Krueger looked over, and Trev pointed out the enemy guards. Rebecca and Mbutu came up behind the pair carefully, scoping out the opposition.

Both guards were facing away from the survivors. They were peering over the edge of the roof with their rifles. Next to them lay a dead comrade, blood pooling around a nasty head wound. Krueger allowed himself a quick sense of self-satisfaction. That had been his shot.

All four of the survivors advanced slowly on the rooftop guards, stepping heel-to-toe on the tarred surface. They moved silently. Once they were close enough, they looked back and forth at one another, and Krueger nodded.

All four sprung up, pointing their weapons at the two remaining guards.

"Freeze! Freeze! Weapons down!" Krueger screamed.

The two guards were caught completely unaware. They jumped, startled, and spun to face the sudden new threat. One of them immediately threw up his hands. The second went for his pistol, but froze the moment his hand rested on the grip when he realized he was staring down the barrel of Mbutu's rifle. He slowly released his grip and raised his hands.

"Up! Get up!" Krueger screamed again.

The guards took their time complying, slowly raising themselves to their feet. Krueger grimaced, raised the barrel of his rifle slightly, and fired a shot over the heads of the two guards.

"I said get the fuck up!" Krueger yelled.

They picked up the pace, and stood before their captors with raised hands.

Still staring down the barrel of his rifle, Krueger tossed orders to his comrades.

"Trev, Mbutu, disarm them."

The two men approached, pulled the pistols from the guard's holsters and unbuckled their ammunition belts and webgear, tossing it a safe distance away.

"Hey, Krueger," Trev said.

"Yeah?"

"Look what I found," Trev said, holding up a small bundle of zipties. "Looks like we've got handcuffs."

"The jailors become the jailed," Krueger said, grinning. "Tie 'em up. Let's take 'em down to Sherman. He can decide what we're going to do with 'em."

Thomas heard his targets before he saw them. As his group moved down the dimly-lit hall he and the others began to hear growled commands and the sound of shuffling feet and shifting equipment. Thomas slowed as he approached the next intersection, peered around the corner, and spotted his objective.

About twenty feet down the hall stood three uniformed guards in front of an open door. They were busy shoving a pair of females into the room, not caring too much about whether their prisoners entered comfortably or not. As Thomas watched, one of the guards planted a booted foot on the lower back of a young woman and kicked her into the room.

Thomas didn't need a written invitation. With both of the prisoners safely in their makeshift cell, the hall was free of friendly targets. He leaned out from the corner and opened fire with his rifle. His first three-round burst caught one of the guards full in the chest, tossing him backwards into his two comrades. The remaining two had enough sense to fall back, slamming the door to their makeshift prison shut in the process. Denton and Jack stepped out from behind their cover, pouring fire down the corridor. Bullets ricocheted off of the concrete walls in both directions as the guards returned fire.

The four survivors pelted the guards' position with rounds, chipping away at the concrete walls. Return fire was brisk at first, causing Thomas and the others to take care, but as the firefight wore on, the guards' fire slowed. They were beginning to run low on ammunition.

Even as Thomas watched, one of the enemy guards stuck his head out from behind his cover and eyed the corpse of his former companion, with its full ammunition belt and rifle. The corpse lay in the middle of the hallway, smack-dab in the center of no-man's land.

He can't be stupid enough to be thinking of going for that guy's ammo, Thomas thought to himself.

Just as Thomas finished the thought, the man burst out from behind his cover, firing his last few rounds as he ran for his dead comrade's body.

Well, I guess I was wrong, Thomas thought. *He can be that stupid.*

Thomas' next three-round burst caught the guard before he made it halfway to the body of his comrade.

A silence fell over the corridor as the guard fell. The smell of cordite and a pall of smoke permeated the hall. The single remaining guard, still behind cover at the far end of the hall, made a judgment call.

"Hold your fire! Hold your fire!" he called out. His empty hands appeared around the corner, followed by his head and shoulders. "I surrender!"

"Step out and keep your hands up!" Thomas ordered. He gestured for his companions to join him in the hall, and they advanced on the surrendering man. Denton and Jack shoved the guard up against a wall, checked him for weapons, and kept him pinned while Thomas and Mitsui searched the bodies of the two dead men.

Thomas came up with a small keyring after a few moments and stepped up to the locked door in the middle of the hall. The first two keys didn't fit in the lock, but the third did the trick, and he heard the deadbolt sliding back as he twisted the key. He pulled open the door.

Inside sat Anna Demilio and Juni Koji, hands bound with duct tape across their mouths. They looked up at Thomas with fear at first. Anna's look of trepidation vanished almost immediately. She recognized the old Sergeant Major from her dealings with General Sherman, and she struggled to her feet, grinning behind the duct tape.

"Sorry it took so long to get here, Doc," Thomas grumbled, stepping toward Anna. He reached up a hand and grapped the edge of the duct tape on her mouth. "This'll hurt."

Before she had a chance to protest, he ripped the tape off with one swift motion.

"Ow," Anna managed, working her mouth to throw off the sticky feeling of the tape. "Good to see you, Thomas."

"Likewise," Thomas said. He plucked a knife from his belt and held it up. "Mind if I untie you?"

"Please do," Anna said, turning around and allowing Thomas to cut through the zipties that held her.

Juni was likewise freed from her restraints by Mitsui.

With the prisoners freed and the one remaining guard under control, Thomas deemed his situation under control.

"What do we do with this guy?" Denton asked, still pinning the living guard to the wall.

"Same thing he did with the Doc," growled Thomas, holding up a ziptie and the piece of duct tape he'd ripped from Anna's mouth. "Bind him and throw him in the room. We'll figure out a use for him later."

☆ ☆ ☆ ☆ ☆

Mason heard the chatter of gunfire echoing throughout the facility as he did his best to drag himself toward the main corridor. He didn't know who was doing the shooting—or the dying, for that matter—but he hoped it was someone who wasn't going to finish him off when they stumbled upon him.

He could feel a numbness in his chest, and it was rapidly spreading. Each breath was getting harder and harder to draw. From what he knew about battlefield wounds, he knew that his chest cavity was filling with air from his punctured lung, putting pressure on both organs. Soon he wouldn't be able to breathe at all.

One step at a time, Mason reminded himself, and stretched out a hand to pull himself another six inches closer to the main corridor. Behind him he left a trail of blood: some from his bruised and battered face, still more from his two gunshot wounds.

Even as he moved, he knew he wasn't going to make it much further. His vision swam in and out of focus, and he fought to stay conscious. Elsewhere in the facility, the gunfire had died down. Mason wondered who had won the firefight.

At the far end of the corridor, a small group of blurry shapes took form. Mason knew they were people, but he couldn't tell who they were or even if they had seen him.

He managed to croak the word "help" before he spiraled down into darkness.

Mason opened his eyes slowly, carefully. Bright light shone down into them, and he squinted against it. He tried to swallow and found his throat bone-dry. Nearby he could hear the steady beep-beep-beep of a heart monitor, and with some effort he turned his head to the left and surveyed his surroundings.

Mason lay in a hospital room. It differed from the other rooms he'd been in before in that it lacked a window and anything in the way of aesthetics, but it was a hospital room nonetheless. Monitors were clipped to his chest and head and ran along narrow wires to banks of machinery, all working to ensure he remained alive.

For a moment, Mason wondered about his situation. His memory was foggy. What had happened? Where was he? Had the whole pandemic been nothing more than a dream? Perhaps he had been wounded on the job and had been in a coma for a few weeks.

That almost made sense; there was no power anymore, no more hospitals, and no way he could have survived the fight with Derrick that was, even then, coming back to him in bits and pieces. Nothing he saw around him seemed to make much sense.

Hell, he thought, there was even a vase of fake flowers next to his bed.

Suddenly the door to his room was pushed open and in came a young woman pushing a stainless steel tray before her. She looked to be in her early twenties and had dirty blond hair tied back in a ponytail. Mason thought if he was fifteen years younger he'd probably try to flirt with her. Before he could ask a single question, however, she noticed he was awake and launched into an explanation, using the same tone a doctor might use with a confused patient.

"Well, you're finally awake," said the girl, checking over the equipment on the tray she'd wheeled in. "My name's Rebecca, and

I'll be your nurse while you stay here. You were in pretty sorry shape when we found you. You're lucky Dr. Demilio was around."

"The Doc lived?" Mason croaked around his throat. It felt like sandpaper.

"Yes," Rebecca said. "And she managed to get you fixed up pretty well. If this had happened anywhere else you'd have been a goner. It's lucky this building has medical facilities."

"So what happened? Who are you? I mean, where did you come from?" Mason asked. "And can I please have a drink of water?"

"Sure," Rebecca said, turning to a sink and filling a plastic cup halfway with cold water. "I came in with General Sherman's group. We had really good timing—we showed up right as those uniformed shooters started to take the upper hand. We managed to take a few prisoners, killed the rest, and secured the facility."

"Sherman? That's the guy Anna wanted to meet up with," Mason said, gratefully accepting the cup of water and draining it in one gulp.

"The same," Rebecca said. "Anyway, I need to give you a couple of shots before I get back to work."

"Work?" Mason asked.

Rebecca took a moment before answering, busy filling a syringe with antibiotics.

"Well, we're here to stay, at least for a while," she answered, jabbing the needle into Mason's arm. He took the shot without so much as a grimace. "So we've been going around and buttoning up, you know, making sure the windows are covered, fortifying."

"How do we have power?" Mason asked.

Again Rebecca took a moment to answer as she filled a second syringe from a new bottle.

"Solar panels on the roof. They pull in enough to keep this place running comfortably. We've even got air conditioning if we want it. Hell of a place, this research facility."

"Sure is," Mason said as Rebecca administered the second injection. Almost immediately, his head felt fuzzy and his body went slightly numb, dulling the pain in his chest. "What was that?"

"Demerol," Rebecca said. "I gave you enough to put you back to sleep for a few hours. You need rest."

"We all need rest," Mason said, head swimming as the narcotic took effect.

Rebecca was already wheeling the cart back toward the door. She stopped, looked over her shoulder at Mason, and grinned.

"Mr. Mason, we've got this building sealed up as tight as Fort Knox. We can all rest for a while."

With that, she pushed her way out the door and was gone. Mason lay back, resting his head on his pillow and enjoying the sensation of the painkiller. He closed his eyes and exhaled a long breath, feeling the stress of the past few weeks melting away as he drifted off to sleep.

"Just going to rest for a little while," he whispered to himself in the last moments before consciousness escaped him.

Mason slept, safe and secure, in the research facility in Omaha, Nebraska. The two groups that had spent weeks—months—trying to reach one another had finally succeeded. Mission accomplished.

All that was left to do was find the vaccine.

If it even existed.

EPILOGUE

COMMANDER HARRIS HALTED HIS MEN at the edge of town after passing a sign warning them that trespassers would be shot on sight. The sign looked faded and hung loosely, one of the nails holding it to its post having worked its way free. He proceeded cautiously, having his men scan the buildings from afar with their binoculars and spread out into a skirmish line, looking for any sign of activity, either human or infected.

After twenty minutes of silent observation, Harris and his men hadn't seen so much as a rat in a gutter. The town looked utterly deserted.

"What do you think?" Harris asked, standing next to the crooked sign.

"Don't know," Hal replied. He'd walked up behind the commander and was surveying the town with a look of suspicion on his face. "Sherman told me about a place out in the desert called Sharm something-or-other that looked just as deserted. He said that they jumped by infected once they were in."

"Sharm el-Sheikh," Harris said, nodding. "Heard the same story once he came onboard."

"So should we circle it?" Hal asked, raising his eyebrows. "Might be the same kind of situation."

Harris looked conflicted for a moment. His men were running dangerously low on food and potable water, and the town offered them a shot at finding something new to fill out their packs with. At the same time, what good is food if you're dead?

Harris sighed and made his decision. He turned to a Chief Petty Officer standing nearby and began to issue his orders.

"All right, we'll go through. Our sub-machinegunners will be on the flanks—tell them to keep a close eye on the doors and windows of the houses we pass. We'll go right down main street and through to the other side of town. Tell everyone to keep an eye out for any store or warehouse that might have food or bottled water we can take."

"Aye, sir," came the reply. The CPO jogged off to relay the orders, and the sailors assembled in short order, checking their weapons.

"I don't know about this," Hal murmured, but otherwise kept his mouth shut.

The sailors, Harris and Hal moved into Hyattsburg at a slow pace. They took their time, checking corners and darkened doorways. They made it three blocks before they came upon the first of the bodies.

"Sir," called out the CPO to Harris, "I've got a body in U.S. Army gear, here."

Harris jogged over to the sailor and knelt down next to the body to take a look. It was as the man had said: a corpse lay on the street, long dead. Its flesh was dessicated and drawn, but even months of decomposition couldn't hide the man's death wound: a self-inflicted gunshot to the chest. Torn, dried skin on the man's arms and face hinted at an attack by infected. The man had likely shot himself before the infection could take hold.

Harris' CPO reached down and gently retrieved the pistol from the dead man's grasp, the fingers cracking as he bent them out of shape. He reached around his back and jammed the weapon into the top of his pack.

Harris noted the unit patch on the man's arm, a silhouetted black bird with flames in the background, and grimaced. This had indeed been one of Sherman's men.

"Let's keep moving," Harris said, groaning as he stood up. "Whatever caught this poor bastard I don't want to catch us."

As the group continued through the town, they began to come upon more bodies. Most looked civilian, and had been put down with multiple shots. Those, Hal guessed, would have been the infected bearing down on Sherman's group. Others wore the uniforms of U.S. Army soldiers. In a few places, Hal spotted the dark, nearly-black stains of long-dried blood on the ground, but no body to accompany them.

"Harris," Hal said, beckoning over the Naval officer and pointing down at the bloodstains. "Looks like we'll have a couple shamblers in the area."

Harris nodded by way of agreement. The pools of blood had come from victims of the infected, most likely, and since the infected had never been known to carry off their victims, Harris and Hal concluded that whoever had been dropped on that spot had gotten back up a while later and ambled off.

The group continued on in silence. They passed a used car lot where several more bodies lay, all grouped around the outside of the chainlink fence that surrounded the lot. The main gates had been burst outward, with bodies and twisted steel scattered across the road.

"What the hell happened here?" Harris murmured, looking over at the lot as they passed it by.

"Looks like a pitched battle," Hal said, nodding in the direction of the corpses. "Whoever it was probably got a couple of cars from the lot and busted their way out. Look down at your feet."

Harris glanced down at the asphalt and saw skid marks leading away from the lot, deeper into the town. He heard a rustling coming from an alleyway behind him and spun, pistol upheld, but relaxed when he saw it was nothing more than a sheet of yellowed newspaper being blown up against a wall. The headline, which read 'Morningstar Cases Confirmed In New York', was visible for a moment before the paper fluttered away. Hyattsburg was beginning to wear on Harris' nerves.

"Let's get a move on," Harris said. "The less time we spend in this place, the better. It's like walking through a damn tomb."

The men seemed to concur, and the entire group picked up its pace. They passed several more blocks without incident. Harris' comparison to a tomb seemed more than accurate. The buildings were stark and silent, and the streets were just as desolate. If it weren't for the bodies and the occasional sign of violence, it would be easy to imagine that the people of the town had simply picked up and left.

One of the sailors was walking near the storefronts, peering into the windows with an upheld Maglite. Hal narrowed his eyes at the man and let out a sharp, quick whistle. The sailor turned to face him.

"What're you doing, you jackass?" Hal asked, throwing his arms wide. "You want to stir up a nest of those things?"

"Sorry, Hal, it's just that—"

"Hal's right, Seaman, stick to the center of the road. Less chance you'll be spotted by one of those things that way," chimed in Harris.

"But it's just that—"

"No 'Buts,' sailor, just do it," Harris said in an exasperated tone.

"Yes, sir," said the sailor, looking over his shoulder at the store with a dejected and curious expression on his face.

"Wait a minute," Hal said, beckoning over the sailor. "What were you looking at?"

"It was probably nothing," said the seaman, shaking his head as the group continued down the street.

"No, I'd like to know," Hal pressed. "What was it? A body?"

The sailor shook his head in the negative. "It's just that the store back there had this pile of shelves near the back that looked like a fort. I was thinking maybe someone managed to survive, but it's probably just a leftover—I mean, no one could have survived all of this."

No one? Hal thought. *I didn't see Sherman's body anywhere with those Army corpses. Or Thomas'. Or Denton's.*

Hal stopped in his tracks and looked back at the store the sailor had been peering in to. A glance up at the sign showed a poorly-drawn superhero punching through a comic book; it was a hobby shop or comic book store. A nagging feeling tugged at the back of his brain.

"Commander," Hal said out loud, causing the entire column to stop and look in his direction.

"What is it?" Harris asked, keeping his voice lower.

"Maybe we should check out that place," Hal said, pointing toward the storefront. "Your sailor's got a good point—if someone did manage to hole up, maybe we can pull them out and bring 'em with us."

"Yeah," Harris agreed, "and then again, maybe we pull down those blockades and get jumped by a roomful of shamblers, or, worse, sprinters. Maybe someone sealed up the dead in there."

The column of sailors picked up their pace again, moving off down the street.

Hal grimaced, turned away from the shop, and prepared to rejoin the column of sailors. He stopped after taking a few steps.

"Goddammit," he murmured, drawing his pistol. "I'm supposed to be retired. Harris!"

Once more the Commander stopped and turned. "What now?"

"I'm checking out the store," Hal said.

"That's a very bad idea, Hal," Harris said. "Let's stick to the streets."

"You stick to the streets, Harris," Hal said, waving off the sailors. "I have to be sure."

"Damn it all," Harris murmured under his breath. He watched Hal take a few tentative steps toward the storefront, then sighed. "Hillyard! Rico! Wendell! Go with him!"

"Sir?" asked the incredulous seaman next to him.

"You heard me," Harris said. "Back him up. We're right behind you."

The three sailors, swallowing down their own fear, jogged over to walk parallel to Hal as he approached the store. All four had drawn weapons. Behind them, the column of sailors fanned out, covering both sides of the street as the little squad prepared to enter the store.

Hal stopped in front of the main door and took in the state of the place. The windows were blacked out with paint, but the front door was still clear glass. He and the seaman named Rico stepped up to it and peered inside, the sailor shining through a light that he played over the interior of the store. The place was a mess. Most of the comics had been dumped off the shelves onto the floor, creating a haphazard carpet of superheros and villains. The shelves themselves had all been dragged to the rear of the store and rearranged to form a serviceable rampart. Hal could see cinderblocks weighting the shelves in place, and could barely make out the top of a doorframe behind the blockade.

"Whether or not anyone's left," Rico said, "they sure did make an effort to stay alive."

"Amen to that," Hal replied. "Let's see if we can get in."

Hal tried the door and found it to be locked—from the inside.

"Well, that's a good sign," said Hillyard from behind Rico and Hal. When they glanced over their shoulders at him, he went on with a shrug. "Only a living person could lock it up from inside, right?"

"Maybe we should knock?" joked Rico.

Hal snorted, shifted his grip on his pistol, and used the butt of it to smash out the glass in the lower half of the door. The resounding clatter set all the sailors on edge, and they shifted on their feet, looking nervously around the street for any sign of infected responding to the noise. Hal himself froze, waiting to see if his action would draw an attack.

Nothing came running out of any darkened doorway, nothing appeared out of any of the alleys or basement entrances. The only noise on the street was the sound of the sailors' nervous footsteps and the distant chatter of birdcalls.

After several long moments, the sailors began to relax.

Hal reached through the broken glass and felt around on the inside of the door for the deadbolt. He found it, twisted the knob, and unlocked the door.

"We're in," he said to Rico with a half-grin.

"All right," Rico replied, holding up his pistol. "Let's do it."

Hal swung the front door open and entered slowly, followed closely by Rico, Hillyard, and Wendell. Their footsteps crunched on comic book covers and paper crinkled underfoot as they spread out into the shop. They made it halfway across the floor before the tense silence was shattered by the sound of a gunshot from behind the shelves.

The sailors dove to the ground as a round shattered one of the blacked-out front windows. A second shot rang out a moment later, embedding itself in the floor next to Rico's head. He rolled to the side, came up into a kneeling position, and fired three shots of his own into the barrier of shelves.

After that, there was silence. The sailors held their position, as did Hal, and waited to see if they would be fired on again. No further shots came from behind the barrier.

"Think I got him?" Rico whispered.

"I hope not," Hal said. "Never heard of an infected using a gun before. I think we've got a survivor."

Hal slowly stood up and raised his voice to a normal conversational level.

"Hello?" he called out. "Don't shoot; we're not infected!"

From behind the barrier of shelves came the sound of someone scrambling to their feet.

"Holy shit," came a reply, floating over the walls of the makeshift fort. "I thought I was the only one left in this town that hadn't turned."

"Come on out," Hal said. "We're not here to cause any problems. Saw your fort from the street and figured there might be someone inside. Thought maybe you'd like to get out of this town, is all."

"Would I?" came the voice. "I've been sitting in this goddamn store for two months living off of fucking candy and canned creamed fuckin' corn. Hell yes, I'd like to get out of this town."

The shelves shifted suddenly as the person behind them kicked them out of place. One unit tipped over, spilling its cinderblocks on the floor and revealing the man who had been holed up alone since January. He wore faded, stained and filthy BDU's and wielded a beautiful, antique Winchester rifle that he was also using as a cane. His leg was wrapped in similarly filthy bandages, and across from the patch that read "U.S. Army" was a similar patch that said "Stiles." He looked more the worse for wear, his face gaunt and eyes hollow. He seemed malnourished and nervous.

"Well, I'll be god-damned," Rico said, taking a closer look at Stiles. "I remember you from the *Ramage*. You were with Sherman's group, weren't you?"

Stiles nodded slowly, leaning heavily on his rifle. "I was."

"What happened here? Where's the rest of them? What happened to your leg?" Rico asked in rapid succession.

Stiles furrowed his brow before answering.

"I'm not sure where they are now. We got jumped by infected in this town and had to do some quick thinking to get most of the group out alive. They needed a way to distract the infected while they got clear. I was the way," Stiles said, shrugged, and leaned against the countertop behind him with a sigh, rubbing his leg.

"And what happened to your leg?" Rico pressed.

"Bitten," Stiles said.

Immediately, all four men in the room had their pistols pointed at the soldier.

Stiles eyed the barrels staring him down and broke into barking laughter.

"Don't bother," he said to them, still chuckling. "I was bitten in January."

"That was months ago," Rico said, narrowing his eyes. "Why haven't you turned yet?"

"What am I, a doctor?" Stiles asked, shrugging. "All I know is, I got bit, and I'm still here. Fucking thing still hurts like a bitch, though, but I haven't turned. Haven't even gotten the fever yet."

Hal lowered his pistol slowly, eyeing Stiles. "You were bitten but you're not sick?"

"That's what I said," Stiles repeated, nodding.

Hal grinned widely, grabbing Rico's shoulder. "Don't you see?"

Rico looked over at Hal and frowned, shaking his head.

"None of you see? Don't you ever read?"

Stiles didn't say a word; he merely fished around in his pocket for a purloined pack of cigarettes and a new lighter.

"Stiles, you were bitten how long ago?" Hal asked, rounding on the soldier.

"About two months," Stiles responded around the cigarette between his lips. "And it's been shit living here ever since."

"Right, but you didn't get sick after a week," Hal said.

"Uh-huh."

"Oh, you're definitely coming with us," Hal said, still grinning.

"I'm up for it," Stiles reassured him. "But why all the excitement?"

"Look, kid, every time any of us has ever seen anyone get bitten, they turned. You're the first—hell, you're the only—person I've ever even *heard* of who hasn't. Stiles, I think you're immune to Morningstar."

That got the attention of the sailors in the room.

"If you're immune," Hal pressed, "That means you've got antibodies—oh, we need to get you to Omaha and find Sherman as fast as we goddamn well can."

"Why?" Stiles asked, flicking ashes off the end of his cigarette.

"Stiles, if you're immune to the Morningstar strain, that means your blood is a key to a vaccine," Hal said.

That seemed to stun Stiles for a second, and he let the cigarette droop in his lips. "Key?"

"Don't ask me how; I'm a damn retired mechanic," Hal said. "But I do know they'll be very happy to see you once we get there."

"If they made it," Rico said.

Hal turned to the sailor. "They made it. If Stiles made it two months in this dead town, Sherman and the others made it to Omaha. I know it. And now we have to get Stiles to Sherman."

"Well, all right," Stiles said, reaching behind the countertop and pulling a fully-loaded pack from a cupboard. "I've been ready to move out for the past month—I've just been waiting for the right moment. Now's as good as any, I'd say."

Hal was suddenly very glad he'd followed up on his hunch and checked out the store. He'd hoped to find a survivor, and he'd found much more than that: a possible natural vaccine to the Morningstar strain.

"Let's get moving," Hal said, helping Stiles shoulder his pack and buckle it on. "We've got a long way to go, Mr. Immunity."

"I'm with you," Stiles said, "as long as you don't take this immunity thing and use it as an excuse to have me go in any dark rooms first."

"Oh, we wouldn't do that," Hal said, fixing Stiles with a serious stare. "I don't know what Sherman would say, but in my opinion, you're probably the most important person on this goddamn continent right now. You could stop the pandemic if we get you to Omaha in time! What do you say to that, Stiles?"

Stiles seemed slightly overwhelmed by Hal's exuberant exclamations.

"Well...I'd say...bring it on?" Stiles said tentatively.

"There's a quote for the history books from the savior of mankind," Rico chuckled, emulating Stiles' anxious tone. "'Bring it...on?'"

"Hey, this is all new to me," Stiles replied defensively. "And if I'm the savior of mankind, I'm worried for the future of the species."

"Don't worry," Hal said, putting a reassuring hand on Stiles' shoulder. "I'm sure you'll figure it out on the way. Now let's get moving. We should be out of this town before nightfall—then it's on to Omaha."

Permuted Press

delivers the absolute best in **apocalyptic** fiction,
from **zombies** to **vampires** to **werewolves**
to **asteroids** to **nuclear bombs** to
the very **elements** themselves.

Why are so many readers turning to Permuted Press*?*

Because we strive to make every book
we publish feel like an **event**, not
just pages thrown between a cover.

(And most importantly, we provide some
of the most fantastic, well written, horrifying
scenarios this side of an actual apocalypse.)

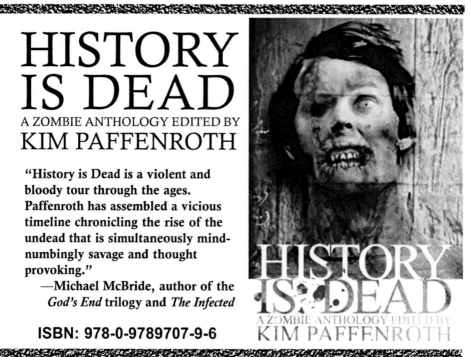

THE UNDEAD

ZOMBIE ANTHOLOGY

ISBN: 978-0-9765559-4-0

"Dark, disturbing and hilarious."
—Dave Dreher, *Creature-Corner.com*

THE UNDEAD

VOLUME 2

SKIN AND BONES

ISBN: 978-0-9789707-4-1

"Permuted did us all a favor with the first volume of *The Undead*. Now they're back with *The Undead: Skin and Bones*, and gore hounds everywhere can belly up to the corpse canoe for a second helping. Great stories, great illustrations... *Skin and Bones* is fantastic!"
—Joe McKinney, author of *Dead City*

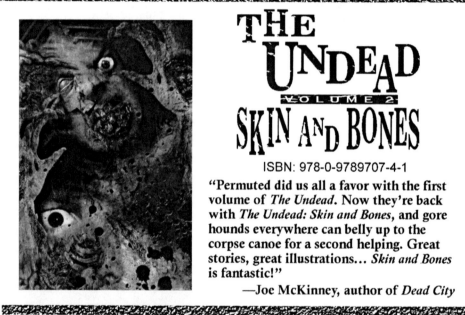

The Undead / volume three

FLESH FEAST

ISBN: 978-0-9789707-5-8

"Fantastic stories! The zombies are fresh... well, er, they're actually moldy, festering wrecks... but these stories are great takes on the zombie genre. You're gonna like *The Undead: Flesh Feast*... just make sure you have a toothpick handy."
—Joe McKinney, author of *Dead City*

JOHN DIES AT THE END
by David Wong

It's a drug that promises an out-of-body experience with each hit. On the street they call it Soy Sauce, and users drift across time and dimensions. But some who come back are no longer human. Suddenly a silent otherworldly invasion is underway, and mankind needs a hero.

What it gets instead is John and David, a pair of college dropouts who can barely hold down jobs. Can these two stop the oncoming horror in time to save humanity?

No. No, they can't.

ISBN: 978-0-9789707-6-5

THE OBLIVION SOCIETY
by Marcus Alexander Hart

Life sucks for Vivian Gray. She hates her dead-end job. She has no friends.

Oh, and a nuclear war has just reduced the world to a smoldering radioactive wasteland.

Armed with nothing but pop-culture memories and a lukewarm will to live, Vivian joins a group of rapidly mutating survivors and takes to the interstate for a madcap cross-country road trip toward a distant sanctuary that may not, in the strictest sense of the word, exist.

ISBN 978-0-9765559-5-7

COSCOM ENTERTAINMENT

Where Imagination is Truth

www.coscomentertainment.com

LaVergne, TN USA
04 December 2009
165962LV00005B/54/P